## ALONG DARK WATERWAYS . . .

Jones heard the echo of hurrying footsteps above her again. Whoever that shadow was, he was good and he followed close. How to lose him? If only some traffic would come, some boat big enough to duck behind. Or if only she could get her engine started quick, take off. . . .

*If only I had one of them "Discreet" engines. . . .*

As if in answer to her thoughts, she suddenly heard the thrumming of a large boat coming fast. Jones jabbed her pole with all her strength and shot straight across the canal, right under the oncoming bow.

A screech of surprise and a furious obscenity followed her as she scraped past, missing collision by a handspan. She recognized the cursing voice: Deiter clan, one of their big boats. But where were the poles? How could their boat make such speed? And then it hit her. *The Deiters got one of them Discreet engines!*

As she pulled into shadowy safety, all thoughts of her pursuer were forgotten in the face of this new and far greater threat. The Ban was broken! And on the waterways of Merovingen, trouble was about to sprout and spread as swiftly as the choking, inescapable tangle-lilies. . . .

# C.J. CHERRYH
## THE ALLIANCE-UNION UNIVERSE

**The Company Wars**
DOWNBELOW STATION

**The Era of Rapprochement**
SERPENT'S REACH
FORTY THOUSAND IN GEHENNA
MERCHANTER'S LUCK

**The Chanur Novels**
THE PRIDE OF CHANUR
CHANUR'S VENTURE
THE KIF STRIKE BACK
CHANUR'S HOMECOMING

**The Mri Wars**
THE FADED SUN: KESRITH
THE FADED SUN: SHON'JIR
THE FADED SUN: KUTATH

**Merovingen Nights (Mri Wars period)**
ANGEL WITH THE SWORD

**Merovingen Nights—Anthologies**
FESTIVAL MOON (#1)
FEVER SEASON (#2)
TROUBLED WATERS (#3)
SMUGGLER'S GOLD (#4)
DIVINE RIGHT (#5)

**The Age of Exploration**
CUCKOO'S EGG
VOYAGER IN NIGHT
PORT ETERNITY

**The Hanan Rebellion**
BROTHERS OF EARTH
HUNTER OF WORLDS

**C.J. CHERRYH invites you to enter
the world of MEROVINGEN NIGHTS!**

# MEROVINGEN NIGHTS

# DIVINE RIGHT

## C.J. CHERRYH

**DAW BOOKS, INC.**
DONALD A. WOLLHEIM, PUBLISHER

1633 Broadway, New York, NY 10019

First Printing, October 1989

1 2 3 4 5 6 7 8 9

Printed in the U.S.A.

# CONTENTS

Because the stories in this volume overlap in time they are, by the authors' consent, printed here in a "braided" format—so that they read much more like a novel than an anthology. The reader may equally well read the short stories as originally written by reading all of a given title in order of appearance.

For those who wonder how this number of writers coincide so closely—say that certain pairs of writers involved do a lot of consultation in a few frenzied weeks of phone calls as deadline approaches, then the editor, presented with the result, has to figure out what the logical order is.

**8** *Contents*

# MEROVINGEN

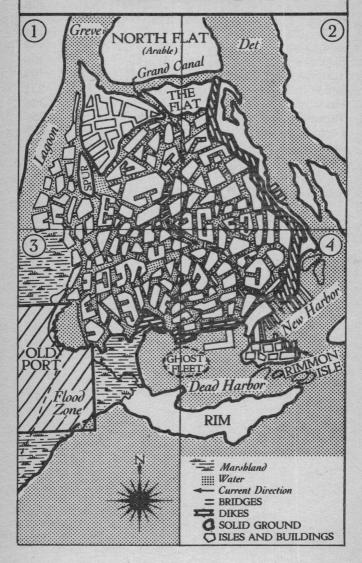

1    Greve    NORTH FLAT    *(Arable)*    Det    2

Grand Canal

THE FLAT

Lagoon

SPUR

3             4

New Harbor

OLD PORT

GHOST FLEET

RIMMON ISLE

*Dead Harbor*

*Flood Zone*

RIM

N

≈ *Marshland*
∷ *Water*
← *Current Direction*
= BRIDGES
Ɵ DIKES
Ɋ SOLID GROUND
⬡ ISLES AND BUILDINGS

# SEEDS OF DESTRUCTION

### C.J. Cherryh

Summer, and Jones' skip nosed its way through West
shoving aside a sheet of floating weed, green, smooth-
leaved stuff that clung to poles with a maddening per-
sistence—not least maddening (and guilt-making)
because Altair Jones had some idea where this sudden
bloom of strange plants had come from. Rif, damn 'er,
and her bag of seeds—a midnight trip in Jones' own
skip.

Do good for the canalers, Rif had said.

Cure the fever.

Make al-co-hol for poor folks' fuel.

Yey, and choke the lighted waterways with a damn
nuisance, so in some places a skip-freighter *needed* an
engine to plow through the crud, except the trailing
feathery roots, tough as cable in the center of the
feather, had a way of tangling up in your propeller—
or wrapping round your pole when you were poling,
or sticking to the sides of your skip and making a nasty
dried mess when you were off-loaded and riding higher
in the water.

Tangle-lilies, folk began to call 'em.

You got cheap fuel, yey, Rif, and you got the damn plants to contend with, ye got engine wash rocking your skip real hard if ye pass some damn fool running his motor in one of the little canals, where a close pass and the wake bouncing off the walls could rock your skip right up—scrape!—against some curb, or, as had happened with old man Cruse, tipped him and his load right over, whole skip-load of flour sacks that damn near broke him, not mentioning what he lost of his personal stuff—after which the Cruses and Gupta Ling were squabbling, both of them having been running under power, but Ling's skip had been passing and passing fast, by what John Cruse swore.

One year everything worked fine and you sweated with the pole and you got around, and the next you had crud clogging up everything and Revenantist canalers wondering what karma they'd acquired that did *this* to them; while Adventist canalers thought generally the stuff must've come in on some Falkenaer ship in from the Chattalen or wherever, and some talked of gutting and throat-cutting; or cutting Falkenaer cables at dock; but some said it was a Nev Hetteker plot, and there was more talk of throat-cutting, hell with the peace-moves the Nev Hettekers were making, sending envoys south, making nice with the governor.

Jones lost sleep over that—knowing what she knew. And she thought more and more that she was morally obliged to *do* something, like 'fess up to the Trade what she had done before somebody got killed: like put the knife to Rif and tell her and her Janist damn 'em friends they done it and they could get rid of it, quiet-like.

Canalers 'stilled fuel off the stuff in pot-stills cobbled together out of about everything, canaler fashion. Engines better than a century old, that had always been saved just for emergencies, chugged along active again, a body having to be competitive, and they broke down, naturally: and parts were always hard come by, but parts got scarce and the price went up and mechanics were full-up if you had to get one—you changed one thing and other things changed, and the ripples kept going like that.

The tangle-lilies slopped up onto the boardwalks in the engine wash and rotted there, to go squish under s me unsuspecting canalsider's foot and send him skidding, bang, down on the walk.

The damn things grew like crazy out in the Lagoon, where there was shallow water and sun got there that never came to the deep underside of three-tiered Merovingen's thousand bridges. You wanted to go out in the Lagoon, you fought your way through a sea of green leaves; if chance be you fell in like old John Cruse, the water was overall cleaner, and maybe you didn't catch the fever and die, but baby deathangels fed on the stuff, and you *never* saw baby deathangel in numbers like that—till the lilies came. Maybe the little 'uns weren't dangerous as the adults that were strictly seagoing, but you didn't want to swim with 'em, no.

And that wasn't all the worst of it, either. Tangle-lilies needed light, and there *wasn't* any light in a lot of the canals, except at high noon, and some places not then. It drifted into cuts and slips and backwaters and up against pilings and just piled up in dead ends and it turned brown and cruddy green and went to jelly when it died, and made this kind of soup that stank and stuck to everything. The governor hired canalers to go along with rakes and get the weeds from wherever they piled up; and you saw skips full of it going up to the Spur—from which the Carswells who had property up to the Flats shipped it up there, dried it on racks and baled it and sold it back to Merovingen all dry and flammable, for landers who had stoves.

Cheaper than firewood. And that made the Dundees furious, the Dundees running the sea-freighters that brought wood from the forests they owned westward along the coast: Dundee was at Carswell's throats over it, and the gossip of the town was how Myrna Dundee had gone after Eddie Carswell at Festival, damn near to drawing knives, and them hightowners.

'Fessing up to dumping that stuff in the canals meant 'fessing up to a scary lot of things; and nailing Rif for it—and Jones was torn between thinking Rif had tried to do good and maybe didn't deserve what might fall on her then; or thinking Rif and her Janist friends might not be friends at all, and doing something terrible in town, with real dark motives.

Altair Jones had run the dark ways all her life, and never ratted on a job; but she never took a job, more to the point, that hurt them as didn't deserve it. She wished to hell she wasn't guilty of this one; and that she knew what to do about it.

She worried and she fretted about it. And it only got worse, so that now there was so much anger built up in Merovingen against whoever was responsible that she had the idea she had already waited much too long to come forward, that it wasn't just Rif the retribution would come down on, now—it was her and Mondragon and everybody she touched; and it wasn't just the Trade would be after her hide: the word would get out all over town.

She could say—the Janes held a knife to my throat. It was all their fault. But that was a lie, and she couldn't hold that up if the questions got close: she wasn't like some, that could lie with a straight face and not a second thought how many folk were going to die for it. She could gut a man outright. She had killed more than one. But that was fights. This was cold and it had to be deliberate and she had to go on lying once she started, and be good at it; or she was going to get other folk involved, and she wasn't the only one could end up knifed or, worse, arrested and taken up by hightowner law—

—after which the Justiciary was going to ask her questions in that awful little room in its basement; and she wasn't the only one they would arrest. Everybody she knew was in danger then—

Especially Mondragon, her and him being lovers, and it no secret on the canals and probably not in hightown where Mondragon moved. The whole town thought he was a Boregy bastard, half a Falkenaer; and the whole town *didn't* know he was Nev Hetterker and that he'd been a friend of Karl Fon and a member of the Sword of God, (before Fon double-crossed him, killed his family and threw him in prison for it.) Folk generally thought he worked for Boregys; but working for Anastasi Kalugin was the real truth, the governor's youngest son—and if Mondragon got hauled in as in any way involved in some Janist plot against the city, Anastasi would shut him up so fast—

Anastasi, who could take either one of them up any time he wanted,—would take her in at the first breath of notoriety; and Mondragon . . .

Mondragon, who had an eel's ways and who could ordinarily protect himself, would be a fool for her sake, and she knew it.

She was seventeen, well, surely she was by now; and she knew things that she wished she didn't know—and she was in a mess of a kind she wasn't sure *had* a way out. Month after month she had told herself it was going to get better and now it was wider and worse, so that Tom Mondragon, who had survived prison and fever and Boregy plots and outmaneuvered the Sword of God itself, might get killed because of a canal-rat who'd taken a fare one night and who'd been fool enough to figure Rif was harmless.

Rif, she'd said, late as last night, you *see* what's going on. You got to do something.

And Rif had said with a shrug, Yey, but you got fuel for your skip, you got no more fever.

And she, with a notion to take Rif by the throat and shake her: Yey, Rif, but ain't every skip's got an engine, and some's taking cargo away from the little 'uns, and we got families hungry that never was, Rif—

And Rif, with a second shrug: Jane'll provide. You got hungry folk, there'll be food.

They ain't takin' charity! she'd yelled at Rif. They'd starve, first! Ye do somethin', ye skit-hearted sherk, ye brung it, *ye get rid of it!*

Which only proved she was in the grip of the hysterics, because when she looked out on a city drowning in weed and rot, she couldn't see any getting rid of it.

She couldn't see herself living with what she knew.

She couldn't see herself living at all much longer, because secrets had a way of coming to the light, like bodies out of Harbor-bottom, and this one was closer and closer to it.


The wood-paneled College hearing room buzzed with voices, clattered with notebooks and echoed with the scrape of chairs—cardinals, and councillors lowtown and high, and secretaries from the Astronomer's office, the Harbormaster's office, and the Deputy Secretary from the governor's office—

Cardinal Willa Exeter gathered up her aching bones and shoved her chair back, feeling as she did so a gentle tug at her sleeve—not her aide, but Cardinal Vincente Cromwell, in company with councillor Rodrigo White-Eber and Devrie Eber from the Astronomer's office.

Cromwell was the surprise. Cromwell was Reform Party, a partisan of Tatiana Kalugin; and Exeter was staunch Loyalist; and while the choice of heirs to the governor was not, by rule, the business of the cardinals, Family was Family, politics was politics, and Cromwell interests were not, either socially or economically, Exeter's.

Except this particularly passionate hearing associated some very ill-assorted interests, irate merchant-families and anguished shippers and the Carswells *and* the Dundees, who had, aside from looking murder at each other across the table, confined their feud to prepared, icy statements. It had all been remarkably civilized—considering the subject of the hearings, which was the complaint of engine noise and erosion of the foundations of the city.

This approach was immediately interesting to Willa Exeter. This—unprecedented—approach suggested both hazards and solutions in the present impasse.

"A word," Cromwell said, and, holding her sleeve, drew her well aside in that company.

Cromwell, Eber, White, Basargin, now, the whole group moving quietly to the cloakroom, Basargin another surprise—especially when Cromwell said, first off, in a low voice, "Exeter, the Trade Secretary would be here with us, but appearances, you understand,—"

Willa Exeter made a noncommittal noise, thinking of betrayals and double crosses.

"Basargin," Basargin said, "will not object to the motion—*if* there's a small expansion of the language—to include distilling."

Willa cleared her throat and tucked her arms in her sleeves, ducking her head.

"It's a hazard," Eber-White said. "Cardinal, a simple statement: that the College suspects unlicensed technology, and supports a bill to require all distillation apparatus be licensed. Not banned. Simply regulated."

"An enforcement nightmare," Willa said, thinking of blackleg police poking into canal-boats, thinking of the ill will and the aggravation of an already restive element. . . .

Thinking of the expansion of blackleg authority, meaning Tatiana Kalugin, who, Lord and the Angel knew, already had enough to threaten the peace.

"Impossible," she said. "I'm afraid we've nothing to discuss on that score."

"It's the responsibility of the College to oversee such matters!" Basargin said. "To sit contemplating one's hands while the city falls apart is not responsible, Cardinal! We have documented erosion and undermining on the walls; we have an economy in upheaval—!"

"And Eber's fuel import business, mmmm?" Willa said in a low voice. "Conflict of interest is written all over this business. Not mentioning you can't enforce it. I can't support this."

"What will it take?"

Willa bit her lip, looked up under a brow and said, with a small smile, knowing the reaction she would get, "College action, not Council. A religious edict, no resort to the legislative. It's after all our province."

"No," Eber said. "We can't support that. If distilling process goes under Anathema—"

"Not refining."

"It could be extended in principle. No. Absolutely we would oppose that."

"We can exempt anyone under our sanction," Willa said, "which of course we would do in your case."

"And could equally refuse it! No, Cardinal. We will *not* accept that. Let's not waste our time."

"A counterproposal," Cromwell said after a breath. "No ban on distillation apparatus. But a simple legislative ban on engine use."

"Excepting," Eber-White said, "the major arteries, yes. Our transports—"

"Port, Grand, West, and Archangel," Basargin said.

"That still leaves us," Eber said, "with those damned—excuse me, Cardinal—the whole question of the stills. They're a fire hazard. They don't meet the storage codes. . . ."

"Then get them for that," Willa said. "You already have the law. Or don't you think it's enforceable? I tell you, m'seri, it isn't. Religious ban, yes, the canalers in general will respect that. I tell you there are suspect influences in this which *are* our business, and that's precisely the question here."

"Tss. But practically speaking," Cromwell said, "the College can issue an Edict, that in principle private distilling is suspect; and it can equally well pass a Resolution, in the form of a bill to Council—to ban engines except in harbor. Both our objectives, you see, very simple. No boarding of canaler boats. And quite, quite satisfactory in both issues, a clear statement of College authority and a legal solution to the immediate problem."

Willa looked at Cromwell in the uncomfortable suspicion of a sandbagging—but it was workable. No blackleg had to board a boat to detect an engine operating. It satisfied the merchants. It meant there would be no strings pulled in the College, where Reformers and Loyalists were precariously balanced.

Still, the Lord knew what kind of provisions Council might add once it got to legislating.

Need to get the aides moving, advise the Family, head off the kind of shenanigans Tatiana, the Reform Party, or, God save them, Anastasi Kalugin's radical supporters might try with a bill like that in their laps.

"I'll support that solution," she said, pursing her lips, "if the Governor or the Astronomer will agree to issue the ban as an immediate Executive Order."

In which case it went into effect as law until the Council could shape its own bill or veto it, —in which case, as an already operating order, it was a damned sight less likely to suffer sea-change in the Council's conniving hands.

It gave the governor power, in that case: if he should reissue it after veto, that dance could go on for another three months, during which there was certainly time to shape a bill Exeter could live with.

And which, of course, maintained karmic balance. The Lord's will be done.

Eber-White said, then, with a little cough, "We do have to consider the fancy-boats—"

God. The launches. The yachts. The powered craft of the Families—historic privilege—

"Charge a license fee," Cromwell said. "Say, —thirty sols gold, annual. To go into the city maintenance fund."

Negligible to a House. Prohibitive to a canaler. "The Governor's staff can work out these details," Willa said. "We only need a statement of policy out of this committee."

At which the others looked somewhat disquieted— Exeter standing high in the Loyalist party, of which, of course, the governor was head.

Out of which Exeter's own interests might derive some benefit, who knew?

# RUN SILENT, RUN CHEAP

*Leslie Fish*

Raven glanced around him at the crowd above Pogy Gate, feeling slightly unreal. The merry canalers on the lower seats, down near the water, looked believable enough: loud, rough-handed, barefoot, dressed in their dark and often ragged canvas and reed-linen, swapping expert comments on the condition and handling of the approaching boats. The little merchants and canalside tradesmen of the higher tiers seemed reasonable enough; with the bets flying free, not to mention an available crowd to measure and peddle at, it was sensible that they'd be here watching the Midsummer Open Poleboat Race come to its finish by the gate. The presence of better-house servants wasn't surprising either; given the chance and the good weather, they'd naturally come out to watch the boat race, make bets and a few purchases, gossip, pursue their petty plots, try for a bit of dalliance—and their fancy high-house liveries wouldn't be at all out of place in the crowd.

But the obviously hightown lady, sitting in the folding chair near the top of the gate, peering out at the

Grand Canal as eagerly as any of them—that was unreal. Hightowners never paid public attention to the Midsummer Open, almost never joined it—not even the wilder hotheads of the fast, young set—despite the promise that it was indeed Open to all and any. Everyone knew that canalers always won, and no hightowner wanted to be seen watching other hightowners trounced thoroughly by the lowest-of-Merovingen's-low.

Nonetheless, the m'sera was here—publicly watching, publicly interested. That was as jarring as the presence of the tangle-lilies everywhere, their golden flowers and pesky foliage floating gracefully all along the sides and slips of the canal. That wasn't part of the Merovingen he remembered. How could a few years' time have changed the city that much?

No, any moment now the vision would shred apart, leaving him sick and feverish and almost likely retching his guts out while May held him steady, back in the swamp. These past few weeks of change had all been part of the dream, this swamp-water vision. Reality was never this lovely, kind, or innocent.

A hand quietly gripped his arm, shook gently, pulled back his wandering thoughts. Raven glanced up and met Yarrow's smile. *Yes,* he remembered, studying that seamed, kindly, rock-strong face. *Yarrow's here, I'm back in town, and I've finally made my contact with the local Janes—only ten years late.*

He sat up a little straighter, reminding himself that Nature's time was not the same as Humanity's. Those years in the swamp, struggling to regain his lost memories, mattered nothing—save for the useful information he'd found there. He'd made his way back into town, caught up to Raj, gone from Raj to his brother Denny, from Denny to Rif—

Raven glanced quickly at the hawk-faced, black-haired musician sitting at his other side. Yes, who better than a street-singer to know all of the odd byways of town? Who better, as contact, informant, agent for Mother Jane? She frightened him, though; a city-wise Jane, especially in Merovingen, seemed an impossible contradiction in terms. Well, no matter. She was exceptionally competent, intensely loyal, and that was all that counted. Especially in Merovingen.

—and from Rif to Yarrow, and the Jane enclave down here in the Tidewater. After all those wasted years, he'd finally come home. And now there was work to do.

Rif nudged him with an elbow and raised her chin toward the hightown woman at the top of the gate. "That's 'er," she murmured. "That's Ariadne Delaney. Our doorway inter hightown. And 'er husband's polin' in this race. Mark 'em well."

Raven nodded and peered at the woman, then down at the water. Aye, mark them well, and think well. Farren Delaney: hightowner but without the usual aristocratic bigotries, bored with his dead-end job in the Harbormaster's office, no young hothead but still willing to join the Midsummer Open Poleboat Race—and with some expectation of winning. Ariadne Delaney: likewise minor aristocracy without prejudice, busily charitable without condescension, ambitious for her husband and sympathetic to the Janes. A hightown couple with ties to the Signeury, moving freely and comfortably down here in the Tidewater: bizarre, anomalous—and the best chance the Janes had found in all their years here.

And desperately needed, now that Crazy Cassie was pouring oil on the fire in hightown, now that the rich and powerful were turning on the poor and numerous with unexpected and undeserved bullying.

*"The guilty flee when no man pursueth . . ."*

A shout drew Raven's attention to the far end of the canal. Yes, there was the telltale flurry of foaming water, then the first boat prows coming into view. The race was coming down to its end, and fast.

The crowd roared and surged to its collective feet, Raven and the two women obliged to rise with it. Raven strained to see over and between the bobbing heads in front of him.

Yes, here they came: two plain boats far in the lead, the rest trailing, all the funny-boats and fancy-boats having dropped out long before. It was a duel, neck and neck—no, one boat nosing slowly but steadily ahead. The two boatmen bent to their poles, shoved, straightened, bent again, in a fast and smooth rhythm that bespoke years of practice: experts both, closely matched in strength and skill. The crowd howled appreciation.

"That's 'im, in the second boat," Rif almost had to shout in Raven's ear to be heard. "That's Farren Delaney. Mark 'im!"

The man poling the second boat was dressed like a common canaler: rough calf-length breeches, bare feet, short-sleeved reed-linen shirt—no different from the wiry young man furiously poling the leading boat.

Only a closer look showed the subtle differences: the smooth and even tan that revealed deliberate care in its acquisition, the balanced development of round and rolling muscles that likewise showed the effects of care rather than need, the trained athletic grace of motion learned by study as much as experience, the absence of scars on the bared arms. Farren Delaney was tall, fair and stocky, deliberately athletic, notably handsome. Raven could hear the man's labored breathing as the boat passed him. This race was not a game to him, not a side issue of some political intrigue; the man really was trying to win the race for its own sake.

The leading boat passed under the suspended ribbon, half a length in front of Delaney's boat, to the roars of the crowd.

Delaney looked up, fatigue and disappointment plain on his face—quickly followed by resignation, then a rueful smile. He shrugged, pulled his boat over behind the winner, and calmly tied on to the nearest ring.

Raven looked up to the top of the gate and saw Ariadne Delaney on her feet, peering down at her husband's boat, wearing the same disappointed/resigned smile. Farren waved to her, then plodded through the crowd to help congratulate the winner.

"Let's go," whispered Yarrow, tugging Raven's hand. "Time to work."

He followed obediently as the women worked through the crowd toward the winner and runner-up, trying to record detail and see patterns, working his rusty Janist observation training. He knew the women would provide the stimuli this time; all he need do was observe, practice observing, learn and relearn by working, and the work was valuable. Raven concentrated his attention on his ears and eyes.

Note: flushed and happy faces, gestures lively with leftover adrenaline but not focused with any anger, only a few drooping tones/expressions/gestures of disappointment—usually as lost bet money was handed over. Note: regretful comments on technique, how this or that contender had failed, no growls of resentment or comments about unfairness. Note how often Delaney's name was mentioned, and with what respect, and how rarely that respect was grudging.

And note: Farren Delaney shaking the winner's hand, slapping him on the back, saying: "—knew I was in trouble when you got inside me on that last turn."

Praising technique: very good.

Note the winner's brief surprise, then gap-toothed smile of appreciation, the affectionate return slap on the shoulder, the easy respect of his reply: " 'Ey, even so, ye made me sweat for 'er, all th' way down ter th' ribbon. Bloody good race, Delaney. Almost fit ter take the trade, ye are!''

Farren Delaney grinned from ear to ear, offered to buy the man a drink, and gestured to the nearest beer-peddler.

*Good. Very good. Perhaps he's only doing this from a devotion to sportsmanship, but very good nonetheless.*

Note Klickett up in the seats, leading a small delegation of her friends and neighbors and clients to offer hands, condolences, and promises of next-year's-race to Ariadne Delaney. Note Ariadne's surprised pleasure in the recognition, and how quickly she adapted to it.

And there were Rif and Yarrow working quietly through the crowd, prodding for comments on Delaney, and the rumored coming ban on fuel-alcohol. Note the comments carefully.

'' 'Ey, it's the rich wants the ban, an' not fer our good. They wants us ter keep buyin' high-price petro from *them*. Screw 'em, I says.''

''Not jes' them. It's the landlords, too. They don' like all the backwash from fast boats sweepin' hard on the Isles. She washes out their underpinnin's, and they don' wanter have ter do repairs.''

''Their underpinnin's'd wash away all the same, an' ye bet yer butt the rich won' give up engines on their fancy-boats. Let the damned landlords fix their buildin's, I says. An' let the canalers keep usin' chugger.''

''Sure, an' with all th' engine wash throwin' water aroun'? Ye heard what happened ter ol' man Cruse!''

''Hell, if fools ain't got the sense ter cut engines when they pass, it's their own damn fault. Get the Trade Council ter stomp on 'em fer their bad manners, but don' bring hightown inter it.''

''But what about the damn boat wash throwin' water everywhere? Throwin' that damn tangle-lily crap up on the walkways, splashin' the water high—''

"That's 'cause o' them cruddy ol' engines most folks use," Rif's voice slid into the argument. "The wash'd be less if ye had shrouded propellers, vortex kind o' engines. An' I jes' happen ter know a place—"

"Ta hell with that! The big boats can make as much speed under power as us little uns, an' they carry more cargo, so they got th'advantage. If they can't use chugger, we got a fair chance again."

"Says you, Jones," one of the Deiter boys cut in. "Y'think they won't keep their stills an' engines under cover? Won't use 'em at night when the blacklegs ain't watchin'? An' don't tell me ye won't do the same. I ain't' seen *you* throwin' yer still an' engine inter Dead Harbor."

"Piss on 'er, I might as well. More use means more wear on th' engine. When she wears out, where'm I goin' ter get another?"

"Hell, I can answer that." Rif elbowed her way into the knot of arguing canalers, handing out small cards from a pack that appeared neatly in her hand. "Looky here. Can ye read 'er?"

"I can read enough." Jones, glowering under her low-pulled cap, grabbed the proffered card and glared at it. "She's . . . a map showing the way ter, hmm, a shop right near here." She turned the card over. "An' here it says . . . Yossarian's Repair Shop. So what's that, hey?"

"Oh, nothin' much." Rif tossed a wide, knowing, conspiratorial grin at the knot of interested canalers. "That's jes' a place what happens ter be sellin' cheap, simple engines. Simple turbine-vortex jobs. Real quiet, real simple. They don' make hardly any noise, they don' hardly ever break down er wear out, an' they don't raise near as much wake as yer old clunker. That's what. Y'interested?"

"*I* sure am!" The Deiter man grabbed one of the cards.

Jones threw Rif a poisonous look, but she didn't hand back her card.

"New engines?" Another canaler took a step back. "New tech?"

"Ney, same old tech," Rif laughed. "Jes' new-made. Yossarian wants ter unload 'em fast. He's even willin' ter trade-in. Bring 'im yer old clunker, he'll give ye a good bit off—maybe even trade one-fer-one—on a new one."

Other canalers shouldered closer, some of them reaching for the cards.

"Ye seen these engines?" Jones asked, suspicion radiating off her like a halo. "Ye know what they're like?"

"Yey, I seen 'em." Rif smiled back, meeting her eyes. "Real nice. All sizes. Good performance. Simple ter operate, burns any kind o' liquid fuel, and . . . they're real easy ter hide on even a small boat."

"All sizes?" The nervous canaler took a step forward, and shyly took a card. "Easy ter hide?"

"Sure. Jes' depends on how well ye want 'er hidden." Rif shrugged eloquently. "Do ye want ter keep 'er real discreet, might be ye could put one behind a false bulkhead in yer hidey. More work, more time in the shop—ye make yer own choice. But do ye put 'er in with a couple hours' work, ye got somethin' the blacklegs wouldn' find, do they come lookin'. An' the price is good."

Jones turned away, stuffing the card in her breeches. Other canalers crowded around Rif, snatching at the remaining cards. The pile shrank quickly.

"Tell ye, though," Rif added, just loud enough for the immediate crowd to hear, "I'd get 'em quick before the ban passes—an' before blacklegs come inspectin' yer boats ter confiscate visible engines."

"Ye don' think they'd . . ." a boatman gasped, going noticeably pale. He snatched two cards, fast.

"Why not?" Rif curled her lip. "Mebbe 'nother reason fer the ban is, the hightowners don' want us canal-rats ter have fast boats. Mebbe they wants ter be sure we can't get away from 'em, whatever they're plannin' fer us. Ye've heard how Crazy Cassie's turnin' 'em on us. Who knows what they got in mind?"

The worried muttering spread through the adjacent crowd. Canalers with cards began hurrying away. Others came to take their place and grab cards.

Raven smiled and shook his head in appreciation. So that was how they did it. So fast, so efficient: the word would be all over lowtown by nightfall. So would the address of Yossarian's Repairs. The shop would have to move soon, before the word leaked up to hightown and the College, but the rush had started.

A hand touched his arm, and he turned to see Yarrow smiling at him.

"Shall we go?" she said. "Dinner waits."

*And more plotting and scheming.* Raven smiled. "I do believe I've worked up an appetite," he said, stepping into place at her side.


"Those cards will be all over lowtown by nightfall," said Yarrow, nibbling delicately at her slice of grilled yellowtail. "By tomorrow, Yossarian will be selling the new engines hand over fist."

"If the College ain't there first, screamin' 'Anathema!' " Rif commented, past a mouthful of fillet. "Won' take long fer the word ter get ter 'em."

"Long enough, with the misleading rumors our people have spread up there already." Yarrow smiled reassurance. "Besides, you don't think we put the real supplies and machine shop at that address, do you?"

"Ney, but then how do the customers—"

"They'll be led by the hand to where the installation is really done. The shop is just the, um, filtering plant that combs out the undesirables from the customers.

If the College howlers show up, all they'll find is a perfectly respectable repair shop—and maybe one or two engines clearly made from parts of old ones. 'Much cry and little wool,' as the Falkenaers say.''

''An' if Yossarian gets hauled in?''

''Then he does as Master Milton did, when the College hauled *him* in over that fireworks display. You remember how well that worked out.''

''Oh, yey!'' Rif rolled her eyes and put on a burlesque stupid-sincere expression. '' 'But it's a *common* trick down in the Chattalen. *Everybody's* got it there. They're way *ahead* of Merovingen on all that stuff. They could run *rings* around us.' Hee-hee!''

''Yes, nothing like appealing to civic vanity—and paranoia. Deflect their attention elsewhere; always deflect.''

''Do you think Yossarian will have enough supply for the demand?'' Raven spoke up. ''There are lots of canalers, and almost every canalside lander has some sort of boat.''

''He has over a hundred sitting in storage, waiting to go,'' said Yarrow. ''Actually, I'm more worried about lack of demand. A lot of the more religious types may stay away from fear of tech, the College, karmic debt or whatever.''

''I made a big point o' sayin' it was same ol' tech, just newer-built,'' Rif noted. ''An' ever since the College's been backin' Crazy Cassie, lots o' lowtown folks've turned sour on the priesthood.''

''Let's hope enough are interested to sway the rest.''

''Hell, they will. One thing folks want less'n a new engine is an old un that don' work, an' chugger use has put lots o' wear on them old engines. There's plenty o' folks jus' *got* ter get new ones.''

''New engines for old,'' Yarrow grinned. ''I hope you're right. I hope by next week Yossarian has a warehouse full of old engines and engine parts, ripe for recasting—though, of course, they won't be doing that in town."

"I won't even ask," Raven murmured, "about the size of your smuggling operation."

"All I can tell you is that it was the first thing we set up in Merovingen—right after the observation teams."

"Which I was supposed to help with." Raven looked down at his half-emptied plate.

"Don't worry." Yarrow patted his arm. "The information you brought us from the swamp is invaluable. We sent the samples north on the first ship out, and by now our labs are no doubt studying them down to their molecules."

Rif and Klickett looked at each other, and shrugged.

"Oh, that reminds me." Raven lifted his head. "The ecology of the swamp—those water-weeds of ours, 'tangle-lilies' the boatmen call them—a lot of the native life of the swamp lives off the sewage of Merovingen. Clean up the canals, and how will it survive?"

"No problem," Yarrow reassured him. "We examined the flow of the water table there; most of the swamp's water comes from the Greve Fork, not the canals. It actually gets very little of Merovingen's sewage, and that only from the westernmost Isles, filtered through the lagoon. Cleaning the water won't affect it."

"The lagoon's full o' tangle-lilies now," Rif considered. "Baby deathangel feed off'n 'em. Bad business, them fish."

"No doubt, but we have to study the creatures. We'd like to get some full-fledged adults, but the local waters are nearly fished out, thanks to the new fad for them." Yarrow sighed. "If we can't spare a boat to go out in deep waters, we'll just have to catch some young ones from the lagoon and ship them out for study. That will take time . . .''

''But damn, what if the tangle-lilies get into the swamp?'' Raven insisted. ''Won't they upset the balance there?''

''No, they can't compete with what's already there. Those swamp plants of yours won't give them a millimeter of foothold. Besides—'' Yarrow flicked a glance toward Klickett. ''What the young deathangel don't eat, the, uh, skits make short work of. No, those weeds of ours can't do very well outside the city.''

''They're growin' well enough in-city.'' Rif frowned. ''Canalers complain 'cause they tangle up the water so much. Folks're already out cuttin' an' brewin'an' burnin' 'em, but they're still clutterin' up the water.''

''Better'n ye hoped,'' Klickett added. ''By next spring, I reckon, they'll be growin' as far north as The Rock 'imself. No way ter root 'em out o' Merovingen now.''

''An' a whole lot o' folks got free fuel an' real cheap firewood,'' Rif added. ''But there's still grumblin' over the stuff.''

''I suppose we can hurry the next phase,'' Yarrow considered.

''Ey? What's that?''

''We introduce a . . . sort of water flea that eats the dead and rotted weed—and then we bring in some nice, very edible crabs that eat the water fleas. We did want to wait until we were sure the water was clean, but if the weeds are becoming a plague . . .''

''Ney, let 'er wait 'til next year,'' Rif decided. ''Already there's folks gettin' good work rakin' an' haulin' the stuff fer the Carswells—an' ye heard how well the Carswells're doin' sellin' the dried stuff. Let 'er ride, Yarrow. Let canalsiders get the idea o' copyin' Carswell—cut, dry, bale an' sell the stuff, or keep it fer themselves. Let's not rush the plan.''

"I can just see all the roofs of the Tidewater spread with drying weed," Yarrow smiled. "Imagine the bribes paid to the people on the upper stories."

"Imagine the smell," Raven considered.

"Better'n the canals used ter," Rif countered. "Folks're beginnin' ter notice that when ye fall in the water nowadays, ye don' necessarily get sick an' die."

"Back ter them engines," said Klickett, digging into her buttered roots. "That's the next big step, ain't she? Ye can call 'er 'old tech' an' swear it makes no difference t'yer karma, but ye know folks'll be wary."

"An' greedy," Rif reminded her. "Ye know other boat shops'll be on 'em like flies: buy one, take 'er down, figure how ter make 'em themselves. They're real easy ter figure, real simple after all. That was the whole point now, wasn'it?''

"Of course," said Yarrow. "We already dropped a word in the right ears at Foundry. Long before flood-tide, the knowledge of making and repairing those simple 'same-old-tech-just-new-built' engines should be all over the city. There's no guessing how many of the poor will take the idea and run with it, but the knowledge *will* be available to them."

"Mhm," said Klickett, reaching into her bag for her ever-present knitting. "And how's these engines ter be sold without the College's stamp of approval on each one, hey? Enough of a step, buyin' a new engine—even if the tech's supposed t'be old stuff—without seein' she's illegal, too."

"No problem," Yarrow waved away a fly. "Yossarian has a lovely collection of College stamps—exactly like the real thing—just waiting to be plastered on any engine that isn't, hmm, *discreetly* placed. They all have beautifully forged signatures of various College clerks—all of them in Cardinal Boregy's division, I might add. If the old snake ever takes a notion to inspect boat engines and examine the stamps, he'll end by suspecting—perhaps purging—a good fraction of his own staff.''

"Nice," Raven approved, over the others' laughter. "Is there a chance the College will actually try to ban engines, old or new?''

" 'Cept fer themselves, o' course—an' their hightown friends,'' Rif chuckled.

"Unlikely, but let them," Yarrow smiled cruelly. "The best way to make a new technology widespread and underground is to make it popular—and then ban it.''

"That'll sure make folks go fer 'discreet' engines," Klickett considered. "An' what the blacklegs can't see, the sharrh surely won't. But what I want ter know 'bout is the metal.''

"Eh?''

"Metal—fer parts, fer engines, fer stills an' all that. Ye know how much the stuff costs down here. Where's it ter come from? Fer that matter, where'd Yossarian's new engines come from in th' first place?''

"No problem," Yarrow said again, reaching for the beer. "This really isn't a metal-poor world, you know. If it were, everyone would have died of anemia generations ago. The problem with metal is knowing where to find it—and the Friends of Jane preserved and regained enough knowledge of geology to know where to look. Among other things, I can tell you, our folk found a good iron deposit in an old volcanic crater, some years back. No one else knows of it, and it's far enough out in the wilderness that no one's likely to stumble on it. We mine, process, and sell the metal . . . discreetly. Lately we've been selling a good amount of it here in town. Where did you think a lot of our funds came from?''

Rif yelped with laughter. Klickett smiled, and hurried through three more stitches. Raven looked thoughtful.

"I hope we're not selling any in Nev Hettek," he said. "You know what they'll make with it."

"They'd make weapons anyway," Yarrow shrugged. "We *have* sold metal in Nev Hettek, I'll admit, but we've taken care to drive prices up, not down. Besides . . ." Her smile turned grim. "The news from Nev Hettek is, they're having some sort of plague problem—striking in high places, too. Gossip says it came from trade with Merovingen, which tends to discourage interest in further contact with the city. It's begun to make serious inroads into Karl Fon's troops—and bureaucracy, too. It's enough to keep him too busy to use any weapons he may have bought."

Rif nodded thoughtfully. Klickett shrugged and looked away. Raven chose not to ask for details, but applied himself to his beer.

"I hear from elsewhere," Yarrow went on, "That certain midtown families have gone into heavy use and production of chugger. We're busy dropping word to them that the tangle-lilies are very good for brewing the stuff. Naturally they don't care for the coming ban. The counterfeiters are getting ready to mass-produce special permits—complete with Boregy's signature—as soon as the ban's in force."

" 'Law after law breeds a multitude of thieves,' " Raven dredged up from his slowly-clearing memory. "Might add, 'counterfeiters,' too."

"Amen," said Klickett. "But what's yer uptown cell say 'bout the backwash from engines hurtin' the underpinnin's o' the Isles? How's the landlords takin' ter that, hey?"

"They don't like it, but general opinion is that the buildings would need repair anyway, and might as well do it now as later. The lower walkways can use some backwash-curbs, too, especially with flood-tide coming on. Also . . .'' She grinned. ''One of the local building-repair families just got a shipment of a new . . . but not called that, of course—brand of cement that sets underwater. Of course, they also got contacts for more—and so did their smaller rivals.''

''What, we've got a cement maker's too?'' Rif marveled. ''Where— Ney, I shouldn' ask. But how d'ye hide an operation that big?''

''By putting it underground, of course—like everything else we do. Mine, lime-kiln, everything—all underground, complete with smoke traps. Nobody knows where that is, either.''

'' 'Dig Down Deep,' '' Rif quoted, raising her cup in salute.

'' 'Unseen Is Unfettered,' '' Raven echoed, finishing his beer.

''And 'Look to Life Itself,' '' Yarrow finished. ''I swear, it's a crime against science that humans have lived six centuries on Merovin and learned so little about its ecology. By Jane's will, we'll remedy that.''

''Well, the Scourin' didn' help much,'' Klickett reminded her. ''Folks scramblin' just ter stay alive don' have much time fer studyin' the wildlife.''

''That might excuse the first surviving generation, even the second.'' Yarrow's seamed face tightened. ''But . . . for six hundred years? Sweet Jane, but I sometimes think the old Union first colonized this world with a crop of idiots. Who else would place their major city and spaceport right over an active earthquake fault? There are stories, from the old records, that they bred men in laboratories—cloned them in job lots, trained them on nothing but tapes, carefully taught them not to think for themselves but only do what they were taught. Jane knows what kind of gene pool we started with, and how brain-dead a culture.''

''Some was smart enough—an' feisty enough—ter hide out from the sharrh themselves,'' Rif reminded her. "We're the descend'nts o' wily survivors, r'member. The good obedient types left with the ships."

"True, true," Yarrow admitted. "They just didn't leave us with a culture that encouraged study or progress. Hmm, and speaking of that, we have another problem."

The others shoved their dishes aside as Yarrow fumbled in her pockets for some notes.

"Here we are. Yes. The ban forced us to speed up our schedule on those engines. This means the workshop school needs to train up lots of mechanics to work them. So far, no problem; the word is already out that Brecht's—no visible connection with Yossarian, of course—is hiring. No need to mention that it's also training. The problem is school space; he has to expand fast. We've got to find a safe, cheap, large enough place to put the school and still make it look like nothing but a crude tool shop—and not possibly big enough to compete with Foundry. Workspace is hard to come by in this city. Does anyone have any suggestions?"

There was a long thoughtful silence around the table. A mouse took the opportunity to skitter across the floor. Rif aimed a halfhearted kick at it, then smiled suddenly.

"DeGrasse's barge," she said.

"Barge?" Yarrow sat up, mind already working on possibilities. "Out on the water?"

"She's been sittin' at East Dike fer almos' two years now, doin' nothin'. Harbormaster can't sell nor rent 'er, seein' she's too big fer the canals an' not fit fer sea, an' 'e's not ready ter cut 'er up fer firewood jes' yet. She's got roof stakes, an' it wouldn' take much ter fix 'er up fit fer a tool shop—or a schoolroom."

"Aye, and I've heard that Farren Delaney's bored ter tears with 'is job in the Harbormaster's office," Klickett put in. "Y'know 'e's got a likin' fer us canalsiders an' water-folk. I daresay, 'e'd like a chance ter do somethin' charitable.''

"Hmm, yes," Yarrow purred thoughtfully. "And . . . I've heard that Farren is to be kicked upstairs soon, given a Prefecture of his own—Waterways, I believe it is. If he helps us before that happens, he may take the promotion as an omen that he's on the right track, helping the poor . . .''

"Ariadne'll love it," Rif beamed. "Put the word in 'er ear, Klickett, an' she'll put 'er in his. 'E gets our job done, then 'e gets promoted, an' we boost 'is name aroun' canalside. 'E gets a faction an' a promotion, we get our school an' a better foothold in hightown.''

"Aye, I'll do 'er," Klickett beamed back. "Ariadne's droppin' by my shop t'morrer, not that she needs any new sweaters. She likes the way yer book's sellin', too, Rif. Don'tcher think it's time ye gave 'er some better way ter contact ye than jes' my shop?''

"Already done," Rif grinned. "I asked Rattail. She knows some good addresses near the College, an' we picked un fer a mail drop.''

"One o' the student taverns, 'ey?''

"Now, how'd ye guess?''

"Uhm, isn't that a problem?" Raven spoke up. "I mean, if you're traveling in hightown circles, isn't it dangerous to . . . well, spread rumors and address cards and so on, down in lowtown, the way, er, we were doing today?''

"Ney, no worry," Rif laughed. "Klickett here can tell ye, Ariadne Delaney an' her hightown friends've never seen me the way I really look, nor Rat neither." She shifted her position and . . . *changed:* voice, expression, enunciation, gestures, posture, everything.

"Aye, m'dears," she said, her accent not quite hightown, only suggesting a beguiling hint of The Lower Depths, "I assure you, neither Ariadne Delaney nor her most charming friends have *ever* seen me as I truly am.''

On the instant, she dropped back into the same-old-canal-rat-Rif, and grinned broadly. ''She's even better with the clothes, hairdo, an' makeup,'' she said. ''Takes us more'n an hour ter put 'er all on, me an' Rat both. But when we're done, when we go out there ter play fer Ariadne's crowd an' knock 'em dead, I swear, ye wouldn' reco'nize us. An' when we leave, we make *damn* sure nobody follers us back t' the Tidewater.''

''But if anyone really bothers to make the connection . . .'' Raven worried.

''What'll they find, 'ey? That me an' Rat sometimes sing in lowtown dives, an' there's rumors we've picked a pocket er two in our time.'' Her eyes slitted in hard thought. ''Ain't but two people outside o' here know I'm a Friend o' Jane, an' won't neither o' them talk.''

''You're *sure?*''

''Yey. Jones won't 'cause she knows I could tell 'bout her—an' drag in her man as well. B— The other won't 'cause . . . well, he's a sympathizer, an' I got 'im in on that Master Milton deal, 'mong other things.''

''Well, make damned sure of him, Rif.''

''Aye, I got 'im . . . clinched.'' Rif smiled into her beer.

''You'll need more links in middle- and hightown,'' Yarrow went on. ''Ariadne's little arts program can help there, not to mention helping your career a bit. I daresay even Old Iosef will remember you, with Ariadne's help. You may need such links soon.''

''They say the governor's sick,'' Raven worried. ''He can't last forever, and the next governor—Jane knows who that will finally be—certainly won't be as favorable to you.''

''I'll work those links,'' Rif promised. ''But don'

worry 'bout the Old Man's health. He always gets some kind o' sick when there's a contr'versial bill comin' up that he don' want ter say yey or ney ter—like the College's chugger ban.''

"Still," Yarrow considered, "Soon as we can, we'd best tie in with one of the heirs.''

"Not Tatty!" Rif snorted. "Sooner bed a skit than that Sword-lovin', blackleg-shovin' bitch!''

"Certainly not Tatiana," Yarrow agreed. "Other cells are arguing the merits of Anastasi and Mikhail, but the majority argument swings with Mischa the Tinkerer.''

"Mischa?" Klickett shook her head. "He's 'is daddy's darlin', right enough, but he hasn't the brains of a yellowtail. Hightown loves 'im, 'cause they figure they can shove 'im. Besides, he's gone mushbrained over Crazy Cassie. What good'd 'e be t'us? He can't do nothin' but play with 'is little machines . . .''

Klickett stopped right there, catching the implications of what she'd just said.

"Right," Yarrow smiled. "Of all the heirs, he's the one most likely to favor tech. And . . . he badly needs friends. Particularly, he needs a friend who can steer him fairly through the wilds of city politics.''

The other three looked at each other. "Farren Delaney!" they all said at once.


"How was your day, dearest?" Ariadne asked as she poured the after-dinner tea. "Are they treating you decently at the office?" She didn't add: *since the race*.

Farren shrugged eloquently, not catching the implication. In fact, no one in the office seemed to know about his lowtown hobby. "Too decently, if anything. Aside from signing the papers the clerks bring me, there just isn't a blessed thing to *do*." He let his eyes wander to the windows and the view of slow sunset over the rooftops of Merovingen. "Of course I've studied all the papers they bring me, trying to see the applications and implications, as Father always said—and blasted if I can find a thing. I've the sinking feeling that I've been shuttled from one dead end to another for years. Er, not that it's your fault, dear," he added hastily.

"But there are possibilities inherent in the position," Ariadne murmured.

Farren caught her tone and looked at his wife. "Ah, you have something in mind, my dear?"

"I did hear something this afternoon, though it quite slipped my mind until now." Ariadne put down her cup. "You know, there's a charitable fellow named Brecht who runs a tool shop down in the Tidewater, and he's made a point of hiring poor children—but not really to work much, certainly not at anything dangerous. What he really does is teach the children basic reading, writing and figures—and then he has them do a little assembly work, enough to justify his paying them, and also to teach them basic mechanics."

Farren laughed delightedly. "Oh, I can see it! A school, disguised as a workshop! Of course; canalers are too proud—hmm, or too nervous of their karmic debts—to take anything for free, but offer to pay them . . . How brilliant!"

"Yes, it's his way of paying some karmic debt or other. But in fact, he's been so successful that he needs room to expand."

"Hmm, hardly my jurisdiction, Addie." Farren guessed where this was going.

"Ah, but it might be." Ariadne leaned forward, the hint of a gleam showing in her eyes. "An ideal location for his shop-school would be the old DeGrasse barge at East Dike."

"Really?" Farren rubbed his upper lip, seeing possibilities. A school for poor children: he'd thought once or twice about founding something like that. Always before, he'd run up against two problems: first, any public school would be inspected and fussed over and eventually run by the College—which would not endear the school to Adventist parents; second, canalers and lowtown landsiders needed their children to work, rake in the copperbits—and couldn't see the use of spending/losing precious coin on sending their children to school, especially when they'd managed to survive without school themselves. This fellow Brecht, however, had neatly found a way around both problems. On-the-job training wasn't the same thing as an official *school,* really, and paying for the children's presence would mollify the parents. Very clever. One had to admire a mind like that. "A school on a barge? Isn't that rather a dangerous place to have children about?"

"Not for canalers' children; they're born and raised on their boats. The problem is getting the permits from the Harbormaster's office, which technically owns the barge. Now East Dike, and the barge, would fall under your jurisdiction, don't you think?"

Farren laughed heartily, seeing connections click into place. "Yes, it does. Oh, it does indeed. Who could argue with having such a reliable tenant as a tool shop? Hmm, and it wouldn't hurt for me to show activity in office once in a while. At the very least, I'd find out which of my clerks are obstructionists."

"Not to mention gaining more fame and popularity among the Shoeless," Ariadne put in. "They really appreciate anyone from hightown taking a kindly interest in them—especially these days."

"Lord, yes." Farren frowned and shoved his teacup away. "I don't know what the College thinks it's doing, encouraging that insane Boregy woman. She's preaching something close to class war, you know. As if the poor needed any more abuse! Can't the College see that it's actually alienating the faithful down in lowtown? Or don't those fools even care? I suspect that woman's damnable 'prophecies' are behind this fuel-alcohol ban the College is proposing; crush the poor, slap them into proper humility—as if that sort of thing ever worked. Damn that fool Ito! He has no idea what he's playing at. I rather wish *he'd* have himself an overdose of deathangel, and put us all out of his misery.''

Ariadne pursed her lips and put that comment aside for consideration later. "No doubt the ban will simply draw lowtown farther away from compliance with the law—or any law. Someone has to heal that breach, dear.''

"Yes, yes indeed.''

*Someone like you, dear.* Ariadne smiled demurely and took another sip of her tea.

Moghi chewed his lip and studied the card for long moments after Jones had stopped talking. "The man's either a fool or smarter'n a whip,'' he finally said. "Same old tech, nothin' new, just simpler an' new-made, hey?''

"That's what 'is shill said,'' Jones agreed. "I think she's damn dangerous, Moghi. How'd 'e get the College t'approve them engines, put their stamps on 'em? Ye know 'e most likely didn't. That means, folks what get 'em, uses 'em, they're like ter get took up by the blacklegs fer unlicensed tech. Y'got ter warn folks, Moghi.'' She didn't tell him about the real danger, that the shill had been Rif, and these engines were most likely Janist work, tied in with the same plot that brought the damned tangle-lilies to Merovingen. *And never mind my part in that!* She shivered.

Moghi tapped the card on his teeth. "Maybe he did get 'em licensed somehow, maybe he makes 'em 'discreet' enough nobody'll find 'em. There used ter be ways, y'know, ter keep engines quiet. Mufflin', or baf-flin' or somesuch, I think they called it . . . Won't know 'til . . . we actually see one.'' He cocked an eye toward Jones. ''I got a friend'd like ter see one o' them engines. Ye interested in makin' a trip ternight, Jones?''

''Not ter Yossarian's!'' Jones almost squeaked. ''I'm jes' tellin' ye what's afloat, Moghi; I ain't gettin' mixed up in 'er. Get somebody else.''

''Ain't like ye ter be so pusey, Jones. What's eatin' ye?''

''Goddammit, Moghi, someone's been followin' me around!'' Jones slammed a fist on her thigh. ''Noticed 'em days ago, but can't make out who nor why. Could be from Megarys; maybe they figured out who called vengeance on 'em after they snatched me. I got ter be careful, don'tcher see?''

Moghi thought on that awhile. ''So what's t'see?'' he said, unimpressed. ''Ye go t'a shop, fetch a cargo, bring 'er here. Ye stay with crowds, he ain't goin' ter snatch ye nor anythin' like it. Do ye want, I'll send one o' my boys with ye. Jes' buy the engine, keep 'er covered, bring 'er back here. No sweat.''

Jones squirmed, knowing she'd have to give away a dangerous chip of information to get out of this. ''Moghi, ye got ter know; I think them new engines is Jane work. I don't want ter go near no Jane place.''

Moghi raised an eyebrow again, then put it down. ''Jane work, Rev'nantist work or sharrh work, what's the difference? They're just another seller, an' ye're just another buyer.''

''I don' want ter get mixed up with no Janes!''

Moghi missed nothing. His eyes slitted, pinned her. ''Ye had dealin's with 'em before, Jones?''

''Dammit, Moghi!''

''Yey or ney, Jones.''

''All right, yey! I did! Just twice, simple fer-hire jobs, ferryin' folk aroun' the city—that's all, an' that's enough. I don' want ter get no more o' their business, specially not now with this tail on me.''

Moghi nodded knowingly. ''Simple fer-hire jobs, an' ye wouldn've known they were Janes. This have any-thin' ter do with them holes in yer skip last Festival Moon?''

''Moghi . . .''

''An' that stuff in yer bilges, smelled like the change in the water?''

''It was barrels!'' Jones almost yelled. ''They had me fetch some barrels, then they dumped 'em in the water. Somebody took potshots at us—I dunno who—but we spilled some in the skip.'' *Rif* . . . ''They tol' me what was goin' down, 'cause I didn' want ter risk my hide without knowin' what I was gettin' inter.''

''What was in the barrels?''

''I dunno, they didn' tell me—jes' said it was some-thin' ter stop the plague, kill the fever in the water.''

''And there *was* no plague this fever season.'' Moghi rubbed his jaw, thinking long. ''All right, I'll get someone else ter go. An' I'll keep eyes out fer this tail ye've picked up.''

''Thanks, Moghi.'' Jones shivered again. Now Moghi knew about the Janes, and her connection with them. Maybe this meant her chances of living to flood-season had just gone down another big notch—or maybe it meant they'd improved. No way to tell, ex-cept that Moghi had hinted, just hinted, at a bit of protection.

Raven almost tiptoed down the corridor, package clamped nervously under his arm. He wasn't used to all these enclosing walls, the presence of so many peo-ple just out of sight, even though he knew that half this Isle—and certainly all this floor—was a Janist safe house. He glanced left and right as he came to the door, saw no one, knocked quietly.

Soft footsteps shuffled inside. The door unlocked, and May peered out. Raven was struck again by how different, how much better, how much younger she looked with decent washing, decent food, decent clothes. He ducked past her, turned and shut the door quickly.

"Somebody after ye?" she whispered.

"No." Raven ducked his head and grinned sheepishly. "Just old habits. I'm not used to . . . all this."

"Hell, neither am I. Sure is a lot more comfortable than the swamp, though." She led him back into the little apartment. It was sparsely furnished, but cozy. The abundance of lamps was reassuring. He noted that their flames burned blue at the root, that the fire in the little heating stove fed on blocks of pressed and dried tangle-lily. May rubbed her hands, appreciating the warmth. "So what'cher got there?" she asked.

Raven smiled and held out the package. "New sweater and pants," he said. "And some soap, and other things."

"Oh, ye shouldn't have . . ." May pulled off the wrappings and dug through the contents. "Cookies! Oh, Lord and Ancestors! So long since I've tasted cookies . . ."

"Some advantages to living in town. There's a bottle of wine there, too."

Crooning with joy, May spread out a threadbare cloth on the bed, brought two cups and a plate, and set them an impromptu picnic. Raven joined her, grateful for the softness of a real mattress under his knobby bones again.

Two cups and half the cookies later, May got around to asking him for the latest news.

"It's going fast and well, May. Our samples have gone north, and it looks like the school-shop will get the barge."

"Mhm," May commented around a mouthful of

cookie. "I saw the boats lined up at Yossarian's shop when I poled 'round the city t'day. Looks like he'll have all the business he can handle—an' maybe better move soon. Seen Raj, too; he's doin' fine, really in good with Kamats, goin' t'school at the College an' all. Spotted Wolfling shadowin' 'im like a faithful guard dog. The cell got any plans fer him yet?"

"Not yet." Raven stretched until his joints crackled. "Let him keep on guarding the boys, and I'll keep an eye on him."

"We got to start buildin' our own cell pretty soon. I could go out on the water, work as a canaler herb-healer, collect a cell there. What'cher think?"

"Hmm, wait on that until you've gone the full course of Yarrow's medical classes. Then ask her. It sounds like a fine idea to me."

"Heh! I'm teachin' her and 'er other students as much's she's teachin' me!"

"That's the way it's supposed to go, my girly."

"Oh, hush. Heard any rumors from hightown?"

"Just more garbage about Crazy Cassie. Mischa the Clockmaker's going to see her again soon, which is probably bad news."

"There's got ter be a way t'lure him away from that witch."

"We're working on some ideas . . ." Raven drummed his fingers together, wondering just how to put this. Cells had to communicate, spread information, but no one must mention names, dates, times or places of meeting: basic security. "We've got . . . a good contact in hightown, a good-family woman with a husband in . . . hmm, I can't tell you which office. He doesn't know anything about us, but he sympathizes without knowing it. She's certainly a sympathizer, though she doesn't know exactly who we are, and she's a . . . charitable type."

May only grunted, not terribly impressed.

"Point is, she's got easier access to Mikhail than anyone else we've got. When we come with a workable idea, we can pipeline it through her."

"So," May guessed. "Mikhail's the heir we're backin'?"

"Heh! Aye, you're still sharp, May. It's to be Mikhail."

"Why him? They say he couldn't find 'is bottom with both hands."

"Three good reasons." Raven ticked them off on his fingers. "One: Mischa's the apple of the Old Man's eye, but Iosef's worried for the boy's future and would bless any decent Hightowner who'd side with the boy, protect and guide and back him, and we've got a likely prospect. Two: despite his slobbering over Crazy Cassie, Mikhail favors tech; that means he'd give us more leeway than his sister or brother ever would. Three: right now he's low man on the political totem pole, despite daddy's favor; whether he knows it yet or not, he has the most need of allies—and again, we can provide that. Besides, if his star rises without help from the usual old fossils on The Rock, it'll throw the whole town's political games into confusion—and we can make use of that."

"Aye," May chuckled. " 'Aye, we're good at dancin' on the waves, Dancin' on the waves of the storm.' "

"Damn!" Raven sat up. "Where'd you ever learn a Janist hymn? I never taught you that!"

"Off'n a Falkenaer lad, when I was young. It always stuck in my mind. So did he, fer that matter. Pretty blond thing . . ."

"Easy, woman. I'm still young enough to be jealous."

"And I'm old enough not t'wait around fer sailors." May ran a ticklesome hand down Raven's chest, making him smile. "Hmm. Tell me, d'ye think Mischa the Clockmaker's gettin' . . . hmm, sufficiently laid?"

Raven laughed shortly. "If nothing else, his daddy would see to that—even if he had to deliver willing women on the doorstep, along with the morning tea and news report."

"Then 'tisn't itching balls sends Mischa pantin' after Crazy Cassie; 'tis somethin' else. Hmm." She thought long, then grinned. "Y'know what I think would do Mischa the most good?"

"What, my toothsome wench?"

"Respect. A *real* friend—one what's practical, and sensible, and gets things done, and what actually *respects* the boy. That'd pull 'im away from pantin' after prophets an' mysteries, now wouldn' it?"

"May, my love," Raven murmured, seeing possibilities, "you're an absolute genius."

Black Cal stood waiting by the railing of Coffin Isle, a black silhouette against the dim-lit sky, when Rif came trotting over the bridge. They met, hands interlocking smoothly as fine gears, turned and strolled unhurriedly to the shadowed door and the stairs beyond.

They said no word until an hour later.

*Lord, but I'm lucky,* Black Cal thought, pulling a lock of Rif's hair away from her bare breasts. *To find another artist in this ugly city, and one who loves—at least likes me . . .*

No, he couldn't ask her for the word. But he had to ask her for something.

"Rif . . ."

"Mmm?"

"Sing for me?"

Rif blinked at him, but gave no other sign of surprise. She thought a moment, hummed experimentally, then launched into a quiet song.

*"Word came out of the sky*
*To our forebears long ago:*
*'Leave this planet or die.'*
*So many rose to go.*
*But a few were stubborn of soul*
*And would not quit their hard-won ground.*
*They hid and stayed through the winter's tide*
*When the Scouring-time came down."*

*Stubborn of soul, yes.* Black Cal smiled to himself.
*Not necessarily smart, just stubborn. But then, so is*
*life itself.*

*"And how do we survive?*
*How do we keep alive?*
*Where do we go from here?"*

Black Cal listened thoughtfully through the lines of
the song, guessing it was a Janist hymn even though
no names were mentioned. He'd grown good at iden-
tifying Janist themes.

*There are worse factions to run with. You have to*
*get into the boat sometime.*

Rif finished the song, snuggled closer and ran her
fingertips up and down his near thigh. "So, how've ye
been?" she murmured, not expecting a specific answer, just wanting to hear his voice in turn.

*Go with the tide.* "I've been keeping my ears open.
Word around the Signeury is that Iosef's going to sit
on the alcohol ban, string it out as long as possible.
You've got some breathing space; maybe until flood-
tide, maybe only a month, depending on how hard the
College wants to push this."

Rif sat up, eyes widening in amazement. "Ye really
do want ter get involved, Cal? Enough ter run news?"

*Maybe more than that.* "I told you I liked the Janes'
style. I suspect the Old Man's angry at Ito for letting

Mikhail get caught up with Cassie Boregy's crap. No love lost there.''

''Mhm.'' Rif pulled her hair back from her shoulders and shifted mental gears. ''Then he might do well ter hype the number of deaths from deathangel ODs, slap a ban on the damn fish, or ownin' or sellin' the same. Won't stop 'er, of course, but he'd jam a stick in Ito's wheels. Gods, if only somebody could slip Tatty an' her boyfriend an overdose of deathangel . . .''

''Or Ito himself,'' Black Cal smiled. ''It wouldn't do any good to OD Crazy Cassie; her harm's already been done, and that would clinch it.''

''True. Better ter discredit the bitch somehow. If we could come up with a counter-prophet, or some other fashion-fancy miracle . . .'' Rif frowned, thinking. ''We've been tryin' ter get our hands on some live deathangel, study 'em, figure out how that stuff works. Trouble is, with all the fashion fer the damned things, local waters're damn-near fished out. We haven't been able ter spare any long-distance fishin' parties ter go hunt 'em in deeper waters. Maybe by flood-tide . . .''

''Take too long.'' Black Cal eyes focused on the ceiling, then beyond. ''Maybe I can do something about that . . .''


Farren Delaney came home for lunch, which was unusual enough in itself. He was also whistling cheerfully, which was odder still. He also had a small gift for his wife, which he handed her—with an elaborate flourish—over the lunch table.

Ariadne took out the little gift with fingers that trembled in awe and bewilderment. ''My dear Lord, Farren, these are rainbow-shells—and already set—and enough to cover a whole collar and cuffs. What in the world. . . ?''

''That, my love, is merely the introduction.'' Farren settled on the nearest chair and reached for the basket of rolls. "The real gift is, your beloved school now has its barge. Right here—" He pulled a thick, folded sheet of official paper from his inside pocket. "—is the lease-form, signed and sealed and about to be delivered. Could you do that, darling, when I go back to the office?"

"Of course, of course . . ." Ariadne took the paper, opened it and stared at the writing in amazement. "But how on Merovin did you—"

"Hah, sheer overkill." Farren happily broke and buttered his sweet roll. "I went to Punabi's office with arguments enough to storm The Rock, but he crumbled without a fight. He was so grateful to find anyone who'd take that wreck off his hands, he practically kissed my feet. I dare say he thinks of me as the man who can answer his prayers about all such similar headaches in the harbor. And no, I had no obstruction from the clerks at all. Yes, I'm making friends and allies in the Harbormaster's office. Pass the jelly?"

"Oh? Yes, yes. Here it is. Farren, this is utterly wonderful. M'ser Brecht will be overjoyed, and doubtless so will the families of his students. Dearest, by flood-tide you'll have a reputation as the True Friend of the Poor. Everyone in Merovingen will know it, I swear."

"Hmm, gently, my dear." Farren's gaze swept out the window again. "Give me a reputation like that, and I'll have to live up to it, every blessed day. This is a small thing, but what can I do for an encore? It will have to be bigger and better, and at the moment I haven't the least idea what it should be."

"You'll think of something," Ariadne promised. "Hmm, I really would love to see these on my new formal sweater. I'll have to take them out to be sewn on professionally . . . and I can stop by the shop on my way back from Brecht's."

Farren cleared his throat. "Ah—my dear, I don't have to be back for a while. I was thinking . . ."

Ariadne demurely set down her teacup. "The children won't be home for hours," she hinted.

Smiling delicately, they rose and moved toward the door that led to their sleeping quarters.

Just then a servant entered the door behind them and coughed discreetly. "A messenger has arrived, m'ser—from the Signeury."

Ariadne and Farren turned toward the servant, identical thoughts darting through their minds. *What's so important that it can't wait?*

"Oh, let him in," Farren grumbled, flicking an apologetic look at his wife.

The messenger turned out to be a harried-looking youth with a stack of vellum envelopes under his arm. "So sorry to disturb you, Sub-Prefect," he dithered, "but I was told—by the governor himself—to deliver this to you, in person."

Farren took the proffered envelope as if it would explode at any moment. Ariadne watched as he opened it and read the message, barely daring to breathe.

Farren's face lit up with a triumphant smile. "Tell the governor," he said, "that I have received his message, and I will be delighted to accept the post."

The messenger bowed, turned and trotted off to his next port of call.

Ariadne waited until the room was cleared before pouncing on the seal-encrusted letter. *"What* position, Farren? Your promotion? Has it finally come?"

Farren beamed at her. "My dear, you are looking at the new Prefect of City Waterways," he chortled.

Ariadne looked blank. "Waterways? Oh, that isn't another backwater, is it?"

"No, Addie; it's freedom—freedom and power." Farren began to pace, across the room and back, across and back. "It's a full Prefecture, and my own Department, with no interference from anyone but the governor himself. Addie, love, I don't know how you did this, but it's all I need. Now I can show what Merovingen can do, if we but put our minds to it."

"Oh, yes, dear," Ariadne breathed, watching her husband with adoring eyes.

# FARREN'S FOLLY:
# MEETING OF MINDS

*Roberta Rogow*

Mention the name of Farren Delaney in Merovingen and you would get an amused smile, a contemptuous snort, a blank look, or a knowing smile, depending on the status of the individual questioned. In the eyes of fashionable Merovingen, Farren Delaney was the adjunct of Adiadne Delaney, thrower of parties and espouser of charitable causes. In the world of merchants and traders he was just one of the many bureaucrats in the Signeury whose seals were necessary on documents before business could proceed. To the canalers, Farren Delaney was an eccentric sportsman who could hold his own at boat-poling. In no case was Farren Delaney considered a thinker (save possibly by a handful of devotees of Mother Jane, and they kept their opinion to themselves. . . .).

Merovingen considered Farren Delaney (when it considered him at all) to be a lightweight chair-warmer without an idea of his own—unless that idea had to do with pretty shop-girls or boating. His cousin/wife Ariadne's maneuvering on his behalf had landed him in his own office with the high-sounding title of Prefect of Waterways—his predecessor now being Prefect of Docks and Harbors, a much more lucrative position, since no vessel could use Merovingen's public facilities without that all-important Docking Permit, and the fee for the permit could run quite high, under the table, as it were.

All that the Prefect of Waterways controlled was the water in the canals, the Det, and the currently lily-logged lagoon . . . and that, as everyone knew, was virtually uncontrollable except by the slow process of sweeping and the hope that the bloom was a fluke of nature, to vanish with first frost. . . .

Brought in on some Falken ship, perhaps. An unintended import from the Chattalen.

Winter would kill a soft-leaved plant: spring and first sprouting was the time to attack the problem, perhaps with oil, who knew?

So Farren sat in his new office and considered his options, and smiled grimly at the canal below him—well knowing, to be sure, how he had arrived at his present position: his wife had a luncheon for the old and ailing governor Iosef Kalugin, shortly after which m'sera Secretary Tatiana had found herself outmaneuvered, her man shunted out of the office she wanted a thumb on and into Docks and Waterfronts, while he, Farren, had the office, the title, and the stipend of a minor prefecture—far above his former position.

He could, of course, continue to do as he always had—which is to say, to do nothing. For most of his thirty-six years Farren had done that and done it very well—smiled his way through his schooling and managed to marry his cousin Ariadne, no beauty, but through her mother possessing Connections to most of the important Families in Merovingen-above . . . and from her mother possessing this fascination with Cul-

ture. (Ariadne's latest fancy had been to present a pair
of canalsider singers to Merovingian society as artists
and poets: she had, over the ten years of their union,
taken up the causes of neglected canaler orphans and
bridge-brats and stray cats—and between Children
(they had five), Charity (innumerable), and Culture (of
all sorts), Ariadne Delaney-Delaney had left her husband more or less to his own eccentric amusements.)

Farren glanced out the window, a mere slit in the
wall, but a major perk nonetheless—his previous office
having been a cubbyhole scantly screened from other
cubbyholes, windowless and very nearly airless, where
he had read documents by the light of a flickering lamp
and shoved them on to the next cubbyhole. As Prefect
of Waterways, he possessed an office, a desk and two
chairs, had the use of an official boat—had (Farren
checked out his supplies) papers, pens, ink.

All he needed now was something to do.

Farren started to doodle on the cheap newsprint
(someone, he thought, was trying to save a pennybit
or two by giving the lesser offices inferior paper) and
wondered how to apply himself—

The plants, perhaps.

The rash of fires in the last months—about Megary's
reconstruction: so far no one had been seriously hurt,
but there was always the possibility one of those ma-
licious fires might not be minor; might skip into the
upper tiers of this wooden city that was so vulnerable
to fire.

Farren scratched busily at his growing doodle, unaware that the door had just opened. The new Prefect
of Waterways shared the secretarial services of a Bright
Young Girl with the elderly Prefect of Ceremonials
and the Prefect of Standards. She was obviously not
available for watchdog duty, otherwise why would the
Prefect of Waterways be interrupted at his labors? Farren glanced up—

Then jumped to his feet. The governor of Merovingen was not in the habit of paying social calls on his underlings in the Signeury.

"Governor! Forgive me! To what do I owe this honor? —Please, sit down!" Farren pushed the spare chair toward the governor, who smiled gently and stepped aside so that Farren could see the younger man in the doorway.

"Delaney, have you been introduced to my son, Mikhail?" Iosef Kalugin nodded at the lanky young man who was trying very hard to melt into the wall.

Farren assessed Mikhail: rumored as more than slightly eccentric, considered by some to be an idiot and by others to be the Last Hope of the Kalugins. Whatever Iosef wanted, Farren decided, he would get, —although it was hard to see what use the Prefect of Waterways could be to the governor and his son.

"I haven't had the pleasure until now," Farren said, bowing.

Mikhail smiled back, briefly and faintly.

"He's been solitary for too long," Iosef said. "Time he got out of that damned workshop and got to know people. I thought he could start here in the Signeury, learn the offices. Your wife tells me you do a good, conscientious job—show Mischa how to go on. Introduce him 'round. Let him get to know people, let them get to know him."

Farren glanced at Mikhail. The prospect of meeting a hallful of minor bureaucrats did not seem to thrill him: he was edging around behind the visitor's chair and over to the window.

"I'll do my best, m'ser," Farren said, as Iosef muttered, "Good luck," and let himself out.

Mikhail slumped into the chair.

Farren's smile faded. So much for having a wife active on one's behalf: this, then, was the price of the fine new office and its fine title—nursemaiding this

gawky nincompoop through the mazes of the bureaucracy. As for the Idea, the brilliant Idea that had come
on him this afternoon as he sat . . .

"What's this?" Mikhail asked sharply, turning Farren's doodle-sheet around.

"Oh, —a small idea."

"Mmm?"

"The fires we've been having . . . you're aware—"

"I know. Mostly Megary's. One of m'sister's lovers
got caught in that one." Mikhail giggled. "I don't like
him, not a bit. —What are you going to do, mount a
pump on a ship? Draw out of the canal?"

Farren blinked. "Yes. That was the idea. Plenty of
water—but what we have to do is get it higher, up to
second tier and third. I thought a pipe and hose . . ."

"Won't work," Mikhail said flatly, reaching for a
pen and an inkwell. "Not enough give, too much pressure and flex with the boat bobbing around, no way to
control it. . . ." Gone was the giggling, awkward
hobbledehoy. Farren nodded as Mikhail sketched out
his refinements on the Idea with quick, sure strokes of
the pen.

"What you need is something flexible, long enough
to reach, hoist it up—can't be pipe, you'll tip, for one
thing—and how do you clear the bridges? Has to be
light, else you have a lot of weight on that skip, water-
weight when she draws . . . maybe brace on the walls,
hold her steady— How many crew?"

"Six, seven . . ." Farren was impressed. "More
ashore, of course."

"Take training to use this thing. Lot of gear, small
space, y'know, like as not bump into each other—"

Farren stared at the sketch. The skip now held an
oversized pump amidships. Two large wheels flanked
the pump. Ladders rested on a rack to the side.

"Beautiful!" Farren breathed. "Mikhail, my friend,
you're going to be an asset!"

Mikhail shifted his position in the chair and coughed. "I don't know anything about Waterways."

"Waterways includes what goes on the water," Farren reminded him. "We're just expanding the meaning a little."

"Are you going to build this boat?"

"I have access to city vessels," Farren reminded him. "Of all classes. All I have to do is remodel one. Redesign it, so to speak. And I can tell you know all about that."

He did indeed, Farren said to himself. *Mikhail may have a reputation as a gormless tinkerer, but he's been studying, watching the way things work. . . .*

Mikhail rubbed his nose. "I'll need materials," he said. "I'm not sure about the hose. Canvas reinforcing, maybe? Tarred between layers, to keep it watertight? I can requisition most anything. A pump that size is pretty major, though—"

Farren chortled. "And they call you a fool! My friend, you build the hose and the couplings. Let me worry about the pump."

# RUN SILENT, RUN CHEAP (REPRISED)

## Leslie Fish

There was someone pacing behind her on the walkways.

*Damn!*

Jones dug in her pole, shoved a little harder, listened for the footsteps above and weighed her choices. If she could reach some safe patch of shadow, hide just long enough to rack her pole, get to the engine, pour in the chugger and start it . . .

But that old engine was noisy, and the unseen stalker could follow her by the sound.

She could pretend to ignore the tail, go right ahead past Calliste Isle and Ventani, then to Moghi's place and safety . . .

But did she really want to lead that shadow to Moghi's again? He just might be from Megary's after all—maybe Megary had figured out who was behind all that fire and damage, which had cost them a pretty penny to repair, and more money for all the guards on Megary's Isle these days—and that could be really bad trouble.

No, not toward Moghi's. Somewhere else, but where?

Calliste Isle lay close now. Could she swing hard around the corner without being seen? Try it.

Jones leaned hard into the pole, wishing for just a little more speed as she darted her skip around Calliste corner and into the narrow Calliste-Ventani canal.

Damn, no, there was the echo of hurrying footsteps above her again. Whoever that shadow was, he was good and he followed close. How to lose him? Where?

Under Pardee-Calliste Bridge? No, no good hiding place under there, and besides, he'd guess where she'd gone.

There was a narrow slip beyond that bridge, though, unseeable from this side or above. If she could get into that, she could wait the scumsucker out—or tie up, sneak out on the lower walkway, cut through Pardee and walk the rest of the way to Moghi's. That'd work.

But how to lose the shadow in that stretch of open water between here and the bridge? From the footsteps, he'd be to her right; too much easy viewing from there. If only some traffic would come, some boat big enough to duck behind, block vision long enough. Or if only she could get her engine started quick, take off . . .

*Or if I had one of them "discreet" engines . . .*

Jones squelched the thought, slowed her skip as the bridge approached—as if she were planning to tie-up under it—and waited for any change, any break of luck.

There— Lord and Ancestors, was that the sound of oncoming boat-wash? Yes, and a large one, to judge by the echoes. But coming so fast and quiet? She must be powered under several poles, but where was the sound of poles dipping? And what was that deep thrumming sound, so low it was felt in the bones more than heard?

No matter. Use the chance.

Jones set her pole, jigged the skip sideways a bit as if making room, and watched for the first sign of on-coming bow-wave.

There, under the bridge—and *wide*. A damn big skip, and moving fast, fast. The deep thrumming sound hung around it like a cloud of mist.

Jones jabbed her pole down with all her strength and shot straight across the canal, right under the oncoming bow.

A screech of surprise and a furious obscenity followed her as she scraped past, missing collision by a handspan. She recognized the cursing voices: Deiter clan, one of their big boats. But where were the poles? How could their boat make such speed? And what the *hell* was that bone-deep noise around it?

No matter, not now. Jones shot under the bridge and past it, pole jabbing bottom for all she was worth, past the Deiter boat and the bridge, through the shadows on the black water and there, going by memory more than sight, into that shadowed slip beyond.

Safe—and a final jab of the pole to stop motion, still the skip. She turned to look back at the darkened canal, just in time to see the Deiters' boat fade into darkness. Just in time to see the faint but steady turbulence at the stern, and only two poles visible—just enough for steering.

*The Deiters got one of them Discreet engines. Already.*

Jones tied up in the slip with hands working automatically, ears strained for the sound of footsteps, mind working on something else altogether.

The rope pulled tight, holding the skip safe in darkness.

The distant footsteps echoed across the canal, slowed, baffled. They paced halfway up Calliste-Pardee Bridge, paused a long while, then turned and went back again.

Jones sat very still in the skip, thinking about that big Deiter boat with its new engine already, probably bought from Yossarian's the very day of the boat race, probably within an hour of the first sight of those cards.

*So much for the Ban.*

Boats as big as the Deiter clan used, already supplied with those chugger-burning engines that stayed hid, gave no sign, ran fast and quiet in the dark. The Ban wouldn't slow them down. Any advantage the small-boat canalers had hoped to get from the Ban was doomed before it started; big boats carried engines the same as little ones, ran them after dark just like the little ones. Maybe by daylight, when nobody dared use the engines for fear of Ban and blacklegs, a small boat could get the advantage of poling-speed and maneuverability, but after dark all bets were off. No advantage then in being small, except maybe negotiating the smaller waterways.

That meant small jobs, or sneaky jobs. It meant getting deeper and deeper into that dark, vast water termed "illegal," and "underground."

It also meant that chugger was here to stay.

Just like the tangle-lilies.

*Damned Janes thought of everything!*

Yes, there was a knot of the damned lilies right here in the slip, dead and turning brown, ripe for brewing in the still or drying and burning in the stove.

*"Cut 'em, Jones. Harvest an' use 'em. That's what they're for."* With a whispered oath, Jones yanked the stuff up with her boat hook and threw it on the bow of her skip. Still it or burn it, she'd deal with it later. Have to deal with it later.

With another blistering curse she got up and untied the skip, and set off for Moghi's.

Rif wakened slowly to the feel of long fingers combing gently down her back. She stretched, purred, rolled over and looked up into Black Cal's green eyes. He was smiling. It wasn't his usual fleeting smile, certainly not that toothy hunter's grin: more playful, secretive.

"Y'got somethin' in mind?" she asked, expecting anything from political news to kinky suggestions.

Black Cal smiled wider, and nodded. "Get dressed," he said. "I have something to show you, over at East Dike."

Intrigued, Rif raised an eyebrow at him and reached about for her scattered clothes.

Fifteen minutes later they were out on the waterside of East Dike, pacing along by the short docks south of the big shipping slips. A small wharf lay there, and at its far end, overshadowed by the height of the piers, almost impossible to see from anywhere else, was an odd low boat under a worn tarpaulin. Black Cal went to it and hauled the tarpaulin away.

Rif gasped in recognition as she saw it plain. Three narrow hulls joined by an arrowhead-shaped deck, three raked masts with drawn-up booms, furled water-gray sails, all painted water-blue-gray above and surface-silver below the waterline, small and light and inexpressibly graceful, built totally for secrecy and speed: it was the perfect smuggler's boat.

"There are three of Yossarian's smaller engines inboard," Black Cal pointed out. "They're well hidden. You can reach them only through a false bulkhead, which may cause problems with coordinated steering. She'll run well on the central engine alone, certainly well enough on sails alone. The still, brewing tank and fuel cans are hidden in the hulls."

". . . Master Milton's boat," Rif whispered, remembering. She didn't dare to add: *you got engines that you know damn well aren't approved by the College, don't carry real tax-stamps or seals; you did that, Black Cal.* "D-did ye get the designs from him?"

"No. I just remembered what I'd seen, made sketches, found a . . . discreet and willing boatwright." He didn't add: *not one who works here in town, and might gossip.*

Rif shook her head in amazement. "Ye do have talent, Black Cal, and fer more than shooting." She gnawed her lip for a moment, knowing her next question was dangerous but had to be asked. ". . . Cal, ye didn't . . . compromise yerself ter pay fer this, did ye?"

Black Cal smiled again, a quiet and peaceful smile. "No, I didn't. Even an honest blackleg makes enough pay to live on. I had years' worth of savings, and nothing to spend it on . . . until now."

"Still, a boat like this . . ." She marveled again at its smooth lines, perfect joins, metalwork. *Metalwork?* "Cal?"

Black Cal shrugged. "Besides, I finally got a reward for being good and faithful." He turned to meet her eyes. "A messenger—in Signeury livery—came up to me a few weeks back and gave me a package. No note with it, just a seal."

"Whose?" Rif whispered.

"Iosef Kalugin's."

"Oh."

"He appreciated my warning about Tatty's boyfriend."

"I . . . see."

"He appreciated your part in it too, Rif. Inside the package was a copy of your songbook."

"My . . . my *book?*"

"Right. And there were a lot of coins set between the pages of a certain song."

"Which one?"

" 'The Ballad of Honest Rowan.' "

"Oh," Rif said again, and hurriedly looked away, blinking back a sudden rush of unexplainable tears.

Someone, where it mattered to him, had finally appreciated Black Cal. Not to mention herself, which just might be a valuable ace in the hole someday. She turned her gaze back to the trimaran. "Does she have a name?"

"Not yet." Black Cal glanced away, almost blushing. "I was thinking of calling her . . . the *Rafaella*."

Rif drew a sharp breath and turned to face him. This was an incredible love-gift, and it was too much: dangerously too much. "No," she said. "Cal, she can't be just mine, not considering . . . how she was bought. She's got ter be . . . *ours*. Not mine alone. Give 'er a different name."

Black Cal thought that over for a long time while the words "honor among thieves" rolled back and forth in his skull. "All right," he said finally. "But you name her, then."

"I'll think on 'er . . . Wait." An idea blossomed of its own accord, a beautifully ironic sequel to a scrap of ancient history. "Call 'er the . . . *I'm Alone Two*."

Black Cal cocked his head and puzzled at the mystery. That name had resonances he didn't understand, but somehow guessed he would appreciate if he knew them. Rif would doubtless tell him at some quietly appropriate time. "Wait here," he said. "I'll go get some paint and a bottle of wine."

"Moghi," Jones said as soon as the door was closed, "the Deiters already got one o' them Discreet engines. Lord knows who else does. It's starting."

"Yey, I know." Moghi turned a bland smile on her. "That all ye got ter tell me?"

"Moghi, this is deep trouble! Does th' College find out folks got them new engines, folks're goin' ter get their engines confiscated, maybe their boats, maybe get themselves disappeared. Somebody's got ter warn folks, stop this!"

"Ye think it's a problem, go tell it ter the Trade."
Moghi shrugged.

"Dammit, Moghi, I know ye got plans with yer
'friend' ter sell them engines! Ye want ter get folks
arrested, make trouble with the Trade?"

"Maybe no trouble at all." Moghi smiled wider, a
grin that made Jones shiver. "Tell me, how'd ye know
the Deiters got a Discreet engine?"

"One o' their big skips nearly run me down, is
how."

"So. An' did ye hear 'er comin', Jones?"

"Ney, there was jes' splashin', an' somethin' like a
deep drum-rattle when they was right a-top o' me.
That's how I knew."

"No engine noise. Right. So how'd ye know they
was under power?"

" 'Cause they was goin' so fast, an' had only a couple poles out, an' nobody makes that kind o' speed
without a damn-sight more poles! Any canaler knows
that! Besides, there was that funny deep rumble . . ."

"Any canaler would know. But would a blackleg?
Or those Crazy Cassie-kissin' fools up at the College?"

Jones felt her jaw drop. "Th-the canalers'd
know . . ." Her words trailed off. She guessed what
Moghi's next words would be before he said them.

"Can ye see any canaler *tellin'* a blackleg—or the
College—how ter spot, an' screw, another one o' the
Trade?"

"Right, right." Jones rubbed her forehead. "Some
landsider might, though. Might know enough, have a
grudge, maybe 'bout all the boat-wash . . . Moghi,
ye've seen one o' them engines, an' workin',
ain'tcher?"

Moghi ignored her second question. "So, somebody squawks an' the College sends blacklegs ter
check 'er out. How many times've ye said it? Black-

legs'll turn fer a penny. They turned fer what canalers could pay, over that fun an' games with Megary's.''

"Lord,'' Jones almost wailed. ''That was diff'rent, Moghi. Nobody loves Megary, an' they're doin' illegal work anyway. This is goin' right up against the damn College! Damn few on the water can 'ford ter pay what a blackleg'd want fer turnin' on that. There's folks goin' ter be hurt bad on this.''

"Maybe not,'' Moghi said again. ''So somebody squawks, the blacklegs come lookin', they don't turn, an' they manage ter find what they're lookin' fer. They get that far, finally see one o' them engines, ye know what else they're goin' ter see? Nice, neat seals of approval from the College, right there on th'engine housings, every last one.''

"Lord,'' Jones whispered this time, feeling the blood drain from her face. ''College seals . . . on them engines? How . . .'' The implications were awesome.

"Yey, I seen 'em myself. Pretty things. Either somebody's paid off really big up ter the College, or somebody's the best damn forger I've ever seen.'' Moghi's smile turned tight and ruthless. ''Either way, that's . . . interestin' action. There's profit in gettin' a piece of 'er.''

*Lord, Lord, who'll they rope in next?* ''Moghi,'' Jones tried feebly, ''they're Janes. Ye can be hung from the bridge jes' fer *bein'* a Jane.''

"Aye, an' it ain't unlikely we'll get shot jes' fer bein' lowtowners, way the College is goin' with Crazy Cassie's prophecies. Y'ever think o' that, Jones?''

She numbly shook her head.

"I ain't goin' ter tell ye my life story, but let it be, I've seen blood-crazes get started before. Never mind where, neither. Crazy Cassie's whompin' up another one; I know the signs. This time, by all the Ancestors, I don't mean ter hide in the bilges 'til the fire burns out, hopin' it won' get me.'' Moghi was no longer smiling. His face was as tight and ruthless as a sherk's. "Way I see it, Yossarian or Janes or whoever, they bring us a way ter get out fast or fight back when the blood-craze comes, an' I don't care who they are—I'll deal with 'em. All I see is, they come jes' in time."

Jones shook her head again. *What would he say if I told him I think they brought the tangle-lilies, too? Hell, he's in the brewing business! He'd probably laugh and thank 'em.*

"Don' worry 'bout me, Jones. I can take care o' myself. An' I'll keep watch fer yer watcher."

". . . Right. Thanks, Moghi."

Jones wandered out into the growing night, wondering who she could turn to now, who she even dared talk to now. Mondragon, maybe? Lord, not yet!

And there were still those weeds on her skip. Dry them or brew them? She had chugger enough for all the use she expected to need in a good while. Where could she dry the damned things?

She glanced automatically at Moghi's place, up at all the protruding gables and porches of Ventani Isle— and saw the edges of drying tangle-lilies hanging over the nearest gutters.

# FOGGY NIGHT

*Bradley H. Sinor*

A smooth white stone went flying out, struck the water, skipped twice and disappeared into the fog. A second and a third followed, leaving uneven ripples on the murky surface of New Harbor.

"Not bad, not bad at all." Seventeen-year-old Rafael Ceti Morgan, Rafe to his friends, had a deliberate hint of pride in his voice, not that anyone was about to hear him down here beneath the piers on the edge of East Dike: the number of people who normally would have been abroad above and harborside at this hour of the night was cut to almost nothing by the heavy fog that had wrapped itself around Merovingen.

From his pocket Rafe pulled a crumpled sheet of paper. In the dark it was nearly impossible to read it, not that he needed to, the message being brief and simple, and several hours past.

*Eight o'clock.*

                              *L.*

Sitting on a rock beneath the pier at East Dike was certainly not the finish Rafe had foreseen to this night. He held the paper up and sniffed it. Just the slightest hint of perfume clung to it, a scent that belonged to none other than m'sera Leanora Jherico, of the almond eyes, short brown hair, and enticing smile. They had met when she had stepped out of a shadowy corner at a walkway wedding this evening up at Kass second-tier—when he had been at some odds with a gate-guard over an invitation.

After which, pleading illness, the m'sera had packed her contract husband, one m'ser Hardin White, off to the subsequent reception. The problem was that a few minutes after midnight m'ser White had come walking through the bedroom door.

With the safety of an hour's time and several isles' distance, Rafe could chuckle about the whole thing. Hard to say which of the three of them had had the most surprised expression when Hardin White had walked in.

"But is climbing down a drainpipe at midnight the way a true gentleman should leave his lady?" he asked himself, picking up a handful of loose gravel. He let fly with the stones.

Most of them splashed into the water and were gone, some skipped several times, while a few clattered short, on the stones at water's edge. Mixed in with those sounds was the quite distinct *chink* of one of them hitting metal.

Rafe got up, walked out, searching along the edge, kicking stones. The water lapped close here. Summer and low water exposed long-drowned stones.

*Perfect ending for a perfect night*, he mused. *Step on a dragonelle or a skit out here, most like.*

That there might not have been anything at all but his own imagination had occurred to him more than a few times in the past several minutes.

But it had to be fairly straight-line along the dike. The pebbles hadn't scattered all that far.

*So let's make another try, old thing. . . .*

While the dike was more solid than any construction in the city, much of it near the water was rubble covered in mud and ooze. That forced Rafe to search more closely than he would have preferred, crouching and peering under old rocks, a little from putting his foot in the water.

But he spotted a golden shine from that angle; a little metal corner poking free from the ooze, under a rock inches away from the water. He reached. The first time he tried to get a grip around it, he came away with a handful of mud and very nearly sent himself into the water. The second got it.

For a couple of deep breaths Rafe squatted there, hefting the unexpected weight of the thing. The chill from the fog, the wind, and the water cut through his thin clothing so he had to fight to keep his teeth from chattering. Only after several long breaths did he dip it in the water and rub it with his sleeve.

Gold, beyond a doubt. Rafe lifted it to the faint harbor lights. A thin smile crossed his face when he saw the engraving on the lid.

The evening proved profitable after all. And not alone in the pawn value.


From the shelter of a doorway, Rafe watched Rohan. The affair seemed fairly straightforward. Drop off the box, collect a reward and then head for Moghi's.

But dealing with hightown—one was careful.

No lights showed in Rohan, no guards, nothing. For the better part of a quarter hour the only thing he'd seen from this vantage had been a pair of cats, one gray, one black and white, hissing and growling at each other as they dashed in and out of the mist.

Wait till morning, maybe.

But there was the wedding uptown. Rohan might well be in attendance—only servants left to keep the door; and he had no notion of dealing with servants. A poleboat glided past, with well-dressed partiers. Voices grew loud and diminished.

He heard approaching footsteps on this second-tier walkway then and pulled himself tightly back around the corner. A woman with two bodyguards emerged from the fog and the timbers at Rohan Middle Bridge. One of the men walked a few steps ahead of the others, the lantern in his hand marking their path.

Rafe caught only the briefest glimpse of dark hair as the woman and her companions passed within a few feet of where he stood. She was small, wrapped in a heavy cape against the chill, but she moved with a sureness and an entourage that meant hightowner; and stopped at the door that meant Rohan beyond a doubt.

"M'sera!" said Rafe, stepping out onto the walkway.

The two bodyguards were on him, swords drawn, alert lest this prove a thieves' diversion. Rafe walked slowly forward, hands held open for their inspection.

"What's the likes of you doing here, boy?" one of them spat out at him.

Rafe relaxed, but not by much, and forced his voice to show the calm his gut didn't feel. "Got business with Rohan."

"What kind of business could you have with Rohan?" demanded the other bodyguard—while the woman stood silently at the door.

The first man gestured with his sword. "At this time of night, the m'sera got nothin' to say to the likes of you or anyone. I don't care if it were Governor Kalugin himself. If ye really got business with Rohan, then come round in the morning, like any honest gentleman would."

"The m'sera is Rohan?" Rafe asked.

"You might say that," laughed one of them.

"M'sera Tanith Rohan," the woman said from the doorway. "You, m'ser?"

"This is personal. Can we talk inside? I have something of yours." Moving very slowly, so as not to alarm the men, Rafe brought the box out where they could see it.

The m'sera held out her hand. One of the men accepted the box and carried it to Tanith Rohan, who studied the box, her face betraying some reaction, but Rafe couldn't tell what. The slightest of nods was the only gesture he could see.

"She wants to see ye, boy," said the man who'd remained next to him.

Rafe's stomach twisted in knots as he walked toward the m'sera and the door. He stopped several feet in front of Tanith Rohan and bowed. He could feel her eyes moving over him, taking in his mud-stained breeches, the shredded remains of his silk shirt.

"I see that I am not the only one who keeps late hours this night," she said. "What's your name?"

"Morgan, m'sera, Rafael Ceti Morgan."

"Of what House?"

"None lately, m'sera."

"And you know this mark?" she said, holding up the box.

Rafe nodded. "They still tell stories about your grandfather. Some say that he could sell Janist bibles to Sworders and leave 'em wanting more."

"That he could. Two silver bars with a gold between. Yes, this is ours," Tanith Rohan said. "And where did you steal it, Rafael Ceti Morgan?"

"I've done many things, m'sera. But by every karmic mark that stands against me, I didn't steal that box."

"Where, then?"

"East Dike. Beneath the pier, near the water's edge."

Tanith Rohan stared at him, her eyes pale in the lantern light. "Marcus, Norman," she said, "teach him a lesson."

At which she turned and went into the house.

The nearer of the two men drove his fist into Rafe's stomach. The second hit him from behind. The last thing that Rafe heard before he blacked out was the gentle lapping of canal water against pilings.

Rafe's breath came in harsh gasps. There couldn't have been more than a few square inches of him that didn't hurt. Tanith Rohan's bodyguards had done a very professional job.

Common sense said that the best plan would be for him to forget the whole thing. Drowning his pain with some of Moghi's whiskey seemed quite inviting at that moment.

Pride and anger, however, had very little to do with common sense.

Instead of going down a drainpipe as he had earlier in the evening, this time Rafe shinned up one, the gate being shut and guarded on Rohan's third tier.

*They started it, but I am damned well going to finish it,* he repeated to himself as he risked a look through an unshuttered window of the Family residency; resort to a small square-ended blade and a certain skill with windows tripped the aged latch.

The window gave, the sound muffled with his shoulder. Rafe lifted it ever so quietly and slipped into a darkened hallway. The air from inside was musty, smelling of dust and incense. He dropped to the floor in a crouch, holding the jimmy in a clenched fist.

He had not planned on anyone being awake.

But light came faintly from a room far down the T; a guard, perhaps. Or simply a nightlight. He padded along the boards and put his shoulder against the door-frame to sneak a look.

The far end of the room was dominated by a huge desk. A tiny oil lamp sat on one corner: its flickering added as much of shadow as light to the room.

And fell on a woman's bowed figure, sitting at the desk with her face resting in her hands.

She did not react; she did not look up; in fact, she barely moved. In the silence Rafe could almost hear her breathing.

An empty brandy glass was on a corner of that desk. So was the gold box from the harbor. Rafe watched for a long time; and knowing the open window was not that far and that surprise and the burglar's iron in his fist were advantage enough—

He entered the room: he walked to the desk; but before his fingers could do more than brush across the surface the woman looked up.

Rafe found himself staring into Tanith Rohan's startled eyes.

"I've been waiting for you," she said.

Only this wasn't Tanith Rohan! This woman was thinner, a webwork of deep wrinkles criss-crossed her face. The same face—the same crown of braids, deep black, eyes so pale they seemed colorless.

"M'sera?" he asked.

"I know you." Pale eyes stared at Rafe, unblinking. A hint of a smile crossed her face and rearranged the wrinkles.

"Know me?" Rafe said.

"My memory was never that bad. You've come for this," she said, tapping the box. "And what's in it."

Rafe nodded.

Either this elder m'sera Rohan was crazier than a swamp rat, or she was as wily as any of the hightowner Families that he'd ever met. Right then he wasn't that certain which.

"Open it, then," she said coolly.

Rafe sighed; he'd tried that almost as soon as he'd found the box, only with as much corrosion as the years had laid along the silver fittings, the thing was effectively sealed. But the look on m'sera Rohan's face was impossible for Rafe to resist. He applied the jimmy to it. This time the lid came free.

A rotted cloth lined the inside of the case. In one corner was a tangled ball of metal; a knot of gold chain wrapped around a half a gold coin. Picking the thing up with two fingers Rafe had to shake it several times before the chain gradually began to untangle. The half coin twisted freely in the air in front of them.

"Put it on, Klive, put it on."

Rafe looked at her, but demanded no explanation for the name. She was clearly crazed. She made no shout for the guards. He played her game. The metal was cold as the Det itself. But the chain felt right around his neck.

Smiling, m'sera brought a second box from inside the desk, a box except for the corrosion identical to the one Rafe had discovered . . . was it only hours ago? Watching her produce a second necklace and jagged half coin, Rafe realized he'd been holding his breath.

"You promised that you'd come for me, Klive, and you have." A protest about that name died in Rafe's throat. M'sera slid the chain over her head as she rose and stepped out from behind the desk.

M'sera's eyes never left Rafe's as she slid her arms tightly around him. In spite of her aged appearance, this was a sensuous woman whose lips sought his—a woman in love and a woman who knew what she wanted.

And as suddenly as the kiss had begun, it ended.

M'sera went limp. Rafe had to catch her—panicked suddenly, with the notion of a dead hightowner on his hands. He dragged her back behind the desk, set her back into her chair. If it were possible, m'sera's face looked paler than it had before. Her head fell as he propped her up.

"Is she dead yet?"

Tanith Rohan might have been inquiring after a lost scarf rather than the m'sera's life. Rafe suspected by that look that she had fantasized it so often that the actual doing of the deed seemed a letdown to her.

"Your work?" he said, standing up and gesturing at the m'sera.

"Of course." Tanith smiled as she took a pair of tumblers from a nearby cabinet. She filled them both with amber liquid from a dusty carafe. "I think we both can use one of these," she said, returning, and handed one of the drinks to Rafe.

He hesitated. Tanith laughed and took a sip from her own drink. "Really, you should be more trusting," she said. "If I wanted you dead, there are a lot better ways than wasting sunwing on the likes of you."

"That cost you a pretty penny." Sunwing was native only to the deserts of Canberra. People said it was deadlier than deathangel, without any of its hallucinogenic side effects—and virtually impossible to detect afterward.

"Oh, yes, it did, a fortune. The results were worth it, though. A few months of it, mixed in with the brandy to cut the taste, and she's been getting weaker and weaker. The shock of having that necklace returned—surely speeded things up a bit. I'm sure her doctor will agree."

"She thought I was Klive."

"Her one true love. I imagine you made her happy for a couple of minutes," grinned Tanith as she refilled her glass. "All that stress; heart attack, you know. Mama was getting so fragile."

"A mortal dose. And in one quick sweep it leaves you as Househead."

"That was the whole point."

"Who was Klive?"

"The other half of a love story. My grandfather was planning to marry her off to Klive Straun, to cement a trade alliance with his family out of Nev Hettek. But there was brother Gerrard, my uncle; seems that he and Klive hated each other. Klive Straun disappeared. No one could prove it, but they knew Gerrard was behind it. Gerrard died. They never found the body either. —Of course, it wouldn't be the first time that a body disappeared in this city. Would it?"

"What about these?" Rafe said, touching the chain.

"Klive had them made by an uptown jeweler, one for him, one for my mother. As for the boxes, they came from her."

"And she thought that I was him."

"You just helped make me Househead that much sooner."

*"I think not."*

Rafe and Tanith both turned back to stare at the huge desk. The chair behind it was empty, still moving slowly. Rafe heard a gasp from Tanith.

It was no ghost that stood near the bookcase, holding a single-shot pistol. M'sera Rohan was still as pale as she had been, but now she radiated an air of strength and certainty that had been missing before.

"You were dead," Tanith stammered. "The sunwing, there's no antidote."

"That was always your problem dear, believing in absolutes when there are no such things. I've known about the sunwing since the second night you ruined my brandy with it. I'm afraid that it didn't cut the taste quite as much as you had hoped. By the way, I must thank you, dear, for arranging to get the sunwing. I can definitely put it to use. Will you leave this House? Or do you want to dispute the case tonight?''

The younger woman, who had gone as pale as her mother, turned slowly and walked out of the room.

M'sera Rohan stared after her daughter. And eased down the hammer of the pistol.

''You've definitely got style, lady, definitely.'' Rafe had eased himself toward the door. This seemed as good a time as any to make an exit.

''I wouldn't do that if I were you.'' M'sera Rohan's voice cut the air like a knife.

''M'sera?''

''You might have been in my daughter's hire. I thought that might have been the case. By rights I should turn you over to the blacklegs. However, I am willing to discuss that point, —Klive.'' Her tongue traced the edge of her lips as she spoke. ''You *are* Klive. You'll have everything you want, dear boy. And I've waited for you—so very long.''

# SEEDS OF DESTRUCTION
# (REPRISED)

## C.J. Cherryh

Jones poured more sugar on the tea, stirred it vigorously, added some more—early on, with Mondragon, she had had real qualms about extravagance, but, Lord! it was damn Anastasi's money, and if she could cost him, she cost him good and proper. She had butter and berry jam on her toast, she had ham and not fish, she had a few fresh berries with the ham, too—sweet, stay in your mouth a long time kind of taste, so she just shut her eyes and thought about it. She had been sixteen before she ever tasted berries or ham or butter, and she never did gulp them the way Mondragon would, who thought they were ordinary—who could eat like this all the time, except he was real irregular about cooking—man would wash a best iron skillet, for Lord's sake, in soap and water—and he kept only plain stuff in the apartment for when he had to cook.

But when times were slow and the mood was on him and he was tolerably sure *she* was going to be there to do the cooking, back he came from hightown shops with stuff like this.

So he'd come down to Moghi's last night to tell her,

just showed up on Moghi's porch when she picked up to go, said he'd go partners on the run if she'd go partners later and besides, he'd bought groceries.

Ye got 'er, she'd said, wondering then exactly what kind of mess he was in and what news he was getting her softened up for.

But they made the run to Harbor, they made the run to Hafiz' Brewery, they made the run back to Moghi's with the whiskey (and the stuff that wasn't whiskey, too, but came in barrels) and she asked him finally flat out what he was into and if she was supposed to be mad at him.

Hurt his feelings, she did.

But they made it up, in his bed with the starchy fine sheets, trail of clothes all the way to the bath and trail of towels all the way to the bed, there was, Denny being the only houseguest now, Raj being off somewhere between Kamat and the College and Denny being out with friends, the little sherk—I'll break his neck, was what Mondragon said, after he had to let them both in and he found the note that said Gon With Frens. OK—Deny.

But that was near the door, they were both wanting a bath real bad, and if Denny was off catting around, then, good riddance, was Altair's own brief thought in the matter—brief, because directly she and Mondragon had other interests than a skinny bridge-brat.

Except this morning, that every noise outside and every bird that landed on the roof got this little twitch from Mondragon, just this little dart of the eyes: he was plainly thinking it was high time Denny was putting in an appearance.

"He'll be back," Altair said, around a tiny, savored last bite of ham. Damn 'im, the kid was doing his best to spoil breakfast. She wiped the grease off her plate with her finger and licked it. "Hell, I tried to drown 'im once. Couldn't. Kid floats."

"I've told him," Mondragon said. "I'll break his neck." Lord, he was pretty with his jaw set like that, pretty hands, hair all curling around his face—

Altair sighed over her tea, and thought maybe they could be just a touch later getting about the day's business. Morning rush was past. She could afford a lay-out, or lay-in-bed, or whatever—

Getting damn comfortable, was what, having ham and berries and sugared tea and all: Mondragon wanted her off the water, wanted her under a roof, and that she wouldn't do, *couldn't* do, couldn't live that way—but she worried about herself sometimes, that she really got to like a mattress to sleep on and a tub of clean rainwater to scrub in, and clothes that smelled like sunshine instead of mildew.

But if Mondragon was there with her the best thing in the world was the heave of the water and the stars over the Rim, and them making love on the half-deck, so far out from anybody it was just the warm wind for a sheet and the moons for a nightlight—

And ham and berries couldn't outdo that.

But that was rare, that she could get Mondragon out of town to the Rim—last night, for instance: "Pack up the groceries," she'd said, "and we'll sail out to the Harbor and I won't even work t'morrow. . . .

And Mondragon: "Can't. Can't, Jones." With a kiss, a straying of his hands, a hasty, breathy, "I've got things doing, I can't leave right now—"

She'd tried to ask. He'd stopped that cold. So it was Anastasi's work, or Richard Kamat's, which was where his money came from—a lot of it, which worried her sick in one sense.

And she never had taken money from him, but nowadays when he wanted to give it to her, she said all right, and she took it right down to Moghi and put in on account there, good as any bank, for when he might be broke again and desperate: then she'd say, Well, I got it, —and hand him enough this time, that it might mean something. More than a skip-freighter got in a year she had tucked away in that account, and it might not stand Mondragon to a clean shirt of the kind he wore uptown, but it sure as hell would buy somebody dead on waterside, or buy a stay in Moghi's upstairs Room and a run to the Harbor if Mondragon got himself in that kind of situation.

You listen to me, she'd said. You save yourself a bit of that, dammit, Mondragon, ye spend like a Falken sailor, ye got no notion yet what money's worth—

I know better than most, he'd said back, in that kind of tone that said there was values and values, and what bought him wasn't money.

Wasn't what bought her either, so she understood; but the damn fool hadn't missed enough meals in his life, when the shaded canals were near frozen and the Trade wasn't moving and the fish weren't biting, and you only had enough oil for heating up the stove an hour or so in the night. Money was what kept you from that. But in Tom Mondragon's mind, being hungry was just temporary, and it didn't scare him; and in hers summers were for storing up against winters you knew would come sure as the Retribution—surer, since she'd seen sixteen of them for certain and the priests just promised the other.

So here they were in the kitchen with as good a breakfast as the governor himself, and Mondragon just ate his ham like it was ordinary.

And worried about a damn kid.

Which he wasn't saying, particularly, but she saw him twitch again—you got these little sounds when somebody would walk by, boards creaking and all.

And she wasn't going to get him back to bed when he was like that, distracted at every damn bird landing on the roof. So she sighed and put her teacup down and said, "*I'll* find 'im. Probably he's showed up to

work—'' Over at Gallandrys. ''—swear like a bishop
he was only thinking not t' wake ye, the damn sneak.
*Probably* was drinking and knew you'd catch it on
him.''

''I'll go—'' Mondragon began; but there was a
thump! from upstairs, that was the roof fire-exit, and
another thump! in the kitchen as Mondragon shoved
his chair back.

Denny was late to work, was what he was. Denny
sounded to be moving in a hurry, pounding down the
stairs—Denny and shoes being unacquainted, the same
as any canaler; and Altair put herself on her feet and
went right behind Mondragon to the hall as Denny
came pell-mell down the steps—

Out of breath and scared out of his mind.

''Tom!'' Denny gasped. ''They're after Raj—'' And
as Mondragon grabbed him by the arms and Denny
got another breath: ''The blacklegs—they're going to
arrest him!''

''For what?'' Mondragon asked, giving him a shake.
''Where is he?''

''K-Kamat. He's at Kamat. We was just standing
down by John's—''

''College district,'' Altair said.

''—an' we was talkin', Tom, I swear, we was just
jokin' around—an' this sherk of a blackleg come up
and said, 'What's yer name?' an' this fool said—''

''Who said?'' Mondragon asked.

''I dunno, this girl, she was from the College—she
said she didn't have to give 'im anything. Then this
other blackleg come up, an' asked what was goin'
down, like we didn't need help, and Jimmy—''

''That skuz!'' Altair said, and whacked at him with
the back of her hand. ''I told ye not to hang out with
that 'un!''

''—Jimmy said shut up, she was bein' a fool, but she

was, anyhow, she said as how the blacklegs was Insti-
gatin' and ever'body on that walk was witnesses—''

"God," Mondragon said.

"So most ever'body got scarce right off, and they
was shovin' her up against th' wall, and Raj— Mondragon, I tol' 'im, come on, I says, —while she was
screamin' at 'em and they was bashin' her, but my
damn fool brother— 'Let her go,' he says, like they
was going to, and she says, 'You better listen to him,
he's close with Richard Kamat—' ''

"God!" Mondragon said.

"An' we run, I got 'im safe t' Kamat topside an'
he got in—but he's in trouble, Tom, he's in bad trouble, they was writin' down what ever'body was sayin',
an' they're goin' t' show up there, m'ser Tom, they're
goin' to take 'im to the Justiciary and that room in the
basement—''

Mondragon let him go. Mondragon was headed for
the living room, looking for his boots, and Altair
grabbed a fistful of Denny's sweaty, sooty shirt.

"Ye damn fool! What was ye standin' around for?
What was ye doin' with them damn College fools?"

"They was friends of Raj's— We just met up and I
was goin' t' get back home, but Raj was at John's and
I just—''

Mondragon had found the boots; he was halfway
into them. Altair shoved Denny off and said to Mondragon, "I'll go down there, f' Lord's sake—if they're
lookin' for him, they don't need to see *you* show up."

Mondragon looked up, looking scared, just plain
cold scared, the way he could admit to that with her,
sometimes, when things were coming too fast for good
sense.

"You're right. You'd better. Get down there, see if
you can talk to Richard. . . .''

Surprised hell out of her with that.

Surprised her again when he got up and grabbed her arm at the door.

"Be careful," he said, "for God's sake be careful. If it's getting that bad, that they're after kids—"

Meaning the They that ran things, meaning the governor and Tatiana and them that knew things weren't going all that smooth, and people weren't all that happy, and they were arresting kids for saying, the way kids would, This ain't right—

"Yey," she said, feeling a little queasy feeling. "But he's in Kamat. He's all right. Ain't no way they're going to drag 'im out from there."

"Just be careful, dammit, Jones, don't tell me what they can't."

"Yey, yoss," she said. Dead right in that one. Mondragon knew those waters, real well.

# SECOND OPINION

## *Janet Morris*

Summertime, and Merovingen stank to high heavens
from the weed choking the canals and rotting where
the sun couldn't reach it, which was everywhere the
disadvantaged lived in the shadows of hightown.

Thomas Mondragon couldn't fathom why the hightowners didn't realize that this plague of water-plants
down below was going to crawl up the tiers and choke
them in their comfy beds. But they didn't. Not yet.
And Tom Mondragon was too smart to go running
around advertising his connection with the Sword of
God by predicting where increased hardship canalside
and increased regulation (read: repression) by hightown was bound to lead: right into the hands of Nev
Hettek's revolutionary Sword of God.

Merovingen already had Cassiopeia Boregy prophesying fiery revolt; it didn't need another prognosti-
cator, even though Mondragon's words would have
carried more weight, since he wasn't doped out of his
mind by a faction of the Revenantist College.

Mondragon couldn't—wouldn't—take the risk of being the messenger with the wrong message, not here

where people Disappeared for less all the time. He hadn't lived this long against all odds by neglecting his own best interests.

The trouble was, the hightowners couldn't see past their pocketbooks. Chance Magruder maneuvered his Sword agents like a virtuoso conducting an orchestra; the tune was the Insurrection Waltz; the audience, Merovingen-above.

Mondragon had helped bring revolution to Nev Hettek and watching it happen here all over again was making his skin crawl. He just couldn't figure out how Magruder had gotten those weeds into the canals. It was a stroke of genius—or (if Magruder hadn't been behind the seeding) a piece of luck that was good enough to make you believe in karma.

As yet, not even the stink of the rotting weeds was evident among the upper tiers, and that galled the pole-boaters and the canal-rats even more as their blisters bled and festered in the heat wave and the edict came down from hightown that you couldn't even use your motors but on Grand Canal, West, Port, and Archangel. If you were lucky enough to have a motor, you took serious umbrage at that, when you were down at Moghi's or anywhere it was safe to take umbrage.

If, like so many, you didn't have a motor, you just blistered and bled, trying to pole through the weed-choked mess of canals that were once the circulatory system of the tiered city. Mondragon's heart went out to Jones and her proud canal-rat friends, but he couldn't do anything for them. And times were too dangerous for him to let his feelings show.

People were beginning to talk about Merovingen as if it were the rotting corpse it smelled like. The medical students from the College likened it to a fat old man with arteries clogged from dining too high on the hog—this ''hog'' being everybody who sweated on the lower tiers, and one of those students being Raj. Raj had a real knack for shooting off his mouth in the wrong places, and soon after he'd done so, a blackleg three-team had come knocking at Kamat's door "investigating rumors of treasonous rhetoric."

Richard Kamat had had his hands full smoothing that one over—which meant that Tom Mondragon did.

So he was down here on Ventani this evening with a pocket full of gold sols—thirty, to be exact—to be handed to a particular blackleg watch commander so that Raj's metaphor would be stricken from memories and report books and the kid's foot could be surgically removed from his mouth.

The tongue was costlier than the sword in Merovingen this season. For that kind of money, Mondragon could have Disappeared the complainant in question and a few well-chosen friends to make his nonverbal message abundantly clear. He would have done so, personally, and kept the money himself, if Richard Kamat hadn't anticipated the obvious solution and expressly forbidden it.

Maybe in the old days, Mondragon would have done it anyway—to keep his sword arm in practice, to vent some of the frustration he felt, and to teach Tatiana Kalugin's greedy blacklegs a lesson they badly needed, a lesson about who muscled whom and how hard.

But Mondragon was nothing if not a professional survivor and his professional opinion was that bloodshed wasn't going to solve anything, or even slow down the rush of Merovingen toward revolution.

Well, the Merovingians revered that damned Angel of Retribution, sword in hand, whose statues watched over Hanging Bridge, and over the harbor. They believed in karma, in debt and debit, in all manner of paranoid fantasies. That was what "paranoia" really meant: seeing causally unconnected events as a pattern organized to your benefit or detriment.

You'd think that somebody of a Revenantist bent

could see the pattern of revolution—of real societal change brought about by Sword of God agents at Karl Fon's behest—now that it was all around them.

But revolution moved slowly among a populace at first, like a communicable disease. And who was to say that the disease was worse than the cure? Was hightown society worth preserving? By now, Mondragon had been too close to too many corrupt Merovingian houses to tell himself he believed that.

Neither did he believe in Karl Fon's revolution anymore, because the rebels in Nev Hettek had set up a government more repressive than the one they'd supplanted, one based on subtractive reasoning that made a larger part of the population equal by lowering the standard of living sufficiently that almost everyone was poor, so there was no longer an entrenched middle class to envy. And as for how the ruling class lived . . . that was the business of the revolutionary council, and nothing for anyone to envy: you had to have a government strong enough and rich enough to treat with other governments.

So maybe Mondragon didn't care if revolution came to Merovingen. Or maybe he'd get out of here before it did. After flood season, if the fires really started in Merovingen-below, he'd flee the riots that only Cassie Boregy saw coming. More truthfully, he'd flee Sword vengeance, which would fall on him like a shroud once Magruder didn't need him to report on the goings-on in hightown mercantile society.

Merovingen-below was going to go up like a tinderbox, if the licensing fees survived the Council's legislation and Tatiana turned her blackleg police loose on the poor bastards who couldn't pole through clogged canals, couldn't afford the licenses, and couldn't afford not to have motors because their boats were their livelihoods.

Waiting for his contact among the shadows of Ventani Pier, Mondragon wondered if there was any use in trying to explain all this to Jones. The trouble with Merovingians, hightowners and canal-rats alike, was that they didn't think beyond tomorrow; they were too busy surviving today. That was something the revolutionaries turned out by the Sword's training program counted on. The revolution was based on creating terror, creating chaos, creating change by making the status quo unstable.

It worked every time. Or at least it had worked when he'd been on the planning staff in Nev Hettek. And it was working now, in Merovingen, or else Chance Magruder was the Angel of Retribution himself and karma was using the rest of them, one and all.

God, he'd been here too long. Been waiting too long for the blackleg he'd been sent by Richard Kamat to meet. Been waiting too long for Magruder to slip and give him an opening to find a way out of this trap. Been waiting too long to find a way to stop caring about Jones and her brood of doomed youngsters.

Been waiting too long to get his strength back. Thomas Mondragon kicked a barrel as he stepped out of the shadows and moved off down the pier, thirty gold sols in his pocket.

He was as doomed as any of them if he stayed here. He had enough gold on him to get out. Now. Right now, if he just headed out tonight. He wasn't helping to preserve the power structure; he wasn't helping to bring about the revolution; he wasn't helping himself by playing every side of this game.

He was going to get himself mangled and crushed in the inevitable collision to come. He moved faster, the long muscles in his legs beginning to burn from the effort of not running—or from the effort of just moving. He wasn't old, he'd yet to turn thirty. But he wasn't young any longer, five years in a Nev Hetteker prison had seen to that—and Merovingen-below took its toll on you. He'd paid that toll last winter and found that recovery was a relative term. He was relatively healthy, relatively secure in relatively improved circumstances, and relatively capable of assessing the stability of Merovingen.

If he was even relatively honest with himself, he'd get the hell out of here before he got himself relatively screwed from tarrying too long where he didn't belong.

He could go to Tyre, where nobody knew him and insurrection was still offshore: buy a boat and take his chances with the Strait of Storms. Or he could play it safe, sail down the coast to the Chattalen.

But it would be hot as hell down there, this time of year. And as far as Tyre was concerned . . . Jones would never go, and he'd be wondering for the rest of his life if leaving her and hers to face revolution on their own made him a complete and utter coward.

Did he care that much? This night on Ventani, he told himself, he didn't. He couldn't. He couldn't afford to care.

It was just luck—or karma—that the blackleg he'd been waiting for crossed his path just as he was leaving the rendezvous, on his way—once and for all, with Jones—or, more likely, without her. . . .

"You're late," he said to the blackleg. Then, half-heartedly: "Too late. Deal's off."

"My ass," said the other man, a black, backlit shape he knew by a limp like none other, from an old wound in an old skirmish.

They all had too many wounds from too many skirmishes. Peacekeeping was a young man's game. Revolutionary movements were, too, unless you were high in the power structure. If you were high enough, then the young men weren't your friends any longer: they were your pawns, the faceless underclasses who'd die for the right to be freer, or at least for the rhetoric of freedom, while you and yours got richer and more powerful with every pint of blood shed.

The dark shape held out a demanding, greedy hand and took a step sideways to block Mondragon's path: "Give. The deal's struck. You're just the courier; unless you want me to take a closer look at who you are and what you're trying to do . . . bribe an officer of the Kalugin—"

"Don't even finish saying that. Don't tempt me. Don't give me even half a reason to feed you to the canal and keep this money." It was a plea, an honest and rasping bit of counsel torn from Mondragon's lips by some impulse to honesty he didn't understand.

Fortunately or unfortunately, it came out sounding like a threat.

The blackleg shifted his weight and a bit of errant starlight, cascading down the tiers, caught the whites of his eyes. The two men stared at each other for the time it took to take three breaths apiece, breaths of which each man was jealously conscious.

Was it worth fighting over: thirty gold sols, the unguarded bravado of a College student, the good name of Richard Kamat, the unsurprising revelation that blacklegs took bribes on a regular basis?

You felt your pulse at times like these, felt it in your veins like an old friend you didn't want to lose. Your body pumped itself up toward readiness while your mind judged everything: escape routes, your chances, the other man's temperament, any telltale sign of weakness, of aggression, or strength.

Suddenly Mondragon was absolutely unwilling to give his life on Ventani Pier for Raj's waggling tongue or a chance to risk it again, trying to negotiate the Strait of Storms in some second-rate boat he might be able to buy on the spur of the moment.

Yet there was no way out, if the blackleg wanted to push matters.

Just as Mondragon was opening his cottony mouth to give them both a chance to back down, the blackleg said, "Look, friend, just give me what I came for and we'll both walk away from this, no hard feelings. My word on it."

"Your word's good enough for me," Mondragon said in a nearly inaudible voice from a mouth with no spit in it.

His hand shook when he held out the leather sack of sols and handed it over.

The other man didn't seem much steadier, taking it.

The blackleg turned jerkily on his heel and strode off as fast as he could, saying he was late for an appointment; the dark shape moved stiffly until it was swallowed by the night.

Mondragon stood there and watched until no movement could be discerned in the deep shadows of the tiers.

Scared spitless by a blackleg. Damn, he had to get hold of himself. It was hellish to see everything falling into ruin around him and not be able to do anything but wait.

If he'd moved a little quicker, decided a little earlier, he'd have been on his way to buy that boat. . .

But who was he kidding? He could steal a boat, if he had no money, anytime; steal one from the Kamats or one of their business associates. With one well-chosen hostage or a blade at the right throat, he could comandeer a sweet yacht at a hightown party, any night of the week.

He hadn't yet. It didn't mean he wouldn't. It meant, though, that right now he couldn't. Whether it was karma, bad luck, or Altair Jones, Tom Mondragon was stuck in Merovingen like a fly in varnish, and he couldn't seem to do a damn thing about it.

The night brought the riverboat *Detbird* into port as if nothing out of the ordinary were happening. She was made fast at Chamoun Shipping's cargo dock, right between the *Detfish* and the *Det Queen*, on schedule and without a hitch.

A runner was sent to inform Magruder, and the three passengers sat in the riverboat's big salon, awaiting further instructions from the bridge or from the shore.

Danielle Lambert could hear the baby crying in her stateroom; she ignored it, rebellious and full of the past, staring at the doorway through which Karl Fon was as likely to walk as Chance Magruder.

If she knew Magruder, he'd send staffers, silent men with ready weapons and orders not to engage in small talk. Talk was the only thing Chance was afraid of—except emotions. She hadn't been able to get anything more than a surface briefing out of Karl; expecting more from Chance was ludicrous, and she knew it.

Still, the past ought to count for something. Enough to excuse the fact that she'd been shipped down here pregnant, and arrived with a new baby in tow, and everybody had known that was likely to happen. Well, the revolution had to come first. Except sometimes it didn't, not with her.

It did with her two companions, young and hard, creatures of the revolution who still were unknown to her, despite the interminable boatride from Nev Hettek—despite the fact that they'd helped, under her less than professional direction, deliver her baby en route.

Fon and Magruder must simply have assumed that, being an obstetrician, she could handle any complications that might arise if she gave birth on their damned boat.

Still, she wanted to blame somebody for all the pain and for having looked through her spread legs at the machinist and the metalworker who shared the cabin and the wait.

Sword agents had to handle whatever circumstance

threw at them. She had to handle whatever mess Magruder was making down here; she'd promised Karl personally that she would.

But with a new baby she hadn't really wanted in the first place?

If she could have stayed in Nev Hettek another month. . . .

but the revolution came first. She'd have that graven on her tombstone, if she was lucky enough to die where she'd get a decent burial.

She was going to make Chance regret asking for her, if it was the last thing she did. She'd called the baby Hope, after Magruder's mother. It was only fair.

"You all right, ma'am?" asked the machinist/mechanic/assassin named Kenner, with a flicker of nervous eye toward her, then away, to the generator he was worrying with blackened fingers.

"M'sera," she corrected primly, to remind him who was boss. "Might as well practice up." Kenner was her hole card here, if Magruder got out of bounds, Karl had told her—and him. The protocol would hold, despite the baby's birth, despite everything.

"Sorry—m'sera Dani," Kenner replied, again with a flick of a glance that had to pass for respect offered to a superior officer. Kenner was only five or six years younger than she, but a lot depended on how old you were when the revolution hit the streets in Nev Hettek.

Kenner had had his own death squad when he was nineteen. In a way that she could never be, he was a child of the revolution she and Karl and Magruder and the others had made.

Kenner was lean and dark in a way that had nothing to do with skin tone or hair color: those were merely nondescript. This was a deeper darkness. His eyes didn't stay long in one place, never on a face . . . except in a crisis. He'd watched her carefully, attentively, while she was grunting in pain like a sow. She had to think of Kenner as a weapon at hand—her weapon. Otherwise, this quiet, coiled killer was going to scare her to death.

Damn that baby, for coming when she had and giving Kenner a chance to feel male and protective and to take charge. The Sword agent *liked* her, for godsake. She was going to have to do something about that.

Jacobs was another matter: sitting beside Kenner, you could see the difference between the two. The dark efficiency of Kenner was all calculation; Jacobs was lighter, still unformed, a pale man who topped Kenner by two inches in height and a good ten kilos in weight. Baby fat augmented by a tendency to nibble when nervous. He'd been under fighting age when the revolution took hold. He wasn't now, and the Merovingen action would make or break him.

Jacobs knew it, and he was struggling to take everything Kenner threw at him in stride. Her labor had nearly been too much for him, and Kenner had upbraided him unmercifully.

Not what you'd call an auspicious start to this "study and observation" mission. Not at all.

Danielle Lambert sighed and pushed up and away from the table where they were sitting. "I'm going on deck. Don't leave without me."

Kenner rose to follow.

"Stay," she said, showing him the flat of her hand. It sounded wrong. But then, she was feeling wrong.

Postpartum blues was what it was, of course. The professional in her knew that, and it rankled her that she had to make allowances.

She'd made few enough allowances for poor little Hope, swaddled in a half barrel with some batting and watched over in turn by whatever steward could be stolen from other duties.

She'd never wanted the baby; she mustn't take it out

on the poor thing. She climbed the stairs determinedly, ignoring the instinctive urge to check the child, a demand that pulled on her as if she were still tied physically to the new life in her stateroom.

On deck, the night was cooler. Merovingen rose like an impressionist painting of a skyline, teetering up through the mist with lights ablaze and flickering crazily into the sopping air. A stilt city leaning this way and that, the humidity blunting all its ugliness, it was a fairyland city and looking at it took her breath away.

But then the pilot came out of the wheelhouse and down the stairs. When he reached her, he slid an arm around her loose, stretched waist.

She jerked away. "Don't do that."

"Whatever you say. How's it going down there?" His words came through a beard he'd been growing for the whole trip. From anyone else, the inanity would have been something she could take at face value.

From this man, it was a command for a report. "Kenner's got everything under wraps, me included, he thinks. Morale's reestablished, now that the baby's no longer an issue. Magruder's people are late by my reckoning, but I don't suppose it's more than Merovingian inefficiency."

"He'll come himself. He'll have to shake loose of whatever's pressing."

"You're so sure? I thought you said he didn't know you were coming—that nobody's supposed to know you're here . . ." She turned and looked up, into the eyes of revolution, shadowed by a visored cap and bracketed by the black beard climbing his cheeks.

"I'm sure. He doesn't know about me, but he knows you're on this boat. . . . He'll come," Karl Fon told her with the surety that had moved them all so far, so fast.

"You overestimate my allure," she said stiffly as he

touched her again, this time on the shoulder, letting his arm slide companionably across her back.

It was just tune-up, she knew. Though security concerns had kept him in the wheelhouse throughout her labor, Karl wanted to make sure she remembered that he cared. Things were getting very complicated. "I wish you'd just treat me like anybody else," she said through clenched teeth.

"You aren't like anybody else, even Chance Magruder knows that."

"What is it you're going to say to him?" If Karl could be unprofessional, so could she.

"That I want to know why he thinks that the best way to handle things here is to give the locals this much help—setting up a machine shop and bringing down mechanics . . . let alone you, a personal obstetrician, courtesy of Nev Hettek, for this Cassiopeia the Prophetess. I want to make sure he hasn't been co-opted by the governor's daughter. Helping the canalers weather the crisis might not be in Nev Hettek's best interest."

"You're going to tell him that?" Dani blurted, her eyes squeezing shut. When Magruder and Fon went at it, she didn't want to be in the middle.

"No, I'm telling you that. I'm going to ask him to explain himself, that's all."

"And I'm supposed to do what, when he asks me what I know?"

"Use your judgment. Give me independent reports. On balance, things are going so well here, either we're inordinately lucky or we're not hearing the whole truth."

"You always said luck makes you nervous," she reminded him. "Maybe it's just the way Chance says it is."

"Maybe." Karl Fon tipped back the bill of his cap

in an unconscious gesture and stared at the wall of tiers with their sparkling lights.

"I think the baby should go back with the boat," she said at last, having found a way to voice it, if tentatively.

"I don't," he said. His hand dropped from her shoulder and slapped her bottom. "Too unusual. Women have babies all the time and the world doesn't stop. Its presence will make you less threatening to the female heirarchs."

"Don't you care about Hope? Things are pretty unstable here. . . ."

But of course, he didn't. She shouldn't have said that. She'd regretted it the moment she had said it.

Karl turned and looked at her and said very precisely, "Dani, are you trying to tell me something?"

"No," she said. "Lord, no, just that it's a Nev Hettek citizen and I've got a job to do that I could do better without some brat to worry about. . . ." She couldn't have him thinking that the baby was his.

The architect of Nev Hettek's revolution blew out a noisy breath. "Good to get that settled. Maybe Chance thinks it's his, the way he insisted on you, despite or because of the pregnancy. I never know with him."

"None of us do. That's what makes him so good at this sort of thing," she managed. Sound as if you don't care. Sound as if it's none of their business. Don't let him think he can demand answers to personal questions. Don't give him an inch. And don't let him see how hurt you are.

But her emotions got the better of her, and she had all she could do not to shout: Can't any of you count? Chance last left Nev Hettek on—

Karl Fon interrupted soothingly, "My apologies, Dani. I shouldn't have pressed you on it. But I need you prepared in case Magruder does impute some intimate connection. I *can* count, you see. Could have been his, if certain assumptions of mine are true, given how late you were.''

''You're no doctor, Karl. Just drop it, if you won't do as I ask and take Hope home.''

''Where would I put her? In the Residence? A child should be with its mother.''

''You sanctimonious bastard.'' She punched him, harder than was playful, in a belly which once was leaner than these last few years had allowed. ''We're all getting fat and complacent, you know that?''

''Perhaps you are, and I am, but I assure you that Chance isn't. I wasn't kidding when I said I want independent reports couriered home—bimonthly, if you can manage it; oftener, whenever you see fit.''

''I still think that a biosolution is the best response, if we want to help these canalers at all. An herbicide . . .''

''That's why you've got Jacobs. Do it covertly, without Chance's knowledge, if you think it's appropriate and his reasoning doesn't ring true.''

''He wants to set up a machine shop, fix engines, build metal cages for propellers, charge exorbitantly, give credit with interest, forgive the debt. Then he's got a karmic hold on whomsoever. It seems straightforward enough to me, in a Merovingian way.''

''I don't know about karma. I know about revolutions, and we want these people to think of us as a resource, not think of us as moneylenders or karmic bankers.''

''It's a different culture,'' Dani reminded him. ''One that can wrap around you like this water-weed they're fighting. Evidently young Chamoun found that out.''

''Don't let him know everything you're doing, just—''

''Don't let who know what?'' came a voice from behind them.

From right behind them.

Dani jumped and spun around, thinking, *If he's ask-*

*ing that, he hasn't been there long enough to have heard anything damaging.* Not for an instant did she doubt whose voice it was: the husky tone, the humor edged with urgency; she'd heard that voice too many times in her ear.

Chance Magruder was dressed to kill in velvet and brocade and lace, as befitted Nev Hettek's Trade and Tariffs officer and Ambassador to Merovingen. His eyes weren't smiling as he held out his arms to enfold her in a brotherly hug, then did the same with Karl Fon.

"You're late," Fon said. "Any trouble?" Fon ignored the fact that no one had warned them that Magruder had come aboard, as he ignored Magruder's question.

"The usual spread," Magruder shrugged. "Nothing special. Although I never got the dispatch that said you were coming yourself, so I'll ask you the same question: anything wrong . . . Protector?"

"Cut the crap, Chance, or I'll start calling you 'Ambassador.' Nothing's wrong besides the fact that there was too much paper on my desk and if I left I could delegate somebody else to see to it. Haven't been out of the city for far too long. And I'm still a devout Paranoid, so I didn't send a dispatch. Just taking a riverboat ride, posing as a pilot. I can still steer one of these, or we wouldn't be here."

"I never doubted it. Good to see you. How long are you staying?"

"Just long enough to load some cargo and make things look unremarkable. Don't bother with the details. Everyone knows what they need to know. Just spend a few minutes with me while Dani gets her people together."

"Dani," Chance said, turning his attention to her, "you look . . . wonderful. I thought you were—"

"I was," she said. "I'll leave you two alone. Karl,

it won't take us long to gather our things, unless you want it to. . . ?''

"No, don't dawdle," said Fon. "This won't take long either."

She left them. Let Karl tell Magruder about Hope, if he chose. This whole business of going into an operation with a new baby was something that made her exceedingly uncomfortable. If she were only a little stronger, she'd have insisted on leaving Hope behind. She probably could have made it stick. But she wasn't that strong. She loved the baby, no matter how she felt about his father, or how little she needed a baby to worry about, coming into a new venue where an old lover was running the show.

# SEEDS OF DESTRUCTION
# (REPRISED)

## C.J. Cherryh

"I dunno," Mira said to Jones, scaling fish, the silver bits flying like so many coins away from the knife. "Rif said it was like this, the old metal's val'able, an' they chop th' old engine up an' make it into two new 'uns, that's why it's even trade."

"Yey," Jones said sullenly, sitting on the halfdeck rim, her skip and Mira and Del's tied together, down by Fishmarket: it was old Mira and her man Del Suleiman's deck, at the moment—Tommy, the kid they'd adopted, was off across the bridge making the restaurant deliveries; and picking up orders: not so bad for the old couple nowadays, with strong help, Del's back was better, and Mira's legs likewise. They had Tommy now, who'd been potboy at Moghi's once; but once they'd wanted her for a daughter, and, fact be known, now they'd given up pushing that idea, if there was any kin she had on the Water (there was none she knew about), they were closer to it than anybody else.

And, damn, she hated that worried look on Mira's face, and knew Del was worried, the way he threw in from the other end, where he was shucking clams, "Som'thin' o' work in it, though."

Meaning karmic balance. Debt. Meaning him and old Mira tied to Rif's lot in their next life. They were like a lot of canalers, taking a little religion from here, a little from there: no canaler liked to be in debt, that was a fact; and with the Revenantist priests saying as how when you owed, you got tied to this world if you got reborn—even if you were pure Adventist, you had to worry a bit, especially if you were old.

Whether Mira and her man knew in this case it was not only dangerously close to charity, it was charity from Janes—that, she wasn't sure, and she wasn't sure about keeping her mouth shut on it. A lot of people didn't know what Rif was, them that knew wasn't saying, of which she was one, and she didn't know why—

She was just scared, maybe, because she couldn't shake the karma or whatever it was that kept Rif's doings coming back on her, like the weed you kept trying to shake off your pole and it just wrapped every time you pushed it.

"They say you got one o' them engines," Mira said.

"Hell," Jones said, leaning on her knees, to keep her voice down, "don't tell that, Mira. One thing, it ain't mine. I borrowed 'er. Moghi, hear?"

That was enough. You didn't talk about Moghi's business. The word she'd said was enough to send her to Harbor-bottom, except if it shut Mira up: one thing, Mira and Del did gossip—except if you scared them good. And if they had a notion, they spoke it out. "I tell you," Jones said, "my mama had this engine of mine, *her* mama had it, she's good solid iron and I ain't havin' it chopped. Damn new things, you know damn well that College seal's faked. . . . That's *trouble,* you know it's trouble. It ain't like getting caught with a couple barrels o' brandy—that's your engine you're talkin' about, they can Confiscate it right along with your boat. And ye don't even know it's goin' t' work. . . .''

"They're saying that new mek down t' harbor . . .''

"Yey, yey, they c'n fix 'er, but I seen inside one, damn skimpy works, I say. Ye got yerself out in some damn storm out t' th' Rim an' th' wind comin' a norther, an' you got t' run an' run—how's it take a real heat-up? Huh? You don't know. I don't know. I know m' own. She's cranky, but I know 'er ways an' I know she'll run long as you got fuel, an' I ain't turnin' my engine in an' trustin' what some stranger give me. . . .''

"Man of yours could buy outright," Del said. "Ye wouldn't have t' trade. Custom 'er in.''

"Hell. What d' ye think I am, Del? I don't take his money.''

"Ney, ney, not t' take on. She's just a problem, Altair. We're gettin' older, that old engine of ours ain't much, we got to think o' Tommy—''

Tommy going down to that damn Jane school, to learn more than mechanicking, *that* was what it added up to, and she knew that too, or guessed, and some-times she waked up at night with the willies.

"I'd say what I'd do, then, if I was you two, I'd just wait a bit, see how things go, *let* a few fools go run them things hard this winter, see if they hold up—*see* if the College don't come down on it— I ain't bein' th' one t' find it out. Mama'd skin me.''

They'd known Mama. Mira nodded, right sure on that one. And they'd respected Mama: most had, Re-tribution Jones tending to be real definite in her opin-ions and real quick to defend them, yey, no question that shot got through to them.

"Wait-see could be best," Del said.

But there *were* people taking the damn Jane engines, like Deiters had, like Willis, whose engine had been broke down so often he couldn't keep it fixed—took it even trade, he said; so Willis' old tub was running fast as her skip could, *Willis* was competition, Lord! And now there was talk the Nev Hettek embassy had got some cage-affair past the College censors, and there was this shop all set to open up, down by Foundry, space rented—

Wasn't sure it was supposed to be known yet, but the word was out, and local meks had their noses real out of joint about foreign competition. . . .

Word was out it was clean with the priests and all, which meant Tatiana'd cleared the way—most folk knew she was in bed with Nev Hettek; or at least the gossip was out about that about as strong as it was about this metal cage that was supposed to keep your prop clear of weed. . . .

Where the hell was a canaler going to afford *that?* she'd asked Mondragon.

Candle stub off some hightowner's table was worth a supper on canalside; and an iron nail to use for a cotter pin in your engine was worth thirty stubs like that, that you lit for emergencies and sometimes when ou were out of oil and needed heat for tea: that was ne way you reckoned *real* money in Merovingen, and here come the Nev Hettekkers bringing cages to keep the tangle-lilies off.

Hell of a lot of candle stubs that would be. Rumor was out you could do 'er on credit.

*Borrow from strangers,* that meant. That was real scary for a Revenantist. You could die before you got paid off and then you and all your kids could end up reincarnated in some heathen Nev Hettek factoryman's house, that was what—if you believed in that kind of thing, and a lot did, and a lot more like Del and Mira weren't real sure as they got older.

She didn't believe in it. Not really. Mama'd say: Ain't no second chance, Altair. Mama'd say: Ain't no karma but what you pile up in this life. *She* could walk in, like Del said, and pay cash. *She* could keep running and not snarl up in the lilies, then.

With this damn thing on the back of her boat that most couldn't afford and worth enough money to tempt anybody to larceny—and her running safe and hell and away faster than other skip-freighters who didn't want the karma of a debt they knew they couldn't pay—

Hell, she could walk off, leave her skip tied, know there wasn't anybody on the Water was going to lay a finger to anything she owned, and wasn't anybody in the Trade, however much a sherk they might be otherwise, was going to stand by and let any lander mess with her boat either. They'd have a thief's guts on a hook.

But all of a sudden here were the new engines, here were the damn cages coming—all of a sudden here was canalers that had and canalers as couldn't afford, and *that* was bad business, *bad* business.

She didn't like that thought.

She had to talk to Mondragon, she thought. Had to talk real serious to him, make him see what she was seeing.

Lay it out for him about the Janes.

Mondragon would think of something. Mondragon was real good at some things—and maybe (she had never in her life thought she'd think anything good about Anastasi Kalugin) he could explain just enough to Anastasi to let Anastasi fix things quiet-like. Anastasi was smart. Crooked, Lord knew, but he was real smart, and he sure as hell lived here same as anybody: Mondragon could judge what he'd do.

Yey.

# SECOND OPINION
# (REPRISED)

## *Janet Morris*

The Merovingian operation was as precise as clock-work, so far as Kenner could see. The warehouse dis-trict was perfect for his application; the quarters and ^ork space on Foundry Isle were just what he'd have ^en looking for if he were calling his own shots.

Kenner couldn't wait to get into gear. When Magru-der himself took a hand in settling them in, the new-comer was feeling better about things than he had since he'd realized his reporting chain went through a woman—a pregnant woman, then a mother.

Kenner had kept telling himself that Danielle Lam-bert's reputation couldn't be discounted simply be-cause she had the biological need to reproduce. But you didn't think about pregnant women and mothers the way you thought about operations commanders, and that dichotomy had made his own performance spotty, if not poor.

Well, they were off the riverboat and he had a job to do and an area to reconnoiter. He focused in on his

111

personal briefing by Magruder with all the intensity that had gotten him this assignment, and the quarters over this would-be shop in the lower part of the city, where fashionable shops gave way to warehouses.

Maybe Foundry was a slum, and maybe it wasn't. It was in the thick of things, and so were he and Jacobs, with their nice new machinist's shop cum revolutionary bastion. Magruder was loaded for bear: he already had the raw materials laid in, here where metal was scarce and the tools to work it scarcer.

The brunt of the briefing went down while Jacobs was doing a quick inventory of the storeroom, and it went like this:

"Look, Kenner," Magruder told him, "if you need anything, or anything doesn't feel right to you, get with me right away, don't wait. We'll have lots of standing orders for this and that, stuff you can bring up to the Embassy any time, and ask me to sign for it personally because of the disbursement policies being what they are."

"What are they?" Kenner asked, hiking his butt up on a barrel marked "Nails" in the warehouse space he'd have to partition if he wanted an office.

"On the record, you're Nev Hettek citizens working for our government, so you'll be paid in our scrip and we'll convert it to local gold and silver for you, saving you the money-changing percentage. Off the record, you can have whatever you need, as long as you don't start asking for things at odds with your cover. Oh, yeah: no drugs. No deathangel, nothing like that. Keep your head clear until you know the ropes—and thereafter."

"What about the reporting chain . . . I mean, what about m'sera Lambert. I'm supposed to report to her." *Might as well play a card and see what happens.*

"You follow all your orders, whenever possible. Danielle Lambert and I have worked together now and again. She's going to be hard to reach once she takes up her own role here, especially initially, what with being the personal obstetrician of Boregy House. You can't send dispatches in and out of Boregy House. It's too insecure and there are too many players here. You'll drop messages for her at the Embassy and she and I will figure out what to do about the rest.''

''I'm glad you two are comfortable. What with the baby and all, I was wondering how the hell this was going to work . . .'' *Play a second card.*

''Don't push it, kid. I know what you're saying. I can't respond yet. Everything ends up in my lap here, eventually. Do us all a favor and don't get too concerned about command hierarchies. Just do the job the most efficient way. Dani and the baby and her Boregy workload aren't going to be too efficient right away.''

''So you want me to set up shop and keep a list of who buys what, right?''

Magruder started to move around the big, empty space. He crossed in front of a window and Kenner realized that dawn was near: Magruder's shadow showed dark against the view.

''Serve all comers. Extend credit with interest to everybody; get signatures on promissory notes. Listen to the complaints and talk about Nev Hettek only when asked. The blacklegs—Tatiana Kalugin's police—are arresting anybody who says anything inflammatory. You'll have some plants coming by to test you. Don't talk revolution. Just show them how generous and supportive we can be. You're the answer to a canal-rat's prayer. They'll want those propeller cages like they want to get laid. Worse. Lay up a stock of standard sizes, so there's as little waiting as possible. You've got everything you need to do that, don't you?''

''I dunno.'' Kenner turned his head and yelled over his shoulder, ''Hey, Jacobs, got what you need to do the job?''

An affirmative came back through the half-open door. "Okay, then. Do I get to come to the Embassy any time soon?"

"You bet. You'll need more papers, green cards. I didn't bring you more than the basics so that you could come up and meet some staffers. Until you have met some, don't assume that anybody else is friendly, but treat them all like brothers. Clear?"

"Got it."

Magruder came over to him, his bootheels cracking against the floor, so determinedly and suddenly that Kenner slid off the barrel and balanced on the balls of his feet.

Eye to eye, Magruder said, "Don't ever give a document to anyone you don't know by sight. Ever. If you do, and I find out about it, even if no harm was done, you're fish food. Got that?"

"Yes sir—'m'ser.' " Damn, but this guy was prickly.

"It's my personal rule and I never break it for anybody: you screw that one up, you're dead."

"I don't screw up—m'ser."

"That'll be a refreshing change. See you before noon at the Embassy. You may have to wait in line. It only means I'm concerned that we don't make you look too special."

With that parting shot, Chance Magruder left Kenner on his own, slamming the door behind him.

Kenner stared at the door out of which Magruder had disappeared. He'd never encountered Magruder before. Oh, you heard stories, but stories tended to be exaggerated. He rubbed his arms and shook his head once before he set off to help Jacobs. He'd heard rumors that Karl Fon was that tough, though he'd never even seen Fon, wouldn't know him if he fell over him. Kenner had heard rumors that said Fon and Magruder needed some distance between them, like the distance between Nev Hettek and Merovingen. From what he'd seen, he could understand it.

Kenner had set a lot of fires in his day, and put the fear of revolution into more hearts than he cared to count. Stopped a few hearts, as well.

But he'd never been on the receiving end of a briefing like the one Magruder had just given him. And he'd never let somebody threaten him and walk away.

At the time, he reminded himself, it hadn't seemed like Magruder was threatening: just explicating a law of nature. If Kenner did what he was probably going to be ordered to do by Danielle Lambert, sooner or later, and Magruder found out about it, Magruder was going to kill him.

That was nice. It really added sparkle to his morning. He decided he wouldn't tell Jacobs. Jacobs didn't need to know more than not to open his mouth to strangers and not to hand dispatches to strangers.

Ambling back to the door beyond which Jacobs was taking inventory, Kenner had the distinct impression that he had walked into the opportunity of a lifetime: learn survival skills, a la Chance Magruder, or die trying.

One hell of a pass/fail, your first time out in the field. But then, Kenner knew what he was really here for: Fon was giving Magruder a pass/fail of his own.

Life was just so damned interesting these days, he could hardly wait to see what would happen next.


"If Cassie Boregy's allowed to continue prophesying unchecked, about a class revolt and the city going up in flames, only the Revenantist College is going to benefit. Not us. Not Nev Hettek." Magruder leaned back in his velvet chair and, from a china cup, sipped tea strong enough to wake the dead.

"I understand," said Dani Lambert. "That much

was in your report. This place is really extraordinary.'' She craned her neck at the opulence.

"Have to keep up with the locals. We've got an image problem if we don't." *Quit trying to change the subject, Dani. You've been sleeping with Karl, I hear. You've seen some opulence before.* "Mike Chamoun's a good boy. He'll come over and escort you to Boregy House to see his wife. They'll probably ask you to stay there. I'd prefer to have you stay here. It's your choice, once you see how it feels.''

"Thank you.'' She slid sideways in the brocade antique chair and brought up her knees. He could see the slackness from childbearing; in fact, he could barely keep his eyes off her waist, off her heavy breasts. He really wanted her to stay with him in the Embassy, but it was going to cause problems.

When he just looked at her pensively, she asked, "But what about Hope—about the baby?''

"Ah . . . yeah, that's a good question. What about it? Her, I mean?'' *The baby's name's the same as my mother's. Are you going to tell me what I'm afraid to hear? Or are we going to be good players and ignore the provenance issue? After all, it wasn't like you weren't present and accounted for through all of that; not like it was rape or under false pretenses.* Damn, he did want her to tell him it wasn't his. Or tell him it was. "Do you want me to engage a governess for the time being, make room for Hope here?'' Wasn't that what he was he supposed to say?

From the look on her face, it wasn't. She said, "I'll have her with me, wherever I stay. So we'll decide that later. Unless you want to tell me why you insisted that the obstetrician in question be me, in spite of my pregnancy coming to term so soon. And why you couldn't wait.''

This wasn't going to go down well, whenever he

broached it. "Sure, I'll tell you. Just promise not to throw any of this expensive bric-a-brac at me."

She almost smiled, despite herself, and tossed her head.

"I'm serious: promise me, no violent reaction—that you'll think about what I'm about to propose and not react at all, right now. That you'll wait until you've examined Cassie Boregy before you make up your mind."

Now she was cautious; perhaps beginning to surmise where he was leading. Her eyes widened, beautiful light brown eyes that he knew had violent flecks in them. "Go ahead, Chance, say it. Whatever it is, I promise I won't say a word about it until after I examine the patient."

"Cassie's overdue. She's been doing lots of deathangel, and it's toxic. The College has been making huge points from her prophecies. They're not going to let her stop while she lives. You're going to be asked to save the mother, regardless of the child. For all we know, the kid'll be stillborn or deformed."

"You can't know anything of the—"

Magruder silenced her with a raised eyebrow. "Let me continue with my supposition and my concerns: Whatever the state of the baby, it's Mike Chamoun's baby and it's the cornerstone of the Chamoun/Boregy merger, the shipping venture, the Embassy here, the whole ball of wax. If the kid's damaged or stillborn, the Revenantists will read it as a karmic indicator against a continuation of the marriage. We lose the Embassy, maybe. We lose Chamoun Shipping's favored status . . . we lose our in to Vega Boregy and his buddy, Anastasi: we lose the game. I don't want to lose the game. Are you with me?"

She said dully, "You never do want to lose. You can't be sure that the baby's damaged."

"No, that's why you're here. Or part of the reason.

But I'm sure of what I want you to do if that baby is in any way less than one hundred per cent healthy, bouncy offspring. I want you to switch babies. Cassie's too doped up ever to—''

"*What?*" Dani came out of her chair, fists balled.

"You promised, no violence.'' He wasn't smiling. Danielle Lambert was as intelligent, tough, deadly, and pragmatic as any man who'd reached her grade level during the revolution. If he knew whose damn kid it was, he'd have been able to judge how this was going to hit her—or judge it better.

However he judged it, he knew it wasn't an easy thing to ask, or even to contemplate. So he didn't give her a chance to respond with something she might later stick to, simply because she'd said it. "If you hadn't already given birth, I was going to closet you here until you did. The College will probably find out about any switch even if we do our damnedest—*if* we have to do it. But everything we've done here is shot without a live baby, in good health, in Cassie Boregy's arms.''

"The mother could die in childbirth, even in induced labor,'' said Dani coldly, sitting back down and crossing her arms over her own belly. "It's cleaner. Would that solve your problem?''

Lord, he'd forgotten how quick she was. "It would still read like bad karma from Michael's union with her, and they'd find a way to void any inheritance codicils the couple may have made between them. Nope, I need a healthy baby. Can we assume yours is?''

"You can assume anything you want, Chance Magruder.''

"All I'm asking you to do is think about it.''

"And I thought you wanted me here because you were getting old and sentimental and thought maybe the baby was yours.''

"What difference would that make?'' *Come on,*

wouldn't make things that much worse, considering how much harm had already been done. "Somewhere we can talk freely?"

The balcony, revealed when Chamoun pulled back heavy curtains, was awash in the blazing summer daylight. Out in the heat, under a white sky, Chamoun's face looked as waxy as Dani's felt. She rubbed her cheeks, stiff and tingly from lack of sleep, and wondered when she'd get some, and whether Chamoun had had any, lately.

"So?" said the husband.

"So we operate. As soon as I get some sleep."

"If it's that bad, why can't you do it now?" Chamoun crossed his arms over a chest rising and falling too fast for Dani's peace of mind.

"Because my hand has to be steady and I haven't even unpacked my instruments yet. You tell her family we'll need lots of boiled water, boiled sheets, and complete privacy." *Before I do anything more, I've got to talk to Chance, sonny; and so should you.*

"Cassie's the most important one . . ." The young agent sounded truly tortured, squinting beyond her into the morning light as he offered advice counter to his objective here, knowing she'd know the significance of what he was saying. "We can always have another baby."

"Don't be too sure. You two children have got yourselves into quite a mess."

"We're not children," he flared. "We're prepared to face the consequences."

"The consequences are going to be a healthy baby and a mother recovering from drug addiction. I'll promise you the one if you'll promise me the other."

"You'll have to talk to her father, and her uncle, Cardinal Ito, about that. The College gives her the drugs these days, not me." And then he faced her. His eyes were bloodshot. "I don't know how much you think you can do, or what the Embassy did to get you here, but I'm truly grateful. Just save her, m'sera . . . Doctor Lambert. Just save her, hear?''

"You come back with me to the Embassy. I've got lots of questions about her earlier symptoms." You never could tell who might be listening, even on a balcony. "And we don't have much time." *And you'd better let Chance brief you, sonny. You're not in line with the program as I've been given to understand it.*

"If you'll just speak with her father, Vega, first . . . Then I can leave with you. He'll want to know when you're going to . . . operate."

"I told you, I need to go back to the Embassy right away. I want you with me." She sighed. She didn't like being pushed this way; she wasn't sure whether she was talking to a Sword agent or a distraught husband. Maybe both in quick rotation. Chamoun obviously wasn't thinking as clearly as he might. "I'm going to give you something for your nerves," she decided. "And you're not going to argue. As soon as we get to the Embassy. Now, if you must, take me to the father. I'll give him a timetable and tell him what to prepare here." Then she smiled a professional smile, reaching out to squeeze Chamoun's hand. "And don't worry." *It's too late for that.* "We'll pull them both through, mother and child."

Chamoun nearly hugged her. She stepped back, out of the light, into the room where Cassie Boregy was muttering to herself in a waking dream.

How did they get her lucid enough to prophesy? Dani wondered as Chamoun led the way out of his wife's room, stopping only long enough to kiss her clammy forehead and promise that he'd be right back.

The father was having breakfast at one end of a table for twenty. A massive repast was on the sideboard; on his plate was only a piece of toast.

Vega Boregy, a black-haired man with translucently

pale skin, stood up to greet her. "Your diagnosis, Doctor?" he asked without preamble.

She spun her tale of exigency carefully: "I'll operate this evening. We want to get moving on this. No drugs whatsoever today. I want a list of what you people have been giving her, and when any medication was last administered. No food or water, either. I'll take your son-in-law with me to the Embassy, and he'll oversee the transfer of what I need from there to here. I'll want a few hours' rest first. This is going to be tricky, I won't lie to you. But we'll do our best to see to it that you have a healthy daughter and grandchild by tomorrow morning. I'd like the notes of the attending physicians sent over to the Nev Hettek Embassy as soon as possible . . ."

Vega Boregy nodded. "Michael, leave us alone. You'll escort Doctor Lambert, give her every cooperation."

When the Sword agent had left, the father said, "Cassie's welfare is my sole concern in this matter. Do I make myself clear? We Merovingians don't put such a premium on offspring that we'll risk the mother. It's imperative that you understand my position: If there's a choice to be made, there's no question of *what* choice should be made. I need your concurrence on that point before you touch my daughter."

Dani met the piercing gaze of Vega Boregy with her best medical hauteur. "M'ser, I'm a physician. I save life when I can; I'm not a magician. Whatever my choice would be were it up to me, your daughter may die in this operation. Without it, she surely will. I'll do my best to save Cassie; you must give me your word that you'll do yours."

"Of course. Don't be ridiculous."

"I'm not being ridiculous. I'm about to be blunt. If I offend, you may of course take that up with my Embassy. I can't and won't be responsible for Cassie's survival and subsequent recovery unless my instructions are followed to the letter. Do *you* agree?"

"Certainly. Why else would you be here, a stranger, if we weren't convinced your expertise was the finest we could obtain?"

"Fine. Thank you for your confidence. Let me be specific. You've allowed your daughter to become a drug abuser. Why isn't my affair. But it must stop or her life will be the price of it. After the operation, she'll be weak. She'll ask for her drugs. No one is to give them to her."

"You're unfamiliar with the situation here, Doctor Lambert." Boregy's tone warned her off.

"I'm Cassie's doctor, and I'm telling you, she can't survive this interval if I'm not given total control of her. I don't want to see her survive the operation and die of misplaced compassion, or political necessity, or whatever you're trying to allude to—and have Nev Hettek take the blame. Are we communicating, here?"

Boregy rubbed his nose, hiding whatever expression flitted across his face. "M'sera, you'll have our full cooperation. Once the operation is done, if Cassie survives, you'll have our eternal gratitude. And our confidence. Perhaps you'd like to stay at Boregy House with us, where your familiarization with our special circumstances can be accelerated."

"Perhaps that's a good idea—at least the first few nights, so that I'm here if there's some crisis. I'll give a list of what I'll need to your son-in-law, as I said. We'll have my things sent over." *And I'll be right here where you can get your hands on me if anything goes wrong and Cassie dies, don't worry about that.* She wasn't accustomed to such blatant threats. As she'd told Karl, this was a different culture, one where responsibility for events fell on everyone associated with those events.

Vega thanked her. She thanked him, in return, for his kind invitation. It was all very civil, very smooth.

Michael Chamoun, when he escorted her down antediluvian stairs to the Boregy water-gate and into a speedboat, was shivering visibly as he said, "Well, what do you really think?"

"I really think," Dani said, "that you're going to have a recovering mother with a healthy baby in her arms by this time tomorrow."

Let Magruder explain to Chamoun just whose baby that was going to be; and explain to her how they were going to get poor little Hope into Boregy House without anyone noticing.

Because Hope was going to be the baby. In Cassie Boregy's distended belly, there'd been no fetal heartbeat, not a movement, not a sign that whatever was in there had a breath of life in it.

Dani Lambert felt as if she might be sick. She hugged herself as the water-gate rose and the speedboat roared to life, waiting for the rush of anger that ⸻st sustain her, and make her strong enough to do ⸻at she'd been brought down here to do.

⸻Vhen it didn't come, she summoned it: Give her ⸻baby to strangers to raise, on the orders of a man who must suspect he was Hope's father. She was going to make Magruder pay for this, if it was the last thing she ever did.

Chance had his hands full with Tatiana—literally—when a knock on his salon door and a note slipped discreetly under it told him that Dani was back, with Mike Chamoun in tow.

It was one thing to keep Kenner waiting downstairs where he couldn't get into trouble and could watch people come and go and get a feel for how the Embassy worked. That was simple tradecraft; an opportunity taken when it arose. But this was just pisspoor timing.

He was off stroke today, and the daughter of Iosef Kalugin knew him too well for him to be able to cover it.

He came toward her with the note in one hand, his pants in the other. Their lunch lay untouched on the table; she lay unsatisfied on the couch. "We must have been bad little cockroaches in our previous lives," he said, tossing the note between her most honorable breasts. "What do we do? Finish what we've been trying to start here, or eat some of that lunch we haven't touched, or get the state business out of the way? I've got to tend to the obstetrician we brought down for the Boregys."

Tatiana Kalugin raised one muscled thigh and looked at it critically, as if it were more interesting than the note he'd thrown her to read. "So that's what's got you distracted. Cassie Boregy again. We can't seem to keep my father out of our sex life, can we?" She was frowning.

He knew what that meant. He dropped his pants a knelt down beside her. "Tatiana, the governor has on a short leash here." He touched her waist. Sh didn't pull away. He let his index finger penetrate her bellybutton.

She arched against it. "Chance, I hate us not having time for each other like this."

She wasn't going to let him off the hook. Test of strength, proof of intent. The last thing he needed was Tatiana feeling slighted. He said, "Let's spend the night together," and let his hand run down from her belly to the raised thigh.

She reached for him with the hand holding the note. "You're incorrigible."

*Just busy, honey.* But the outrageousness of continuing on with her while Dani and Chamoun waited, and the risk on every side, excited him more than it worried him. His focus narrowed: it was quicker to do what their bodies were urging than to explain why there wasn't time or what was so troubling that he couldn't. And he could.

So he must. As he did, he told himself that the governor's daughter knew him well enough to know he could perform in most crises. And it was safer to leave her happy than resentful. Or maybe it was just that he liked combat, and Tatiana was always that. This was a battle of wills, and one of wits, and the prize was control of Merovingen itself.

In moments like these, with Tatiana more responsive under him than someone with less at stake could ever be, he wondered if it were him she was wrapping her legs around, or the entire Nev Hetteker enemy.

But he wondered what he was doing with her all too often, playing this most dangerous game. When her father had caught them together, Magruder had thought he'd be packed off to Nev Hettek forthwith. But Tatiana's power had shielded him. She was ''m'sera Secretary'' and lots more. She was Anastasi's real rival for the governor's legacy, now that Mikhail was following Cassie Borey like a sheep.

Without Tatiana's support, Magruder couldn't have rammed home the machinist venture, or secured the permits to bring in Kenner and Jacobs, or even acquired the Embassy territory he now controlled.

One of these days, she was going to ask for more than sex. Right now, giving her his full attention was his pleasure.

When she gave a tiny gasp and stiffened, quivered, then relaxed under him, he let himself shudder as well. Women faked it all the time. She didn't need to know that he wasn't about to give up a bit of his edge right now.

She came up on one elbow when he'd slid off her,

after looking exaggeratedly deep into her eyes and murmuring, "Yep, that got the job done."

And she said, watching him dress, "Why are we taking risks like these, Chance?"

He was buckling his belt. "Because we can't not. We live in a damned fishbowl. Even fish have got a right . . ." Then he looked up at her as he reached for his shirt, realizing that her voice was strange, that now, in the middle of all this, she was about to up the ante. "But that's not the answer you're looking for." It came out of him about an octave too low, sounding too much like a duelist's challenge.

She said, "Do you think we're falling in love? Because I can't understand it, otherwise." She raked her hair back from her face. Her words had been tremulous. "I don't need all this . . . with you. My life was nicely—"

"I think we have trouble with that word," he said, knowing he was going to have to declare himself way beyond what he'd always considered the call of duty, or make an enemy. "But yeah, I think you're right, only I'm a foreigner, here on your family's sufferance, and I never could have said it first. Couldn't dare to say it." He took a deep breath and walked over to that couch like he was walking out on a limb he knew was likely to break at any moment. "We're not kids. If I started talking about . . . love . . . and it was unwelcome," he shrugged, "well, you'd have started wondering about ulterior motives and next thing I knew, I'd have been packed off to Nev Hettek as unsuitable, or in a Justiciary cell explaining myself."

"Chance . . ." She got up, that whole long nude and beautiful length of her that was his enemy, and in a moment she was in his arms, her belly pressing against his belt buckle. "What are we going to do?"

"Take our time. Go carefully. We're an item in public. Is it so wrong that there's more to that than convenience?'' *You know there is, and I do too, and it's whatever you want to make of it, lady. There's no words I won't say and nothing I won't do, as long as it makes you happy and relaxed while I get my work done.*

"I don't mean that. I mean, how are we going to handle . . . everything? Anastasi, my father. . . ?"

"Whoa. Put your clothes on, first thing. Get out of here and let me look like I'm gainfully employed for the rest of today, next thing. Let's spend the night here, where we can talk. If your schedule permits?"

"I'll make it permit."

*Great. Perfect timing. You and Dani under one roof.* "Then I'll see you for dinner and we'll have all night to convince each other we shouldn't be executed for letting this happen."

She kissed him on the lips and whispered something. He was almost sure it was, "I love you," but he wasn't sure enough to ask her to repeat it.

He couldn't imagine what the hell was going on in her head, to open matters up like this. Unless she really was in love and not thinking straight.

But you just didn't get that lucky. Marrying into the power structure was something that they'd planned for Mike Chamoun, at a nice, controllable level. If he and Tatiana didn't watch themselves, they'd both end up floating facedown in the Grand. Anastasi and his daddy would vie for the privilege of giving the orders to their personal militias.

When Tatiana was dressed and he'd deemed her presentable, he escorted her out of the salon, through the antechamber, and to the front door himself, all but ignoring Dani and Mike Chamoun.

If Karl Fon hadn't come down to put Magruder on notice that Fon was watching so carefully, Magruder wouldn't have been so worried about appearances, with so much really wrong.

Before he went back to his office, he snagged a
staffer and gave orders to reset the salon for four and
sneak Kenner up the back stairs and in to join them.
Might as well have a party large enough that Dani
couldn't broach anything personal.

He could tell by the look on her face that she'd examined Cassie and realized he was right about the
baby. And he could tell by Michael's face that she
probably hadn't told the kid yet, or Chamoun would
be angry and resentful, not distraught.

Well, the privilege of command included the joys of
making people hate your guts for their own good. He'd
always known that. He'd just never realized that making people love you so that you could destroy them
was part of his job. Or that it would feel so confusing.

He was going to go get drunk with Mike Chamoun,
soonest, and compare notes on what it was like to be
a revolutionary whore.

Next to what he had on his plate, sneaking baby
Hope into Boregy House and sneaking out whatever
Cassie had in her oven was going to be easy. A veri-
table piece of cake.

Or so he thought until he saw Dani's face, stony and
cold, and she announced that she'd be staying with the
Boregys for the foreseeable future. He couldn't imagine why that bothered him the way it did.

But it did.


Dani Lambert's hands were shaking like leaves in
an autumn gale, now that the deed was done. Thank
heavens there'd been no one in Cassie's bedroom during the operation but Michael and the assistant the
Embassy had provided.

Thank heavens, too, that Boregy House had elec-
trics. They'd brought in all they could, and Michael
had added a battery-operated searchlight from one of
his ships.

Vega Boregy had suggested taking Cassie over to the College and using an operating facility there, and Dani had brazened her way through it, saying that moving Cassie would be the worst thing they could do.

She'd blocked Vega's attempts to insert other physicians to help, people from the College staff. She'd said she needed all the room she could get, and the medic from the Embassy was trained in Nev Hetteker procedures.

Given the tension between the two cultures, and the premium everyone put on trade secrets, and the nervous father, she'd managed to push that through against all reason.

She cursed Chance Magruder unto eternity as she set to work.

The worst of it had occurred before she ever picked up an instrument in Cassie's bedroom. That had been the necessity of tranquilizing poor little Hope and toting her over by boat to Boregy House in the middle of a closed trunk. Dani had been terrified that Hope would suffocate.

Only Michael knew that Hope was in there. They couldn't even trust the assistant. They'd sent him out for more boiling water and clean towels as soon as the trunk was brought up. Then Michael and she had gotten out Hope and hidden her in the couple's big armoire.

Hope had been sleeping peacefully, yet Dani had been dizzied with relief when she saw that nothing was wrong.

When Dani put the anaesthetic over Cassie Boregy's half-conscious face, she'd taken a cruel and horrid satisfaction in the process. Maybe the bitch would die under the anaesthetic. If not, she was so stoned she'd never know what hit her. Poor little Hope hadn't known why Mommy was putting that cloth over her nose. . . .

The operation made such a mess that there was no question of anyone discovering the dead fetus. Dani had hardly been able to look at it herself. She'd been wracked by a horrid fear that the thing might be alive, weak but alive.

If it had been, it wasn't alive for long. They'd wrapped it in the middle of the bloody sheets and put the sheets in the bottom of a refuse barrel they'd brought up for the purpose.

Then there was more mess, and the cleaning out of Cassie's womb, and that made more bloody sheets to pile on top.

Dani performed like an automaton through the worst of it. In retrospect, as she sat now in the hallway, it seemed to her that someone else had used the forceps, that someone else had clamped the tongs around the fetus' head, that someone else had sent the assistant from the room at exactly the moment that the head was becoming visible.

"Quick, Michael," she remembered saying. "Now."

Michael Chamoun had been the one to smear Hope with birthing fluids and awaken her with ice cold water.

Then Hope wouldn't scream. He'd slapped her three times before she did.

Dani remembered that Cassie still wasn't awake then, as they put the live baby in the mother's arms, where Hope snuggled, pink and angry looking with traces of artfully smeared blood still all over her face, and mucus in her hair.

*Lord, this isn't going to work. She doesn't look like a newborn. She doesn't.*

But the baby was so overdue, and the family so relieved when they were let inside, and the room such a mess, that nobody noticed.

Or if they did, nobody said anything. Hope's bellybutton was gong to be a telltale, so Dani had put a stitch in it, praying that she could say it was Nev Hettek procedure, if anybody asked. There were stitches enough in Cassie Boregy . . .

It was done then, but for rousing Cassie, and they'd had a rough time doing that. Michael, and cold water when all else failed, finally succeeded.

Dani had wandered into the hall, where she sat on a little velvet chair as the family clustered around Cassie Boregy and her baby, and watched her hands shake. She kept trying to tell herself that it wasn't a bad sign that her memory of what had just happened was a jumble of bits and pieces, incidents out of sequence.

She was frightened, and for good reason. And she was heartsick at what she'd done. And she wanted to go cry on Chance's shoulder, which was absolutely absurd, under the circumstances.

The circumstances: The evidence of the swap was out of the way. If she could just not say the wrong thing, the gambit would succeed.

She was about to endure celebratory parents and myriad congratulations she didn't want.

Dani got up suddenly, went to the doorway, and called to Michael, "Could you show me my room? I'm feeling a little tired. I've had a long trip and a long night."

Everyone made sympathetic noises, and Michael Chamoun was at her side in a heartbeat, wanting to know if she was all right.

She told him she wasn't, when they were out of earshot. She told him she hated what she and he had done. She was nearly out of control, but if she'd been totally out of control she'd have told him she wanted her baby back.

Chamoun looked at her, his tired face full of unspeakable misery and inestimable relief, and said, "I'll never know how to thank you for this. Whatever you need, whenever—just . . . I'm no Magruder, but whatever I can do to help, as long as I live, you've got.''

She wished she could have been gracious. She wasn't. She looked at her feet and the figured carpet under it, and the pattern swam before her eyes. At the door to her room in Boregy House, she grasped the doorjamb for support and said to Mike Chamoun. ''Her name's Hope, you know.''

Chamoun looked away. ''Sorry. It's whatever they decide,'' Cassie Boregy's husband told her as he turned and walked away, down the stairs to his wife and his daughter.

Dani set on the feather bed and then lay out flat without even bothering to take off her boots or her blood-smeared smock.

No sooner had she closed her eyes than a knock came, tentative, then stronger, on the door she'd shut.

She opened it and a stranger was standing there. He was dressed in fancy Merovingian clothes and his eyes were very bright in a thin, pale face.

''I'm Mikhail Kalugin,'' he said, sticking out his hand awkwardly for her to take.

She did. ''You've got the wrong room, m'ser Kalugin.'' The Kalugins were the real power here, she dimly remembered. Mikhail wasn't the one you heard about . . .

''I've got the right room. I just felt I must thank you for saving our dear prophetess. You don't know how much Cassiopeia Boregy means to all of Merovingen. I'm going to speak to my father about seeing that you receive a special honor, a medal for valorous service to the State, and we'll throw a great gala to present you to all of Merovingen.''

''Terrific,'' she said tiredly. ''Ambassador Magruder will love that. You go work it out with him, m'ser Kalugin. I've got to get some sleep.''

The weird Kalugin fellow still had hold of her hand. She tugged at it and he pulled back, raising it to his lips and kissing its back.

Then he apologized for disturbing her and wandered off down the hall.

Well, Chance would love it. And it beat having opened the door to a squad of blacklegs ready to haul her off to the local prison, or seeing Michael standing there telling him that Cassie had gone into convulsions.

There was a possibility of that, of course. One could always hope.

The prophetess of Merovingen was already someone that Dani Lambert didn't like very well. As a matter of fact, she didn't like anything about Merovingen very well.

The least Chance could have done was stop by to see how things had gone. Then she realized that she was disappointed that it hadn't been him at the door. Then she decided she was going to write Karl Fon a long letter about Tatiana Kalugin and Chance Magruder, as soon as she knew what the hell she wanted to say.

Then she locked her door and took a little envelope out of her pocket. She swallowed three of the tablets inside and lay back.

If Cassie hemorrhaged during the night, they were going to have a hard time waking her personal physician, but this way she wouldn't dream.

Danielle Lambert didn't want to dream: not of Magruder, not of Karl Fon, not of home, so far away, and especially not of little Hope, who was now heir to one of Merovingen's greatest houses.

It beat being a Lambert, she told herself.

She just couldn't make herself believe it.

# SEEDS OF DESTRUCTION (REPRISED)

## C.J. Cherryh

God! was what Mondragon had said when Altair 'fessed up to him—not an easy thing to do. Ye don't be mad, she had said, and got him out on the Water, on her skip, which she just reckoned was how she wanted to tell him, not that Mondragon would really hit her, that was what made him scary sometimes— he'd blow up like anybody when he was upset, but when you really, truly made him mad, he just got quiet—and she didn't want anywhere for him to go off to without talking to her and she didn't want him in his fancy apartment to hear it, she wanted him on the boat where he could just look around him and remember what poor was.

She'd been scared when she'd done it. He'd said— *What?* She'd said, Just listen to me, dammit, I'm tellin' ye. And he'd shut up.

He'd shut up so long she'd been really scared he wasn't going to forgive her.

Then he'd just dropped his head onto his hand and sat there like he just couldn't handle that, —like he'd already bashed Raj up against a wall about the black-

leg mess, and the only thing that kept Raj from fling-
ing hisself off Rimmon Bridge once and all with a rock
in his arms was how Mondragon had been real nice
about it— Not entirely your fault, Mondragon had allowed, with his hand around Raj's throat, and bashing
him again, Raj gone all pale. —But you wake up, boy,
you live in dangerous times, and if some fool girl
thinks she can take on the blacklegs, it's *her problem*,
boy, —(bash!)—hear me?

Yessir, Raj had said, trying to pry Mondragon's hand
loose so he could breathe.

You owe me, Mondragon had said. You owe me being *smart*, boy!

Yessir, Raj had whispered, because he was running
out of air.

She couldn't but think of that while Mondragon was
sitting there like it was just one thing more than he
could cope with.

Like he'd trusted her, he'd really trusted her to use
her head, and now she'd just messed things up he was
just—

—just going to break down and cry, was what it
looked like. And that was like a knife in her gut.

So she'd sat there, he'd sat there, a long, long time,
and a couple of times he'd shook his head, not looking
up.

"I'm a fool," she'd said. "I knowed it, Mondragon,
I *tried* to fix it, but that damn Rif—"

He was going to kill Rif, that had been her sudden,
awful thought; he was just going to cut her throat and
she was going to turn up floating, no explanations, and
maybe that was what she ought to have done, maybe
she was a spineless fool not to have—and he'd have to,
if it hadn't all gone too far for anything to help. . . .

But he'd looked up finally, staring off across the
Grand, calm as if he hadn't a thought in his head.

And she'd been too scared to say a word, and he'd

gotten up, finally, and stretched an arch in his back, and looked up the Grand where the bridges cut off the view, but the Signeury was up that way.

So was the Justiciary.

"I'll work the boat today," he said, as if there was nothing wrong; but he hadn't done that in weeks, and she'd thought maybe she'd messed things up so bad he knew he was going to die, and he just wanted to be out on the Water a while, just not thinking about it.

She was scared sick, was what she was, she had supper with him on the skip and he ate just fine, but she choked hers down like it was poison; and he made love to her that night up in his apartment, and she was so cold she shivered.

"What's the matter?" he asked, holding her tight. "Jones?"

"I'm sorry about what I done." With her teeth chattering. "I'm sorry."

He just made love to her. Eventually she stopped shaking. He told her he was thinking about it, and he hadn't known about the seeds, but he'd known what Rif was, and he was, frankly, he said, relieved she understood things, was real happy with her figuring it all out, how the Sword and the Janes both were working, making what he called haves and have-nots, making poor folk *know* they were poor, making them hurt real bad—

Like she'd been so damn slow, and he'd never expected she'd figure things out, but he knew, because he'd been Sword of God himself, and that was how they worked and that was how the Janes worked— because they were so far opposite to each other they met on the backside of the circle; and used the same tricks and sometimes dealt with the same people. . . .

"What're ye going t' do then?" she asked, finally, with him on top of her.

"Just thinking," he said, and kissed her like he hadn't a thought to his name.

*Happy,* for the Lord's sake. . . .

So when, a couple of days later, he came walking down the front of Ventani and said he had something to show her, she scrambled right up and untied and expected they were going to go do something dangerous, so her gut was in a knot, but she was ready for whatever it was.

She expected he was going to say to take him uptown.

But he wanted to go to the harbor.

"Quiet-like?" she asked, meaning engine or not, and he shrugged and said it didn't matter.

So she flung up the cover, put down the tiller, cranked up her balky old engine—she had it running the best it ever had, for pride, for one thing; and the last couple of days because she was sure she was going to need it—and they motored on down to the harbor, down through that black maze of pilings to the area of the Customs House, where he worked for Kamat.

"Got a surprise," he said, and didn't tell her what it was, just said come on.

So, totally puzzled and no little worried, she tied up to a ring and followed him off the skip and down the wooden dock where mostly lighters and canalers tied up.

A few berths down he stopped and waved his hand out to the water, said, "There she is," and she looked out to the harbor, expecting some ship was coming in that meant something hopeful to their problems.

But if there was anything out there she couldn't see it.

"Where?" she asked.

"Right in front of you," he said.

There wasn't anything in front of her but an old canaler-boat, that hadn't moved in two years.

"What?" she asked, looking for canvas on it, something newer than the little heap of canvas that was rotting away on it undisturbed, on gray-brown slats all eaten up with worms. Whatever it was, was well-hidden.

"The boat. It's mine. Just got the motor license."

Her mouth was open. She looked around at him, thinking, *Lord, he's joking or he's cracked.* But he looked just plain pleased with himself.

"Mondragon," she said, "—this boat ain't *goin'* anywhere. I *know* this boat, Mondragon, ever'body knows this boat: she's th' old Manning river-runner, Manning's dead an' th' creditors got th' boat, but they ain't been able to sell 'er—she's got *dry rot,* Mondragon, ain't no fixin' 'er."

"Few new boards—one of those new engines—"

"There ain't no sound wall to fix it to! She ain't wood, she's *punk,* f' th' Lord's sake! You mount an engine on that stern, she'll pull her bolts right through the wood if ye ain't fell right through the deck first time ye step on it! Who'd ye deal with? Mantovans?"

"I can just put a little bracing on the stern wall—"

"Lord an' my Ancestors!" He *had* cracked. Everything he'd done for days was like he was sleepwalking. She sorted wildly through recent memory, trying to see if this made sense, or if she should maybe get him back home, get him to bed, get him to rest a few days. She wanted to cry, she outright felt tears coming, and she raked her cap off and twisted it in her hands, because she wanted to strangle the crooks that he was dealing with, and all the folk of the Trade that were going to laugh themselves sore when the word got out her man had bought the Manning boat.

"It'll take some fixing," Mondragon said, "but it'll

be good—working with my hands a while, get some exercise—''

''Oh, shee-*it!*'' she cried, and just sat down with her head in her hands.

She didn't even care people were going to laugh at her; it was his life she was worried about, how he was ever going to take care of himself. She just felt sick.

''Jones,'' he said.

He sounded sane. He sounded real sane, all of a sudden, and she looked up at him standing there like an Angel himself, with the sun behind his hair.

Like God was on his side.

# FARREN'S FOLLY: MEETING OF MINDS (REPRISED)

## Roberta Rogow

The evening bells signaled the end of the working day. Farren led Mikhail down the stairs to where the official skip rode in its own docking space. "Can I drop you anywhere?" Farren asked.

Mikhail stared at the little boat. "You pole yourself?"

"Good exercise," Farren said cheerfully, slipping out of his shoes and moving into position. "Could do with a bit. Hop in, and I'll row you over to the bridge."

Mikhail eased himself gingerly into the boat, while Farren rolled up his sleeves, took up the pole, and slid the boat into the going-home traffic without as much as a splash.

A pretty girl waved from the lowest tier; Farren grinned up at her and waved back.

"I love this place," he said, half to himself and half to Mikhail. "There's nowhere else like it."

Mikhail had never been this close to the actual canals or the canalers. He usually traveled in a much larger barge, where he was safely isolated from the riffraff of the canalside. Cassie Boregy warned against these people. They were not to be trusted, she said . . . yet, here in the sunlight, with the waves lapping against the boat, they didn't seem so fierce or so sinister. The stout woman who shouted a greeting to Farren . . . hard to think of her as The Enemy. Nor the gap-toothed boy who smiled from another boat, nor the man who offered a fishcake from off his tray "for luck."

Mikhail stepped back onto dry land as Farren pulled up to Archangel Walk. "I've been thinking," he said diffidently from the shore. "That pump. How are you going to pay. . . ?"

"Don't worry, my friend, I have an idea about that. Do you like music?"

"Music?" Mikhail echoed, bewildered at this sudden turn of the conversation.

"My wife's having one of her Musical Evenings tonight," Farren explained. "And your father asked me to see you met some people. No better place to meet people than one of Addie's Musical affairs."

Mikhail thought that over. "Am I invited?"

"Just come. Tell old Seymor at the door you're mine."

"But . . ." Mikhail stammered, as Farren swung his boat around and headed across the canal, cutting sharply in front of a parked barge bearing the flag of the Kamats.

Richard Kamat was checking over the last load of raw wool when the skip pulled up to his dock. He frowned at the boatman, then realized that the bare-armed canaler at the pole was actually his neighbor, Farren Delaney.

"Way-hen!" Farren called.

"Good evening," Richard replied curtly. God. Neighbor visits. From eccentric Delaney. He was hungry and dinner was waiting.

"You seem to be doing well, Kamat."

"Business isn't too bad," Richard said carefully. "And I should congratulate you on your promotion. Prefect of Waterways, isn't it?"

Farren smiled modestly. "It was bound to happen, sooner or later. Addie's arranged a little entertainment tonight to celebrate. I would very much like you to come . . . bring your sister, and your mother, too, if you like. How is m'sera Andromeda these days? Addie's missed her work in the soup kitchen."

Richard's frown deepened. "Mother isn't too well," he said slowly, "and Marina's got her hands full taking care of things . . ."

"In that case, come yourself," Farren persisted. "There are a few things I'd like to talk over with you."

"What's wrong with my office?" Richard asked.

"I wouldn't like to keep you from your dinner. Just drop by. Seymor's my doorman: he'll show you right up."

Farren waved a farewell and poled himself off again, leaving Richard staring blankly after him. Raj stepped out of the shadow where he had been observing the scene.

"Who was *that*, m'ser?"

"Farren Delaney. He wants me to go to a party tonight."

"Will you?"

"I just might . . . if only to find out what he's up to."

Ariadne Delaney's Musical Evenings drew as many of the idle artistic rich as could wangle an invitation, and a number of somewhat surprising other invitees as well. No one knew what might get served up by

Ariadne: a new dancer or a mime troupe or an elderly (but still active) poet found starving in a hidey, forgotten until Ariadne revived an interest in his Great Epic of the Scouring.

At the moment the stars of the evening were the singers Rafaella and Rattaille, those balladeers who (it was rumored) had begun their careers in canalside dives. Now they were in Fashion, thanks to Ariadne, and Merovingian leisured society filled the Delaney ballroom to hear them.

Ariadne waited at the door to the ballroom to greet her guests with a smile or a word or a very occasional kiss on the cheek.

"Sonia, so good of you to come; very glad to see you, Prefect . . . Letty, I hope you will be entertained. . . ."

While Farren smiled at her side and led this or that guest to the buffet table, where the spread was lavish without being ostentatious.

The smile suddenly stiffened on Ariadne's lips as she realized who was making her way up the stairs.

Cardinal Exeter, draped in the austere burnt-orange robes of the College.

"Good evening, Your Eminence," Ariadne said, recovering her poise. "I'm *so* pleased you could come. I always send you an invitation, but I know how busy your schedule is. . . ."

Willa Exeter smiled, raking the room with a glance that did not partake in frivolity. She said, sweetly: "I've heard so much about these singers of yours, I felt I should find out for myself if the stories are true."

"Stories?" Ariadne asked brightly, thinking frantically, *I hope Rafaella knows there's clergy here! God, don't let her do the Poleboater song—*

"Oh . . . exaggerations, surely. You, of all people, would never harbor heretics in your house!" Willa moved into the ballroom, accepting the bows and greetings of the other guests as she went, bestowing the occasional blessing. Farren bounded over to his wife.

"What's she doing here?" he hissed.

"I *always* invite the clergy. A courtesy. I had no idea she'd decide to come— Is something wrong?"

"No, not at all . . . just a little unexpected . . . ah—" Another blink of startlement. "Kamat!"

"Addie, you don't mind? Kamat's a neighbor, after all. . . ." Farren virtually hauled Richard past her into the ballroom, with an almond-eyed boy trailing along behind. The boy gave a nervous bow, said: "Raj Tai, m'sera," and slipped into the crowd in Kamat's wake. Ariadne moved over to the buffet, certain that the last of her guests had arrived.

Farren dived back past her to the door—and the last-comer standing hesitantly in the arch. All conversation stopped dead. The man in the doorway started to retreat, but Farren had reached him and led him gently across the room.

"Mikhail Kalugin! Glad you could tear yourself away from your workshop. There are some people I want you to meet . . . this is Richard Kamat, *the* Kamat . . ."

Cardinal Willa Exeter stared, tried to keep her face bland as she watched the governor's eldest, *her* party's candidate for the succession, shambling across the ballroom arm in arm with one of the most useless, brainless pieces of furniture in the Signeury . . . or so she had thought.

How had Mikhail gotten snared into this company of dilettantes and bohemians? *That* certainly bore looking into. . . .

Araidne clapped her hands for silence. "Dear friends, in honor of Farren's promotion to Prefect of Waterways, we have prepared a brief entertainment. Would you come into the music room?"

Farren managed to get between Richard and Mikhail as the crowd surged forward.

"Could you manage to drop over to the Signeury on some pretext?" he murmured to Richard. "Mikhail and I have a little business proposition to put to you, but we would prefer not to have it widely known just yet."

*Aha!* Richard thought. *He wants money! Or backing for some scheme or another.* Aloud he said, "I have a few minor fees to pay; I was planning to come over around noon."

"We'll be there," Farren promised, as he steered them to adjoining seats. We. Richard noticed that. "I think you'll like these singers. The tall one's got a good, strong voice . . .'

Behind them, Cardinal Exeter smiled blandly, and wondered just what Farren Delaney thought he was doing. And wondered whether Ariadne knew how close those singers were to being declared heretic.

Or whether she should simply refer them to her bodyguards down at the water-gate, and bring them to her office. . . .

Not yet, she thought. And took mental notes, who applauded at what.


Farren's tiny office seemed more crowded than ever. Gathered around the table were Iosef Kalugin, Richard Kamat, Cardinal Ito Boregy, and Cardinal Exeter. Mikhail had wedged himself into a corner, while Farren demonstrated with the little wooden model on the desk before them.

Mikhail had worked all night after the party modifying one of his precious model boats. Now it held a pair of outriggers, with a ladder mounted on each one. The engine had been expanded until it nearly filled the stern. A length of twine represented a hose, coiled around a wheel, mounted on the pump assembly.

Farren explained the mechanism, as Mikhail had explained it to him: "You see, the water is pumped up through this intake, into this compressor, which shoots it through the reinforced hose at high pressures with an adjustable nozzle, to direct the flow. The extension ladders reach the upper tiers."

He manipulated the model, and pulled the tiny ladders upright, extended the braces. "To keep the boat from tipping."

Cardinal Boregy's normally glum face took on a sour frown. "Noisy. A very *large* engine."

"In use only in emergencies, Cardinal."

"You know the dangers of technology, Delaney. This is a *large* machine, a large *public* machine."

"Existing technology—"

"We do quite adequately—without this monster."

"A spilled lantern could devastate an Isle. Consider Megary. . . ."

"Karma."

"With all respect, Cardinal, the karma of the neighbors—"

"Do you lecture me in religion?"

"No, Your Eminence. Absolutely not. But—" An inspiration. "To know how technology can prevent tragedy and not to do it—what about the karma of lives and property?"

"*Existing* technology," Mikhail said from his corner.

"Lives and property." Farren threw fervor into his voice. "Think of it, seri. What if a stray spark ignited the grain stores? or the archives? Everything gone in a flash, records gone—and it might have been prevented by this equipment, in the hands of a well-trained crew."

"Ah, yes," the governor purred. "The crew. Just who were you planning on hiring to run this little . . . experiment?"

Farren turned a desperate smile on his three doubters. "I put it to you, seri: who is most likely to know the canals? Who is best-trained, almost from birth, in the handling of all sorts of water-craft? Who knows the backwaters and byways of the city? and most importantly, who is most in need of steady work?"

"Cheap," Richard muttered.

"Folly!" Boregy exploded. "Machinery of this size —should not be in the hands of canalers. It puts tech in unlicensed hands. I assume you'll keep this firewatch on duty around the clock? And the money— Who would take money for putting out fires? It's a civic duty. *Pay* for that is immoral. A corruption. Give canalers that windfall and they'll be *starting* fires to make themselves necessary. If you think the fires at Megary are coincidence—"

Farren cleared his throat and looked at Richard. "Exactly. That's why I asked my neighbor, Kamat, to this meeting. You see, I thought that the merchants have the most to lose by fire, and the most to gain by a firewatch. Let us suppose that each merchant with a warehouse or shop fronting on the canal contributes a small sum . . . say, a lune or two . . . to a general fund, administered by whomever you care to choose—" Me. "—with the—ahem!—Signeury and the College contributing matching funds."

Sullen silence from Boregy.

"Each contributor would place a token on any buildings covered by the investment. In the event of fire, those buildings with tokens would receive priority attention, although—of course—saving life is always our first consideration."

The governor frowned, took the model up, looked at it, looked at his son. "Yours?"

Mikhail stared stolidly back. Nodded.

Iosef Kalugin set the model down in front of him. Folded his hands and looked briefly at Exeter, sourly at Boregy, last and with a lift of his brow at Farren. "Ingenious, Delaney. Kamat?"

"The merchants stand to gain."

"Certainly the Signeury can match funds. Your Eminence?"

Boregy scowled, shot a glance at Mischa, who was attentively picking a hangnail and did not look up.

"Your Eminence?"

Boregy inclined his head then with cold deference, pulled the Variance toward him and sullenly affixed the College seal.

Mischa grinned, looking up under one eyebrow, winked at Farren and bit the offending nail.

# RED SKIES

## Lynn Abbey

When man first looked up at the skies he reluctantly concluded that bad weather was more inspiring than good. Clear skies made the sun rise and set without fanfare. Add clouds—add weather in any interesting form—and patterns of glowing, shifting beauty emerged. The Ancestors had an adage: Red skies at night, sailor delight; red skies at morning, sailor take warning. It was as useful a piece of wisdom as could be wrung from the dynamics of rotating bodies, and it had followed mankind through the stars. Even to Merovin.

Richard Kamat leaned on the railing of the Salvatore high bridge. Sunrise colors ascended to mid-heaven. There were roses and ambers, golds and pinks, and at the foundation of it all the blood-red sun. It was slack-tide; the waves slapped gently against the city's pilings. To the uninitiated, it might seem that a peaceful day had begun, but no one in harbor-straddling Merovingen above the age of five was uninitiated.

A flickering breeze touched the back of Richard's neck: a warm breeze for this time of day, and onshore as well. It carried a reminder of tangle-lilies rotting in every damp shadow of the city. The more delicate among Richard's peers had taken to dangling a cinnamon-orange from a silk-ribbon bracelet. A sensitive nose was not an asset in a dyeworking House. Richard judged the taint no worse than sheepdip and considerably less pungent than the mordant brews simmering in Kamat's cellars.

He frowned and pushed away from the rail. There'd be a storm by mid-afternoon, a rafter rattler from the colors on the horizon. It might bring an end to the stifling heat; one could always hope. Even a Revenantist on Merovin. He descended the stairs leeward of Ramseyhead into the sunlight and the Ramsey Bell's cul-de-sac.

The unassuming tavern opened at dawn and closed in the depths of the second watch. In the course of a day it served the heirs of the mercantile houses, their agents, and, finally, the customs laborers themselves. The regulars took care to keep their brawls away from its taps, and the nonregulars were icily encouraged to take their trade elsewhere. Richard hadn't been a regular since his father died. He was recognized as he came through the screen door and accorded a narrow stare from the barkeeper. Richard's presence here couldn't be casual, it had to have a reason, and spying out that reason might be worth something to someone.

Mutely acknowledging his changed status, Richard walked past the window table where he had once eaten two meals out of three.

"Is your oil boiling yet?" he asked, propping one elbow on the worn wood of the bar.

"S'past dawn, ain't it? The fish be floured, an' the chips ready, too."

Richard nodded. The keeper tossed two white fillets and a handful of taters into the fryer. There were dozens of taverns in Merovingen where rumors were spawned. Moghi's on the Ventani waterside was a likely place to learn something worth knowing—if your silver was pure and your karma was up. The Bell was a good deal brighter than Moghi's. It smelled better, too, especially on days like this, but its real business was about the same.

When the oil was seething steadily, the keeper returned to the bar. "What brings you back this way, m'ser Kamat?"

"A sudden craving for breakfasts past," he replied with a laugh that was more good-natured than cryptic.

Richard wasn't about to tell the barkeep why he was here; he wasn't comfortable admitting it to himself. It wouldn't do for a Househead to confess that his gut was lob-tailing and he'd spent half the night beside the commode.

He'd come a long way since his father's untimely death, hadn't he? He was the driving force—the visible force, at least—behind the Samurai. He was trading with Vega Boregy and Anastasi Kalugin: personal trade, Family trade. Kamat's handshake was worth five hundred gold sols, and people listened when he talked. Of course, Vega and Anastasi were each inclined to say *you and I, Richard, against our untrustworthy partner,* and the three of them never got together.

That was still trade. Boregy or Kalugin hadn't kept Richard up all night; that honor belonged to Tom Mondragon. Mondragon, the archetype of treachery; Mondragon, the father of Marina Kamat's unborn child; Mondragon, the man who guarded Kamat's back. Against all instinct Richard found that he was comfortable with Tom. They could betray each other six ways from Sunday, and the knowledge was somehow reassuring. But late at night, when the House was quiet, a hysterical whisper of sanity would interrupt Richard's thoughts: *You're trusting Mondragon. You're*

*taking his advice. You're sharing your secrets*—his
*karma.*

Thomas Mondragon definitely had karma. He also
had enemies and obligations. One of those obligations
was currently living in Kamat: the youth, Raj Tai.
Richard had swallowed Raj Tai like he'd swallow an
oyster: quickly and thoughtlessly—because spitting it
out wasn't going to resolve anything. For a while everything had gone smoothly. The boy seemed as intelligent as he claimed to be—until last week when
he'd gotten drunk; when he'd mouthed off near the
wrong ears; when he'd compared the rotting lilies to
the idle rich in terms no one could possibly appreciate.
And now Kamat had paid a bribe to the blacklegs—
Tatiana's blacklegs—and Tom Mondragon had been the
go-between.

Thirty sols.

No matter what Richard did, he couldn't get the
memory of those coins out of his head. As blackleg
bribes went, it was exorbitant. But if Tatiana had meant
to put the screws to Kamat, thirty sols wasn't a quarter
turn. It simply didn't make any sense, and one thing
Tom had taught him was that treachery *always* made
sense to someone.

Mondragon and the boat made sense in a crazy way.
*Mondragon* said he wanted the exercise. *He* offered Mondragon a *real* boat, because getting Mondragon out of
Merovingen was the most sensible thing to come in
with the tide in the last five months. But Mondragon
refused. Anastasi had his hooks in Tom deeper than
Boregy: now Boregy was stalking Tom. Vega put it
bluntly: *I've canceled that trade, Richard. I'd advise
you to do the same. I'd hate to see you go down when
he does.* Richard hadn't canceled his trade, and neither
he nor Tom had gone down—yet.

At ten Richard would meet with Vega Boregy to
discuss the Samurai. It was their usual Thursday

morning meeting. Richard had the usual receipts and reports in his satchel. There was nothing to say that today would be any different than last Thursday.

The Signeury bells gave their first peal of the day. The barnlike doors of the Merovingen Customs House across the New Harbor canal opened for trade. Here was the key to the Bell's popularity: an eagle's vantage of the custom dock and the counting hall inside. Every legitimate import or export stopped at both places. A skillful observer could learn as much by how goods did, or didn't, pass through the customs house as he could by eavesdropping on The Rock.

The barkeep stood on his toes to see the pallets waiting for their assessments. It was reasonable to guess that there might be something special, even something contraband, down there on the dock to account for a Househead's presence in his tavern. Reasonable, but wrong. Richard had only a passing interest in the pallets. Instead, his attention was focused on the men standing beside each pallet and at regular locations within the counting hall.

"They're a tidy bunch," the barkeep allowed, once he'd taken the angle of Kamat's gaze.

A layer of tension slid from Richard's shoulders. He was proud of those men, those Samurai, standing in their faded blue chambrys. They were making a difference in Merovingen. Trade had cleared its throat and was moving freely again. If Kamat had made enemies, they'd made friends and allies, too. Richard had done something his father could not have imagined, and he'd done it well.

The Samurai were a counterbalance to the unreliable blacklegs—the municipal blacklegs under Tatiana Kalugin's de facto control. The Samurai answered to the mercantile community. After three months they were fully subscribed; every House Kamat approached had anted up its share, and, to Richard's proud surprise, ten Houses that had previously scorned three-generation Kamat contacted him directly.

He'd spawned a burst of civic responsibility. The Signeury Waterworks was offering subscriptions in a municipal fire department. Even the College's initiative to ban motor traffic on the smaller canals acknowledged the damage high wakes did to the pilings as much as it reflected the conservative concern with the summer's burgeoning crop of noxious weeds in the canals.

Everyone had an idea how to improve the city, but the Samurai were already doing something. They'd put a stop to the uncontrolled smuggling. Tradestuffs moved as their shippers intended; silver on the barrelhead reached the right pockets. Vega Boregy had greased the financial skids, but it had been Anastasi Kalugin who'd wrung the biggest coup from his father's hands: Samurai countersigned each bill of lading as it passed through the counting hall, and they had free access to sealed goods awaiting shipment.

"Heard that you're ready to hire another two dozen?"

"First of the month. We're expanding to the regular warehouses. A House will contract for however many men it wants, piece-wise or weekly. But the Samurai directors will make the rosters and sign the pay chits."

The barkeep nodded. He could make a profit with that tidbit, or pass it along gratis to those of his acquaintance who had earned the privilege. Men and women who wouldn't have joined the blacklegs on a bet were willing to wear Samurai blue.

A gust of wind blew over from Grand. The Bell's faded signboard creaked on its hinges. The summer smocks the Samurai wore filled up with air. Richard tightened his lips. Marina had come to him with a handful of designs before the need for a uniform had entered his mind.

*Don't make them look like thugs or servants,* she'd urged. *Give them their own clothes better than they thought they could be. So they're proud to wear it, and they're wearing it for themselves.*

The idea made sense, or at least it had made as much sense as any Richard himself was likely to come up with. Mostly he'd been glad to get Marina doing something useful with her time. His family's rising public fortunes were undermined by domestic turmoil. No sooner had his mother, Andromeda, recovered from her second bout of deathangel addiction than his sister had gone melancholy. Carrying Tom Mondragon's child under her ribs was turning out to be less than the idyll Marina expected. She had the appetite of a storm-tossed landlubber, but, mostly, she didn't have Tom.

Richard knew more about Marina's love affair than she would guess or he would ever admit. Mondragon wasn't the confiding sort, but he was human and Richard had enough readings to plot a general course. Tom was taking his impending fatherhood hard. Mondragon didn't love Marina, but there was another woman—Richard didn't know her name—who'd cracked the Nev Hetteker's facade and left him vulnerable where he'd thought he was dead past mourning.

Marina, on the other hand, blamed Tom for supplying Andromeda with enough deathangel for three incarnations. She hated Tom almost as much as she still loved him.

Richard figured he'd have to send the baby away for its own good, with or without his sister. Still, Marina had been right. She'd made the Samurai recognizable and familiar. Merovingen-above or below didn't give its trust easily, but they didn't distrust the Samurai, and he owed his sister for that. . . .

"Kamat wool?"

It was the second, if not the third, time the barkeep had asked his question. Richard physically shook his sister's image from his mind and scanned the customs docks for something that looked like bales of wool.

He found it unloading from a motor cart. The gusts had become a stiff breeze; the stevedores were hard-pressed to get the pallet from the deck to the dock. Two of the Samurai came forward to help after taming their smocks with knotted ropes. The pallet was safely stowed on a customs cart. The Samurai returned their rope belts to their pockets.

There was hardly a canaler in Merovingen who didn't keep his pants up or his shirt down with a length of sheet rope. Angel knew it was a practical solution to the problem but not the image Richard wished his Samurai to project. "Sashes," he murmured, unaware of his own voice. "A wide red sash . . ."

The barkeep stroked his wiry, tan beard. The Ramsey Bell had been in his family for generations, always catering to the particular needs of the Customs House workers. He prospered as his clientele prospered, and he was genuinely protective of them. He knew his regulars as well as their families and competitors did, perhaps better since his needs were always simple and well-defined. He was a sponge taking everything in, yet rarely giving anything away.

This would be a rare day.

"I think not, m'ser." He spoke softly though they were still alone and there was no one around to overhear. "There's more to be done with leather of a certain width and texture." He meant to sound mysterious, yet buyable, and he succeeded.

"Of what texture?" Richard took the bait.

The barkeep stepped back so Richard could see him from the hips up. He unclasped his belt. The only remarkable thing Richard noticed was its length: it was too long by half and whippy as a snake. With well-practiced gestures, the barkeep laid the tongue across his left wrist, then, moving too fast for Richard to follow, he whirled the leather along his arm from elbow to wrist. Grinning proudly, he flourished his arm. The hook of the steel clasp extended a knuckle's length from his armored fist. The whole procedure, from waistband to flourish, had taken less than ten seconds.

But Richard was slow to grasp the significance of what he had been shown.

"Got it from a Chat merchanter, all decked out in silk and uncommonly fearful of it bein' cut to ribbons. How many's the time yer out alone and yer apt to be rousted? Maybe he'd got a knife. Maybe there's two of 'em. An' yer not the sort who wears a sword for temptation. If ye've got enough time to sneeze, you can get yer off arm out there in front. Thicker'n any glove. Parry hard, maybe nick his knuckles with the buckle or snag his knife altogether . . ." The barkeep crouched down, warding with his left arm and feinting with his empty right hand. "S'easy enough, with a little practice."

Somewhere on Yucel there was a *salle d'armes* that taught two-weapon work. Not a particularly respected *salle*. Richard's tutor had always stressed the wisdom of doing one thing with great competence rather than two with less. And he had never, personally, been rousted.

"Works on dogs, and rats. Skits, too."

There was something about the indigenous skit that invariably brought a grimace to a human face. Maybe it was the subtle alienness of the beasts. Most other natives were either basically familiar or utterly strange, but the skit, shelled like a crab, tailed like a rat, and adaptable enough to eat *anything* brought out the xenophobia. Earth genes just reared back and said *unclean* on a primal level. Nobody wanted to touch one.

Richard wiped one hand against his trousers. The

red sash had been a fleeting thought at best; no match for the mental imagery the barkeep had aroused. The barkeep, sensing that the deal was clinched, straightened his arm. His open palm caught the falling coils of leather. Richard reached out to feel the goods for himself.

"Don't suppose you'd let me have it as a model?"

The other man shook his head. "Shirt'd be filthy by noon."

"A lune would buy a new shirt."

"But not a new belt, m'ser."

"A lune would buy two or three."

The barkeep's eyes glazed with swift calculations. "A lune would indeed buy two . . . after tomorrow morning, if there's a job in it for a friend of mine." He hadn't selected the friend any more than he'd bought the unworked leather, but neither would be a problem.

"If your man's fit. If he can read and cipher, and carry himself right, there's a slip behind East Dike—you'll know it by the Red Turban signboard. There's a hall at the end. Send your man there Monday next and he'll get a fair deal."

Four days to winnow through his relatives and acquaintances. "Done," the barkeep extended his hand as soon as he'd refastened the belt around his waist. "How many?"

"Fifty to start."

The barkeep's eyes widened. "I'll need a mite more time . . . and a show of earnest."

Richard nodded. "Two weeks, and a tenner?" He showed the bright gold coin.

Not for the first time, nor the last, the barkeep marveled at the casual way the hightowners handled their money. The Ramsey Bell was worth a tidy, golden sum, but his liquid capital was all in copper and silver.

He'd not rest easy until the coin had passed safely through his hands.

The outer door banged open and stayed that way. The barkeep secreted the tenner in his breeches and removed all hints of excitement from his demeanor. Richard did the same as Grev Martushev tossed a satchel on one of the window tables. A fringe of lead seals jangled against the wood, telling Richard, and the barkeep, that the bag held diplomatic, and likely secret, correspondence.

If showing a pocketful of gold was risky, leaving a sealed diplomatic pouch untended was pure provocation—and very much Martushev's style.

"Just the man I was looking for—" Grev advanced on Richard with a theatrical grin and an extended arm.

Richard felt his pulse quicken. No one could have, or should have, expected to find him here. Years of practice under his mother's socially exacting eye paid off. His smile was as natural, or unnatural, as Martushev's. Martushev and Kamat had been rivals since his grandfather, Hosni, had bought a Merovingen island from the bankrupt Adami clan. As with all such rivalries, they knew each other better than they knew most of their friends. But familiarity didn't make for comfort. It took all Richard's will and poise not to draw back as Grev surrounded him with a back-slapping handshake.

"You're a lucky man, then, m'ser. I hadn't expected to stay this long myself." Richard shrugged off the forced camaraderie.

"Uncle Sorghus had to go out at midnight to put his seal on a detention writ."

Grev let his arm fall, but the smile remained on his face, and Richard grew distinctly nervous. All the reasons he could imagine for that grin added up to bad news for Kamat. He held his peace and let Martushev play his next card.

"Seems your blue boys were on the ball. Caught some lowlife fingering the goods from a Falkenaer tramp-ship. Don't mind telling you that we'd be in a world of hurt if what's under those seals had fallen into the wrong hands—"

Martushev hadn't subscribed to the Samurai prospectus. They hadn't said that they expected it to be filled with Kamat stooges—they weren't foolish enough to imply something that might offend the Boregy bankers—but they'd implied enough. Even now, Grev's arched brow and narrowed eyes implied equal amounts of surprise that the satchel had been returned intact and disdain for the same lily-pure reason.

"The mandate was completely impartial—if you bothered to read through the prospectus."

Martushev shrugged. "Too much risk for the return. Have to reconsider now. That's what I was looking to tell you. It's hard to ignore success and it seems as if you've cleaned up the Customs House. If you're interested in private work, it begins to look as if blue might be more trustworthy than black."

The same restraint that controlled Richard's suspicions now blocked all expression of his elation. Where Martushev led, Takezawa and Khan followed, and behind them a raft of families so well-established that their mercantile roots were almost forgotten. Families that didn't need to be impressed by a Boregy countersignature. It was more than he'd dared to hope, and more than enough to offset the minor concern that Kamat's rivals intended only to hire Samurai, not underwrite them. Almost enough to keep him from wondering if Martushev knew that he and Anastasi Kalugin were plotting ways to disperse the Samurai throughout the city. Wondering which Kalugin Martushev would line up behind after Iosef. Publicly they supported Mischa the Clockmaker. Then again, publically so did Kamat.

With a final smile, Grev Martushev returned to his table and his satchel. Richard went to the other window table where his old friends were gathering. If the Samurai leaked secrets, they would leak from the top. The organization had been his idea, and he had signed the prospectus, but Richard Kamat had no delusions about his status. Boregy was wilier and cagier than he, but at least Kamat and Boregy were playing by the same rules toward the same goals. His other partners were not bound by rules at all.

Kamat knew what Anastasi Kalugin's goals were. All of Merovingen, from Iosef on down, knew that. The goal was the only thing Anastasi didn't keep secret. The youngest Kalugin stored a few of his secrets in the Samurai; not even Vega knew the full extent of Anastasi's involvement—and certainly not the extent of his alliance with Tom Mondragon.

Richard caught himself frowning again. The idea for the Samurai had come to him when he'd realized the municipal blacklegs were no longer working in the interest of Merovingen and its merchants. He hadn't wondered why Anastasi was so helpful until Tom had laid it out for him late one night in a subtle exchange for a two sol advance.

*You're his karma*, Mondragon explained, mentor to Richard's student. *Anastasi needed you. He needed something to use against his sister. Something so legit that neither Iosef nor Tatiana could stop it even if they figured out what it could do for him. And you brought him the Samurai. Nothing you want goes against what he wants. Nothing he needs interferes with trade as usual for you and your friends. Everybody profits— except those who counted on you merchant princes not looking up until it was too late.*

Too late for what? Richard had asked, but Tom's expansiveness vanished as suddenly as it had appeared and the conversation ended. At the moment other questions were gathering in Richard's mind. Anastasi needed Samurai because *his* blacklegs couldn't operate in the city where his sister controlled law and enforcement. But Anastasi had the makings of a fair army in the outlands where Merovingen had its colonies . . . Untrue—*Merovingen* didn't have anything. *Kalugin* had estates; Kamat had estates; Martushev had estates— and Anastasi's blacklegs were the muscle the Houses relied upon to keep things that way.

And Mondragon sweated, bare-backed in the sun, bracing up the stern-wall of a rotting boat—an old river craft.

Were Merovingen's merchants dangerously naive? Were they inattentive to the realities of their city and their world? In four short months Richard's world had turned upside down. He knew secrets his father, he was certain, had never suspected, and he lived in constant fear that his House's face was rising faster than its substance. The Vega Boregys and Tom Mondragons of the world were at home on thin ice. Richard Kamat wasn't. There were days when he reveled in the excitement, but mostly he fretted in silence.

Gavin Yakunin and Franck Wex, men who had been Richard's friends and peers since childhood, came into the Bell. They greeted him with cheer and the events of their days. Richard caught himself recoiling from them, cloaking his thoughts behind politeness as he had with Martushev. He nodded and laughed on cue, and said nothing of the thoughts swirling in his mind. His stomach churned acid. When the barkeep set the steaming plate on the table in front of him, his mouth was as sour as the canalside air. Gavin and Franck were still children doing chores, unaware of the larger picture through which they moved. They were no longer his peers; he wasn't certain if they were still his friends.

There was nothing left for Kamat at the Ramsey

Bell. Nothing for Richard Kamat. He might as well make it official and give his young cousin Gregory his old duties, his old friends. The young man had been itching for status since his graduation, and Richard had been dragging his feet. Gregory wasn't ready, but neither were Gavin or Franck, or Grev for that matter. Nor had Richard himself been ready.

*The Houses train their children, but no Househead expects to die.* He didn't want Gregory to know what he knew. He wanted to keep him young, innocent . . . and ignorant. Just the way his grandfather had kept his father and Uncle Patrik. Just the way his father had kept him.

He turned on the ghost of Nikolai Kamat in his mind. *I'd never have been ready. And if you'd lived to a ripe old age, House Kamat would have turned to dust in my hands. We'd have been like the Adami, selling out to the highest bidder, the next wave. But now I've got a chance . . .*

"He's put out to sea!" Gavin joked, prodding Richard in the shoulder just enough to dispel the ghost. "Next his hair'll turn white and his stomach'll be too weak for wine."

Richard came into focus. He laughed heartily at his own expense, then put a stop to the merriment. "It's not the wine in ser Vega Boregy's office that puts your stomach to flight." His tone was as bantering as Gavin's had been, but even that served to emphasize the gulf between them: Vega Boregy didn't see the heirs in his office. Richard pushed away from the table with a good show of reluctance. "But there's no helping it."

There was nothing formal about his leave-taking, nothing to say that he would never return to the Ramsey Bell, yet there was something in the farewells he exchanged with his old friends. The room fell quiet.

"Good luck, ser Kamat," Grev Martushev saluted. "You'll need it wherever you're headed."

Their eyes met as if by mistake and swiftly parted. Richard stepped out onto the plank walk and suppressed a shiver in the gusty, fetid air. Karma—or the promise of karma. He wondered if Martushev had felt its cold fingers on his spine. Worse for Grev, Richard decided, if he hadn't, because something had been passed between them, and something would someday be claimed.

Richard emptied his lungs hoping to empty his mind of karma and Martushev's green-gold eyes. He got rid of the man, but not the dogma. Philosophy clung to him like the air as he made his way from island to island, and the air, despite the wind, was thick enough to slice with a knife. Richard forced his thoughts toward the weather. The air was pregnant with a storm, but the winds were wrong, and the temperature, and the sun in the sky. Not even a storm could visit Merovingen before its time.

Karma.

The best route from Ramseyhead to Boregy—not counting a poleboat through the Grand—went right past Kamat's high door. As he saw his Househead coming and had the door open before Richard was off Wayfarer's Bridge.

"You're back early, m'ser—"

"No, not back at all. Just passing by."

"Shall I summon a boat?"

"No, walking's fine."

Which was a lie. Richard's clothes were limp from the humidity; his face was blotchy with sweat. He should go inside, should change his shirt at least before meeting with Boregy, but if he went inside he wasn't sure he'd come back out until the storm had passed.

"What about lunch, m'ser. Shall I have the kitchen wait lunch for you?"

Houses were bound to their servants, just as servants were bound to the house. Richard had to stop where he could see the stairs that led, ultimately, to the sanctuary of his office. "No, Ashe, I don't know when I'll be back—"

"Is something wrong, m'ser. . . ?"

"No, Ashe, nothing's wrong. Nothing."

Richard hurried toward the St. John stairs without having convinced either himself or Ashe. He stopped when Kamat was out of sight and did his best to make himself presentable: refolding the pleats of his sleeves, mopping his face with soft linen. He wasn't a *believing* Revenantist—he didn't know anyone, including the cardinals, who was—but he was a behaving one, and if you behaved long enough, believing didn't matter.

On the other hand, eventually all karmic anxiety gave way to fatalism: what would be, would be. Every act contained all its consequences. Each man's stream flowed toward the sea, and it was best not to swim upstream. What would happen had already been spun out by karma's wheel. There was no use worrying. There was nothing that m'ser Vega Boregy could do to Richard in person that he couldn't do just as easily from afar.

Richard's breath steadied. He crossed the bridge to Boregy's island with a firm, resolute stride and gave his name to the doormaster. The woman glanced at the appointment register.

"We're a bit behind today, m'ser Kamat," she grimaced. "What with m'sera Cassie, you know."

In point of fact, Richard did not know, but he was heartened that Boregy's servants would think he did. The ramrod doormaster ushered him into the dim library where, until his eyes adjusted, Richard thought he was alone.

"Did you get rid of the bitch?"

Richard was on his feet, fists made, peering into the darkest corner.

"My humblest apologies, m'ser. I mistook you for someone else."

Confounded by what he saw, Richard's mind filled with irrelevancies. Revenantism, he realized, was a winter religion. How else to explain the high boots, puffed vests, and embroidered collars? A cardinal or a professor at the College might strip down to chambrys— Family dignity was, after all, deeper than religion. But the sweaty pear-shaped man was only a deacon, and his careful enunciation couldn't quite conceal his canalside origins. All he had, everything he hoped to be, was woven into those garments; he dared not remove them, even though, in this weather, they made him look like a melting art-candle.

Richard relaxed, and grew instantly curious. Deacons were useful creatures, but hardly the sort of folk he expected to find taking up space in Boregy's library. Moreover, who was the *bitch* and who had he been mistaken for? "*My* apologies, per. I was lost in my own thoughts. I had a ten o'clock meeting with m'ser Boregy. Now . . ." He frowned with his best co-conspiratorial concern. "They said m'sera Cassie. . . ." Not that any low-College functionary was likely to call Casseopeia Boregy a bitch.

On cue the deacon leaned forward in his chair. "The baby's whole, unmarked, and healthy," he confided, which was news enough to Richard who had not heard that the widely-discussed pregnancy had finally come to its conclusion. "What more do *they* need? The cardinal told them that karma was vindicated—and that there was no need for that Nev Heretic to remain."

"Her husband?" Richard asked. The only other Nev Hetteker he knew with connections to Boregy was Tom.

The deacon's face puckered sourly. "Doctor Danielle Lambert, Nev Heretic Obstetrics and Lying-In, with her tool chest full of glass, metal, and *plastic*."

Richard suppressed a sad grin: as far as the College was concerned, no good, not even the saving of innocent lives, could come from such unnatural technology as plastic. He knew who the bitch had to be. "Everyone was very worried about Cassie. I'm sure m'ser Vega only did what he did through a father's natural worry—"

"The Angel Himself watches over m'sera Casseopeia. He has given her great work to do. M'ser Boregy would do better to worry about his own karma if he can't see that for himself." The bloated little man was full of the self-righteousness of those who will never be heard or obeyed.

There were two windows in the library. Both were wide open, but they caught none of the morning's wind—only the stench of tangle-lily rising from the canal. The air was as heavy as the fried food churning slowly through Richard's stomach and, quite suddenly, he knew he'd better sit down.

The deacon misinterpreted both the gesture and the grimace that spread across Richard's face. Belatedly he realized that he might be speaking to someone of importance. "I'm Bryan Neil, Cardinal Ito Boregy's amanuensis," he stressed his own insignificance. "I was with the cardinal when m'ser Vega sent word that m'sera Cassie was delirious. We came shortly before dawn. They've been together in the chapel since then."

A war began in Richard's gut. The first volley was fire, the second was a crab with claws that pulled and twisted. He hid one hand behind the other, massaging the spasm, and tried to concentrate on the deacon's nonsense.

He'd been to one of Cassie's carefully-staged oracles, and been repelled rather than awed. Kamat knew deathangel addiction when he saw it, because he'd seen it every night in the family dining room, staring out of his mother's eyes. No man, or god, had the right to destroy a soul as deathangel did. If the Angel of Merovingen spoke through deathangel, then Richard would prefer to rot in a Sharrist hell. Twice he'd sent Andromeda out of the city, but both times when she'd returned to the house, she'd returned to the drug as well. In the end he'd turned to the College for help.

"Did the cardinal bring the dysmutase?"

Bryan Neil turned white and swabbed his face with a scented handkerchief. He still didn't recognize Richard, but he'd begun to realize he wasn't orating at another secretary. Deathangel toxin wasn't, strictly speaking, illegal—but addiction to the toxin was illegal, sinful, and usually fatal. Officially, the College held that deathangel addiction was its own reward— just like karma—and equally irreversible. Officially. Unofficially, more than one cardinal had succumbed to the drug's recreational temptations, and so the College brewed up a cure for its afflicted brethren: dysmutase.

They extended the cure, for a price, to that segment of Merovingen whose discretion could be trusted absolutely. The rest of the city barely suspected the enzyme's existence. To mention it out loud, as Richard had done, was a naked declaration of highest privilege and status.

"No. Cassie fits the cardinal's plan. The deathangel is a means to an end. The child is *healthy*—karma— everybody's karma: Cassie's karma, the cardinal's karma, all Boregy's karma, *everybody's* karma—is served by what Cassie can do. But Vega's fallen prey to Adventist heresy, first with a Nev Hettek contract for her, now with that damned obstetrician and her mechanic friends. . . .

"The girl herself understands."

The agony in Richard's gut subsided to a persistent ache. He tried to stay perfectly still, fearing that any movement would restart the battle, and knowing that if he felt better he'd throttle the sanctimonious little prig.

He'd never cared for Boregy's Heiress. She was pretty enough. She knew everything that she was supposed to know, and not an iota more. As exasperated as Richard could get with Marina, he'd rather have a dozen lively women like his sister under his roof than one decorative, obedient female like Cassie. He imagined Marina in Cassie's place and a shiver shot up his back.

"More power to m'ser Vega, then, if he's the only one who values Cassie's life and sanity. And if it takes a Nev Hettek doctor, then more power to her, too. Have you ever *seen* what deathangel can do to a person, Bryan Neil?" Richard leaned over his folded arms. Pain added extra intensity to his expression. "Maybe it is a miracle that the child's not addicted, too, but if it'd been left to me, I wouldn't have taken the risk. No addiction. No baby."

"That's heresy, m'ser."

Richard was in no mood or condition to be lectured by a fat, sweaty deacon who rolled his R's. "That's the right of the head of Kamat or any other House to preserve and protect itself. A man's House is his castle. Our right; our karma. No College and no heresy."

Neil reassessed the situation: so this was Richard Kamat, the young turk whose stock was rising fast and whose name had reached the inner sanctums of the College itself. He didn't seem particularly impressive at that moment, in fact, he looked a bit like a man with a deathangel problem himself. The deacon saw an opportunity that might never pass his way again.

At the cardinal's insistence, Boregy had opened its salon to the better class of true believers during Cassie's labor. Neil and others had been there leading prayers, holding hands, taking attendence. Marina Kamat had been there from the beginning; the House staff said she'd been alone with Cassie earlier in the evening, before all the excitement began. But she wasn't there when word came that the baby girl was whole and living, and she hadn't joined in any of the prayers.

No one thought anything of it. Marina was pregnant herself, and brooding women—especially brooding women who didn't seem to have a lover or a contract— were notoriously hysterical. Neil's talent—the sole reason Ito Boregy had lifted him out of the gutters and sponsored him to the lowest level of the hierarchy— was an innate ability to transform circumstance into scandal.

"And does your sister feel the same way? About deathangel and abortion?"

Kamat's outrage was boundless—notwithstanding that he didn't know where his sister had been any night since Sunday. A volcano erupted in his stomach. An earthquake tore through his gut. He wanted to crush the deacon's neck with his bare hands until the viper's tongue turned black and his eyes bulged out of their sockets. And he would have, had there not been something that he absolutely had to do first.

With a growl Richard bolted from the library.

The founders had left Merovin with legends of star-travel, of worlds beyond imagination, and of technology that lifted mankind above bodily needs. Schematic drawings for self-contained organic recyclers, molecular incinerators, and flush toilets were still preserved in the College library, but the best anyone in Merovingen could hope for was an oubliette with a bright porcelain bucket or, more likely, a malodorous shaft descending straight to the canals.

Every house had dozens of them, and there was sure

to be one within dashing distance of the library, but Boregy, like Kamat, took great care that the little rooms did not advertise their presence. Richard scanned the paneling, looking for a latch, a knob, a handle—*anything* before it became too late.

The world was turning gray and he swallowed bile before he spotted the one piece of molding that stood apart from the rest. He lifted the dog's leg and slammed the door behind him. The worst was over before he found the oil lamp and the hand sparker lying beside it. On the second try he got the lamp lit and was completely dismayed by the sight revealed in the mirror. He looked like a student after his first flask of Suvalen whiskey—except Richard's stomach had never betrayed him so thoroughly while he was at college.

And neither had Marina.

It was not quite unthinkable that his sister would have brought an abortificant to Boregy. Doctor Jonathan's simple cautions that a pregnant woman should avoid recreational drugs had grown like the tanglelilies. Marina had become a fanatic about her own diet and a crusader against deathangel since the beginning of the summer . . . And she'd been to every one of Cassie's public performances.

Richard had been reduced to the dry heaves by the time he'd convinced himself that Marina could not have actually done anything. He stripped to the waist, then sponged off in the basin to reconstruct his appearance and his nerves. He hoped to slip out of the house unnoticed, but there was an unfamiliar face staring at him as he opened the door.

"You had another five minutes before I called someone to break down the door," she greeted him. "You gave the cardinal's pet quite a scare."

"M'sera Lambert?" Richard guessed from her accent and her manner that she was the Nev Hettek physician Deacon Neil had described so unfavorably.

She frowned slightly. "*Doctor* Lambert, thank you. I've been asked to make certain you're not contagious or apt to die before you leave Boregy."

Richard shrank in his shoes. "It wasn't anything. I'll leave my apologies for m'ser Vega and just go home. You don't need to bother."

"I'll be the judge of that. We're both guests here, and proprieties are so very important in Merovingen, aren't they?"

The deacon would hardly have gone running to the Nev Hettek doctor on his own. He'd have gone to the House servants, or perhaps the cardinal. Either way, Vega Boregy would have been told that Richard was indisposed in the library oubliette. Doubtless Dr. Lambert knew exactly who he was. There was no point in arguing and he followed her meekly up the stairs.

They stopped in Cassie's sitting room—judging by the adolescent frills and thick piles of absorbent cloths. The doctor produced a leather satchel not unlike Richard's and studied him as if he were a dissection specimen. Richard remembered that she'd been brought here for Cassie.

"For your sake," she said with a touch of wry humor, "I certainly hope you're right. I haven't given a medical examination to a man in a good, long time. Off with your shirt."

Danielle Lambert chose her words carefully. She was no stranger to men's bodies, though she'd had little cause to examine them in her professional capacity. Under different circumstances she might have been tempted to set her duties aside. Richard Kamat, stripped to his skivvies, had nothing to be ashamed of. He was a good ten years younger than she, but that in itself wouldn't have been enough to deter her. In the end she turned away and told him to get dressed.

Richard obeyed as he had obeyed her other commands. For a moment, while she had the horn against his chest, he'd feared that things were about to get out of hand; he was just as glad that they hadn't. There was something about her—something that reminded him of Tom Mondragon. They were both from Nev Hettek. Richard didn't know many people from upriver, but it was odd that she didn't remind him at all of his mother.

"You'll live," she said with her back still turned. "No thanks to your breakfast, though. If you don't want to wind up like half the men in this city, eat your fish broiled—not fried, and not smothered in cream sauces."

"I have it plain . . . sometimes." He tried to remember the last time he had.

"And I'll bet there's someone in your house right now with his foot on a pillow. How much brandy do you drink each night? One glass? Two glasses? Half a bottle?"

Richard buttoned his shirt and masked his discomfort. Both his father and his uncle Patrik suffered from gout; it was one of those things a man of a certain position had to expect. As for the brandy . . . He found himself in sympathy with the deacon. Merovingen physicians—House physicians—healed their patients; they didn't lecture them. He headed for the door.

"Ser Vega wants to see you before you go."

"How do I get there from here?" He turned around for the instructions.

She told him which corridors to take, then, while she still had his attention repeated her warnings. "You're a young man, ser Kamat, don't waste what you've got."

He reassured her as he would have mollified his mother, and with about as much sincerity. He told himself he wouldn't remember a thing she'd said, and knew that meant he'd be unable to forget.

Vega Boregy's private office was larger than Richard's. The younger man had been duly awed the first few times he'd been admitted to Boregy's inner sanctum, but after a dozen or more visits he understood the carefully constructed drama and was unmoved by it. He ignored the leather chairs that looked so comfortable and guaranteed he would be looking *up* whenever he looked *at* Vega, and towed a rail-back chair from the corner by the door instead.

A mechanical fan kept a breeze circulating though nothing could completely purge the reek of tangle-lily from the air. For a moment Richard thought his stomach was going to churn again, then when he passed Vega the financial report he calmed down.

Richard Kamat might never learn the intricacies of intrigue. He might never be able to meet the Vegas, Anastasis and Tom Mondragons of the world on their own grounds, but he was very good at what he did. The Samurai were efficient. They weren't profitable yet, but he hadn't intended them to be. They were right where they were supposed to be and Richard knew that no other man could have done better.

Vega Boregy grunted his confirmation as he scanned the columns of figures and paragraphs of analysis. "You're right on target, Richard." He squared the paper and put it on a shelf behind him. "Now, in your own words, what next?"

Clearing his throat and sitting erect in the chair, Richard began his recitation. It was like being in college again—but what Vega taught couldn't be learned for any price in the Revenantist College. The young man unveiled his plans and measured their wisdom by the minute changes in his mentor's expression. He described his encounter with Martushev; his hopes for assignments in the private warehouses; the dyes Kamat was developing which were proof against the most common forgeries. Vega smiled and nodded.

"We've double-hired some customs clerks—"

Boregy shot up in his chair. "Who's *we?*"

Not *why* put clerks on the Samurai payroll without taking them off the customs payroll. Not *what* did he hope to accomplish by such subterfuge. Not even *when* had he done it. Richard gave himself a passing mark for attention and a second one for covering his tracks.

"You and I, acting on behalf of all the subscribers."

"Just you, then, making the decisions, no one else? No one on the roll or off?"

Everyone knew that a heartbeat could make all the difference in a duel. Vega had taught Richard that the same rules applied in trade. Now Richard applied those rules. He lied, not fully understanding why it was necessary to lie, and assured his mentor that he was working absolutely alone.

"You know, Richard, what's going to make the difference between the Samurai and the blacklegs is how clean they are. Your men have got to be clean down to their soles. It's a very delicate situation there at the Customs House—making certain that everything goes where it's supposed to go. Not every man understands where something's supposed to go . . ."

Vega Boregy didn't usually ramble, but, then again, Boregy didn't usually play host to a cardinal; a Nev Hettek obstetrician; an addicted, oracular heiress; and his first grandchild. Richard stopped listening and started watching. The signs of stress were there on Vega's face: nothing major, but enough that a well-taught student could read.

Angel knew, Boregy and Mondragon had been on the outs for months. Richard knew some of the details from Vega, and a few more from Tom; he didn't want to know the rest. But, to date, Vega hadn't been subtle. He'd been emphatic that they had better ways of scenting the Nev Hettek wind now that they knew what Cassie had married. Deal with Anastasi—because Anastasi was the better Kalugin; deal through Chamoun—because he had more to lose than Mondragon.

". . . There's more trade coming downriver from Nev Hettek." The magic word refocused Richard's attention. "They've got things I want. Things we want . . ."

*What sort of things, Vega? Who really asked Doctor Lambert to come to Boregy? How do things stand between you and your brother-in-law, Ito? Is this trade, or your daughter? Have you truly sold Tom this time, or just threatened to? Who's scratching your back, Vega?*

"There's a place for the Samurai at the end of all this, Richard, but it's got to be done cleanly."

The wind had died down. The only air moving came from the fan, and that breeze passed by Richard. It should have kept the sweat from Boregy's face. Richard was comfortable. He'd graduated. There were still things to learn from Vega Boregy, but they were equals now.

"I think I understand, Vega," Richard replied, using his counterpart's given name for the first time. "You have my personal guarantee that nothing's coming out of the shadows."

"And that nothing will interfere with anything that *has* to be done?"

Richard hesitated and Vega stared, then Richard let the silence lengthen into drama. "For all our sakes," he said softly, "it would be better that anything that *has* to be done is done well enough that the Samurai don't have to interfere . . ."

Vega Boregy nodded stiffly and reached for a different pile of paper.

The meeting at an end, Richard was escorted back

to the main hall. He glanced in the library as they passed it. Deacon Neil was gone, and the cardinal, too, most likely. Whatever was twisting Boregy had religion written as largely upon it as it had Nev Nettek. Nev Hettek's power in Merovingen was still an open issue, not so the College. Higher and richer families than Boregy had been brought down by a well-directed charge of heresy. Vega's advice was wise, as far as it went, but it would be wiser to cast a calculating eye on Boregy itself.

Then he was outside the house. The air was utterly still and thick as day-old cream. The sky was a dirty gray from one horizon to the other with the sun a burning white smear at the zenith. The plank walks were almost empty, and those few who had to get from one island to another were walking slowly. Shopkeepers and canalers found some comfort in their wide, straw hats, but hats weren't stylish this year in those strata where style was more important than comfort. Richard wiped his forehead on his sleeve and headed home.

In other years—in the years before he'd been Kamat's Househead—he, Marina, his mother, and just about everyone else who could be spared, left town the First of Quinte to spend the summer somewhere—anywhere—else. Last year they'd been in mourning. This year everybody had some excuse for staying. Especially Marina. Richard was going to have to do something about his sister—but when he saw her ahead of him, he decided to do something about Tom Mondragon instead. He sped down the stairs and hailed a boat from the St. John slip.

"East Dike above Delaree," he said to the poler, catching his balance as a wake took the poleboat across the beam.

They both stared daggers at the motorboat and took their positions at opposite ends of the boat. Richard closed his eyes and wondered when they'd decide who had the authority—or the balls—to ban motors off Grand. There just wasn't anything in all Merovingen that needed to move faster than a poleboat could get from one place to another—especially in Sixte or Septe. And no damned excuse at all for churning up the damned lilies. Cut through a vine with a propeller and the next day you had a dozen healthy vines, and the day after that you had another stinking, dying scum choking the House slips. Maybe they weren't winter-hardy, but if they weren't, then they'd all die at once and the air wouldn't be fit for skits . . .

"This'un okay?"

Richard squinted into the shadowless sunlight. "It'll do."

He paid for the ride and stepped up onto the docks along the cityside of East Dike. The poleboat heeled around to join the skips and such waiting for a load on the incoming tide. Richard lost himself in a lethargic crowd, waited a few extra moments, then opened an unmarked door. Kamat's storerooms were a good distance away but East Dike, despite its blasted rock foundation, was as porous as any other Island. Richard made his way to familiar bales and barrels, and from there into dustier passages where no one came uninvited.

From the beginning he and Mondragon had agreed that it would be best if he were never seen near the back room of the Red Turban where the Samurai did their hiring. Fortunately, this had been easy to arrange, and Tom possessed a nondescript key that admitted him both to these corridors and to a small, shuttered room abutting the Turban. He usually showed up every day or so, whether the Samurai were hiring or not. Tom didn't have the only key to the bolthole, and Richard never left messages for him anyplace else.

They had met there by accident before, but always at night when Mondragon was apt to be more active.

Richard opened the door carelessly and thereby saved his life. Tom had been polishing his sword and had the point leveled steadily at Richard's throat before the latter had wit to react.

"Expecting someone else?" Richard stammered, but he didn't dare move.

Tom had the good manners to appear embarrassed. He laid the sword on a table beside its scabbard and left it there. "Not expecting anyone, least of all you."

The room, warm and stuffy in the depths of winter, was like a sauna. Tom had discarded his shirt and confined his singularly golden hair in a striped shibba scarf. He might well have been a different man, only the winter-sea eyes said he wasn't, and Richard never could look straight into Mondragon's eyes. There were pale scars on Tom's shoulders and his arms. Richard had endured his fencing lessons; he'd passed his final exam and drawn blood from his teacher. He even had a hard, white line across his right shoulder where he'd gotten careless showing off with Pradesh St. John. Richard thought he knew dueling or brawling scars when he saw them—and he wasn't seeing them.

"Me neither. I was going to leave you a message. I've been to see Boregy."

"And?"

Tom casually threw his leg over the edge of the table and leaned on it. He made no move toward the shirt dangling from the back of the room's one chair.

"I didn't like what I saw . . . what I felt. I thought you should know."

Answering Richard's silent prayers, Tom reached for his shirt. He used it as a towel, then threw it over one shoulder. "I'm old news to him," he muttered, but his eyes said he was still interested.

Richard accepted the inevitable and the empty chair. He began with Deacon Neil, both what he said and what his presence implied about Cardinal Ito Tremaine Boregy. Then he related his meeting with Boregy almost word for word. Understandably he skimmed over his encounter with the doctor, but that was where Tom returned with his questions.

"What did you say her name was?"

"Lambert, Danielle, I think. She didn't say, but that was the name inside her satchel."

"Describe her."

Richard shrugged. What he remembered best was least translatable. "Ordinary, I guess. Older than me—middle late thirties, but I'm lousy guessing their ages. Dark eyes, hair—just a hint of gray. She knew her business, that much I'll say for her."

"Would you say she knew more than her business?"

"Ancestors, how would I know, Tom? I was with her all of a half-hour, at the outside. She gave me as good an exam as old Doctor Jonathan ever did, but she's at Boregy because she's a woman's doctor, or is that what you meant?"

Tom's eyes went flat, a sign that Richard knew from experience wasn't good. "Just her?"

There was an abrupt comment on the tip of Richard's tongue, but he swallowed it. Mondragon was a dangerous man, not an annoying one; his questions had a purpose. "She didn't say, but I gathered from the deacon that she wasn't alone. She'd come downriver with some others—men, I guess—he said something about mechanics. To tell the truth, I was mostly fighting my stomach, not listening."

Mondragon's eyes went to his sword and, knowing Tom even a little, that couldn't have been an accident. "Friends of yours?" Richard asked, meaning the opposite.

"Might be. How's Cassie . . . Chamoun?"

"Didn't see either of them. Neil said the baby's healthy. Boregy loves his daughter, he'd trade with Nev Hettek to get her off deathangel."

Tom said nothing for a moment. "Yey, *anything*. You're on the right course, Richard, if you're keeping a safe distance between Boregy and Kamat. If Vega thinks he's had trouble up to now, he could be in for a few shocks."

He hooked the scabbard to his belt and slid the sword home. A sealed envelope remained on the table.

"I think it's about time for me to make myself scarce. You won't be able to find me for a while, Richard. A few days, maybe a week."

Richard had intended to suggest the same thing, based on what he'd found at Boregy. But the envelope gave the lie to Kamat's influence. Whatever Mondragon was going to do, he'd decided before Richard had opened the door. Tom didn't bother to deny it.

"Just in case. Call it my last will and testament if something happens." He pushed it toward Richard.

"The boat?" Richard asked, and feeling foolish for it.

Mondragon's lips twisted into a half-smile. "Can't figure that, can you?" He shook out his shirt and tugged it over his head. "You're a smart man, Richard Kamat, but you can't see around corners for your soul."

From any other man that would have been a fighting insult, but from Mondragon it was only the truth. "I know my trade. Most times, that's enough. I keep my promises and, thanks to you, I've learned not to make very many."

The smile broadened. "That's why I didn't ask you not to open the envelope the moment after I leave. Can't have too much karma piling up."

Richard shrugged. "I won't open it until I think I have to." He'd been planning to do just what Tom described, but now—and without any explicit promises or trust—he wouldn't.

Tom didn't talk about Nev Hettek or what had

brought him downriver to Merovingen. The thin scars didn't tell Richard anything he hadn't already guessed. Most times Tom seemed infinitely older, wearied and hardened by his secrets. Richard had laughed the first time Marina referred to her erstwhile lover as sensitive and vulnerable. How could a man who didn't trust his own shadow be either? But he was. Not trusting, not caring, not taking friendship when it was freely offered took more out of Thomas Mondragon than Karl Fon and all his prisons.

"Write to me care of Anastasi after you get there," Richard tried to make light of the gloom that had settled around them.

"I'm not leaving, Richard." There was no humor in Tom's voice. "And you're not leaving without that envelope."

Richard shoved the paper in his satchel and headed for the door.

The sky was the same color as the canals by the time Richard got outside, and both of them were gunmetal gray. A steady wind was blowing from the west. There were two-foot waves slapping against the rock breakwater and none of the boats double-tied at the docks took notice of a displaced hightowner looking for a ride home.

The storm Richard had scented in the morning was in spitting distance of the city. Any man with a mite of sense would have gone back into the warehouse and counted barrels until it blew over. Richard had the sense, and ignored it, hoping instead that Tom, who still didn't know leeward from windward in a storm, would stay put.

By the time he reached the deserted promenade behind Gossan the sky was black and the wind was gusting a full gale. The tide was nearly in and waves were hitting the dike with enough force that Richard was soaked with salt before the heavens cracked open. He grabbed the rail and let the cool rain splash against his face.

He didn't dare linger. Given a choice, lightning usually chose one of the many metal-clad spikes rising from the city's roofs, but lightning, like everything else on Merovin, was known to be perverse and a single man standing on the wet, windswept promenade had been a target before. Richard bent into the wind and hurried toward Nahar and home.

Ashe saw him coming and handed him a towel as soon as he came through the door.

"Will you wish to shower, m'ser?" Kamat's doormaster inquired.

"I *have* been showering since Gossan," Richard replied. The storm had refreshed him. He shook like a dog, not caring where the water landed, and toweled his hair until it stood on end.

"Gossan, m'ser?" Ashe got another towel and mopped the water before it could spot the wax. "Do we have trade on Gossan?"

Gossan's Family was Gossan's landlord, nothing more, and Adventist to boot. No elite Revenantist Family could match its house servants for snobbery. Richard sighed. He handed the sopping towel to Ashe and resumed his proper dignity. "I'll be in my office if anyone needs me."

The storm continued to rage. Richard felt Kamat sway from the wind and the pounding of the waves. His storm-fed exhilaration was as out of place as Ashe's snobbery. Any storm like this could become a disaster. In addition to earthquakes and floods, Merovingen was blessed with a hurricane every few seasons, and when they came they came like this. This one had come from the west, a land storm, meaning large-scale destruction was less likely, but even a land storm was disaster for someone.

He sprinted up the last two flights. The top of almost every island in Merovingen was reserved in some way for its dominant family; Kamat was no exception. Beneath the lightning rods and ringed by a "widow's walk," the Kamat's tallest spire contained Richard's private apartment and an octagonal office with a view that was second to none in the city. When Richard entered it, however, it was as gloomy as any interior suite with its shutters tightly latched and the oil lamps buried up to their hips in sand.

Darkness was no problem for the young Househead. He knew where everything was—or thought he did. His bark of surprise, pain, and anger was lost in a thunderclap. Then, rubbing his shin and hobbling, he found the hand sparker and brought light to the mystery.

Everything had been shoved toward the walls to make room at the center. The unopened crate was more than a meter long and almost half as high with strapping irons at the corners and seams. It must have taken two or three men the better part of the day to get it up from the canal. By accident or design they'd left a pry bar behind. Like a child on 10 Prime morning, Richard forgot everything else and set to work.

He made as much noise as the storm. Whoever had sent whatever it was—despite the customs tags and addressing label there was no clear indication of the crate's origin—had meant it to arrive intact. The outer box was lined with straw. When Richard pawed through the straw, he found another crate as secure as the first. The office was too filled with antiques and other objects of value for utterly indiscriminate destruction. Richard was forced to slow down, and was glad he did.

The second box was lined with woven raw silk that would itself fetch a handsome price for salvage. Within the silk was a third box of fine-grain hardwood from the rain forests of Temaii. Richard lifted it reverently and carried it to his desk. The hardwood was finished with a triple lock, but the latch was loose. Richard held his breath as he lifted the lid.

Raw silk had protected the case, silk brocade of the highest quality cradled the sword within. It was a samurai sword; Richard recognized the design from the plates in the BOY'S BOOK OF HONOR that had inspired the name of his security force. Not illogically, he assumed it was a gesture of support from someone in Merovingen. He assumed, as well, that it was a reproduction from such a drawing. A costly reproduction, but it had been six hundred years since the Scouring, and, Ancestors knew, how little had survived that holocaust. Still, Richard couldn't bring himself to lift the scabbard or remove the blade, and so it took him a while longer to notice the scroll deep in the folds of the silk.

He broke the seal and began to read. After a few moments he sat down. The storm passed its peak. The winds died and the peals of thunder were replaced by the steady rhythm of rain against the shutters. When he finished, the scroll fell unnoticed to his lap. Richard Kamat stared into the silk with awe and disbelief.

The katana wasn't a reproduction, and the man who had sent it knew nothing of Richard's Samurai. Stunned by what he had learned, Richard navigated slowly past the discarded crates and yanked the servant-bell. The cord was still wrapped around his fingers when Ashe's voice came faintly through the horn.

"Find . . . Find Raj Tai and bring him here." His voice echoed, then the room was silent.

There were dozens of places where Raj could legitimately be. There wasn't any good reason to assume that he was on the island. The young man was on scholarship at the College now, off and on overnighting at Kamat and he applied himself to his studies with a diligence that both amused and impressed his sponsors. It could be hours before Kamat's men found him.

Richard had dragged the discarded crates and the straw down to the landing beneath his office. He measured and folded the raw silk. Knowing now where it came from, salvage was out of the question. He'd pass it to Marina who would design something suitable to make from it. He closed the hardwood case, then he sat in his chair, listening to the rain and waiting. A high door had been revealed and opened, but he could not go through until he'd met with Raj . . . with Rigel.

Time passed. They summoned him to dinner, and he had them send the meal up. He could imagine the rumors that swirled when he refused to let the maid set the tray on a table but took it from her on the landing.

"Have they found Ri . . . Raj yet?" he asked the wide-eyed girl.

"No, m'ser."

"Tell them to keep looking. There's a place on Petrescu; ask Marina, she'll give you directions."

"Yes, m'ser." She curtseyed and tore down the stairs.

The Petrescu address was Mondragon's flat, which Richard had never admitted he knew and where he had never gone. But the boy had brought Tom and Marina together, and Kamat was getting impatient: Mondragon could find him, if no one else could. Belatedly, then, he remembered the envelope. It seemed less important now and he put it in the safe with hardly a second thought. He picked at his food because there was nothing else to do, and tried not to make plans for the future.

The plates were clean—except for a mound of cream sauce—by the time there were footsteps echoing on the stairs again. Richard leaned forward, hoping; there was a light, hesitant knock, and he told the boy to come in.

"You wished to see me, m'ser."

It had stopped raining, but the shutters were still closed and the only light came from the oil lamps on the mantle. Raj was plainly terrified and his eyes never wandered toward the hardwood box on Kamat's desk.

"What have you learned about Kamat—about our trade, what we do to survive?"

"You're dyers, m'ser. You make First-Bath once a month. And you have lands to the southeast, where you came from, and you own some sheep."

A shadow-smile crossed Richard's lips. *Some sheep.* Kamat owned sheep for every man, woman and child in Merovingen three times over. He knew he was teasing the boy, and that it wasn't absolutely necessary. He could tell Raj about the scroll and the sword without saying anything more. The boy was going to have to make a decision tonight whether he understood or not, and he'd live with that decision the rest of his life. Maybe it wasn't teasing, was necessary so in later years he'd remember that there'd been no secrets.

"You understand, then, that we have the sheep, the shearers and the weavers and the fullers. We have the indigo plantations and the rendering mills—and all of these are outside the city. Only the dyeing is here, because that's the most critical part of the making, and the most expensive as well—for *us*."

Raj knew this was important. He was all eyes and ears, taking it in and remembering it though clearly he couldn't understand why he was in Richard's office or why he felt like he was balanced on the edge of a sword.

"We make good products, and a fair profit. Do you know why our profits are not as good as our products?"

"No, m'ser."

"Mordants."

Raj wanted to be a physician. He borrowed Dr. Jonathan's texts and memorized lists of diseases, symptoms and cures. He didn't know what a mordant was, but he guessed that like morbid, mortal, moribund and murraine it had to do with death and dying.

"Just dyeing," Richard corrected. "Mordants control how deep the dye penetrates the fiber, how much and how long. They even determine what the final color will be. There are as many mordants as there are dyes—and we're always looking for new ones, cheaper ones. The best we've got is alum, but the only proven alum deposits are down in Chattelan land."

Raj could extrapolate a bit from that: Chat trade was expensive trade.

"We sell them some cloth, but we won't sell them the raw dyes, so they see to it that we pay in gold and silver for their alum. They don't quite bleed us dry, they're too smart for that, but the trade is never quite even, and whether in Merovingen, Nev Hettek, the Falkens or anywhere else, dyers are always at a disadvantage. They tighten the spigot every twenty years or so, and dyers all over Merovin fall into their hands."

"Even Kamat?" Raj knew they were relatively new to their wealth, but it had been considerably longer than twenty years.

"No, not Kamat, because we pay on delivery and we always pay in cash, and because we could shut down the dyeworks and live on the backs of the sheep for a year or five if we had to."

"You're very wise, then."

"We're cautious—which is not always the same as wise. From the water all of Merovingen-above must look the same, but the Families are not equal, and Kamat has never been of much concern or importance. Until now."

"Do you mean to be less cautious, m'ser?"

Richard smiled again. He'd taken his risks already with the Samurai, with Boregy and Kalugin, with Tom Mondragon. What the boy could offer was a way back to the familiar, cautious pathways the family had followed before.

"Suppose the Chattelan didn't have all the alum. Suppose someone else had a proven deposit, but had kept quiet all these years. They weren't dyers but metal workers and no one noticed that they didn't buy what little alum they needed. Suppose, besides, that they weren't sure they wanted to tip the balance their way—considering where they were—"

"You're losing me, m'ser."

"Suppose there was another Family in another city. Suppose they had more alum than they needed, but that they'd never told anyone they had it because there was always the chance they would need it some day. Suppose that day came, and to get what they wanted they offered an exclusive license to all their alum for five years—with a provision for renewal. Do you think I would be wise to give that family what they wanted?"

"I can hardly say, m'ser."

"But you must say."

Raj stared at the ceiling, at the floor. He raked his hair and tugged his earlobe. "I guess so, m'ser—if this alum is everything you say it is."

"Suppose this other Family came from Nev Hettek. Would it still be a good idea?"

"I don't know, m'ser. It might be. There's good folk in Nev Hettek. Good Families."

"That's right." Richard feigned surprise and insight. "Your mother, you said, came from Nev Hettek, and you grew up there for a time. What would you say about Takahashi? Are they good folks?"

The boy was speechless.

"Come now, Rigel Takahashi, surely you remember

your grandfather. What was he like? Is he the sort of man Kamat should trade with?''

Raj's eyes widened and glistened. There might be tears in a few seconds and Richard knew he'd gone too far.

''There's a box on the desk,'' he said more gently. ''Open it and read the scroll inside.''

Moving like one of Mikhail's automata, Raj stumbled toward the desk. The dusky glow through the shutters reflected on the case that the boy did not seem to recognize nor be able to open. Richard began unlatching the shutters. He eased the screens quietly into place. The office filled with the red, orange, and amber light of the sunset.

There were tears when Raj finally got his hands to raise the lid. They stained the brilliantly crimson silk. Richard waited and watched until the boy touched the sword. He wouldn't be able to read the scroll.

''Hideo Takahashi, Takahashi of Takahashi, has learned that we have given shelter to one of his house. He says this boy is the eldest son of his eldest daughter, and that he has endured both worry and helplessness on account of this boy and his brother . . . You've never mentioned a brother, Rigel, you must tell me about him.

''Your grandfather wishes he could bring you home, but if that were possible now it would have been possible before. He is a proud man, your grandfather. He does not ask for anything, but gives me his sword, calls me his son and offers me alum, only then does he speak of honor.

''Did you know him well?''

Raj nodded, more tears fell onto the silk. His hands trembled; wire rings rattled against the scabbard as he replaced it in the silk.

''Then I think Kamat will become a Takahashi partner, and vice versa. Welcome home, Rigel.''

Richard extended his hand—man-to-man, trade-in-trade, and friend-to-friend. Raj seemed not to know what to do and for a moment Richard felt foolish.

There was still much he and Kamat didn't know. The katana wasn't a gift. The alum alone would have bought Kamat's cooperation; Takahashi knew that. If Richard remembered the BOY'S BOOK OF HONOR correctly—and he'd pull it off its shelf once he was alone again—that sword meant more to the Takahashi than any one son or grandson, unless . . . Unless Hideo were dying; unless the situation in Nev Hettek were deteriorating so fast that all Takahashi might choose to die. And if that were true, then Rigel and his sudden brother were all that would be left.

Raj raised his arm toward his face. He considered the impropriety and took Richard's hand. It was better, when sealing one's fate, to keep one's tears on one's face rather than on one's sleeve or hand.

"You won't regret this, m'ser. I promise—"

"And I promise you that neither you, nor your grandfather, will regret it, either."

Light struck Richard's desk. A crimson glow reflected upward between the two men and merged with the blazing sunset.

Red skies at night; sailor's delight.

# SEEDS OF DESTRUCTION (REPRISED)

*C.J. Cherryh*

"His Eminence is in meditation," the servant said; and: "Thank you," Willa Exeter said sweetly. "Bless you, my son," all the while thinking of flaying-knives and a slow fire for the servant, the whole effete staff his *Eminence* kept around him, and in particular Ito Boregy himself.

Three times she'd had the requisitions on his desk, three times his damned staff had screwed up, failed to notify Budget, failed to convene the Council a sufficient three days in advance, finally some fool had overset an inkpot on the stack of copies and thank *God* Pardee hadn't destroyed the plates yet: they could run another batch.

Damned bunch of incompetents, Boregy's pretty pets—half of them stoned, she suspected, but couldn't prove, as she *suspected,* but couldn't prove that Boregy wasn't in meditation at the moment, because he didn't want to talk about the baby and the Nev Hettekker doctor and the petition for Inquiry—

She walked into her own offices, got her hat, two servants and the folio she had assembled over the last

196

several weeks, and ordered a boat to meet her at the water-gate.

It was not spur-of-the-moment. It was so far from that she'd already *made* the appointment with the governor, because she *knew* Ito Boregy was going to duck the issue.

And in Iosef Kalugin's office in the Signeury, she laid that folio on the desk and said, "Iosef, I'm not here as your priest. I'm here as your friend. And I have to tell you, we have a problem."

"Mischa?" Iosef said wearily.

Willa frowned and folded her arms into her sleeves. "The College understands a talent like his. Difficult, very difficult, and prone to a certain—difficulty of cohesion—"

"Scatterbrained. Don't mince, Willa. What's he done now?"

"Head over heels for Cassie Boregy's little seances."

"I know it." Iosef ground the heels of his hands against his eyes. "I've got a watch on him. *He's* not doing any past-lives foolishness."

"The curiosity that drives him—"

"I have him tailed. I know his contacts."

"*I* know them. Are you aware His Eminence the Boregy is doing regressions? Are you aware he's counseled with your son? Are you aware these regressions involve—"

"Deathangel. Yes."

"Mikhail *lives* for curiosity. Not to experience something—"

"I know it, dammit! You can talk till Retribution, Willa, you can't change Mischa, all you can do is watch him!"

"Let's be frank. You know and I know the quick solution—get rid of your daughter and promote 'Stasi. . . ."

"I plan to die of old age, Willa, not a knife in the back."

"Anastasi's dangerous because he *wants* power. Give it to him—"

"And you, me, and Mischa will be dead before the sun sets," Iosef said, with a grim, calm stare that reminded her where Anastasi got it. "He's *my* son. You think he'd trust you—or anyone who'd ever opposed him? You think we're not alike?"

"Then let 'Stasi have an accident!" she muttered, but she knew Iosef's answer before he said it:

"He serves a purpose. He's a focus—just like my daughter."

"And coalition is the only hope," she said, old argument. "Mischa's the only hope. Yes. But Mischa's only useful if he's in *our* direction. If he's under Boregy's—"

"Don't you think I don't know that?"

"That's evidence." She picked up the folio and dropped it squarely in front of him. "Those are names. I'm telling you—there's leverage there. It may agitate some Families. But those are accurate reports. Servants—talk to their priests. So do scared kids, in the provost's office. Or lovers. Or the dying. We have our records. Disciplinary interviews. Young fools. And old sinners. There's *power,* Iosef. I know how to use it. I assure you His Eminence does. And our Mischa is putting more and more of it into his hands."

Iosef opened the folio and leafed through it.

Slowly.

She sat down, folded her hands in her lap and watched his face go white.

# TURNING POINT

### *Mercedes Lackey*

*I send into the keeping of House Kamat one of the honor-blades of Takahashi, in token of the bond now between us. Young Rigel will know how it is to be cared for.*

\* \* \*

Raj held his breath, and with all the concentration he could command, placed the centuries-old *katana* reverently in the cradle of the special rack he'd asked M'ser Richard to have made.

\* \* \*

*"Your grandfather says you know how to care for this sword."* M'ser Richard regarded the *katana and* Raj *with equal curiosity. Raj nodded, not able to speak. There was a volume of message there from Elder Takahashi, message m'ser Richard could not possibly read. Raj knew—and the implications had turned his life upside down in the single span of time it had taken Richard to free the blade from its silk wrapping. But m'ser Richard was no fool—if he could not read the message, still, he knew that one was there, and that it must be portentous for his House. So he took*

*Raj's nod at face value, and set the* katana *back down in its silken nest. Takahashi silk; Takahashi steel. Takahashi honor. "Tell me what you need," Richard said simply. "I gather this isn't the sort of thing you just hang on a wall."*

\* \* \*

Raj stepped back two paces to scan his handiwork with an apprehensive and critical eye.

\* \* \*

*"A—place," Raj stammered then. "I need a place for it, somewhere where it's safe, but where it can be seen by—by—" He flushed. "—by the Househead. You, m'ser. You're—supposed to be reminded by it, m'ser."*

*Richard nodded, thoughtfully. "Will that do?" he'd asked, pointing behind and to Raj's right.*

*There was an alcove between two of the windows, an alcove currently holding an unimpressive sculpture of the Revenantist Wheel of Life. The alcove was approximately a foot wider than the blade was long.*

*"Yes, m'ser," Raj said immediately. "Yes, m'ser— that's perfect."*

\* \* \*

He'd inspected and cleaned the blade of the *katana* this morning, that being a small ritual in and of itself. Somewhere in his conversation he'd told Richard that in Merovingen's damp climate, he'd have to inspect the blade once or twice a week, and that he preferred *not* to have to move it too far from its resting place. He'd been a little apprehensive about that, since this was clearly the Head of Kamat's private—and very special—sanctuary. But Richard had nodded his acceptance of that, gravely, and then he'd taken the undyed tassel off the hilt, keeping it, *not* giving it to a servant to be dealt with. This morning he'd returned the tassel to Raj, now the deep and unmistakable midnight-blue of Kamat First-Bath. That was all Raj had needed. The *katana* was now ready to take its place in the heart of Kamat.

He knelt again, and reached out to adjust the blade so that the silk tassels hung side-by-side from the hilt, neither obscuring the other. The Takahashi-scarlet and Kamat-blue tassels hung gracefully, shining as only heavy silk could.

Takahashi silk, Takahashi steel.

Raj wore both, now. A main-gauche and rapier of more common design on his belt, sent by Granther, and Takahashi silk (so Marina had told him) on his back.

Dyed First-Bath blue. Marking him as under the hand and eye of Kamat for all to see.

\* \* \*

*"It is your Grandfather's opinion—which I share— that you would be far safer in the public eye, where harming you would be noticed and acted upon."* Richard Kamat's gaze weighed and measured Raj before he added—

*"Both of you."*

It took all the eloquence that Raj possessed to convince Richard that he did not *want* Denny—not-entirely-ex-thief, bridge-brat Denny—inside Kamat. At least not for now.

*"Tom Mondragon's the only one that can control him, m'ser,"* Raj pleaded earnestly. *"I can't. And you might as well try and tell the tide not to come in, for all he'll heed you. Tom Mondragon can keep him safe until he grows into a little more sense."* He clenched his hands in anguish on the arms of the chair. *"Please, m'ser—Lord and Ancestors know I love him, but I know him. He's been on the street since he was eight or nine. He's Takahashi blood—but he's bridge-brat taught, and it'd be like trying to tame a wild kitten. Tell Tom to bring him around to be civilized. If any-*

body *can make Denny see sense, it'll be Tom Mondragon.''*

*Richard Kamat scowled at the mention of Mondrag-
on's name, then nodded again—this time reluctantly.
''I can't say that I like it, but you know your brother.''
His mouth firmed. ''That makes it all the more impor-
tant that we fulfill our obligations toward you, Rigel.''
He surveyed Raj's clothing with a critical eye. ''And
one of the first things will be an appropriate wardrobe.
I'll have my mother see to that—''*

* * *

But in the end it had been Marina, not Andromeda,
who had outfitted him. Andromeda was indisposed,
and Raj had yet to actually see her except at meals.
She seemed ill, and looked as frail as a creature of
lace and spun glass. He much doubted she'd seen *him*,
not really; he'd kept his head down and his eyes fixed
on his plate, and he never spoke. That *wasn't* because
the Kamat cousins were unfriendly; mostly it was because he didn't know what to say. The intricacies of
polite social conversation were still a mystery to him.
And what could he talk *about*, anyway? The joys of
swamp life? The best ways to break into a house? Poi-
sons of preference when assassinating an enemy? What
it was that Tatiana *really* had in her bed? Lord and
Ancestors—his age-peers were so *innocent* in some
ways that it shocked him. They had no *idea* what they'd
let into their midst, and Raj didn't think it was any
business of his to enlighten them, when it wouldn't do
any good.

So he kept his mouth shut, and let the Kamat cousins steer him through the maze of dancing, religion,
and etiquette lessons, let Marina guide him through
what it meant to be a House scion, let Tom Mondragon
*try* to show him how to keep himself *alive* with that
Takahashi steel—

And let Marina outfit him. In leather, silk, and wool

and the finest linen, clothing like he hadn't worn since Nev Hettek, the kind where the cost of one sweater would outfit a canaler for years.

The silk of a sleeve slid caressingly along his arm as he adjusted the positioning of the black-lacquered sword-rest by a fraction of an inch. The stand itself was adequate—the best Richard could do on short notice. The cabinet maker had been given a more exact design, and instructions to paint the stand with no less than twenty coats of lacquer. *That* kind of work took time, and Raj was content to wait for it.

The black-lacquered table it stood on, though, was perfect. Rescued from the Kamat attics, its clean, pure lines could have come from the hand of a Takahashi craftsman. Perhaps it had—Andromeda had brought some furnishings with her from Nev Hettek, and the Takahashis signed only their steel.

Raj had looked long and hard for something to hang on the wall behind the *katana*. In the end, he'd found a painting—a marshbird very like a crane, standing in a clump of reeds, all silhouetted against a scarlet sunset, in a spare, spartan style. It wasn't a scroll, but it was the closest he could come. Odd that it happened to be a work from the hand of that Gregori artist. . . .

Raj looked again at the scabbarded *katana,* and shivered. The second sword of Takahashi, that he'd last seen on its own rest just below the *first* sword. It brought with it levels of meaning as intricate and interleaved as the folded and refolded steel that made up the *katana's* blade.

* * *

*"The sword of Takahashi is the soul of Takahashi,"* Granther said, with Rigel kneeling attentively beside him.

*"This sword—"* Rigel turned wide eyes on his grandfather. *"—is as old as Takahashi?"* He could

*not imagine it; the tally of years made him dizzy to contemplate.*

"*Not* this sword," Granther sighed. "*Although this one, and its brother below it, are relics of Earth. In uncertain times, it is sometimes wise to send a second soul out with the heir to seek a new home, so that Takahashi will continue. This is the fourth blade that—*"

Beside him, Denny wriggled and yawned audibly.

"*Father, this is boring* me *to tears,*" Angela complained. "*I can hardly imagine the boys—*"

"*Exactly,*" Granther had snapped. "*You can hardly imagine anything. Exercising your mind is evidently beyond you.*" He rose to his feet, his face gone cold with anger, and pointed to the door behind her. "*Go, get out of here, and take your impertinence with you!*"

\* \* \*

That was what Granther had meant, sending the sword. That things were deteriorating in Nev Hettek. That he feared for the clan, and was taking steps to ensure its survival.

That he, Rigel, was now the recognized heir.

Takahashi honor.

Richard Kamat couldn't know these things, but he had evidently understood that the coming of the *katana* meant far, far more than mere courtesy to a new ally, a new trade-partner, or even the Family that had assumed guardianship of his grandsons.

\* \* \*

"*You realize—we've had to change our original plans about you,*" Richard said—reluctantly, as if he regretted having to tell this to Raj. "*We were going to sponsor you into the College in anticipation that you would eventually replace Doctor Jonathon. He's getting old, he's been hinting for some time that we should start thinking about finding him an 'assistant.' But now—*"

Richard shrugged, helplessly.

*"I'm sorry Rigel, but it's really out of the question. It simply isn't done, having a son of a Family serving another Family, even in so honored a position as Family physician. Oh, I see no reason why you can't study medicine, go right ahead, and we'll go through with our sponsorship and support, but—"*

Rigel nodded. *"I understand, m'ser,"* he'd said quietly. *"That's just the way it is."*

\* \* \*

Takahashi honor.

Takahashi *responsibilities.*

There was no running away from this. And he had learned, finally, the folly of running. Even Tom didn't run from problems—because he had taken on responsibilities. So there would be no "Doctor Raj" living canalside, helping the canalers and the poorest of the canalsiders.

Still—Doctor Jonathon, a kindly man, had been letting him *be* something of an assistant, so long as it was within the House. And he'd been listening, carefully, to what Raj had poured out to him about swampcures. That information—slowly, carefully, and with no clues as to the source—was something Doctor Jonathon had taken to leaking back into the College. It *wasn't* heretical, since it certainly wasn't tech—and Raj had seen evidence that it was coming *back* down to canalside, as the herb-hunters were pointed to new plants, and the results were coming into the drugshops. So he'd done that much good—

And there was something else. He'd been *watching* these hightowners, and from the inside vantage point. No one thought any the worse of the Househeads for having hobbies—some of them pretty odd. Old Man Fife cultivated entertainers. Dao Raza studied Merovingen insect life. Pradesh St. John played the flute. Fieval Masud made *lace,* for Ancestors' sake! So long as it didn't obsess you, the way Mikhail Kalugin's clockwork toys did, a hobby was actually considered genteel.

There was no reason why the head of the Merovingen branch of Clan Takahashi *couldn't* indulge himself in a hobby of medicine. And if he chose to treat the impoverished canalers and canalsiders, well, the medical establishment would be relieved that he *wasn't* taking away potentially *paying* patients, and his peers would consider it no more than mildly eccentric. He could work it out with the priests by explaining that he was discharging karmic debt. As for having the time to do this, he'd been watching Richard, and yes, he was *busy,* but he did have some leisure time. It was possible.

And the opportunity to so indulge himself—the training to be able to do so—would have come without any strings attached other than those of duty to his clan. Not Janist, not Kamat. There were other ramifications—of potential benefit to both Takahashi and Mondragon. He could earn loyalty and gratitude for Nev Hetteker Takahashi down along canalside that no amount of money would buy. He could earn *friends* for his Family, and ears for Thomas Mondragon. He'd even worked it all out when he'd thought it was going to be just him, consulting with Del Suleiman.

"I'm kind of lost here," he had been saying to his patients, or his patients' parents. They knew by his accent that he wasn't canalside born, though what they made of him, he couldn't guess. "I don't *know* canalside. I need friends in the Trade, friends who'd tell me when somebody's setting up to cheat me or hurt me. Not spies, Lord and Ancestors, no! Just friends— who'll give me a ride now and again, give me warning if there's a bullyboy on my tail, and tell me the common gossip everybody knows, but nobody else would tell *me*. That's help, honest help, worth more than silver, worth more than enough to clear any karmic debt.''

Those who'd insisted on *paying* him with goods instead of that asked-for help he'd had leave the stuff in front of Wolfling's hole. It kept disappearing, so he assumed Wolfling was getting most of it. He doubted anyone else was; Nayab had become mysteriously free from crime of late. . . .

He sighed, and got to his feet. It was hard, trying to think out all the ramifications of something. He was so used to living one day at a time, not thinking beyond the needs of the season. Now—

Now it was time for dancing lessons.

Andromeda Casserer Garin, m'sera Kamat of Kamat, paused in the stuffy, darkened corridor, pressed her right hand to her aching temple, and supported herself against the corridor wall with her left. The perfume in the single lamp along this stretch of hallway could not mask the faint odor of mildew, nor the fishy origin of the oil it burned. Her stomach knotted.

It had *not* been a good day.

She'd been in the workroom late this morning, supervising the replication (in four different color schemes) of one of her sweater designs, and completing another new beaded design herself. There had not been enough garnet beads to finish the design she'd plotted, even though she was *positive* she'd made certain that there had been before she charted it. Her headache had started within an hour of rising, and she had experienced an odd sensation of floating awareness, as if she was not entirely in control of her body. The beads themselves kept slipping away from her fingers, and her fingers had trembled so uncontrollably that she'd stabbed herself more times than she'd cared to count. Her fingertips felt like ill-used pincushions. She'd been too nauseous to eat lunch, and Alpha Morgan had scolded her. Then Marina had taken exception to something she'd said, and had a blazing and spectacular row with her right in the middle of the workroom, right in front of the women workers. Morgan had leaped to the defense of her lady, and sent Marina off to her room in a flood of tears.

*Then* the headache had begun in earnest.

It had gotten worse, not better, with every remedy Morgan offered. It sat just behind her eyes, pounding in time with her pulse, and bright light seemed to increase the pain. Finally she'd just dismissed them all for the day, Morgan included, and began threading her way to her room through the darkest of the private corridors.

She *told* them that she wanted to take a nap. What she *really* wanted, with all her heart, was Nikky. *He* would have known how to deal with a pregnant and hysterical daughter; *he* would have known how to handle Richard's insistence that he *needed* the heartless Thomas Mondragon to command his Samurai.

*He* would have known how to protect his wife from the vagaries of her own children.

And one of those vagaries had cost her the deathangel dreams that brought him back to her.

Light flickered up ahead as a door opened and closed again, and she winced away from it. "Who is it?" she snapped in irritation; this corridor was only supposed to be used by *Family*.

"Your pardon, m'sera." The voice out of the vague gray shadows was either a low alto or a high tenor; musical, but not gender-specific, nor familiar. "I'm afraid I took the wrong turning somewhere."

Echoing footsteps, light and balanced, heralded the approach of the other, and a face swam into view in the dim, watery light.

Almond eyes, high cheekbones, long, straight black hair. A familiar face—

—though *not here.*

The face of a ghost, for Andromeda knew that her schoolmate Angela Takahashi was dead. Once a member of the Sword of God, she had been murdered by the Sword of God, Karl Fon's adherents. Like her aunt Dolor.

Horror frosted her heart, and thin sweat dampened her brow and arms; her mouth dried with fear, and she stepped back an involuntary pace, backing into the wall.

Alarm filled those oblique, black eyes, and Angela reached forward as if to touch her. Andromeda stifled a scream, and shrank back further from the touch of the dead.

Angela *could not* be here, *should not* be here. Not dead. Not looking the bare seventeen she had been when Andromeda had last seen her. She was *dead,* as dead as last year's flowers, as dead as Dolor, as dead as—

Nikky.

The hall spun, whirled away, became another time, another place.

*The guests were not looking at the laden feast-tables, nor at Andromeda and her family behind them—they were staring, surprise turning to shock, at something just behind her—*

"Your pardon, m'sera," Raj said humbly, "I'm afraid I took a wrong turning somewhere."

His night sight had always been good; he had no difficulty seeing who it was that accosted him. M'sera Andromeda—and she didn't look well. Her skin was grayish, and a vein throbbed in her temple. And her eyes seemed to be all pupil. Prudence said that he should go back through that door and leave her alone. Concern and the healing instinct said that she was in no shape to be *left* alone. He moved quickly to her

side, footsteps sounding hollow in the uncarpeted corridor, intending to ask if he could be of any service to
her, since he'd inadvertently intruded on her privacy.

But she began trembling the moment he came into
view, stared at him as if he was a sharrh, and crowded
back against the corridor wall—and when he held out
his hand to steady her, she shrieked, spasmed, and fell
to the floor.

Prudence dictated that he find help; Doctor Jonathon, or Richard Kamat.

*And by the time I find it—*

He was on his knees beside her in an eyeblink, then
cradling her in his arms to protect her from injuring
herself with the convulsions she was suffering. He held
her head against his shoulder, and pinioned her wrists
in one long hand. She was so frail, it took next to
nothing to restrain her.

"*Nikky!*" she cried, shrilly. "Nikky, *no!* Not again!
Dear God, not *again!*" She writhed in his arms, trying
to free her hands, trying to reach for something. "Angela, you were my *friend*—help me save my Nikky!"

Dilated eyes, racing pulse, clammy skin. Sweat
beading the brow, and hallucinations. By that throb-
bing vein in the temple, probably a blinding headache.
Symptoms tumbled together in his mind and formed
an answer.

Deathangel dreams. Either induced, or flashback; it
didn't much matter which. And in a patient as obviously weakened as this one was, if someone didn't *do*
something, *now*—she was in very real danger of never
coming out again.

And if he left her alone to get help—she was in very
real danger of hurting, or even killing herself. Only
yesterday some hightown fool caught in deathangel
flashback had thrown himself off Hanging Bridge and
drowned.

There was only one choice; try and talk her through

it. He'd done it more than once, with Raver. If he could just get her attention fixed on him—

"Andromeda—" *Now* was not the time for "m'sera Kamat"; she wouldn't respond to that. He slipped her farther down so that she was lying against his upright knee and slapped her cheek, lightly. "Andromeda, say something. Tell me you hear me." He slapped her other cheek. "Tell me! Talk to me!"

Her eyes wandered, seeing things he couldn't; tears poured down her ashen cheeks.

"Andromeda! Talk to me!" He shook her, and dredged up her few, hysterical words, looking for a clue to get into her dream. "Andromeda, if you *don't* talk to me, Nikky will be very *angry* with you!"

Her eyes focused on him for a moment. "A-Angela?" she faltered, her face twisted, her mouth a slash of pain. "Angela, you *have* to help me! They're your friends—they're killing Nikky—"

God and Ancestors—she thought he was his mother. That must have been what threw her *into* this in the first place! Nikky—that must be Nikolay Kamat, Richard's father. He'd wondered about the portrait in the study, so like Richard, but plainly older; Richard had identified it, then said something about his father dying from an accidental fall.

*God—could she have seen something no one else did? Is that why—never mind. I'll get her out of this first, then worry about Kamat secrets.*

There were only two ways of dealing with deathangel dreams—*direct* the dream, or break it—

And somehow Raj knew that if he directed the dream from the nightmare she was in into something pleasant, she'd never leave it again.

"Nikky is *dead*, Andromeda," he said savagely. "He's been dead more than a year. You *know* he's dead. And you can't change the past. You think you can, but the past you create is a *lie*. And Nikky doesn't *like* lies, Andromeda.''

Her eyes widened, and she whimpered in the back of her throat. He continued on, as stern and unyielding as the Angel, his morning's religion lesson giving him another weapon to break her out of her hallucination. ''He's very *angry* with you, Andromeda. You're muddying his karma, trying to hold onto him like this. He sent me to tell you that if you *really* loved him, you'd let him go!''

She cried out in denial, freed her hands from his, and tried to push him away. At the end of the corridor another door opened and closed, and there was the sound of a footstep—two. Raj didn't dare look up—he had Andromeda's attention now, and if he broke eye contact with her, he'd lose it.

''No,'' she moaned, as a gasp from the direction of the door reached him, and he heard running footsteps. ''No, Nikky would never say that! Nikky wouldn't—''

''He would, and he did. You're *hurting* him, Andromeda, you're holding him back.''

Marina's voice, sharp and shrill. *''What are you doing with my—''*

''*Shut up*, Marina,'' he hissed, regaining Andromeda's wandering attention by shaking her again. ''Get the doctor!''

She at least had enough sense not to argue with him. Running feet retreated, and the door slammed open and shut again. Andromeda beat at his face and chest with hard, bony fists; her blows were wild, but she got him a good one in the nose and just under the left eye. Raj tried not to wince; ghosts feel no pain.

''I don't believe it!'' she was crying. ''I don't believe *you!* Nikky would never believe such—''

''Nikky is *Revenantist*. Do you want to be responsible for dragging him down?'' The religion lesson gave him another barb to use on her, and forced to be cruel by desperation, he dug it in. "Do *you* want to be the one that forces his rebirth as some nameless bridge-brat? If you die, if you lose yourself in deathangel dreams, Andromeda, that's what will happen, and it will be *all your fault.*"

"*NO!*" She shoved him away, hard enough that he lost his hold on her, and he lost his balance as well. He hit his head on the wall with a sickening *crack*, and saw stars—

He struggled against darkness, still not able to see but fighting off the dazzle, and more footsteps pounded up the corridor. As his eyes cleared he was shoved summarily out of the way by Doctor Jonathon, and a wiry woman he recognized as Andromeda's maid. A hand grabbing his elbow helped him to stand; when he turned to render thanks, he found himself staring into Marina Kamat's profoundly unhappy, dark-circled eyes.

He froze, unsure what to say, as behind him he could hear her mother's muffled sobs, and the comforting murmur of her maid.

He stood that way for an eternity. Marina reached out toward his face, as if to touch his swelling nose, then stopped herself. She seemed at as much of a loss as he was.

"Rigel—"

He turned, grateful for the chance to look away.

"Rigel, whatever you did, it was right," Doctor Jonathon said, getting painfully to his feet, while the maid held Andromeda against her shoulder, letting her cry herself into calmness. "You broke her out of her hallucination—"

"I—she thought I was someone she knew," Raj said carefully, not sure how much of his background the House had been told. "My mother; her schoolmate back in Nev Hettek, and she knew that my mother is dead. I guess she never got a good look at me before this. I think I might have thrown her *into* the hallucination in the first place. I—I'm sorry. I certainly didn't mean it.''

''Of course you didn't,'' the doctor said soothingly, one eye on Andromeda as her maid helped her to rise. Andromeda turned a tear-streaked face toward the sound of their voices, and blinked.

''Who—are you?'' she asked, voice hoarse with strain.

''This is Rigel Takahashi, Andromeda,'' Doctor Jonathon interposed smoothly. ''You remember; Richard told you. He's going to the College under Kamat sponsorship, and Elder Takahashi made some trade agreements with us in return.''

She pulled away from her maid, and looked at him with wondering eyes. ''*Rigel* Takahashi—you must be Angela's boy—''

He bowed to her. ''Yes, m'sera.''

''It's uncanny,'' she said, ''You look just like her.''

''So I've been told, m'sera.''

''I—'' her eyes clouded for a moment, then cleared, and she drew herself up, taking on a dignity and poise that reminded him sharply of his grandfather, and a beauty that had nothing to do with tear-swollen eyes, blanched cheeks, and trembling hands. ''I believe I owe you a debt of gratitude, at least—''

He interrupted her, gently. ''M'sera, you owe me nothing. You were ill, I simply stayed with you until Marina could bring the doctor. That *is,* or will be, my duty—I'm studying medicine, after all.'' He was amazed at himself; he sounded *years* older, and he wondered where the words were coming from.

They were evidently the right ones. She flushed a little, and lowered her gaze.

''Andromeda, you should go rest,'' the doctor prompted.

"Yes," she replied vaguely. "Yes, I should. Forgive me—"

As the corridor door opened and closed behind them, Doctor Jonathon cursed savagely. "I'll have Guptal's head for this—he *swore* the antitoxin would prevent—Marina, where is she getting it?" He stopped, then, as if only now realizing that there was an outsider not *of* Kamat standing awkwardly at his elbow, privy to every word he said.

Raj cleared his throat. "It's none of my business, Doctor Jonathon, but—that looked like deathangel flashback to me."

The doctor pivoted, face blank with surprise. "Deathangel *flashback?* What in the name of the Ancestors is *that?*"

Raj flushed, and stammered. "I-if you take enough deathangel, it changes your head. Even if you never t-take it again, you can get thrown into hallucinations by any s-strong stimulus." He shrugged. "Th-that's why a l-lot of swampies are c-crazy. S-stuck in death-angel dreams."

Doctor Jonathon closed his eyes, and cursed again. "So *that's* why—thank you, Rigel. Again. I trust we can rely on your discretion?"

Raj managed a feeble smile. "What discretion, m'ser? M'sera Andromeda had a dizzy spell, and I just stayed with her until you could come. Nothing terrible, and she certainly didn't say anything to me except to thank me."

"Good boy." The doctor clapped him on the shoulder, and he staggered a little. "I'll go see what needs to be done."

That left him alone in the corridor with Marina.

Now she wouldn't look at him.

"You've heard enough that you might as well know all of it," she said, bitterly, staring at the polished wooden floor, twisting the hem of her sweater in white hands. "When Father died, she took it badly—she'd been in love with him, really in love, and she couldn't bear to be without him. She started taking deathangel so she could see him—" Marina looked up finally, and gestured her helplessness.

"Where was she getting it?" Raj asked.

Marina's eyes blazed. "Thomas Mondragon," she spat—and burst into tears.

Once again Raj wound up sitting on the floor of the corridor with a lady of Kamat in his arms—this one crying out onto his shoulder all the things she didn't dare tell mother or brother. About how she still loved Mondragon—and hated him. About how her mother's valet, Kidd, had been the go-between. About how she'd put two and two together when she realized that Kidd had known *exactly* where to take her the first time she'd met with Tom—which could only mean he'd been there many times before.

And that she was pregnant with Tom's baby.

None of this—except the business with Andromeda and the deathangel—was any surprise to Raj. It was pretty obvious from her intermittent hysterics that Marina was "not herself," and adding those frequent visits to Tom gave anybody a good cause. But that she thought Mondragon was the source of the drug—

Lord and Ancestors.

He didn't know quite what to say or do, so he just let her cry herself out—something she evidently needed—then helped her to tidy herself, and helped her to her feet.

"Thank you, Raj," she said, shyly, a little ashamed. "I didn't mean—"

"That's what friends are for," he told her. "We *are* friends, aren't we?"

"I'd hoped so—but after—"

He shrugged. "I learned things from that whole mess—and it got me *here*, didn't it?" He delicately declined to mention how much that fiasco had placed him in Mondragon's debt.

"Then we *are* friends." She offered him her hand with a sweet smile that could *still* make his heart jump a little, even if he *wasn't* in love with her anymore. He took it, squeezed it—and they parted.

The summons to Richard Kamat's office at sunset could only be tied to the near-disaster in the private corridor this afternoon. This time Raj followed the servant to the top of the house with only a little trepidation. He had, he thought, handled the whole mess fairly well.

The east windows framed a sky that was First-Bath blue, spangled with tiny crystal star-beads. The west held the sun dying a bloody death. Richard was a dark silhouette against the red, unconsciously like the crane in the picture in the sword shrine.

Raj cleared his throat. "You sent for me, m'ser Kamat?"

Richard did not turn around. "It seems," he said dryly, "that you have fallen into a muck pit of Kamat secrets. Doctor Jonathon told me a bit—Ree told me more."

He seemed to be waiting for a response.

"Every House has secrets," he replied carefully. "You know more'n—more than a few of Takahashi's."

Now Richard turned, though he was still nothing more than a sable shape to Raj. "Well. I will admit I had been toying with this notion for a while, but—I didn't quite know how to phrase this delicately, yet I also did not want you to have any deceptions about what I was going to offer. Ree told you, she says, that she's—"

"Expecting," Raj supplied.

"And who the father is." Richard coughed. "We are in something of a dilemma. It just isn't done for a

House daughter to have an—unacknowledged child.
Yet we can *hardly* look to Thomas Mondragon to do
so. It would seem best for Ree to make a contract
marriage, but frankly, there wasn't anyone she wanted
to confide in—really, no one she truly didn't find re-
pugnant even for a short-term contract." He paused,
significantly. "Until today."

Raj was considerably less a fool than he had been a
half-year ago, but this was still something of a shock.
"You mean—" he gulped. "You mean me."

"It would be of great benefit to Kamat," Richard
admitted frankly. "A contract marriage with Takahashi would get us out of an awkward situation—and
not incidentally, give us a chance to negotiate for a
longer lease on those mines." His voice was wry. "I
do have to think first of Kamat as a whole before I
think of Ree—but if I can benefit both. . . ."

"Was this Marina's idea, or yours?"

"I suggested it after she told me about this afternoon; she seemed to welcome the idea. She does like
you, Rigel—so, I think, do I. I'd be quite pleased to
have you further tied to my House."

He could have Marina—and if he just kept his mouth
shut, she'd continue to blame Tom for her mother's
addiction. That would, eventually, break the hold he
had on her heart. Which would please Jones, and
maybe Tom, too.

Takahashi honor.

"M'ser—two things," he said, carefully choosing
his words. "The first is—I'd like to think about this.
I'd like—to get out of the House for a while. I'll suggest a few things that I know of to Doctor Jonathon,
but while he's trying them, it might be a good idea if
m'sera Andromeda wouldn't be in a position to *see*
me."

Richard nodded, as the scarlet behind him faded.
"Did you have anything in mind?"

"Well—my friend, Justus Lee, was talking about there being a suite open in Hilda's. He was kind of wishing he knew somebody he could trust to split it with him. I *think* he was hinting, me. He's Father Rhajmurti's protégé, in art."

Richard nodded again. "A good choice. I think we can arrange that. What's the second thing?"

This was daring, but— "Thomas Mondragon isn't where m'sera got her drugs. There isn't much he *hasn't* done, but that's not one of them." He coughed a little, shamed, but offered the confession to balance the secrets he'd stumbled on. "Couple of months ago, during all the—fuss—I had reckoned on maybe doing some drug-selling myself. Lord knows I know the swamp, what's out there. I wanted the money to pay for the College, and I figured, if fools are going to spend their money, I might as well get it and do something decent with it." He coughed again, and flushed. "So I wasn't thinking real clear, well—I know better now. Thing is, Tom got wind of what I'd figured, and he just about beat me bloody for even *thinking* about it. I couldn't sit for a week. I can't *prove* it, not yet, but—it wasn't him."

"So?" Richard's voice was neutral.

"Before I say anything to m'sera Marina, I want to be able to prove to her that it *wasn't* Tom. I want *everything* clean between us."

Takahashi honor.

He sighed. "I want her making her choices without any lies. I messed her up with lies before; I don't want to do it again. If she knows the truth—she might make different choices. And that's her right."

Richard folded his arms across his chest; the sky behind him deepened to blue, and the first stars sprinkled across it. "I can respect that," he said, a certain warmth coming into his voice. "I can respect that, and I can understand that. Very well. You seek your proofs, and I'll see about getting you moved out of Kamat so that you can have your time to think.''

"Thank you, m'ser," Raj replied quietly, and turned to go.

"Rigel—"

He stopped, and turned back.

He could just see Richard's grim smile in the blue dusk.

"Welcome to Kamat, Rigel."

# SEEDS OF DESTRUCTION (REPRISED)

*C.J. Cherryh*

"Ho! Yoss!" Jones yelled, and eased her skip forward as gentle as she could feather the throttle. It was still a hell of a jolt on the cleat when the slack took up and the rope came taut between her and the old river-runner: but you couldn't muscle anything in a tow that big, you just eased into it and hauled, and you might not think you were going to budge it for a minute, and you might be tempted to put the power on, but you were likely to pop a cleat or snap a rope if you got hasty. You just took it slow, because that old hulk once it did gather way was something to stop.

Which was what Del and Mira were doing back there, close in with another rope on the 'runner's bow as she came away from dock.

"She holds!" she yelled at Mondragon, on the 'runner's stern. "Port ye, *port all!*"

Mondragon put the 'runner's tiller over, fast, soon as she said it, because the current was tricky here, and crowded with other boats, and it was a real dicey piece of work backing her out and getting her squared away.

She let the speed fall off then and gritted her teeth while Del Suleiman nosed his skip through the needle's eye of the 'runner's bow and a river-barge's mooring cable, got himself through and just timed it to take up the pull without too much jolt, though sure as was, he and Mira and Tommy were hanging on tight when the pull hit.

"Hard yer starb'd!" she yelled at Mondragon. "*Yoss,* now! *Yoss!* —Del, ye're out o' room!"

As the old 'runner came within a spit of crossing that barge-cable, and an easy pitch of drifting into the moored boats. She had her hand on her throttle, holding her breath and finally seeing Del's pull win out. A cheer went up from skips that had come to watch the show. Bottles passed. Bets got paid.

They'd had a little misgiving about Mondragon being at the tiller—but it was a matter of pride, that was the way she saw it and that was why she talked Del into it—

If you were going to own the biggest laughingstock on the Water, if you were Thomas Mondragon and Altair Jones, and you knew canalers from one end of town to the other were talking about Mondragon's Fancy-boat, and laying bets whether it was going to founder in the Grand before it ever got to its berth up by Kamat's Pardee warehouse, why, hell if you didn't do it with all the style you had—

Damn right he's going to take 'er! she'd said to Del. He c'n do 'er. Man's got a right, don't 'e?

Del understood that. Any canaler would understand that—would understand it too, if Mondragon had asked for somebody else to manage that tiller, because it was a real dicey thing, a boat that size, with other traffic and bridges and the currents and all, and no engine— wasn't anybody on the water didn't know that was a tricky job in itself.

But the Trade accepted Mondragon: most landers, if

they ever laid hand to a pole or tried their hand at a skip, Lord! somebody'd do 'em a dirty trick: they'd find their path crossed or their pole fouled and maybe, if they got into some canals, find out canalers didn't like landers getting beyond themselves—lucky if they only got dunked in the Det, and not something worse. Mondragon, though—

'Ware! she'd yell, when he'd foul somebody, and she'd wince and beg pardon for him; but the Trade'd allow for him—like they allowed for kids learning to pole: Hey, they'd yell. And he'd blush—few things could make him do that, but banging into somebody's boat would do it every time—and yell out, Sorry! Beg pardon, Lewis! because he knew the names, and no lander did; and more than that the Trade owed him blood.

So Del knew why he took the tiller himself, even if it scared hell out of her.

And there was a real groan from the spectators on the water when he came close to that barge, and so many other people shouting advice she'd shouted herself hoarse, afraid he wouldn't hear her over the rest; and people were laughing and collecting bets when he made it—

Most famous thing to happen on the Water all summer, Jones and Suleiman doing some tricky maneuvering and Jones' man steering that old boat right into the Grand and right through a cheering lot of spectators.

It was a damn parade all the way up the Grand: *Hoooo—ooo!* canalers yelled, and raised bottles to them and yelled that that was the biggest damn poleboat anybody ever saw—it having no engine, and no poler alive being strong enough to move a 'runner against the Det's current.

Parking it drew a crowd too, Lord! hightowners too, come to see what was going on, and canalers piling up on the bridges and walkways so heavy on Pardee North to get a good look at where it was going to park, it was scary. Fools were so thick up there they were straining the second tier braces.

But parking was why she was back here: it was in some ways trickier than the harbor, getting slowed down and fighting the Port Canal current to coax that big boat up against the side of Pardee.

There was Mintaka Fahd, drunk and standing up in her skip-well to cheer them on.

"There's me handsome lad!" she yelled. " 'E done it, didn't 'e?"

"Move 'er, Min!" Jones screamed at her. "Ye're complicatin' us!"

Blacklegs were out, conspicuous on the lower walkway, worried about the crowd.

But they had their permit to tie up a big boat there, cleared, stamped and sealed: a five day permit, *For overhaul and repair,* it said.

They missed Min by half a foot. They missed fool Rama Pardee by inches, when he came up on the walkway to supervise and didn't realize a 'runner was going to overhang the walkway a foot with its beam.

But they did it. Mondragon was white as a ghost when he jumped down off his boat, and canalers were offering him and Del and Mira and Tommy drinks from one bottle and the other before he ever got to show his Permit to the officers—bottles came her way too, Min's being one of them, and she was tolerably feeling it when the crowd just sort of carried them down to Moghi's.

Much more noise than Mondragon liked. He looked downright scared—the same as the blackleg had, who'd had to ask him for that tie-up permit. Mondragon even when they got to Moghi's didn't seem real sure how it had all gotten this far out of hand, or why people were slapping him on the back and buying him drinks and getting drunk and dancing, but she knew—

It was because it was hot and the canals were clogged up and people were feuding and there was so damn little to laugh about this summer—and because all the hightowners who came to watch had no idea in the world why canalers all over town were falling down laughing.

# DRAW ME A PICTURE

## Nancy Asire

"You aren't listening, Alfonso," the voice accused.

Rhajmurti turned away from the open window where he had been standing in a vain attempt to catch a breeze. His apartment was stifling, but none of the other priests, except the most exalted, fared much better these muggy summer days. The stench coming up from the canals was at its worst: summer had dropped the water level to the stage that he wondered how the canalsiders could endure the smell.

To say nothing of the stench raised by the new floating greenery choking the backwaters of the canals, dead and scummy in the shadows.

"I'm listening," he protested, turning to face his slender visitor. "I'm paying attention to every word you say."

"Sorry." The fellow spread his hands in apology. "As you might suspect, I'm rather nervous talking freely like this. Ah, no . . . I don't mean that I'm nervous talking in front of you. Gods, Alfonso! We've known each other too long for me to fear *you* have a loose tongue."

226

"And I don't." Rhajmurti met the startling blue eyes of his fellow priest. "But you'd best choose your audience with care, Trevor . . . exceeding care."

Trevor waved a hand. "You think I'm stupid?" he asked. "I know who I can talk to and who I don't dare approach."

"All right." Rhajmurti walked to his sideboard and poured two glasses of wine. He extended one to his guest and sipped from his own. "It's not that I haven't thought the same things as you, and I don't think I'm the only one here in the College who's entertained similar notions." He met Trevor's eyes. "I'm not blind. I've had a chance to see who goes in and out of Cardinal Ito's rooms these days."

"Rama bless!" Trevor began to pace, his wine forgotten in his hands. "What's become of us, Alfonso? Where did we lose sight of our calling? We're *priests*, dammit . . . not petty bureaucrats jockeying around for a higher place in the line to kiss someone's . . ." He stopped, threw his head back, and contemplated the ceiling. "We've forgotten what we're here for, some of us. And those of us who haven't are getting lost in the shuffle."

"I know, I know," Rhajmurti said, leaning back against the sideboard. "I feel the same way. But I'm only a teacher, Trevor, and I—"

"You're a priest first." Trevor's eyes blazed as they caught the light from the window. "A priest who dedicated his life to the service of the Lord and the holy gods."

"Yes, that's true. But I don't have the same power you hold. You've always astounded them, haven't you, Trevor? The brilliant mind . . . the one they held— and still hold—such high hopes for. Even if I *did* complain about the abuses of those in high places, few would listen to me."

"Every voice added to mine gives my own words

power.'' Trevor walked to the open window and gestured with his free hand at the canal below. ''Take
those godforsaken plants. We *think* they were seeded
by the Janes, but we can't prove it. They can be used
to create cheap fuel and benefit the poor. Ha!'' His
laugh was brittle. ''All they've done is polarize Merovingen into two warring camps. And where do we
clergy come in? Are we giving scriptural advice to
either side?''

''Not many of us,'' Rhajmurti said.

''You're damned right, not many of us. And now,
certain cardinals are talking about issuing an Edict,
dammit, outlawing the plants. And have they chosen
this course of action to benefit the people? Not a
chance. It's because certain Houses—and I don't need
to mention names—are opposed to the plants because
they cut into their profits, and *their* profits mean gifts
to the College. Shiva take them! We're being sold out
to the highest bidder!''

Rhajmurti lifted a hand and glanced toward the
closed door, bidding his guest lower his voice. Everything Trevor had said was true. Ito Boregy fed deathangel to Cassie Boregy, her baby survived, and the
debate as to the veracity of her Past Memories raged
unabated. Mikhail Kalugin was one of the more illus-
trious followers of every word that dropped from
m'sera Boregy's lips. The entire College waited with
ill-disguised alarm to see what she would say regarding the plants. *Whatever* her pronouncement, it would
set one side at the other in a debate that raged beneath
the calm surface of the College.

And the cardinals? Even teaching fathers like himself had found themselves caught up in the tightening
spiral of events. One could not live in the College
without being touched by what transpired in the apartments of the highest of the high.

''So,'' Rhajmurti said. ''I agree. We've lost sight of

our calling. We've let ourselves be led down pathways we would not have chosen.''

''Some of us,'' Trevor inserted, lifting an eyebrow.

''Ah, there's good and evil in all men—''

''Which our karma should alleviate after living so many lives.''

''What do you want?'' Rhajmurti asked. ''What do you *want* us to do? To say?''

Trevor sighed heavily and took a long sip of his wine. He lowered his cup. ''I know what *must* be said, if we're to regain our purpose, but I don't know how to say it.''

''Or to whom, or when.''

''Yes.''

''How many priests have you talked to as freely as you're talking to me?''

''At least twenty,'' Trevor replied, ''chosen with extreme care, as you stated was the correct course of action.''

''And their reactions?''

Another long sigh. ''Much the same as yours. They agree with what I've said, and they don't argue that something must be done to clean up the College, but they don't know what to do.''

''Nor do you,'' Rhajmurti reminded gently.

Trevor nodded. ''I wish I had the guts to call a Convening. I wish I could stand before every single cardinal and tell them what I've told you.''

''But you like looking at the topside of the canal rather than bottom.''

''That's truth.'' Anguish showed in Trevor's eyes. ''What do you counsel, Alfonso? You're wise.''

''Wise? As are all men at some brief periods of their lives.'' Rhajmurti shook his head. ''I can tell you what you *shouldn't* do. Don't let your cause run away with you. Talk only with those you can trust. If and when you've talked to enough of us that you feel fairly comfortable with the numbers, call *us* together, not the priests you know for your enemies. Maybe among the entire lot of us, we can come up with some ideas.''

''Lord! That could take forever!''

''Merovingen wasn't built overnight.''

Trevor growled something into his glass.

''You want reform,'' Rhajmurti said, ''and I don't deny that reform is needed. But I understand enough of the way the world works to know that what you *don't* want is to destroy the good along with the bad. Take it slower, Trevor. What we've fallen to hasn't happened overnight, either. A quick cure might kill the patient.''

''You're full of sagacity, aren't you?''

''You *asked.*''

''I did, I did.'' Trevor smiled slightly. ''It will probably please you no end to know that your opinion is shared by all the brothers and sisters I've talked to so far. Not a one of them has urged me to move *faster.*''

Rhajmurti walked to his friend's side. ''Don't take it so hard,'' he said, setting a hand on Trevor's shoulder. ''Everything has to start somewhere. At the risk of another aphorism, the largest river starts out as a small stream.''

Trevor's smile widened. ''You must know a *million* of those old sayings. How do you keep track of them?''

''That's a secret.'' Rhajmurti let his hand fall. ''Be careful, Trevor. You're playing a very dangerous game, and there are more than a few of the powers in the College who would take great pleasure in calling your hand.''

Justice Lee stopped in the hallway, a heavy portfolio of his latest sketches under one arm, and his other arm clutching a basket filled with rolled canvases.

''Dammit, Sunny! Make up your mind,'' he growled, glancing down at the large gold cat weaving in and out between his feet. "Keep moving, or get out of my way."

"I'll get him."

Justice grinned widely as Raj Tai bent down and scooped up Sunny, then flattened himself against the wall so Justice could pass.

Sweat rolled down Justice's face, down the back of his neck; the underarms of his shirt were soaked. *Only a few more trips to make*, he thought, *the Lord be thanked for that*. Moving had to be one of the most obnoxious pastimes he could think of.

There was *no way* he could have accumulated all that . . . stuff, for better lack of a word. His room was surely too small to hold it. Granted, he had stowed much of what he owned under his bed, on top of anything that had a top, and filled his standing closet to the stage that its door nearly burst off its hinges. He thought of Raj with a certain degree of wistful envy: medical students kept all *their* supplies at the College, textbooks, and notebooks being the only things they brought home with them. Now an artist, on the other hand—

"Do you want me to bring that stack of books behind the door?" Raj asked.

Justice glanced over his shoulder and nodded, then turned his attention back to his goal, a door just down the hall from his old room.

His old room. He shifted the portfolio and sidled in through the open doorway. He never thought he would leave the room he had rented from Hilda for so long, but a change in his fortunes had made that move possible.

Since meeting Sonja Keisel, and being accepted by her hightown friends, he had been able to sell many small works of art he knew would have otherwise gone unnoticed. Rank had its privileges, most of them financial. Adding what he made from the sale of small commissions and other simple works to the allowance his aunt gave him, Justice felt flush for the first time in his life.

And then there was Raj. Raj, whose own life had taken an astonishing turn lately. Raj . . . no, Rigel Takahashi, scion of the House of Takahashi in Nev Hettek, recognized by House Kamat as representative of a trade agreement between the two Houses and the two cities. Sponsored to the College by House Kamat to study medicine, Raj had lived in the family mansion, had worn new clothes provided by his sponsors, and had—by all the Ancestors—even started taking dancing lessons, all of which were calculated to prepare the young man for life in hightown society.

Even down to the rather handsome allowance granted by the Kamats.

Raj had told Justice the whole story of who he really was and where he came from, admitting he was heir to one of the powerful Houses in the north. He had seemed embarrassed as he had spoken, his eyes pleading with Justice for understanding; he in no way wanted Justice to treat him differently than he had in the past, when he was, for all practical purposes, just another poor lad eking out a living with the rest of Merovingen-below.

Of course, there was much Raj had left out of the story—why he had moved out of House Kamat, for example—but Justice had not pushed, astounded enough by his friend's story.

So, the combination of Justice's own money, Raj's new-found funds, and their liking for each other had prompted them to discuss rooming together. Fortune had smiled on them, for one of Hilda's roomers had graduated and moved out of his rooms. Rooms, plural. The fellow had not been a hightowner, but his parents were successful merchants and all through his schooling they had given him enough money to rent the suite Justice and Raj were moving into.

Suite. Justice shook his head, paused for a moment in the room he had entered, and looked around. Prime property, this: two large rooms, each bigger than the room he had lived in for years, entered from a small outer room that came complete with two chairs and a table. He grinned and walked to the room that opened off to the left and set his portfolio against the wall. A bed, a standing closet, a desk, a chair . . . all much the same as what he had left, but with so much more space than he was used to.

He groaned. More room hinted of future stuff to come.

"Justice?"

"In here," he called, setting his basket down on the desk. Lord and Ancestors, there was even space against the wall for a small bookcase!

Sunny trotted into the room, and sniffed perfunctorily at the bed. Then, leaping to dead center, he curled up to watch everything going on around him with total feline disinterest.

"Where d'you want them?" Raj asked, standing in the doorway with an armload of books.

"Obviously not on the bed," Justice replied. "It's already occupied."

Raj laughed and set the books on the floor, in the very place Justice had staked out as a home for his possible bookcase.

"I wish I were you right now," Justice said, glancing around the room which was already beginning to fill up. "You didn't have to move *half* the stuff I've got."

"Courage. You've only got about two more trips."

"I can't believe this is really happening to me. I've only *dreamed* about having this much space."

"It *is* a large suite," Raj agreed, "and well away

from the noise of the common room. I think I'm going to like it here."

"Ha! That's a laugh! *One* of the rooms in House Kamat would equal the space of these three."

"Maybe so, but it's ours now." Raj waved a hand toward the sitting room. His dark eyes began to twinkle. "And it's large enough we can have company. Maybe even Sonja Keisel."

Justice felt his face go hot and he turned away, hoping Raj had not seen.

"You're still going to help me with my fencing, aren't you?" Raj asked.

"You'll outstrip me soon enough, what with the teachers House Kamat provides. All I know is the basic handling of a sword, not the finer points of fencing."

"So to speak." Raj turned in a full circle, eyeing the room. "You're going to have more room here than you ever did in your old place."

"That's for sure." Justice drew a deep breath. "Let's get the rest of the stuff, Raj, before all my good intentions vanish."

"Then how about a beer?"

"Lord and Ancestors! That sounds so good, I'll try to pack two trips into one just to get out of here." He mopped at his forehead. "Damn! I wish we had windows."

"That, my friend," Raj said with a wink, sweat beading his own face, "is something Hilda's doesn't offer. We'll just have to wait, you and I. Someday, we'll both have our chance at windows."

The time between semesters at the College alternated between having nothing to do, and frantic preparation for the coming classes and students. Rhajmurti stood at the edge of the stairs leading down to the entry hall of the College, watching the traffic.

He nodded to several cardinals who passed him on their way upstairs, then caught sight of a familiar face: Father Alexiev, the priest who had warned him about the abuse of deathangel.

"Lord Rama's blessing," Alexiev said, joining Rhajmurti at the railing. The stocky priest hunched his shoulders, and ran a hand through his hair. "Did you hear about Ivan?" he asked, his voice so low that Rhajmurti barely heard him.

"Which Ivan? The College is full of them."

"Mhaharaju."

Rhajmurti lifted an eyebrow. One of the hightown students, a good lad, faithful to his studies, but a bit on the wild side. "No, I haven't. What about him?"

"Dead." Alexiev's bushy eyebrows came together in a frown. "Deathangel."

"Gods." Rhajmurti bowed his head momentarily, offering a prayer that Ivan Mhaharaju would be reincarnated with more brains in his next life. "When?"

"Last night."

"Vishnu protect! At one of those godsforsaken parties?"

"No. This time he took the stuff in the privacy of his own room. One of his friends found him this morning, stiff and cold." Alexiev warmed to his theme. "He must have had a bad time of it, Alfonso. He'd clawed at his face, and scribbled gibberish on the walls with the blood."

Rhajmurti grimaced, his mind busy sorting out all of the young Mhaharaju's friends. He had never seen much of Ivan, as the young man had chosen accounting as his major—

"Damn!" Rhajmurti smothered his oath, but Alexiev was not listening. Accounting. Krishna Malenkov. He remembered seeing the two of them come out of a class they took together.

"You say he was alone when he took the stuff?"
Rhajmurti asked, putting on his best innocent face.

"That's what I heard." Alexiev shrugged. "There
were a number of parties going on that evening, but
from all we can tell, he didn't attend any of them. The
last time his friends saw him, he told them he was
going home because he had a headache."

"Who were the friends?"

"The usual group he ran around with. Jorge Whit-
man, Titus Pruvinski, Krishna Malenkov. . . ."

Rhajmurti shut his eyes. Gods. Krishna again. Did
that young fool have nothing better to do with his brain
than fry it? And after Rhajmurti had punished him for
drug dealing—or *attempted* drug dealing—by having
him wash dishes in Hilda's kitchen for ten days,
Krishna should have known better than to come close
to drugs.

Obviously not.

And what of Justice? Rhajmurti rubbed his forehead. He had faith that Justice would not become involved in the drug traffic going on at hightown parties.
Justice was too damned smart for that. Besides, Sonja
Keisel had made it plain she would not put up with
drug-taking in any form whatsoever, and Rhajmurti
felt certain Justice would not jeopardize his blooming
relationship with Sonja over a bit of deathangel.

Still, with Krishna more than likely involved again,
it might be a good idea to look in on Justice.

Despite it being moving day, when even a teaching
father might be asked to carry a thing or two.

Raj sat across from Justice in Hilda's common room,
his mug of beer forgotten in his hands. He glanced at
Justice, but the lanky artist sat slouched in his chair,
his head leaned back, a look of utter exhaustion on his
face. Moving day was over at last: the two of them

were now in possession of one of the best set of rooms Hilda's possessed.

It was fortunate they got along so well, because Raj foresaw times in the future when their relationship might become strained. Though Justice strove manfully to hide it, Raj knew his friend was unsettled at learning who Raj Tai *really* was. He had done everything he could to make Justice realize that a change in name and fortune had not altered the person who was Raj and, he hoped it never would.

It was not his revealed identity but rather what went on between himself, Jones, and Mondragon that might strain the relationship. He had never told Justice any more than he had to about his business. Justice already knew Jones; he had spoken with her often enough to allay her native distrust, and had won her grudging respect in the nighttime ride to Petrescu with those damnable papers. As for Mondragon, Raj had never mentioned Tom's last name, simply referring to him as "Tom." The commonality of the name *could* hide his identity; also, Mondragon was a Nev Hettek name and, versed as he was in his knowledge of hightown Merovingen, Justice might not recognize it.

Denny, however, was Denny. Raj shrugged, thinking of his brother. By Raj's choice, Denny had not made the move to Kamat, staying instead with Mondragon on Petrescu. Maybe, someday in the future, Denny would mature enough to abandon his bridgebrat, roof-runner ways. Then, and only then, could Raj support Denny's entry into House Kamat.

Raj glanced at Justice again and took a long sip of his beer. The last thing he wanted to do was to involve Justice in anything dangerous, or to put Justice in the position he had faced the night he had made the secret delivery of papers to Petrescu. But Raj knew as well as he was sitting in Hilda's common room that he could only protect Justice so far. Thank the Lord Justice had a level head on him and was no slouch when it came to a fight.

Raj ran a hand through his hair and took another drink. He was out of Kamat now; he did not have to endure the agony of seeing Marina every day, *or* of listening to the innuendos and outright accusations she brought against Tom.

Lord and Ancestors! Marina, pregnant.

By Tom.

Jones was like to kill him.

If the rest of his enemies did not get to him first.

Tom would no more give drugs to Andromeda Kamat than he would fly; Raj was certain of that. Living as he had in House Kamat, and having Marina confide in him as she used to, he had learned more about what went on in the mansion than he cared to know.

Andromeda Kamat was taking deathangel, diluted in brandy, in an effort to see her dead husband. Raj had seen enough swampies suffering deathangel flashbacks to recognize what affected the matriarch of House Kamat . . . had seen enough to advise the House physician that this was what had Andromeda Kamat in its grip.

Afterward, Marina had told Raj the entire dark story, adding that one of the retainers in House Kamat had provided the deathangel.

A newcomer by the name of Kidd.

No one knew where Kidd hailed from, only that he was a new face and new name in the House.

*And* Andromeda Kamat's valet.

But the person Marina accused of providing the deathangel to Kidd, who, in turn, gave it to her mother, was none other than Thomas Mondragon. She had arrived at this conclusion through a twisted trail of logic: Kidd was a stranger; he had given the drug to Andromeda; and when Marina had wanted to know where Tom lived, Kidd had taken her there with no hesitation at all. Therefore, she had concluded, he *must* know Tom, and since he did, Mondragon (in her eyes) had become the obvious supplier of deathangel.

Raj's hands clenched on the mug. Damn that Kidd anyway! He would give a lot to find out where the fellow came from. If he could do that, he might be able to prove to Richard Kamat that Mondragon was innocent, *and* let Mondragon know what was going on with Marina. There was a hint in Kidd's speech pattern that spoke of Nev Hettek and, on a leap of logic of his own, Raj was very much afraid Kidd could be Sword of God.

He was fairly sure Mondragon had never seen Kidd, so Tom would not be aware he might have a new enemy in town . . . as if he needed any more. If there were only some way Raj could get Mondragon in a position to see Kidd. . . .

Kidd always ate supper at John's, the canalside tavern where Raj and Justice had first come to know one another, but getting Mondragon to have dinner at John's was totally out of the question. Raj contemplated luring Kidd over to Petrescu on some errand or another, then discarded that idea as equally stupid. If Kidd knew where Mondragon lived, it was entirely possible he knew Raj had lived in the same apartment . . . or at least the same building.

Sweat broke out on Raj's forehead. Everywhere he turned, he came face to face with the Sword. And being Mondragon's friend hardly assured him of a long and peaceful life.

Back to Kidd. He could easily describe Kidd to Mondragon, his perfect memory calling up Kidd's face, speech, and mannerisms, but that was a far cry from having Mondragon actually *see* him.

"Hey, Justus."

Raj looked up from his mug; a student stood next

to Justice's chair, a young man Raj vaguely recognized.

"Have you got my portrait ready yet?" the student asked.

"I'm getting it framed," Justice replied. "Should be ready in a day or two."

The student smiled broadly. "Marvelous! That's really going to make my mother happy. You know something, Justus . . . you're damned good. I can't believe how much it looks like me."

Raj saw a flush creep up Justice's neck.

"Thanks."

"Drop me a message when it's ready, will you? I'll stop by and pick it up."

"Fine. And if I'm not here when you come over, tell Hilda who you are. I'll make sure she gets it to you."

"Thanks again. I'll see you later."

The student nodded at Raj, turned and left.

"Who's that?" Raj asked.

"Gregor Talens. He's a second year student in literature. He saw some of my artwork at a party one time, and asked me to do a portrait of him."

Raj sat up straighter.

A portrait.

And Kidd would be at John's tonight.

Raj drew a long breath. "Say, Justice, would you mind doing me a favor? It'll only take about an hour."


It was late afternoon when Rhajmurti finally got free of the College. He was still not sure what he would say to Justice regarding the possibility that Krishna was dealing drugs again, but it was a subject he knew needed further discussion.

As for Krishna, Rhajmurti had all but written him off as a complete and utter fool. Single-handedly, Krishna was ruining his privileged life, along with his chances for the future. The young man possessed a streak of self-destruction Rhajmurti had seen in other hightowners, stemming perhaps from their idle life, and their knowledge that they would always be provided for.

He shook his head and entered Hilda's Tavern, looking for Justice at his usual table.

"Greetings, Father," Hilda said from her spot behind the bar. "Huntin' for Justus?"

"Yes." Rhajmurti glanced at the empty table again, but Sunny was its only occupant, curled up in a chair, fast asleep. "Have you seen him?"

"He just left, Father, him an' his friend, Raj. Not all that long ago, either. Said somethin' 'bout goin' to John's for dinner." She lifted an eloquent eyebrow. "Now what John's got that I ain't is beyond me."

John's? Rhajmurti rubbed his chin. A rather rough place, but one many students frequented, for the food was not bad, and it was cheaper than a lot of other taverns.

"Thanks, Hilda. I'll catch up with him there." Rhajmurti turned to go, then glanced over his shoulder. "Have you seen Krishna?"

Hilda made a face. "That 'un I don't *want* to see. Been downright surly lately, he has. Ye'd think he had nothin' better to do than insult honest folk." She took out a wet rag and began wiping an already spotless bartop. "Must be my karma, Father, for me to have to put up with the likes of *him*."

Rhajmurti struggled to keep the smile from his face. "He'll be graduating before you notice, Hilda."

"Huhn. Not soon enough for me. And knowin' *my* luck, I'll get another one just like 'im. You tell Justus to watch himself canalside. It's damned rough down there. They's been trouble—"

"I'll tell him."

The walkway on second level Kass was crowded at

this time of day with citizens off to do last minute shopping, or out to dinner. Rhajmurti joined the flow of people walking up and down the wooden walkway, his path cleared for him by virtue of the saffron shirt he wore that marked him priest.

Crossing Kass Bridge to Spellbridge, Rhajmurti paused to talk with two priests he knew, then headed toward the steps that led down to canalside. It was good that Raj had moved in with Justice, though the heir of Nev Hettek's House Takahashi could be something Justice might find difficult to deal with. Nevertheless, the two young men seemed to get along well, and it was high time Justice had a male companion who was nearly his age.

But John's? Riffraff and radicals. Rhajmurti hoped it was momentary lapse of judgment—not young Takahashi's influence.

The interior of John's Tavern was dimly lit as usual, for its proprietor saved on oil for his lamps like every other canalside businessman. Justice stood outside the door, Raj at his side, taking a good, long look at the gathered clientele. He seldom came to John's unless his cash was running low, for the crowd that gathered here was far rougher than that which patronized second-level businesses.

He checked his dagger in its sheath at his back, and felt the reassuring weight of another small knife strapped to the inside of his left wrist. Carrying such arms was not totally unreasonable, especially looking back on the fight where he had met Raj and Denny. And Raj seemed uncommonly nervous.

Nothing inside the tavern seemed amiss. Justice turned and lifted one eyebrow in Raj's direction, indicating things looked normal enough. He was clad in his usual black shirt and pants, his College sash the only mark of color. Raj had followed his example, only his clothes, upon close inspection, were of finer quality and new, not showing the wear of Justice's. Like Justice, Raj carried two knives, one worn openly and one concealed; in addition, he carried his sling-shot.

"Now who is it we're looking for?" Justice asked, leaning close to Raj's ear.

"A nondescript fellow. You'd not notice him . . . he'd disappear in a crowd. I'll let you know if I see him."

Justice shrugged and led the way into John's, watching the faces turn as customers looked up to see who had joined them. Finding nothing threatening in the two students, John's patrons turned back to their drinks or dinners.

"Ain't seen ye in a while," John said, nodding to Justice from his place behind the bar. "Where ye been?"

"Studying, mostly." Justice looked around and found a free table. "We'd like dinner—silverbit and greens—and two beers."

"Ye got it," John said. "Enjoy."

As John turned away to take their order to the kitchen, Raj led Justice toward a small table at the rear of the room. It was a dimly lit position, but one situated so that anyone sitting there would have a good view of everyone else in the tavern.

"Now, tell me again what it is that you want me to do," he said, leaning across the table as Raj sat down across from him.

"Not much. I just want you to get a good look at this man . . . a *good* look. Then, after we've gone back to Hilda's, I'd like you to do a sketch of him."

"A sketch, I take it, that will be good enough to let someone who's never seen him recognize him later."

"Right."

Justice sighed quietly. Such a drawing would tax his

talent; it was one thing to sketch someone while looking at the subject, and another to reproduce that person accurately from memory. The mind often did
strange things: a nose could become a little too long,
hair might turn a shade too light or dark, or the bone
structure of the face could be just enough off to change
the total combination.

*Why?* he wanted to ask Raj. *What are you up to
now? And how dangerous will it be for us?*

But he kept his questions to himself and patiently
awaited dinner.

Raj, meanwhile, was carefully looking at the tavern's patrons, his expression now one of idle curiosity.
Justice admired his friend's ability to look totally dis-
interested when he was the exact opposite.

"I don't see him," Raj said quietly, "but he'll be
here. He's *always* here for dinner."

"Maybe John knows him," Justice ventured.

"Maybe. But I'll bet he doesn't know what *I* want
to know." Raj's dark eyes were steady in the lamplight. "I'm sorry, Justice. I know you're dying to be
let in on what's happening here. I don't think I can tell
you without involving you in things you really
*shouldn't* know . . . that could be dangerous for you."

"Oh, well. As I've said before, don't enlighten me
any more than necessary to keep me out of trouble."
He patted his belt pouch. "What about this? I've got
my pocket sketchbook and a pencil. Think I can sketch
him here?"

Raj shook his head. "Not if he's who I think he is.
He'll be primed to notice anything unusual going on
around him. Hypersensitive, if you know what I
mean."

"Well, shit. I'm an artist, a student. I'm *always*
sketching."

"Maybe somewhere else and some other time. Trust

me, Justice. This one you'll have to do from memory.''

A waiter came to the table and set down two plates of steaming silverbit and two mugs of beer. Justice reached for his belt pouch, then stopped as Raj shook his head.

''This one's on me. You're doing me a favor.''

He subsided back into his chair and watched the tables around him as Raj paid for the meals. The usual group of customers filled John's—students mixed in with canalers, poor shop owners, and other men who looked much rougher. Justice cut up his fish and began to eat.

And caught, out of the corner of his eye, a familiar face.

Krishna!

Lord and Ancestors! What the hell was Krishna doing in a dive like this?

''Raj, don't turn around. Krishna's here.''

Raj lifted both eyebrows. ''What's *he* doing canalside? Way he acts, you'd think he couldn't breathe the air down here.''

''That's what I'd like to know. He's been gambling a lot lately. Maybe he's wasted his allowance again and has to live frugally.'' He took a drink of beer. ''I don't like it, Raj. For some reason, his being here bothers me more than it should.''

Krishna had not seen Justice or Raj in their dark corner, and took a table on the opposite side of the room. He had dressed down for this trip canalside, leaving his expensive shirts and weapons back at Hilda's. That, in itself, rang an alarm bell in Justice's mind. That Krishna Malenkov, duelist and hightown bully, would be seen anywhere without something to mark his station . . .

''How many blacklegs did you see on your way down here?'' Justice asked Raj.

Raj lifted both eyebrows. There was a sudden spookiness about him. A hint of panic. "The usual number, I'd guess. I wasn't really paying attention. Why?"

"Just wondering. Keep on your toes."

"Ummmm," Raj acknowledged through a bite of fish. Panic faded. Then his eyes narrowed. "There," he muttered, pointing slightly with his chin toward the door. "That's him."

Justice looked up at the man who had entered John's. As Raj had said, there was not one outstanding feature on his face: he was dark-haired (but then so was nearly everyone else in Merovigen), clean-shaven, dark-eyed, of medium height, and walked with no telltale gait. Yes, this man would indeed disappear into a crowd.

Stilling his breathing and trying to calm his mind, Justice set about memorizing every feature of the man he watched. Now that he looked closer, he saw the subtle differences that made this man's face unique to himself. His jaw was slightly longer than normal, and his left eye had a slight tilt to its outside edge, as if a scar puckered the skin. The light was dim enough in John's that Justice could not see the scar, but he thought it was there.

The man stood a moment in the doorway, scanning the crowd. Justice and Raj both busied themselves with their meals, keeping their faces averted. Evidently, the fellow saw nothing that disturbed him, for he nodded to John and walked across the room, his pace neither too slow nor too fast. The man was a perfect medium: his looks were unremarkable, and none of his gestures or walk would stick out in someone's memory.

Justice watched the fellow's progress across the room, his mind focused on anything that could aid him in reproducing the man in a sketch. Then, he nearly choked on his fish.

"What's wrong?" Raj hissed, leaning across the table.

"Damn!" Justice swallowed heavily. "He's going to Krishna's table!"

Raj sat absolutely still now, his attention riveted to the table where Krishna Malenkov sat. Justice felt his heart pounding in his chest. What the devil was the connection between Raj's mystery man and Krishna?

The fellow sat down, nodded in a friendly manner to Krishna, and the two of them sat talking quietly, no more out of place in the surroundings than anyone else. The waiter delivered Krishna's meal, took the other man's order, and walked off.

"What the hell's going on?" Raj asked. "How does Krishna, of all people, know K—that man?"

"I don't know." Justice finished off his fish. "That's what bothers me. First off, Krishna doesn't belong here. The Krishna *I* know wouldn't be caught dead in such a lowlife place. And now, he's sitting there, dressed like the rest of us, talking to someone *you* think important enough for me to do a sketch of." He met Raj's eyes. "What, in the Angel's name, have you got us into now?"

Raj shook his head. "Nothing, I hope. If we sit tight, and don't draw attention to ourselves, nothing should happen."

"Nothing should happen," Justice echoed. "Why doesn't that reassure me?"

"Damn. Don't be obvious, Justice, but look what's going on now."

Justice watched Krishna's table from the corner of his eyes. Krishna had slipped a small packet onto the table, subtly enough that no one would have noticed if they had not been watching. The other man ignored the packet; then, slowly, he leaned closer to Krishna, set his elbow on the packet, and started drawing it toward him.

"Mind if I join you?"

Justice jerked his attention away, saw Raj's face go white, and looked up into the dark eyes of Father Rhajmurti.

"For Rama's sake, Father," Justice said, "sit down quickly! Please!"

A puzzled look crossed Rhajmurti's face, but he drew out his chair and sat with no comment.

"Did anyone notice you come in?" Justice asked, keeping his head averted from Krishna's table. Raj was doing all the looking now, his face gone very still.

"I suppose so, but I've been here before." Rhajmurti watched Raj for a moment. "What's going on?"

"I'm not sure," Justice admitted. "But whatever you do, don't turn around. Krishna's here, and I don't think he's up to anything honest."

Father Rhajmurti drew a long breath. "Drugs?" he asked quietly.

"I don't know. I think so. I think he's making a delivery right now. He doesn't know Raj and I are here, and it's Rama's own blessing that he didn't see *you* come in."

Raj, meanwhile, had not taken his attention away from what was going on at Krishna's table. "He's delivering *something*," he said in a near whisper. "It's a packet of some sort."

"What's wrong with that boy?" Rhajmurti growled. "He's going to ruin himself!"

"Whatever you do," Justice pleaded, "don't stop him."

"I wasn't planning to. That wouldn't be the brightest thing to do right now."

Justice felt his face go hot. "I know. I just don't want him disturbed . . . him or the man he's with."

"Who's with him?"

"I don't have any idea."

Rhajmurti lifted one eyebrow. "For someone who's obviously hip-deep in possible trouble, you know remarkably little." He glanced at Raj. "And you, Rigel? How much do *you* know?"

Raj's eyes fell. "A lot that I can't tell you, Father."

"Oh?"

Raj shifted in his chair. "Please, Father, try to understand. I swear I'm not doing anything dishonest."

"Then why can't you tell me . . . or Justice?"

"Family secrets," Raj said at last. "Things that could damage Family."

Justice heard the emphasis placed on "Family" and read the capital letter on the word. Kamat or Takahashi? He sure as hell was not going to ask.

"Let's just say that I'm here to vindicate a friend of mine who's been falsely accused of dealing drugs. I *know* it isn't him, but . . . but someone else is sure it is. I'm trying to prove that my friend isn't providing drugs to the man who's sitting with Krishna."

Father Rhajmurti stared at Raj for a moment. "Then why do you have Justice here?"

"So he can witness the transaction."

Justice sat up straighter in his chair. That was *not* part of what Raj had told him he wanted him to do. But then, he had never asked, had he?

"And. . . ?" Rhajmurti prompted.

"And, draw a sketch from memory after we get back to Hilda's as additional proof that we saw the right man."

A waiter drifted up to the table and took Rhajmurti's order for a beer, then left.

"Please, Father," Raj said quietly, "don't interfere. We shouldn't be in any danger."

"Dammit, Rigel, coming canalside is dangerous enough as it is. What if this man you're stalking sees you?"

Justice watched Raj's face carefully, but his friend's eyes were steady.

"He might be mildly surprised, but not enough to be thrown into a fright. He knows I'm a student—"

"—*and* the heir to House Takahashi, who's as out of place canalside as Krishna."

Justice glanced back to Krishna's table. Krishna and Raj's mysterious quarry had finished their transaction: the packet had disappeared from the table. Now the two men sat casually in their chairs, talking as if nothing had gone on.

*Damn! I wonder if anyone else saw? And if so, did they care? Is John's a drug house? Does this go on all the time? If it does, how many men here would think nothing of killing someone who might be witness to their business?* He squirmed in his chair, the hilt of the dagger in his belt rubbing his back. *What's Krishna got himself involved in now? And how did I get mixed up in it again?*

"Have you looked long enough, Justice?" Raj asked. "Do you think you can draw the man's face?"

"I suppose I can. But we can't leave now. They'll notice us for sure."

"No problem. We'll stay until they've gone."

"Which could be some time from now," Rhajmurti inserted. "Are you willing to wait?"

"I don't think we have a choice, Father," Justice said. He quickly glanced across the room. "What are you going to do about Krishna?"

"What I promised I'd do the *last* time I caught him trying to deal drugs. I'm going to tell his father about it."

Lord and Ancestors! Krishna's father would have a stroke! Justice was glad for the thousandth time that he was not in Krishna's shoes.

Well, there was nothing to be done now but wait. Sooner or later, Krishna and the other man would leave. Justice knew little about drug dealing, but it seemed to him that it might not be terribly bright to sit around in public too long after making a buy.

"Hsst!"

Raj pointed with his chin toward Krishna's table. Justice looked, saw the flash of gold on the tabletop, and knew that Krishna had been paid for his trouble. Where was Krishna getting the stuff? At the parties he attended? Or was he stealing it from his hightowner friends? That was always a possibility, because he had—

"He's getting ready to leave," Raj whispered.

"Who?" Rhajmurti sat up straighter in his chair; his back was to Krishna's table, and he could not see. "Krishna or—?"

"The man I came here to see," Raj said, his jaw clenched. His eyes glittered coldly. "I think I might be able to prove my friend's innocence now . . . if—" He glanced at Justice. "—you'd be willing to back up my story."

Justice spread his hands. "Sure. Why not? As long as I get out of this evening with a whole skin, I'll be happy."

The waiter returned with Father Rhajmurti's beer, took the coins, and went off to pick up another order.

"I want the two of you to know I'm not very happy about what you're doing," Rhajmurti said, swirling the liquid in his mug. "You may think it's not dangerous, but let me assure you, it is."

"But, Father—"

Three things happened at once.

The man sitting with Krishna rose and took his leave.

Krishna happened to look directly at Justice's table, and recognize who sat there.

And the door to John's Tavern suddenly filled with grim-faced blacklegs.

* * *

"Damn!"

Justice's curse was whispered, but in the deadly silence that fell it seemed overly loud.

The man who had sat with Krishna stopped dead, as did anyone else who happened to be up and walking around. Justice was certain if someone had dropped a button on the floor, the entire room would have heard it.

For a long, agonizing while, the blacklegs merely stood in the doorway, sticks held in their hands, their faces showing absolutely no emotion. Then the tableau was broken.

The blacklegs entered the tavern; Justice counted seven of them, including their captain, big, burly fellows all. No one else in the room moved . . . everyone was staring at the blacklegs, afraid to draw their attention.

Justice glanced at the man who had been sitting with Krishna. He had to admire the fellow's presence of mind, for he stood relaxed, his face totally free of any emotion save that of curiosity.

Then, as the blacklegs came farther into the room, the fellow started edging toward the door, moving so slowly it seemed that he did not move at all.

There was a crash to the rear of the room: all heads turned as a small, dark-clad man leaped up from his table, tipping over his chair as he did so. He rushed toward the open doorway, knocking other patrons aside, and pushing the fellow who had bought drugs from Krishna out of the way.

Amazingly, the little man managed to bolt out the door before the blacklegs could catch him.

"Move!" the captain bellowed. "Catch that bastard, or he's lost!"

Four of his men raced after their quarry. In the mayhem that followed, the fellow Raj had wanted Justice to sketch followed directly on the heels of the black-legs, sprinting off into the dark. The remaining two blacklegs made as if to follow, but were restrained by their captain. Obviously, they were looking for the little man, and had no time to spare for someone who had let their nerves get the better of them.

"Damn!" Raj whispered. "He got away! I can't believe it! That took guts!"

The blacklegs gestured to John who joined them at the bar. Their conversation was hushed, but the black-leg captain seemed satisfied with what John was telling him. He nodded, gestured curtly to his two companions, and they stalked out of the tavern.

An excited hum of conversation replaced the silence. Neighbor turned to neighbor, whispered their theories as to who the little man was, and what chances the blacklegs had of catching him.

Justice sat staring across the room at Krishna, whose face (seen in dim lamplight) looked decidedly pale. It paled even more, as Rhajmurti slowly turned around in his chair to fix Krishna with a steely gaze.

"Excuse me," Father Rhajmurti said, standing. "I think I'm going to have a little conversation with m'ser Malenkov." He glanced over his shoulders at Justice and Raj. "I hope I can depend on the two of you going straight back to Hilda's."

"Yes, sir," Justice said. Raj nodded fervently.

Rhajmurti smiled slightly and slowly walked toward Krishna, who was shrinking back into his chair as far as possible.

"Lord!" Justice breathed. He reached for his mug of beer. "Why is it when we get together we always manage to get mixed up in something?"

Raj shrugged, but his face registered the relief he must be feeling inside. "I don't know. Lucky, I guess."

"The next time we go off anywhere on one of your

missions," Justice said, setting the empty mug down
on the table, "I wish you'd tell me all you can about
what we're doing *before* we get there, not after. Who
the hell do you want me to bear witness to that Krishna
is most likely the one supplying drugs to this man
you're after?"

Raj dropped his eyes, then looked up again. "M'ser
Kamat."

"Richard Kamat?" Justice asked. "Why does he
want—?" He lifted a hand. "No. Don't tell me. I
think I've been through enough tonight without learning more."

"Sorry." Raj grinned slightly. "But you *did* get a
free meal out of it."

Justice glanced across the room to where Rhajmurti
stood glowering down at Krishna. "True. And it's a
damn sight better than what Krishna got."

The torches and lamps shed a flickering light on the
slippery stone walkway. Rhajmurti stood waiting for
a poleboat, Krishna Malenkov at his side. Krishna had
said nothing when Rhajmurti had accused him of dealing drugs; his eyes had gone wide and frightened, he
had nodded once, but that was all. The break in the
young hightowner's composure had come when
Rhajmurti had told him they were going to pay a visit
to the Malenkov mansion on Rimmon Isle, and that
Krishna himself would tell his father what he had
done. Krishna had all but fallen to his knees, begging
Rhajmurti to spare him that, but Rhajmurti had remained undeterred. Now, the two of them stood waiting by the steps to second-level Spellbridge for a
poleboat to take them across town to Krishna's father.

Rhajmurti cursed silently. He did not want to face
m'ser Malenkov with the news that his son had been
dealing drugs. It would be a scene fraught with emotion, and Rhajmurti truly did not know what Krishna's

father would do. Despite him all but giving up on ever making anything out of Krishna at all, Rhajmurti still believed there *might* be something in the young high-towner worthy of salvage.

He sighed. Events had gotten out of hand lately. Between the drug-dealing on campus and among the students, and the reformation movement inside the College itself, he wondered where he was going to find time to teach his classes.

As for Justice and Raj—no, Rigel—Rhajmurti could not help but be concerned. Unwittingly, Justice was being drawn into situations Rhajmurti knew he could not keep him out of. There was far too much going on in the young Takahashi's life that Rhajmurti did not know about. And yet he could not forbid Justice to see Rigel . . . the two of them were rooming together now. He could only hope that the levelheadedness he saw in Justice, and felt hints of in Rigel, would keep them safe.

He turned his head at the sound of someone poling a boat in his direction. Krishna straighened at his side, his eyes fixed on the water of the canal. Those damnable green plants that had washed up from the canal during the day had made the stone walkway more treacherous than usual. Huhn. An additional problem facing Merovingen.

Rhajmurti glanced up, seeking empty sky, a futile attempt from where he stood. If, in this life or the next, he ever had a chance to meet the Ancestors who had doomed everyone to Merovin, all respect and his priestly calling aside, he would probably strangle each and every one of them.

And enjoy the hell out of it, too.

# TURNING POINT
# (REPRISED)

### Mercedes Lackey

Lunchtime for runners saw Denny draped over the lower railing of the Gallandry walkway above Port Canal, absorbing lunch and sunlight at the same time. He was blind and deaf to the traffic behind him, intent as he was on his study of the canal below, until an elegantly-booted foot nudged Denny's leg.

"Hey, kid," drawled a smooth voice, rich with amusement. "How's the Trade?"

Denny looked up sharply from his noontime perusal of the traffic on Port Canal, startled, his mouth full of bread. He *knew* that voice!

Wiry and thin, dark hair falling in a mass of curls to below his shoulders, Gregori Mendelov leaned elegantly on the walkway-rail beside him, grinning, looking very like a younger, darker, shorter version of Tom Mondragon. Denny took in the slightly exotic cut of his clothing, the well-worn hilt of his rapier, the sun-darkened state of his complexion at a glance, before bursting out with his reply. "Greg!" he exclaimed, scrambling to his feet, and throwing his arms around the older boy—boy still, for Gregori was only

256

a year or two older than his brother, Raj. "Where ye *bin?* I was thinkin' the Megarys got ye!"

Greg laughed, and ruffled Denny's hair, but did not attempt to extract himself from the younger boy's embrace. "Had to make a trip south, kid—for m'health." Denny let him go, and backed up a step, looking up at him in perplexity. Greg tapped Denny's nose with a playful fingertip. "Not to make a story out of it, laddy, but m'dear father turned me in to th' blacklegs. Hopped a ship one step ahead of 'em, and worked m'way to the Chat an' back. Didn't have much time for goodbyes."

Denny grinned in delight. "Truth?"

Greg turned his expression to one of unwonted seriousness, and placed his hand solemnly on his satin-covered chest in the general vicinity of his heart. "Truth." Then he dropped the pose, put his arm around Denny's shoulders, and returned the boy's embrace. "So what you been up to, kid? Still roofwalking?"

Denny grinned. "Some. Mostly bin runnin'. Do an odd job fer Rat'n'Rif, fer—'nother feller. Some fer canalers, but that's bin a special—canalers got it in fer Megarys, I bin helpin', like. Mostly runnin' fer Gallandry these days."

*"Gallandry?"* Greg pursed his lips in surprise, and sun struck red lights from his hair, green sparks from his hazel eyes. "Come up in the world, have we?"

Denny flushed with pleasure. "Hey, ain't no big thing. An' it's mostly on account of that feller, th' one I do a bit'f odd work fer. *He* got me th' job. I bin stayin' with 'im."

Greg grew silent, a silence punctuated with the distant clamor of voices on the canal below, the splashing of poles, the regular spat of wavelets on Gallandry foundations. "Denny—" Greg's expression darkened, and his grip on Denny's shoulders tightened. "Denny, this feller—he isn't—messing with you, is he?"

Denny's open-mouthed shock seemed to reassure the older boy, even before he spluttered out his reply. "*Him?* Hell, no, not in a million years! He likes *girls*. Got him one, too. 'Member Jones?"

Greg's eyebrows rose, and his tense expression relaxed. "M'sera Hellcat herself? And a *lander?* Lord and Ancestors, I don't know whether to congratulate the man, or pity him! Who *is* this paragon?"

"Name of Mondragon," Denny replied happily. "Tom Mondragon."

"That's not a local name, at least not one *I* know." The questions in Greg's eyes gave Denny momentary qualms, and he belatedly began to pick his words with care.

"Hightowner, Boregy bastard, half Falkenaer," he said, sticking to the "official" story. "They pay 'im t'keep hisself quiet an' do a job'r two fer 'em."

"To *not* make an embarrassment of himself, and to do what m'ser Boregy doesn't want to dirty his fingers with, hmm?" Greg mused. "I can see where a smart kid like you could be useful to him. Is he treating you all right?"

Denny nodded vigorously. "As good as you. 'Cept he *tries* t' keep me outa trouble."

Greg laughed. "Then *I've* got no quarrel with him. And how are my old pair of nemeses, m'seras Rif and Rat?"

Denny hid another grin. Rat did not approve of Gregori Mendelov, but Rif approved of him even less. *She* considered *him* far too reckless, far too careless— which to Denny seemed rather a case of pot calling kettle. She hadn't liked it when Denny had taken to hanging around with the older boy—she'd liked it even less when Greg had included him in on some of his escapades.

But Greg was something special—a kind of substitute-brother; with his own brother out of reach in the swamp, he'd given Denny someone to tag after, look up to, try to imitate. He'd initiated Denny into the no-longer-mysterious ways of Girls—or rather, Women—just prior to his disappearance. And he'd been something of a protector when there was trouble and Rat wasn't around.

Truth to be told, Greg was a great deal that Raj was *not*. He took risks Raj would not even have thought of, and took them laughingly. Raj was so serious—and Denny grew tired of seriousness, now and again. He didn't seem to know what a joke was—it was Greg's easy, careless good humor that attracted Denny the most. Greg could always find something to laugh at, even when the job went wrong. Mostly, though, nothing went wrong in Greg's hands, and he did everything with a flair and style that Denny could only envy.

"Rat's okay—but ye'll never guess who Rif's playin' footsie with," Denny replied, smirking.

"Mischa Kalugin?" Greg laughed.

"Less likely'n that."

"Less likely—the only man less likely would be Black Cal—" He stopped dead at Denny's widening grin. "You *can't* be serious!"

"Dead serious."

"Dip me in batter and call me fried fish! If Rif's a-bedding with Black Cal, can Retribution be far behind?" His eyes were wide and gleeful. "I can see I've been missing *far* more than I dreamed!" He let Denny go, and regarded him with a lifted eyebrow and a grin that practically sparkled. "I can see that getting caught up is going to cost me at least the price of a dinner. So tell me, my young wage-earner—when do your employers release you for the day?"

* * *

The girl approaching the bench of Gallandry runners was definitely an enigma. Denny couldn't place her in the heirarchy of Merovingen-below or -above. Her clothing (pants and severe tunic-shirt, and boots), though plain to the point of severity, was of a quality—and the First-Bath blue—that fairly shouted money. Yet she walked with the slightly rolling, balanced tread of a canaler. In appearance she was like any one of a thousand other Merovingen girls of seventeen or eighteen; dark, curly hair, dark eyes, dusky complexion—but there was a personality behind those eyes that made you sit up and notice her. Denny chewed his thumbnail and wondered what brought her to Gallandry.

He soon found out.

She walked up to Ned Gallandry's desk like she owned him, desk, and all of Gallandry, and didn't need to flaunt the fact. The saturnine Gallandry cousin sat up sharp when he saw her, and put aside what he was doing. She spoke quietly to him for a moment, too quietly for Denny to hear what she was saying, although he strained his ears unashamedly. But *then* she turned away from Ned toward the bench, and crooked her finger, beckoning. Beckoning *Denny*.

He jumped up and bounced over to her; Ned Gallandry looked him up and down, speculation in his no-color eyes, then cleared his throat. "M'sera Bolado needs a runner—for somethin' special," he said, slowly. "She wants somebody as knows where Raj Tai went. I tol' her that he's not here no more, that he got proper leave to go, so he's not in any trouble with us, an' that you'd know where he is."

"Yes, m'ser," Denny said quickly. "M'sera, I—" He gulped. "I do know where he is, but—"

He wasn't quite sure what to say, and looked at Ned for some clue. It was no *secret*—at least, he'd not been told it was—that "Raj Tai" was now openly Raj Takahashi, and under Kamat protection and sponsorship—keeping the name "Raj" in obedience to the Revenantist priests at the College, who had not much cared for his birth-name of Rigel. But it wasn't something that too many people knew, either. Ned knew—but that didn't mean he wanted the other runners to know.

"Why don't you an' the m'sera take a walk, kid," Ned said. "Make this the last run of the day. The Bolados is good neighbors—"

Lord and Ancestors—*that* "Bolado?" The ones that owned the next isle north?

"—an' can't hurt t' tell her what she wants t' know."

"Yes, m'ser," Denny replied faintly. "M'sera?"

She led him out, into the late-afternoon bustle and clamor on the shadowed walkway, maintaining a strained and complete silence. They moved with the flow of the crowd all the way down to the diNero bridge, without her saying a word. Denny kept glancing at her out of the corner of his eye; she had a funny expression, the kind Jones wore when she was baffled by what to do next. He reckoned by that similarity of expression that m'sera Bolado was an unusually competent woman—like Jones. And that, like Jones, it wasn't often that she found herself at a loss.

Finally she stopped in the little alcove where the bridge met the walkway, a nook built in the side of the building so that people with long burdens to maneuver from the bridge onto the walkway could do so. She finally faced him there, and cleared her throat, awkwardly.

"I'm Kat Bolado," she said, holding out her hand. Denny shook it, noting with surprise the amount of callus there. "Denny Diaz," he replied, keeping to his assumed identity. "Whatcha want with Raj Tai?"

She blushed, much to Denny's surprise. "I—I'd like to send him a note," she said. "But I haven't been able to find him. I—I have a lot of canaler friends—

oh, hell, this is *so* awkward!'' She flushed even harder, from her neck right up to her hairline, and worried at her lower lip with her teeth. Denny shuffled his feet, scuffing his bare toes on the worn wood of the walkway, not certain how to break the impasse they seemed to have reached.

''Would you like a drink?'' she asked suddenly.

Denny managed a tentative smile. ''Wouldn' turn one down, m'sera,'' he offered.

She smiled a little herself, and nodded at the bridge. When he hesitated, she led the way across the bridge, down through the thinning crowd, to a little second-level tavern. It was scarcely more than a hole in the wall, with a narrow entrance, a bar-hatch facing the walkway and four tiny booths crowded behind the bar—but it was on diNero, neutral territory.

The booths were in deep shadow, and none of them were occupied. She bespoke the one farthest in the back; the weary tapster nodded, and gave her the pitcher of beer and two mugs she'd asked for to carry back there herself. He took her money and turned his back on them both almost before she'd picked up the mugs.

She took the farthest bench, settled into her seat, and gave him a long and penetrating look over the top of her beer mug. ''We're New Money,'' she said suddenly. ''Bolado, I mean. My granddaddy poled one of his own boats. Mama says I take after him. I can't abide being—confined.''

Denny nodded vaguely, wondering where all this was leading.

She looked, he thought, distressed. ''I don't—I don't know, I don't seem to fit. Not with the Salazars, the Yans, the Old Money kids. They—spend all their time thinking of parties, who's sleeping with who. Not with the other New Money either, seems like they're busy trying to think up ways to get into the Residency, the

South Bank crowd. That just seems so stupid. So I read a lot, and I got to spending a lot of time on the canals. I *like* the canalers; a couple of them kind of adopted me—now that they're getting on, I help them when I can. Poling. I like it; it's kind of fun. I s'ppose that's 'cause I don't have to do it all the time.''

She offered him another tentative grin, like a gift. Denny grinned back and nodded agreement with that last statement.

''The canalers, though, they're tied to Bolado so they never minded teaching me. They do the light hauling for us. Nadra and Jimi Chen; Jose isn't big enough to be much help with a pole yet, so I'm doin' for them until he is. Mama doesn't much care what I do so long as I don't get into trouble doing it—I'm bottommost of six. She figures Nadra'd whop me good if I got out of line. So I know a lot of the canalers, at least to put names to faces. And that's why I was out on the water when I saw the girl Jones bringing Raj in. And—'' she flushed again, visible even in the shadows. ''And I—I thought he looked—I wanted to—'' She hid her confusion in her drink for a moment, emerging only when her flushes had cooled. ''Then I got all tied up in Family stuff for a while, and couldn't even talk to Nadra, so it took me a while to find out who he was, where he worked. I never did find out where he lived before he just dropped out of sight.''

*Now* it dawned on Denny—this was The Girl In The Boat. Well, no *wonder* Jones hadn't been able to track her down—she wasn't canaler, she was Family! And no wonder no one would tell her where Raj lived—with every canaler on the water knowing he had Enemies.

''And now he's gone—'' She took a long gulp of her beer, and looked at him pleadingly. ''I think I saw you with him, that day. Do you *really* know where he is?''

''Ye, m'sera,'' Denny said slowly. ''I know where

he is, all right. An' I bet you know, too. 'Cause he ain't Raj Tai no more. He's what he was *born* as, now. Raj Takahashi.''

''Raj—'' she went red, then white, then red again. ''—Raj Takahashi? The one—Kamat—oh—'' She hastily emptied her mug, refilled it, and half emptied it again. ''Oh, my,'' she said, weakly.

''Ye, m'sera,'' Denny said, just to fill the silence.

She smiled, but it was shaky. Very shaky. Denny reckoned she would have gotten the same expression if he'd set fishhooks into the corners of her mouth and pulled.

''Well,'' she said, finally, ''I guess I don't really need you to deliver this note. I could do it myself.'' Whispered. ''If I can come up with the guts to do it.''

''Ye, m'sera,'' Denny replied, but she wasn't listening anymore. She stared into nothing for a moment, then just left her mug and the rest of the pitcher of beer on the table, and walked away, in a kind of dream.

Or maybe, Denny reckoned, finishing his beer, a nightmare.

Moghi was watching them out of the corner of his eye, so Denny was doing his damnedest to act Virtuous.

''—I can't believe it,'' Greg said, leaning back in his chair against the wall, and sipping at his whiskey, his eyes alight with laughter. Jep cleared away their plates, with an odd look at Denny, but he didn't say anything. Denny concentrated on being *very* well behaved. This was Moghi's after all, and if he *did* anything, Jones would hear about it. He wasn't even drinking whiskey, though Greg had offered it, nor even beer; he was sticking to tea.

Outside Moghi's open door there were canalers lounging on his porch, mugs and glasses in hand, enjoying the balmy evening. He and Greg had the tap-room pretty much to themselves.

"I just can't believe it," Greg repeated, chuckling. "I leave this town, and the *very next day* all hell breaks loose! And me not here to help it along!" He shook his head mockingly. "I can see I've got a lot of lost time to make up—"

Suddenly he leaned forward, and his tone grew con-spiratorial. "That's where you come in, kid. If you want in. Because I need a lookout and a housebreaker for a little piece of work."

Denny brightened. " 'Course I want in!" he replied softly. "What'd'ye take me fer? What's th' action?"

Greg's eyes flamed with glee. "Who's the richest, *dumbest* man in this city?"

Denny snorted. "No contest. Mischa Kalugin."

"And what does he love above power, wealth, women—everything?"

"His toys," Denny supplied.

"Now—what would he do, do you think, if he'd gone and built a *wonderful* toy just for his daddy to send to Nev Hettek as a kind of present for m'ser Fon—and he'd sent it to the jeweler to get all gilded and prettied up, and get sparklies put on it—and somebody—borrowed it? And told him he'd get it back *only* if he left a *great* deal of money in a particular place—and *didn't* tell anyone about it? *And* told him if he *did* bring in the blacklegs, he'd get his beautiful clockwork toy back in a million pieces?" Greg settled back in his chair with a smile of smug satisfaction.

"He's just *dumb* enough t' do it," Denny acknowl-edged, answering Greg's smile with one of his own. "When and where?"

"Tonight, if you're game. Jeweler just opposite the Pile."

"Blacklegs?" Denny asked.

"Got a distractor. Gave Tree Vasoly a Chat-made

coat like this'n when he drooled over it. *He* thought I was groveling.'' Greg chuckled. ''Then this afternoon I sent a couple of messages to him and Sven Lenski concerning the coat and Tree's manhood. Send one more and I'll guarantee they'll play knife-talk on the Pile bridges tonight.''

Denny chuckled evilly. ''An' if anybody *sees* anythin', all they'll notice is th' coat. So if anybody comes lookin' fer a thief—they go fer Tree. Yey. What is this thing of Kalugin's, anyway? A timepiece?''

Greg snickered. ''I *heard* it's a clockwork whale he put together for his bath.''

Denny sniggered at the notion of a grown man playing with bath toys. ''Let's do 'er,'' he said.

There were more ways into the building than by the door, and Denny knew most of them. He and Greg began their operation with him going over roof and down air-shaft, an air-shaft so narrow even he, skinny as a hoopwee, had a tight fit of it.

But the air-shaft gave on a window that was never locked; the window gave on a storeroom holding cleaning supplies, and the storeroom was shared by both the jeweler in question and his neighbor, a perfumer.

Denny opened the outer door to Greg, just as all hell broke loose on the Pile.

Greg flitted in, Denny out. Crouched in the shadows by the door he kept his eyes and ears peeled for the approach of *anyone*, blackleg or no. Innocents could make as much trouble as blacklegs if they noticed the boy in the shadows, or that the door was cracked open.

Across the canal on the Pile, torches were flaring, waving wildly; there was a clamor of young male voices, shouting, cursing. A girl's scream cut across the babble like a knife through cheese—a scream of outrage and anger, not panic, and the horse croak of a young male in pain followed it.

And Denny saw, weaving through the walkways and heading up the stairs to a second-level bridge, a string of bobbing lights, moving at the speed of a man doing a fast trot.

Blacklegs.

"Greg!" he whispered. A slim shadow flitted out the door, shutting it with agonizing care to avoid the clicking of the latch, a sound that would *carry,* even with the riot going on across the water. A bundle under Greg's arm told Denny everything he needed to know.

He grinned, as Greg took off at a trot, heading away from the Pile, to the bridge that linked Spellbridge and Yesudian. He lagged a bit; his job to guard Greg's backtrail, delay any blacklegs.

*Perfect,* he thought with exultation. *Worked this'un timed as perfect as any'f Mischa's contraptions—*

And that was when everything fell apart.

People were looking out of windows, coming out of apartments with walkway entrances, moving toward the Pile, attracted to the ruckus like skits attracted to food. He and Greg had counted on that, too—it would cover *their* trail—

An old man, looking angry, popped out of a shop door in his nightshirt, halfway between Greg and the bridge. He was holding something down by his side; Denny didn't even think about what it might be, just noted his presence and his anger, and planned to avoid him. He looked like he'd been disturbed and wasn't happy about it—he probably had a cudgel, and he'd take out his pique on anyone jostling him. A lantern carried by someone hurrying toward the fight glared up and caught the gaudy patchwork of the Chat coat Greg wore.

And the man let out an angry yell.

"You punk bastard!" he screamed, raising his hand. "Break *my* windows, will you! *I'll* give you 'protection'—"

Too late, Denny saw that what the man held was a flintlock pistol. Too late he yelled at Greg to duck.

Too late, as the pistol went off with a roar, right in Greg's astonished face. His head exploded, blood fountaining as he fell.

Denny screamed, his cry lost in the screams coming from the Pile, the screams of those around the madman and his victim. "Greg!" he shrieked, and tried to push his way toward his friend, past the people running *away* from the carnage. But something seized on him from behind, and when he struggled, hit him once, scientifically, behind the right ear, sending him into darkness.

He woke with an awful headache, in a dimly-lighted little room that smelled of whiskey, faint perfume, and greasepaint, with Rat bending anxiously over him.

"Here—" she said, helping him to struggle up, pressing a glass to his mouth. He grabbed for it—drank—coughed, his eyes watering at the strong whiskey in it.

"What happened?" Rat asked, as he took a second, more controlled swallow. "The ugliest brute I ever saw in my life dumped you at the back door. He asked for Rif, but she's not here—"

She shut her mouth with a snap at whatever it was she saw in his eyes.

He told her, anger fighting with tears, making every other word break.

She shook her head when he finished, her own eyes gone cold and indifferent. "Told you," she said, standing up and staring down at him. "I *told* you that would happen. And you know what? *Tomorrow morning nobody's going to even remember his name.*"

Denny screamed at her, rising up with clenched fists—and the only reason he didn't hit her was because he knew how much better she was. She let him shriek curses at her with her arms crossed tightly over her chest, and at the first pause, pointed to the door.

"I don't have to take that, not from you, you little punk, not in my own bedroom," she snarled coldly. "Get your ass out of here."

He didn't even remember hitting the door; the next thing he knew, he was charging down the walkways to Mondragon's, dashing hot, angry tears out of his eyes with his fists. He only slowed when he got to Petrescu because he had to talk to the gate-guard, and he *wouldn't* be crying in front of anyone, not if he died for it. So he composed himself, holding his sorrow and his rage under the tightest of masks; opened the door with his key—

Started to. The door opened at the first rattle of key in lock, and he found himself looking up at Mondragon himself.

He just stared, frozen.

"You're late," Mondragon said, grabbing his arm and hauling him inside. "You should have been back—"

*"Let me go!"* Denny snarled, voice cracking again, pulling his arm away so fast his shirtsleeve nearly tore.

Mondragon gave him a startled look, then a measuring one. He let go of Denny's arm and turned back to the door, careful to throw all the locks—and only *then* turned back to Denny.

"What happened?" he asked quietly, neutrally.

He'd told himself, over and over, that he was *not* going to tell Mondragon what had happened—not after Rat's reaction—

But Mondragon was a skillful interrogator; he couldn't resist the steady barrage of quiet questions, not when Mondragon was between him and the door. Syllable by tortured syllable, the handsome blond man dragged the night's escapade out of him, as Denny stared at the floor, smoldering sullenly, determined *not* to break down a second time. He got to know every crack and cranny of the entryway floor before it was over.

Silence. Then, "I'm sorry," Mondragon said quietly. "I'm sorry about your friend."

Denny looked up. Mondragon's face was unreadable, but his eyes were murky with thought, memory, something. He looked *past* Denny for a moment, then *at* Denny again.

"But you know very well," he said, noncommittally, "that was a *damned* fool stunt."

Denny snarled and made a dash for the stairs. Mondragon made no move to stop him. He tore up the stairs, stubbing his toes twice, getting up and resuming his run—got to Tom's bedroom and through it, not caring if Jones was in the bed—to the roof-trap and out, slamming it behind him—

And out onto the roof, into the dark, the night, the sheltering night, where he huddled beside the chimney and cried and cried and cried. . . .

Dawn brought the return of sense, the return of thought.

*Rat was right,* he thought bleakly. *She tol' me an' tol' me. Must'a bin a million times. She tol' me Greg was a fool. She tol' me 'e wouldn' see twenty. She was right. Him an' 'is ideas—"gonna be rich, gonna be famous." So what's 'e come to? Blown away 'cause some ol' fool thinks 'e's Tree. An' ain't nobody gonna remember 'im but me.*

He crouched on his haunches, both arms wrapped around his knees, rocking back and forth and shivering a little. *Ain't nobody gonna remember 'im but me. Coulda bin me. Coulda bin. Bin coastin' on m'luck, just like Greg. Only one day th' luck runs out. . . .*

He stared off across the roofs, to the steeples and turrets of the College. *Raj mebbe got it right.*

He sniffed, and rubbed his cold, tender nose on his sleeve. *What I got? What th' hell good'm I doin' fer him, fer Tom? Granther's gone an' made 'im next in line, poor fish don' even know how t' be sneaky. Just honest—an' honest could wind 'im up just as dead as Mama. There's gotta be som'thin' I kin do. There's gotta—*

His thoughts went around and around like that for some time—until he heard voices below, and saw Jones shutting the door beneath his perch, saw her hop into her skip and pole it away into a shiny patch of sun and past, into the shadows on the canal—

And knew Mondragon would be up.

He unwound himself, and crept on hands and knees to the trap door; lifted it, and let himself down into the apartment.

"I wondered if you'd gone," said a voice behind him as he dropped.

He turned. Mondragon sat on the edge of the rumpled bed, eyes half-closed, but not at all sleepy, fishy-smelling breeze coming in the open window and ruffling his hair.

"No m'ser," Denny replied uncertainly. "I—bin thinkin', m'ser."

He could *feel* Mondragon considering him from under those half-closed lids; weighing him.

"You've been thinking."

"I'm a fool, m'ser. Lucky, but—Greg was lucky for a while."

"And you saw what riding luck got him."

"Yey."

"And what do you propose to do about this revelation?"

Denny couldn't stand looking at that expressionless face. He dropped his eyes to his own feet; bare, callused, dirty, and covered with little scratches. "Dunno, m'ser," he murmured. "Jest—*you* need help, m'brother needs help—an' I dunno how—what t' do. I jest—wanna do it smart, that's all. I wanna be able t' *do* things. An' if somebody d'cides t' put a hole in me—"

He looked up again, his chin firming stubbornly, a kind of smoldering anger in the bottom of his stomach.

"—if somebody d'cides to put a hole in me, I *don't* want it t' be fer *no damn reason!*"

Mondragon licked his lips a trifle, his eyes no longer hooded. "You're asking my advice."

"Yey," Denny said. "I'm askin'. An' I'll take it. I ain't gonna be a fool no more."

"Kamat," Mondragon replied.

Denny wrinkled his nose doubtfully. "M'ser? What's Kamat got t'do—"

"Richard Kamat has been made aware of the fact that there are *two* Takahashi boys in Merovingen. It is only because of my effort and Raj's that he hasn't had his people out to bring you in, regardless of your wishes in the matter." Was that a hint of smile? If so, it was gone before Denny had a chance to identify the expression. "We persuaded him that until *you* wanted the shelter of Kamat's patronage, it would be—a less than successful venture. He continues to inquire about you. He has a very strong sense of obligation—" It *was* a hint of smile. "—has young m'ser Kamat."

"But—Raj, he wants t' be a doctor," Denny felt moved to protest. "I ain't smart, not that smart—what'm I supposed t' do?"

"What did your grandfather tell you to do?"

Denny remembered, as clearly as if he had Raj's perfect memory, the words of his Granther's note. *It is your duty to take care of Rigel; he has no talent for lying, no ability to deceive. This is not altogether bad:*

*there should be one in every generation that under-*
*stands and believes in Takahashi Honor. But those who*
*believe in the Honor need those who understand the*
*price of Honor to care for them.*

''He tol' me t' take care'f 'im.''

''Why you?''

'' 'Cause I ain't good—an' the good 'uns need bad
'uns t' watch out fer 'em.'' That may not have been
what Granther *said*, but it was what he *meant*.

''And if Raj were to become Head of Takahashi,''
Mondragon said intently, his green eyes boring into
Denny's, ''what then?''

Denny thought about Granther; clever, canny
Granther, who understood expediency—and Raj, who
did not—and shivered.

Mondragon leaned back on his pillows a little. ''So.
You see.''

Denny nodded, slowly.

''Then, young m'ser, I advise you to go to Richard
Kamat. And I advise you to ask him to train you in
the ways of business. And I further advise you to *learn*,
Deneb Takahashi. Apply yourself as devotedly as you
did to learning to pick a lock.''

''Yey, m'ser,'' Denny said, in a small, humble voice.
He turned, and started to go—then turned back for a
moment. ''M'ser—''

Mondragon simply raised one golden eyebrow.

''Yer debt still stands, m'ser. You call it in, any
time—I pay it. Roofwalkin' too.''

''That's a little foolhardy a promise—''

''No, m'ser,'' Denny interrupted bleakly. ''It
ain't. 'Cause *you* ain't no fool. Not like—some of us.''

And he picked his way carefully down the staircase,
and out the door, into the dawn sunshine.

He sat on the doorstep of Kamat for a very long time
before the doorkeeper opened the outer protective grate

for the day. The doorkeeper was a withered old man who stared at him with a pride far more in keeping with a Househead than that of a gatekeeper.

"Away with you, boy," he grated, looking down his nose as Denny scrambled to his feet, and clasped his hands behind him. "We don't need idlers or beggars. If you're looking for work, present yourself at the kitchen—"

"Pardon, m'ser," Denny interrupted, looking out of the corner of his eye at the huge pile that was Kamat, and feeling more than a little apprehensive at what he was getting himself into. "Your pardon—but—I got a message. For m'ser Kamat."

"Well?" The ancient drew himself up and sniffed disdainfully. But his disdain was short-lived.

"M'ser Mondragon sent me, m'ser. 'F it's convenient. I'm s'pposed to speak t' m'ser Richard. I'm—" He gulped, and watched the surprise flood the old man's face. "I'm Deneb Takahashi. Rigel's brother. I think m'ser Richard wants t' see me."

# POSTPARTUM BLUES

## *Chris Morris*

It was nearly noon and hot as an oven down on canalside. Kenner didn't need to check the time because Black Cal had just left Kenner's shop, and Cal rousted Kenner every day just before noon, regular as clockwork.

Kenner came around the counter, flipped the flyspecked sign in the window from "Open" to "Closed," and went into the office he'd partitioned off so he'd have a place to sit where he could take a deep breath without wondering who was watching.

He put his feet up on the sawhorse desk and leaned back, grease-blackened fingers laced behind his head. He wasn't hungry, but Jacobs would be bringing in fish and chips from one of the stands at any moment.

You couldn't get away from fish and chips in Merovingen. Kenner kept dreaming about rare steaks, two inches thick, cold in the center, with blood and fat oozing out of them.

The only way somebody with his cover could get a steak was go up to the Embassy on some pretext and sneak one in the kitchen. He was seriously considering what, among recent events, might constitute such a pretext, so that if he got his steak, he'd have the stomach to eat it. Magruder didn't like screw-ups.

Therefore, Kenner was going to need a good reason to go uptown, a reason that wouldn't sound fake to Magruder, who'd conducted his orientation personally and personally warned him that the error factor here was zero.

He hadn't told Magruder that there was no such thing as an error-free environment; if Magruder wanted zero-tolerance, you gave it to him. No quibbles about what was possible and what wasn't. When Magruder looked at you and told you that if you screwed up, you were fish food, you didn't argue. And you didn't screw up.

Since his meeting with Magruder, Kenner's orientation in Merovingen was feeling more like a trial by fire every day. He and Jacobs were working themselves silly in the machine shop, patching up ancient motors and machining new parts where old parts wouldn't fix, as well as cobbling together weed-cages for a range of standard and nonstandard propellers and crankshafts. And that was just his cover.

Every few hours some militiaman would stomp in, trying to catch him doing something wrong, or sidle in dressed like a civilian and ask him leading questions.

Didn't any of the yokels down here realize that if you were dumb enough to fall for that old trick, you wouldn't be what they suspected you were?

But the harassment gave him an opportunity to size up the opposition. He was beginning to be able to tell Anastasi's military militiamen from Tatiana's secret police, and distinguish both of those from old man Iosef's handpicked special agents—by smell if not by sight.

And then there were the real players: the College

marshals and the private stock: every House in Mero-vingen was beefing up its own guard. Private armies were as common here as religious crazies and cut-throats and thieves. Well, nobody'd said it was going to be easy, back in Nev Hettek, when he'd volun-teered.

But if Kenner did well, he'd not only cut himself a piece of the revolutionary pie down here, but maybe even catch the eye of Karl Fon back home. He'd al-ready caught Chance Magruder's attention.

Magruder was a walking textbook, a perfect master, and scary as hell. It had been a long while since any-thing or anybody scared Zack Kenner. Being caught on the wrong side of Magruder was something that happened to you only once.

Being caught between Danielle Lambert, Karl Fon's personal pick for this assignment, and Magruder's en-trenched Sword organization, hadn't been part of what Kenner'd been told to expect.

But that was what was happening here.

Magruder wanted the moon, the stars, and perfect performance. Kenner had run death squads during the revolution in Nev Hettek, and laid down the law pretty hard back then among his boys.

These were different rules, but nothing was impos-sible if doing it kept you alive and winning. Jacobs took direction well; Doctor Lambert was busy uptown with the Boregys; and he was doing what Magruder had ordered: making this machine shop indispensible to the local canalers.

They came in with their desperate eyes and clenched jaws and suspicions, and he gave them just hard enough a time to make the desperation overcome the suspicion. He fixed what needed fixing and sold them weed-cages on credit, at exorbitant interest. Nobody knew yet that, down the line, Nev Hettek would issue a public order that he forgive the debt.

All he was supposed to do was get their signatures on receipts and make them aware that, even with the interest on the time payments, Nev Hettek was doing this out of humanitarian concern for its Merovingian trading partner. Sure thing.

Well, the prices were low enough, if you paid cash. Some did. Some tried to, but in the end, couldn't. Chance Magruder knew his targets' mentality. You couldn't *give* the Merovingians anything. They were devotees of karma, and karmic debt was worse than a pauper's grave.

Weird way to run a revolution, but it seemed to be working. Everybody Kenner met was the right degree of nervous, anyhow.

Except his direct superior, Dani Lambert, who was taking everything personally or else had orders to make it seem that she was, in order to spook Magruder and see if he'd jump the wrong way.

Kenner didn't think Magruder was constitutionally capable of jumping the wrong way. Their first meeting had convinced him of that. Their second, with Dani Lambert and Michael Chamoun, Magruder's protégé, in attendance, had made him wish he hadn't come in here attached to Lambert: she was here checking up on the way Magruder was running things, and she wasn't making any secret of it.

You never really got a clear take on the way the higher-ups maneuvered. But Kenner's instinct was good, and he instinctively wanted to separate himself from Lambert, to make Magruder think of him as an asset rather than a potential liability. You couldn't survive long down here with Magruder thinking of you less than fondly, not when you were Sword of God.

When the tinkle of brass bells told Kenner that the door to the shop had opened, he didn't get up to see who it was: he was expecting Jacobs with the fish and fries for lunch.

So he just waited for his food. When it didn't immediately appear, he realized that the footsteps coming toward the office door weren't sure enough, quick enough, to be Jacobs'. Then he admitted that the cadence of the footfalls wasn't familiar. Must be some customer who couldn't read. There were enough of those here.

Kenner was just taking his boots off his desk when the door to his office swung open.

The man standing there was blond, taller than the Merovingian average, and balanced on the balls of his feet like a duelist. He was dressed in uptown clothes, not the best or the worst tailoring that Kenner had seen.

By the clothes, then, the man was probably in the shipping trade, somebody who lunched at a cafe nearby called Moghi's, that catered to a halfway respectable shopkeeper clientele. In the daytime, anyway.

Kenner said, "What can I do for you, m'ser?" as he got up and moved to the right so that the newcomer wasn't standing in the sunlight streaming in the shop window behind his back. Kenner hated being at a disadvantage—any disadvantage. Having the sun in your eyes and your enemy coming out of it was a classic mistake . . . but this wasn't an enemy, or a combat situation. Was it?

The man answered, "I'm after a propeller cage. Heard you do 'em quick." But the accent didn't ring quite true. And there was something familiar about the underlying patois, something that smacked of home.

"Well, you've come to the right place, m'ser," said Kenner, still maneuvering for position. Now he could see the fellow's face clearly. There wasn't a canaler in Merovingen with a face like that. *Aristocrat* was written all over the blond man.

Was there something familiar about the face, as well? Kenner told himself that he'd been here just long

enough that lots of Merovingians were folk he was
seeing for the second or third time.

"Come on out inta the shop. I was takin' a little
break," Kenner responded in as close to canalside
patter as he could manage.

He had a good ear for dialect. It wasn't what he'd
said or the way he said it that made the other man peer
at him with such keen interest as he slid by to lead the
way.

Out in the shop proper, Kenner felt better behind
his counter. Funny how even the flimsiest barrier can
represent rank and authority. Behind the counter, he
was the proprietor and the other guy was the customer.
Things were in balance. So what was making him nervous about the man?

Maybe his visitor was a militiaman in disguise? No,
too loose. Maybe a private guard, attached to one of
the warehousing concerns? That sounded better. Some
House security type, that must be it.

But the houses didn't need Nev Hettek relief, or
charity, or assistance. And when they were checking
him out, they didn't send their top men—at least none
had before. Again, Kenner said, "What can I do for
you? A propeller kit, is it?"

The man who looked like a Nev Hettek blueblood
gave him specifics; the boat in question wasn't a poor
man's skiff, by any means; but not a yacht, either.
Personal craft, Kenner was willing to bet.

And the guy was still looking at him with that keen-
ness that Kenner didn't like.

Just then he saw a girl, or a boy—a waif—peering
in the window, nose fogging the glass; and Jacobs,
coming back with lunch.

"Hey, Jacobs, lock the door or we'll never get to
eat that."

"Wait till I'm done, if you would," said the customer in a tone that made Jacobs scurry by into the office, leaving the door not only unlocked, but ajar.

"That'll be . . . say . . . ten sols, cash on the barrel," Kenner said, testing the waters. "Or we can arrange credit with a downpayment. . . ?" If this fellow needed time payments, Kenner needed his eyes examined.

"How about half now and half on delivery?" said the blond man, watching him as if Kenner might go for a weapon at any second. He had one, a Nev Hettek ten millimeter revolver tucked against his spine. But it was his fail-safe, and nothing happening here was justifying Kenner's instinct that he was failing, somehow.

"No problem," Kenner said, and got out his sales book. He wrote up the order specs, flipped the pad around, and shoved it toward the customer. Find out whether the guy could read, anyhow. "If it's right, just write your name on the top line there, and an address where you can be reached."

The man took the pencil lying on the counter and said, as he scribbled, "You won't need to reach me. Tell me when it'll be ready and I'll bring the boat down. That way, if there's anything wrong, we can fix it on the spot."

The customer handed the sales book back. On it, in a clear, precise hand, was written, *Thomas Mondragon, c/o Richard Kamat/South Bank.*

Kenner actually blinked at what he saw there, and read it again. Then he looked up, at his customer's face. *Thomas Mondragon?* Bold as brass and in the flesh, staring back at him. Did Mondragon recognize him, when he hadn't had a clue to the other man's identity? Five years in a Nev Hettek prison could change you. . . .

Mondragon said, "Now if you'll sign where it says 'Received,' I'll give you five sols in cash and be on my way."

Kenner wasn't using an alias; his orders had been clear on that. Everybody who was anybody in Nev Hettek had been a revolutionary player; command didn't want to take any unnecessary risks. In case of just this sort of situation.

He signed his name, not bothering to scrawl any more illegibly than usual, tore off a copy for Mondragon, and took the sols the other man counted out.

Well, now he had a reason to go up to the Embassy and get that steak. Only he'd just lost his appetite.

*Had* Mondragon recognized him, by face, name or reputation? You couldn't assume otherwise. And if so, so what?

Only Magruder was in a position to assess the damage, if any, since Mondragon was cool as a winter evening when he left, just folding the receipt and pocketing it as he said, "See you at the end of the week, m'ser Kenner."

When Mondragon was gone, so was the waif at the window, and every shred of Kenner's composure.

He didn't even bother to explain things to Jacobs, just called, "I'm going up to the Embassy; don't know when I'll be back. Close up at the usual time."

Like there was anything usual about Merovingen. Or about completing a polite transaction with one of his country's most wanted criminals. If he'd been anywhere else, he'd have shot Tom Mondragon on the spot.

Only here, he couldn't. If Mondragon was supposed to be dead, Magruder would have gotten the job done long before Mondragon had showed up at Kenner's little shop.

Wouldn't he?

With belated doubt gnawing at his innards that maybe he should have killed the criminal when he'd had the chance, Kenner made his way uptown, to the

Embassy, to sit around and wait for Magruder to make time for him.

Cassie Boregy knew that her husband was Sword of God. She'd seen it in a vision, and her visions were always true. Or at least, they always had seemed true. She'd seen her baby dead, but she had her baby, live and in her arms. So maybe Michael wasn't Sword of God.

If Michael wasn't her enemy, then neither was Danielle Lambert, the obstetrician. But she knew the doctor was her enemy, because the doctor was the one who wouldn't let Daddy give her any deathangel. And she really needed deathangel now, to see through the fog to the truth of things as she lay in her bed with her baby in her arms.

Her baby had hazel eyes; Michael's eyes were lighter than hers. She didn't know why Baby Belle shouldn't have hazel eyes, but she shouldn't.

It wasn't that she didn't love her baby. It was that she needed deathangel. She kept asking for Uncle Ito, but he never came. She'd stare at the cherubs on her wall and yell for Ito at the top of her lungs, but it was always Michael, or Doctor Lambert, or Daddy who came.

But this time, when she yelled for Ito and the baby started screaming so that she had to suckle Belle to shut her up, it was Mikhail Kalugin who came.

Mikhail the Clockmaker came tiptoeing in, smiling his self-effacing smile, his head down and his eyes demurely averted from her exposed breast, asking if he was disturbing her.

"You never disturb me, Mikhail," she lied. She always lied to Mikhail. She'd started lying to Mikhail because Uncle Ito had told her she must, it was necessary for everyone's security. She prophesied in private for Mikhail, telling him what Uncle Ito wanted her to tell him, and Mikhail would look at her with adoring eyes and nod his narrow head and eat up every word.

She really liked Mikhail. She hated to lie to him. In fact, right now she liked him more than Michael. Michael. Mikhail. Maybe karma was trying to tell her something: the right name, the wrong man? But wrong for what?

"Mikhail," she said, pushing herself awkwardly up on her pillows with one arm, the baby clamped to her with the other. "Mikhail, are we the best of friends?"

"Of course, Cassie. I've always told you so. You're the light in my darkness. You and your gift have made my life worth living once again. Even my father's happy with me now, since you've shown me that it's my destiny to take a hand in steering Merovingen toward a new future . . ."

She nodded, trying to focus her eyes on his face. She felt so terrible. What could she say to Mikhail. . . ? The truth was something he deserved from her: "Mikhail, I need a friend now as I've never needed one." The baby gurgled against her breast, pinching her nipple and slobbering so that milk and spit ran down her teat. Why didn't she like being a mother? Why did the baby have to be such a brat?

"You have my friendship forever, dearest Cassie," said Mikhail. She held out her free hand and he took it gratefully, stroking it as if it were something precious.

"Then I must ask your help, and your silence. If you can't help me, you'll tell no one what I ask. Agreed?"

"Agreed, light of Merovingen."

"I feel terrible," she said, and saying it made her want to weep. Her voice thickened. "I've been brave, and I've given everything to everybody, not asking anything for myself, prophesying until it endangered my life and my baby's . . .'' She sniffled.

"Cassie, dear Cassie, what can I do to help?''

"I hate my doctor. I don't trust her. I want a Merovingian doctor.''

"I can understand that,'' Mikhail said, squeezing the hand he held. "I'll talk to Vega.''

"My doctor won't let me have any deathangel, Mikhail, and I've been taking it so long, I need it to get my strength back. Maybe I should stop, but not right now. My doctor's a stranger, she doesn't understand our ways. And she doesn't believe in my Gift. So she's trying to control everything, and she's wrong. I need my deathangel, and I need it now, Mikhail. Can you get me some, without anyone finding out? Doctor Lambert has everyone, including Daddy, frightened to give me any. And nobody will let me see Uncle Ito in private. I want to see Uncle Ito, Mikhail, and I want my deathangel.'' She took a deep breath. "Or something terrible is going to happen.''

"What, Cassie? What's going to happen?'' Mikhail wanted to know.

"Something terrible,'' she pronounced. "I can't see clearly without my deathangel, not right now. I must have it, Mikhail. And I must see Uncle Ito. And I must have a Merovingen physician. I'm afraid Doctor Lambert . . . is our enemy. If she is, and she's here to stop my prophecies before I can save Merovingen from the flames, I'll not be able to stop her on my own. Not while I'm so weak. Not without my deathangel. Not without Uncle Ito. Not without your help, Mikhail.''

"Of course I'll help you, Cassiopeia.'' Mikhail sat up and took a deep breath, thrusting out his pigeon breast. "But what about your husband?'' Can't he—''

"Michael,'' she reminded Mikhail archly, "is a Nev

Hetteker. He'll never believe that Doctor Lambert is my enemy. He helped bring her here.''

"Of course, I forgot. And I hear what you are not saying, my dearest and most revered Cassiopeia.'' Mikhail's eyes were shining like buttons. "I'll see to things, never fear. First I'll go to my father and when I've explained—''

*"No!"* *Idiot!* She'd forgotten how dim Mikhail could be. "First, my deathangel. Find some for me. Bring it here yourself. As soon as you can. Then I'll be able to help you plan a way to get this woman out of my house before she destroys everything.''

"I don't know where to find . . .''

"I'll be able to prophesy again, Mikhail. Just for you. Like old times. Please, Mikhail . . .'' She let a tear leak from her eye, a real tear of frustration. Couldn't this foolish but powerful man just once do something right?

"All right, Cassie. I'll do it. For you and young Belle, and for all of us.''

Mikhail put her hand gently on her coverlet, leaned down and kissed her on the forehead as he'd never before dared to do, and then straightened.

His steps seemed more certain as he left the room, his shoulders straighter. His chin jutted, firm with purpose.

Cassie Boregy slumped back against her pillow and pulled Belle's mouth from her sore nipple. Little succubus. She itched all over; she was sweating, alternately hot and cold, and she had a baby to deal with. She reached blindly up beside her and grabbed the bellpull.

Let the wet nurse come, even if that wet nurse was precisely the woman she least wanted to see—her Nev Hetteker physician, who'd evidently lost her own baby just before leaving Nev Hettek and had valiantly offered to suckle little Belle.

Cassie had refused, of course, precisely because the obstetrician didn't want Cassie suckling Belle. Since Cassie was a drug addict, the baby was, too, according to the doctor, who'd first suggested bottle feeding and then offered her own alien tit.

Well, the baby wasn't looking half so sick as Cassie felt. The baby didn't seem to be sharing any of Cassie's symptoms. But then, the doctor was giving the baby medication she wouldn't give Cassie, because she didn't trust Cassie to follow her doctor's orders.

The woman wasn't stupid, but she was an enemy. Cassie Boregy had been prophesying too long and too accurately not to know an enemy when she saw one. If only Daddy would believe her.

If only she could trust Michael. She loved Michael, she told herself, that was why she couldn't bring herself to declare him an enemy wholeheartedly. And no matter what he was, he was the father of her child and a hero, in a previous life, of the war against the sharrh. If everyone wasn't so jealous of her Gift, none of this would be happening to her.

She was going to be a hero in the next war against the sharrh. She just knew she was.

She knew it as certainly as she knew that the fires of her vision would rise up from Merovingen-below in a cleansing blaze that only the strong would survive.

She intended to be one of the strong. Even though she'd seen in one of her visions that her husband would murder her, she intended to change the future. After all, her baby was alive, and she'd been sure it would be born dead.

So the future could be changed, if you had enough deathangel and enough good karma.

Better not tell Mikhail Kalugin that, she thought, and giggled as, beside her, the hungry baby lifted its searching hands and began in earnest to cry.

When Doctor Lambert came to nurse the baby, Cassie was going to tell her straight out that Mikhail Kalugin was on Cassie's side, that Doctor Lambert couldn't keep Uncle Ito away from her, or keep her deathangel away from her. After all, you had to put these foreigners in their place.

Didn't you?

She told herself that Daddy would be proud of her, when the smoke cleared, for acting like a true Boregy, the way Daddy had taught her.

Tuesday just wasn't going to be Magruder's day, that was certain.

First he'd come back from an unsatisfactory lunch with Tatiana's father, during which Iosef had ranted about some female cardinal named Exeter who was stirring up Iosef's own Loyalist party, and what that might mean. The only thing Chance Magruder had learned about this internecine squabbling in the Council was that Iosef felt threatened. And, feeling threatened, was doing some threatening himself: Magruder and Tatiana had better make sure that there was not the slightest morsel of potential scandal in anything the two were doing, or Iosef would Take Steps.

Magruder had been put on notice to keep his Nev Hettekers squeaky clean for the time being, or Tatiana and the Nev Hettek/Merovingen alliance and, most especially, Chance Magruder would suffer for it.

He'd come back from the Rock wondering just how much the old man knew and how much was a fishing expedition. And there was Kenner, waiting for him in the kitchen, for godsake, hunched over the remains of a steak dinner.

Still chasing inferences squeezed from Iosef Kalugin's masterful display of implication and innuendo, the sight of Kenner made his mouth go sour. The last thing Magruder needed was a petty crisis right now.

Keep his Nev Hettekers squeaky clean. How about

fly to the sun on wax-and-feather wings? Or dump enough herbicide in the canals to solve the problem that Iosef was having with Exeter, send Kenner and Lambert back to Karl Fon because he'd then have no explicit need for either, and let Cassie Boregy raise Dani Lambert's baby on deathangel milkshakes.

If Iosef pushed Magruder hard enough, he was going to do just that, he decided, as Kenner followed him up the back stairs to his office. The possibility of using an herbicide was something Magruder had reported to Fon; that was what Jacobs was doing in Kenner's fix-it shop: waiting for Magruder to give a dump order, or not.

Meanwhile, there was Kenner's problem, which turned out to be infuriatingly nebulous when the young Sword agent finally blurted it out:

"Tom Mondragon came down to the shop at noon and ordered a weed-cage from me," said Kenner, arms crossed, jaw locked, his hair stirring in the afternoon breeze and his eyes looking way past Magruder, out over the rooftops of White and Boucher to where you could see the Signeury spire from here.

"So?" said Magruder softly. The Signeury. The Justiciary. His mind's eye saw the interrogation cells everyone knew were there. *Go carefully.* On a day full of too many questions and too few answers, he didn't need even one more problem. Dani hadn't bothered to send a note back when he'd sent a messenger over there to inquire politely how she was faring. . . . Tom Mondragon was the least of his worries. Or should be.

Kenner turned on the balcony, hands curling on the balustrade, and looked Magruder right in the eye. "So what's it mean, if he's recognized me? I can't judge the situation, sir . . . m'ser. What— How come that bastard's still alive, anyhow?"

Magruder's world hiccoughed, then settled. He said, "Mondragon's alive because he's no use to us dead."

''So he's one of ours?'' There was incredulity in Kenner's voice.

The agent was Dani's creature, Magruder reminded himself. It was just hard to think of Dani as an enemy. But the baby had changed everything—maybe changed things Chance Magruder wasn't capable of analyzing.

''He's useful, at times. Right now I think he's Richard Kamat's. Probably others.'' He considered, finally handed over a tidbit of information. ''That big boat on Pardee Isle. That's his. He's watching you. You're strangers. He may have recognized you.''

''Kamat fits with what he wrote on his charge slip.''

*And if he's Kamat's, he's working with Anastasi Kalugin, kid. But you're too green here to understand what that means.* ''Again: so?''

''So, —do I expect a midnight hit? Who's Kamat? Do I give him the weed-cage, then? If he's ours, am I supposed to help the son of a bitch?''

''You're supposed to keep your cover wrinkle-free. If there's a step-up in harassment from the blacklegs, let me know, that's all. There's nothing Mondragon's going to pick up. Let him look.''

''That's all? What am I supposed to tell Lambert?''

''Whatever you choose.''

''I mean, what's the official line about this guy? Is he actively . . . useful . . . to the revolution? Am I going to be acting as a drop for him, or what?''

''Look, Kenner, it's not that way here. Not cut and dried. If and when I want to do something about Mondragon, I'll make sure you've got point. That's what you want, right? To be the executioner if the order comes down?''

''I . . . yeah, that's what I want. You mean I'm overreacting?''

''Everybody sees things in terms of his specialty, Kenner. Assassination isn't always the answer to a problem like Mondragon.'' *Tell Dani I'm mellowing, if you like. Or losing my edge, which is probably what you think you see. But I've got too much on my plate to make room for Tom Mondragon right now.* "You just keep doing what you're doing. Sell the fool a weed-cage if that's what he wants. Same terms as for anybody else."

Kenner knew when to quit. The younger man started to back away, mumbling that he was glad he'd come up and reported it, anyway, and that he'd keep Magruder informed, when the door to the balcony opened and Michael Chamoun came bursting through it.

"Michael, you remember Zack Kenner," Magruder said as if he'd been expecting Chamoun.

In a way, he had been: nobody but Michael could have gotten into Chance's office without an appointment; none of Magruder's staffers would have interrupted a balcony conference. So it had to be him.

But Chamoun didn't have to be this drunk, not while it was still daylight. Or this upset, not where Kenner could see.

As if reading Magruder's mind, Chamoun said, "Kenner, maybe you'd better forget you saw me here."

Nice thought, but highly unlikely. Chamoun wiped his lips with the back of his hand, stalked by the two of them stiff-legged, and braced his hands on the railing, looking down and away.

So Magruder had to say, "Kenner, why don't you stay. From the look on Mike's face, maybe we'll be able to use some of that special expertise of yours, after all."

Magruder's mind was racing toward a plan built of accident and tactics: Whatever Michael had on his mind, the only safe move now was to involve Kenner in its solution. He couldn't have Kenner running back to Dani saying that Chamoun was out of control, or that Magruder was losing his focus, or his grip.

''Yes, m'ser,'' said Kenner, and stepped back to lean against the building and wait, ready and able.

*Okay, hotblood, let's find something that'll cool you off.* The Kenners of the world thrived on action; without it, they became dangerous to themselves and those who thought to command them. The last thing you wanted was somebody named Kenner doing any thinking on his own. Or going to Dani with questions.

Merovingen was awash in questions, and answers were at a premium. Maybe it was time to field some of the solutions that Kenner could offer.

''Michael, let's hear it: what's wrong?''

Chamoun turned his head like an animal in a trap who sees his torturer approaching. ''She's way out of hand: Cassie. Mikhail was over to see her today, and she told him to get her deathangel, and tell Ito she wanted to see him. I know because Lambert's having a fit. She *sent* me over here to tell you to do something.''

''All right. Calm down.'' *That's not what's bothering you, sonny. We've been together too long for that sort of fabrication to fly with me.* Kenner was another matter. The languid eyes of the Nev Hetteker assassin rested on Chamoun as if Mike were a target. ''Did you get drunk with Dani, too?''

''Nope.'' Chamoun took a breath and turned all the way around. ''Chance, this baby swap thing's messing everybody's head around. I can't handle it. Lambert's way out of bounds, pushing the household around like she owns the place, issuing ultimata . . .''

*Thanks, kid. You just earned your keep.* Magruder slid a glance off Kenner. No expression. But the data was having an impact, Magruder would be willing to bet.

Would bet. ''We'll do something about it,'' Magruder promised.

''What?'' Chamoun wanted to know. His voice was

thick; every muscle in his body as knotted as if he were about to spring at Magruder. "Fight or flight," they called that set of reactions in training courses. Once those reactions set in, you had to flush the stimuli or vent the system, some way.

"I think it's time you and Kenner went out on a night mission together, anyhow. Bonding, and all. And it's surely time we put an end to Ito's meddling. Permanently."

"Chance!" Chamoun was aghast.

Kenner stood up straight, not saying anything, but watching him now with a clear demand for clarification in those killer's eyes.

"Look: It's Ito that got us into this mess, pumping Cassie full of drugs. If he mixes in and spots Dani as a plant, the whole charade could come apart. It's bad enough that Ito pushed Cassie so hard, forced so many dope-induced prophecies, that your real baby was stillborn . . ."

Chamoun shivered visibly. Kenner picked at a hangnail.

9Magruder continued: "We can't have Ito and Dani clashing over the healthy baby you've got, or over Cassie, or over deathangel. Do you concur, Michael?"

That brought Chamoun's head up. "Yes, but . . . how?"

A half-smile flickered over Kenner's lips and his eyes sought the rooftops.

"Let's take Ito out. Tonight if we can. Soonest. The two of you ought to be able to handle it. Zack, Michael knows the College better than I do. You two find your own ways and means. I'm late for another meeting. . . ."

He'd left them to hash out their assassination plot, headed for a fictional meeting. Never thinking that Dani would dare show up at the embassy with her baby—with Cassie's baby—in tow.

And then Magruder had been sure that this was his unlucky day. Danielle Lambert was fire-eyed and white-lipped and clutching the baby to her breast.

And she was furious with him. She wasn't going to put up with this. Poor little Hope was going to be turned into a drug addict. It was all Chance's fault. Didn't he care about the baby? Didn't he care about her? Didn't he have any self-respect?

She paused for breath and he said, "Don't you want to stay alive? Don't you want the baby to live? Don't you care about the mission? About making Karl happy? About not spending the rest of your life in a Merovingen dungeon for murdering the actual child, for the swap, for trying to overthrow the local government, for any number of—"

Danielle Lambert closed her eyes. She didn't cry. She didn't say anything. She bounced the baby against her belly in silence. At last she said, "Chance, I'm not taking Hope back into that den of dope fiends until you promise me you'll do something."

"What, Dani, would you like me to do?" The exasperation in his voice was coupled with honest enquiry. He had no idea what to do to make Dani's conscience easier, or her life bearable, or her fears liveable. He flat didn't know why an experienced professional would do something as stupid as bringing that baby here.

Kidnapping wasn't a petty crime in Merovingen.

"Something," she whispered almost inaudibly, then suddenly came toward him, holding out the baby for him to take. "Hold her. Hold her and look into her eyes and tell me you think we should give her back to that spoiled hop-head."

He couldn't refuse to take the baby. It was warm and its bottom was moist and he wondered if it was wet. It was sleeping. *She* was sleeping. Through all that, and it slept still.

"I'll do something," he promised. "You take the baby back to Boregy House before they have the blacklegs out looking for both of you."

"No." She came forward to snatch the baby back.

He let her, relieved. He looked past her, because he couldn't look her in the eye, and nothing in his office seemed familiar, suddenly.

"Yes," he said. "I insist. I'll work on your problem. If you can't handle it, staying there, stay here. I asked you before. . . ."

She wasn't listening. She had her face down by the baby's, her nose against its nose, and she was crooning to it. He thought he heard the word *Daddy*.

He wasn't going to ask. "Did you hear me, Danielle?"

"I heard you." She raised her head. "You're a bastard, Chance Magruder. Before I take Hope back into that dope den, I want to know what you're going to do about the way they're treating her. And about Cassie. I sent Mike Chamoun over here hours ago, so don't tell me you weren't aware, or—"

"Dani, you don't want to know what I'm doing. But I am doing something. Now, you're staying here after tonight. Tonight you stay at Boregy House, tell them you're coming back here in the morning. Cite the fact that you and Cassie aren't getting along. Say you'll oversee a College physician, but you don't want to—"

"So Chamoun did come to you."

"We're working on a solution that you can't be involved with, not in any way. And you've got to keep in mind that it's to Nev Hettek's benefit to keep Cassie prophesying fiery revolt. So we go carefully, agreed?"

Her pause was too long, her assent hardly more than a sigh: "Agreed."

"Dani, I'm worried about you. You're too personally involved in this. I—"

"Personally involved?" She stepped back and her

eyes widened. "How could I not be? Don't you understand what you made me do? This child is—"

In his turn, he interrupted, before she could say "yours," or "ours," or anything that might be worse. It didn't matter. It was easier to tell himself so, as long as he didn't have to know the rest.

"Go back to Boregy House. Tell them you'll be moving into the embassy tomorrow. Be nice to Vega. Make yourself very conspicuous this evening. You'll have to write up a regimen for Cassie and the baby, at the very least. . . ."

Dani Lambert was backing away from him, toward the door. "You still don't understand. The baby isn't addicted enough to pass muster, not by another physician. You're asking me to give my child drugs, or risk her being found out as an imposter, possibly killed—"

"You're overreacting. Overstating." *Postpartum blues.* "Go back to Boregy House. Have dinner with the family. Let Vega know you're concerned, but not distraught. Put Cassie's welfare first, with him. And stay up late where everybody can see you, at least until after midnight."

She knew better than to ask any more questions. She left him without another word, her whole body telling him that she'd never forgive him for this.

Well, he could live with that. As long as she lived through this. As long as the switch held and they all lived through this.

Damn, why couldn't Dani behave like the professional she was?

For hours after, he kept seeing the indictment on her face. Finally, he gave up pretending he didn't care, and sent a messenger over to Boregy House asking if he might drop over to see Vega later that evening.

Might as well have the best alibi he could concoct tonight. Then he sent somebody to Tatiana to see if she'd join them. No use in leaving her out of the fun, or out in the cold where Anastasi might find a way to lay Ito's murder at her door.

Then and only then was his mind clear enough that he began asking himself what Tom Mondragon wanted with a boat. Like so many other questions this summer in Merovingen, meditation led to no answers, only more questions.

Dani Lambert was tucking her baby into bed beside Cassie Boregy when a knock came on the bedroom door.

She put a hand to the small of her back when she straightened up. She wasn't going to be able to have another baby; her professional assessment was clear on that point.

Now that she'd made a fool of herself, she felt empty, drained, clumsy and flushed, almost as if she'd been crying.

But you didn't cry in her business. Not in either of her businesses.

She went to the door and opened it.

Mikhail Kalugin was standing there, a daft grin on his face and a big, ornate clock cradled in his arms, a pink bow upon it. "Is Cassie awake?" Mikhail, on tiptoe now, craned his neck to see beyond Dani.

"It's time for them both to rest. I've given Cassie a mild sedative . . ."

"Mikhail," croaked Cassiopeia Boregy. "Is that you, Mikhail?"

"Yes, Treasure, it's me. With a present, just the way I promised."

"Cassie," Dani said, still blocking Kalugin's path. "You've got to rest."

"See, Mikhail?" Cassie Boregy struggled up in her bed. "See what I told you?" She turned to Dani: "Get out of here, foreigner. Get out of here while I speak with my countryman!''

''In a moment,'' Dani said. ''May I see that beautiful clock, m'ser Kalugin? You make the finest clocks in Merovingen, so I've heard.'' Still, she barred his way, her feet planted firmly in the doorway.

''Uh . . . Yes, surely. But don't disturb the bow. It's a gift for our wondrous mother . . . and her child, of course.''

Dani's suspicion wasn't based on anything concrete. It was a mixture of Cassie's earlier threats, current demeanor, and something . . . sneaky . . . in Mikhail's face. He reminded her of a boy who'd just smuggled a frog into class.

So she looked at the clock, at its fine ivory face and its carved hands. It was a large clock with a wooden case. And its second hand wasn't moving. She turned it around and heard Mikhail say, ''No! Don't.''

So she did.

She opened the back of the clock, where the workings were, and there it was. A packet of deathangel.

She ripped it out of the cavity, tape and all, and then handed the clock back to Mikhail, shoving it against his chest.

''M'ser, I'm disappointed in you,'' she said as severely as a schoolmarm. ''If you'll come with me, I think m'ser Vega will want to speak to you. And to see what you've brought his daughter.''

She was afraid as she said that. She was more afraid than she'd ever been. This was the son and heir of Iosef Kalugin. She wasn't underestimating her peril. But she had to bull her way through this. The only way to do that was to be authoritative, pejorative, and assume that her instructions would be followed.

She strode past Kalugin, who skittered out of her way, and started down the stairs. ''Come along, m'ser,'' she said in a loud and angry voice.

And, wonder of wonders, the clockmaker followed her, despite the muddled calls of Cassie Boregy, sedated in her bedroom with little Hope cradled by her side.

Vega Boregy had given up on the evening being pleasant. It would be enough were it survivable.

The Nev Hetteker doctor didn't realize, when she brought Mikhail Kalugin down to his study, for all the world like a teacher dragging a student by the ear to his principal, what a can of worms she'd opened thereby.

No sooner had he smoothed things over with Mikhail, pretending that Mikhail had been ignorant of the orders surrounding Cassie's deathangel addiction, than Lambert announced her intention to leave in the morning.

"I can't stay here, with my orders being subverted, my integrity questioned, and my foreign provenance becoming an issue. If I weren't bound by higher standards than I've seen in Merovingen, I'd tell you to get yourself another doctor, m'ser. But since I am, I'll offer this solution: I'll take up residence at the embassy, beginning tomorrow morning, where I'll be available to consult with whatever College physician you engage. I'll want to examine Cassie and the baby myself at least once a week: their health comes first. But under the circumstances, I can no longer live under your roof, although I thank you for your hospitality."

The woman sat down after she'd made her speech, trembling and pale.

The passion in her was fierce and Vega didn't understand that. He went to the marble mantlepiece in his study and stroked the stone.

"We appreciate your feelings, your commitment,

and we sympathize with your difficulties. We also think you're overwrought. Won't you reconsider?''

He was relieved when she declined. Perhaps one less foreigner under his roof was the answer. Perhaps he was getting rid of the wrong foreigner. If not for young Chamoun, none of this would have happened. It was Chamoun whom Ito had introduced to deathangel and regressions, beginning all that had led them to this point in time.

But he had a healthy granddaughter, no matter the whispers and doubts as to how that was possible. And he had a daughter being cleansed of drugs, which was a relief.

Letting the College use Cassie to prophesy their paranoid rabble-rousing claptrap had never been his choice. Perhaps now it would stop.

He told Lambert, "We're having rather an impromtu late supper this evening. Quite a gathering, actually. We hope you'll join us."

"Ah . . . I don't know that I have the right clothes, seeing as you dress for dinner, but I'd be honored." The Nev Hetteker still had not recovered from her outburst.

It showed some sense of decorum, that she was so abashed. Vega would be magnanimous. "We'll find you something of Cassie's, or perhaps Marina Kamat, who's joining us, will have something suitable. I'll send a runner. Meanwhile, get some rest, Doctor Lambert. If we work you to death, your kind Nev Hettek sponsors will take offense."

The woman stood up, composed now and aware that she was being dismissed. As she reached the door, she asked, "Would you mind telling me who the other guests are?"

"Surely: Your Ambassador, the Secretary, Richard Kamat and his sister, and Iosef Kalugin. Quite a stellar assemblage."

The doctor stiffened, then relaxed, as if some names had been unpleasant to her ears, and others pleasant.

Nev Hettekers had a roughness to them that Vega often mistook for guile. He was, truly, grateful to this woman. He was also aware that he would be giving her a chance to defend her actions to Mikhail Kalugin's father, Iosef. Perhaps she was, too.

It wasn't often that foreigners dined at Boregy House—with the exception of his son-in-law, Michael, who had other plans this evening. At least, it hadn't been, until Doctor Lambert had come to stay with them.

He was secretly pleased to see her go. Cassie hated her, and her presence had become a bone of contention with Ito, who refused to set foot in Boregy House until the Nev Hetteker was gone.

Someday, things would change. But now, Vega must deal with parochial attitudes on every side. This was part of the price he paid for spearheading a merger between Nev Hettek and Merovingen.

He wished he found it easier to accept the foreigners' ways: the woman's outrageous treatment of Mikhail Kalugin; Chance Magruder's casual message, in which he invited not only himself, but Tatiana Kalugin, to dinner at Boregy House.

At least, he consoled himself as the woman left his study and he let the smile drop from his dry lips—at least he didn't have to sit through an entire evening with Mikhail as one of his dinner partners.

That would have been simply too much to suffer.

And, for one more night, upstairs, his daughter was sleeping peacefully, free of deathangel dreams.

Considering his worst fears, this evening could rank as a celebration of nightmares that hadn't come to pass.

He determined to make it so, and called the major domo to confer with him on the widening guest list and an augmented menu.

* * *

The night was pitch black; the stars were occluded by clouds.

Kenner had to assume that Chamoun knew what he was doing. Instead of climbing the College walls, they'd walked right in, using identification belonging to somebody named Rog Takahashi, or some such.

An older brother showing a younger brother his school. Evidently, it wasn't that unusual. Or it wasn't flagged, at any rate.

The place was huge. The cloak he had on to conceal his weapons and shadow his features was hot. He kept up with Chamoun easily, yet the other man was breathing hard.

Nerves. Nerves could get you killed in a situation like this. They climbed stairs and stairs and more stairs. They went down corridors and, at one point, across a suspension bridge, badly lit, open to the air.

Then through another door where names were asked and aliases given.

Down more corridors. Up more stairs. Here the smell of incense was heavy and you could hear singing, or chanting, and the smoke of candles stung your eyes.

Kenner checked his weapons. He wasn't to use his pistol unless it was absolutely necessary. He had the weapon of choice, a Nippon-style dagger made of fine steel refolded five hundred times. Whoever had owned it, hadn't given it up without a fight.

But it was good for this mission. Suspicion was obviously going to land somewhere, upon someone, that Chamoun had targeted for the privilege. Or that Magruder had.

They passed unremarked through a group of men in robes. Like certain buildings in Nev Hettek, if you were this far inside, you belonged here. No one questioned you. No one stared.

Their feet made hardly a sound in rope-soled sandals.

When Chamoun stopped and knocked loudly on a stout door, it startled Kenner, flooding his system with adrenaline.

"Ready?" Chamoun said, his teeth gleaming white as he smiled in his hood.

This guy was still a little drunk, and filled with wrath. You usually didn't take somebody this involved on a kill. But Kenner was under orders.

The door opened, and a man stood there. The man was old and fat and jeweled. He was in a velvet robe and he frowned. "Yes?"

"Cardinal Ito," said Chamoun. That was all.

It was the confirmation Kenner had been waiting for.

He moved forward, the blade in his hand, and slit the old man's throat in his own doorway. The move was one that mimicked an embrace.

Once the throat was slit, Kenner didn't care how long the killing was going to take. He just didn't want his victim to cry out.

Ito obligingly stepped back one pace, two. Kenner followed. Chamoun was hissing at him to watch the blood on the floor.

Blood streamed down Ito's vestments. His mouth opened and closed. He clutched his throat and turned, and that was Kenner's first, best chance in the distended time of the murder cycle.

He reached up, grabbed Ito by the hair, and slashed across the back of the old man's neck. He felt the bone grate against the blade, snap as he pulled back on the hair he held.

He pushed the corpse forward with his knee in its back, and retreated, looking critically at the trail of blood. Nearly all was within the room. He dropped the incriminating weapon from his gloved hand, just inside the doorway.

The little bit of blood on the threshold should be covered by the door when Chamoun shut it.

They walked down the hallway, silent but for Chamoun's breathing, and turned a corner. Then another. Then another.

Suddenly Chamoun grabbed him by the elbow and jerked him into an alcove. In it was a door.

They opened it, and hot night air caressed Kenner's flushed face.

Now it was he, not Chamoun, who was breathing hard. He blinked into the night. Out there was freedom, another spidery bridge, a canal below.

Safety.

He didn't wait for Chamoun to urge him to hurry.

Behind them, all was silent, all was peaceful.

As they crossed the bridge, they dropped their robes into the canal. From the College, the bells tolled midnight.

# SEEDS OF DESTRUCTION
# (REPRISED)

*C.J. Cherryh*

The black boat glided under the jaws of the College water-gate, and the shadow passed over Richard Kamat like doom—shadow despite the glow of a garde-porte grating in the shape of the Wheel of Life.

A man didn't like to wake to a message like that—a knock in the night and a visitor who frightened his way past the servant at Kamat's water-gate; a black-cloaked visitor who said simply, "M'ser Kamat, have you a cloak with a hood? I advise you wear it."

The door opened, filled with shadow-figures against a gold glare of lamplight as the boat glided in, bumped gently into the buffers and the boatman/priest jumped ashore in a swirl of black cloth. Richard stood up cautiously, feeling the wobble in his knees—expecting he was not sure what, except the messenger assured him it was only secrecy the cardinal had in mind.

"M'ser." The attendants were courteous, deferential. Richard walked up into the light, into the musty, incense-laden air of the Ecclesiastical Wing of the College, followed the lead of the servants, wondering if he was going to leave this place—or what would become of Kamat if he didn't, or what his chances had been of declining this invitation.

It was too late for what-ifs.

They climbed the stairs to a residential floor. They passed solemn statuary, intricate murals, ornate columns. The servants opened a door for him, and let him into a room where Cardinal Exeter waited behind a desk.

With a short-sword under her hands.

"Cardinal Boregy is dead," she said. "Murdered." She gathered up the sword and pulled it halfway from its black sheath.

A Takahashi blade.

Richard felt his knees go to water. He said, calmly, "Your Eminence, how can I be of help?"

"You know this?"

"Takahashi."

"The murder weapon."

"Nothing from my House, I assure you. Nothing from Takahashi."

But he was thinking about Mondragon, who had such a blade.

"You know nothing about it."

"I assure you, Your Eminence."

Exeter stared at him a long, long moment, while the sweat trickled on his sides. She slid the sword into its sheath. Click.

She extended it to him one-handed. "Take it."

He took it. His hand was shaking.

"I don't know who did it," Exeter said, "yet. But I will. I do know who didn't."

"Your Eminence?"

"Kamat. Takahashi. Leaving that—" She gestured to the sword he held. "—would be stupid. Neither Kamat nor Takahashi would be stupid. Whoever killed His Eminence is either your enemy or Takahashi's."

"Thank you," Richard breathed, and bowed. "Thank you, Your Eminence."

"Fools are an abomination," Exeter said. "Good night, my son."

"Good night, Your Eminence."

The door closed.

Willa stared at infinity, a moment, then picked up a pen, dipped it, and wrote: *I regret to announce—*

Regret, hell.

Kamat owed her major karma. Takahashi did. Even Adventists understood *that* kind of karma. Takahasi's grandson was in her reach and she gave the blade to his guardian. Takahashi would get the message.

She had thought of accusing specific agencies— Janist agents, Sharrists,—the Sword of God.

But she moved into Boregy's chair—and from that perspective, with real power to wield, a wider investigation was much more to her advantage.

*—at the hands of some person, whether acting independently or with others, this Holy Office will seek to determine by inquiry . . .*

# POSTPARTUM BLUES (REPRISED)

## *Chris Morris*

Tatiana had left the Boregys' with Chance and spent the night at the embassy, so she was still there when the College functionaries made their belated discovery.

Magruder had slept fitfully, waiting for the alarm that didn't come until the sun rose.

It was a glitch, but not a deadly one, that no one had discovered Ito until morning. Time of death could be determined.

And it meant that Chamoun and Kenner had gotten away clean, or Chance would have been awakened by blacklegs reporting crimes by his citizens.

Tatiana was shaken, pale. He handed her more tea. "Easy, love. Old Ito had lots of powerful enemies. Your father himself was telling me that some cardinal named Exeter was making a move on him through the Council. Something like this was bound to happen."

*Wrong thing to say, that last.* But it was too late to call it back.

*"Bound to happen?"* Tatiana said. "Nobody's bound to have his throat slit in his bedroom, except

by karma.'' She put her head in her hands, sitting on his rumpled bed. Then she looked up, tousled and beautiful, and said, ''Chance, what are things coming to? When will it stop? How can we dare to think that Nev Hettek and Merovingen can live in peace, when Merovingen wars upon itself?''

He said, ''We'll manage, Tatiana. We'll manage because we must, because we're smart, and because things can't go on this way—you're right about that.''

Without Ito, things were going to be lots easier.

Or at least, he was feeling so much better that he told himself he believed his own line.

Outside, the College mourning bells were beginning to toll.

# SEEDS OF DESTRUCTION (REPRISED)

## C.J. Cherryh

There was a nervousness over Merovingen: the Black Barge made that when it passed. Cardinal Ito Boregy made the trip to the harbor in better style than most, and the bridges were hung with white and with black, Merovingen's folk disagreeing even in the color of mourning.

So back came the official barges, and the Black Barge with all its oars, and back to town came all the hightown folk in their silk and jeweled finery, drifting along the high bridges or motoring back from the funeral in fancy-boats and launches, and back came the shopkeepers and the middle class folk on the middle bridges, not so much glitter there, but staunch respect.

And back came the canalers to get drunk, it being an official holiday and the bars all closed until the funeral was done and Ito Boregy slid off the barge to be fish food. There was respect there, too, if only for the blacklegs standing guard on the corners and the bridges, —to protect against thieves, the word was, seeing as how citizens were distracted by the funeral.

But once the doors at Moghi's were open and once the liquor started flowing there was holiday—

*Boregy's got his!* somebody yelled, and the blackleg standing guard at Pardee Bridge looked sharp for who had said that, but mostly because he was sort of lonely there, Jones figured. Rich folk had gone away to *their* parties, the College was running as usual, and deadlines were coming due, like their Permit was expiring this evening, and Mondragon had already had an exchange with that fellow, who didn't *like* the 'runner tied up . . . obstructing traffic, as he called it, and looking tatty as it did, on his beat, and today being a state funeral and all.

"Can't move it," Mondragon had explained to the man. "Engine's not in."

"What's that?" the blackleg had asked from the walkway, pointing aft.

"That's the engine. It's not in. We haven't got the tanks hooked up, we haven't got any fuel, the shops are closed—"

"Tow it!"

"My permit's valid till sundown."

"Your permit's expired when I say it is!"

"No, it isn't." Mondragon had stood up then, all sweaty and shirtless and holding this big wrench, looking down at this blackleg, and Jones had gotten up and put her foot on the rail looking down at this blackleg, just happening to have this big length of chain in her hand, and Mondragon had said, "Sundown. That's what my paper says."

"You're a public nuisance! We're going to have funeral traffic through here—"

"We were measured for clearance."

"You're an eyesore!"

"Can't fix that. We can drape the bow in black or something. Show our respect."

So off went the blackleg, and back had come a city

crew with black crepe and hammer and tacks and hung the bow in black.

Respectful-like.

So they had kept working. The blackleg had come back by just before the funeral to say, "No hammering during the procession. Hear?"

Mondragon had stood up and loomed over the rail again, wiping his hands with a lace handkerchief. "Absolutely." In his most hightown accent. "I assure you, officer, we'll respect proprieties. —What *is* your name?"

It was Beccard. He had had to give it. That was the law, Mondragon had said, which was funny, Jones thought, because she never had known that.

It had made Beccard real nervous, when Mondragon took on the hightown accent like that. It had made him real nervous when Mondragon asked his name.

"Should be done tonight," Mondragon had said then, all pleasant, wiping his neck with the handkerchief and lazing through the accent. "Promise you, officer, I'll try to hire some more help soon as the funeral's over and get this off your corner."

"No hammering till the last gun," the blackleg had said, and walked off whacking his stick on his leg, as the processional got closer.

Made Jones a little nervous, but Mondragon wasn't, Mondragon was all cool.

And now, the funeral being done, the walkways turning noisy with canalers drinking and hallooing at each other, the blacklegs had their hands full.

So here came some of Moghi's lads, and here came Tommy, and here came Rahman, all the way they'd promised; and here came—Lord! Gran' Min Fahd, bumping up against the hull in her skip and boohooing and taking on about how it had been a beautiful funeral, and how she'd seen fifteen cardinals go to the harbor, and Ito Boregy had had to go in two pieces.

"Cut his head right off—" she yelled, in case anybody could miss it, including the blackleg on the corner

"God, shut her up," Mondragon said, jerking at a bolt.

"Gimme a silver," Jones said. "I'll send 'er for food."

"She'll spend it on booze," Tommy protested, Tommy having come up to kibitz.

"That's the idea," Mondragon muttered, and fished out the silver. "Here."

The sun was going behind Gallandry, throwing a sharp shadow down Port Canal. She saw that and worried. She leaned down off the waterside rail and tossed a silver down into Mintaka Fahd's well. "Here, Min, ye want ter go down t' Moghi's an' bring us back some silerbits?"

"Yey!" Min exclaimed, rocking her skip prodigiously as she scrambled after it, agile for an old woman her size. "Sure will. Oh, thank'ee, Altair!"

"Praise Allah," one of Moghi's boys muttered.

She ducked back to get back to her hose-fitting. Damn, that sun was getting low.

"Ye goin' to make it?" somebody shouted from the Pardee walk. "Hey, Mondragon, how ye doin'?"

"Fine!" he yelled, pulling at the wrench, and muttered, "Damn, we don't need people on here. Jones, leave Rahman the hose, just keep 'em off this deck."

Because everybody on the Water knew that boat had to move today, and it had to move by sundown, and the blackleg was hovering out there on his corner ready to see it did—

"How ye doin'?" people shouted up, a little on the lit side.

"Oh, fine," she said, feeling like her stomach was full of eels. "Just fine."

God! People might forget about it with the funeral

and all; except she'd just sent Min off to Moghi's, and Min's mouth there was no stopping.

"How *is* it coming" she asked, looking back.

"Damn template's wrong," Mondragon said. "*Damn* that Yossarian! Got to drill again, this damn board's going to look like holey cheese, damn, damn, *damn!*"

"Pray she holds," Rahman said, who hardly ever said two words in an afternoon.

More drilling. More cursing. The sun got lower.

People came drifting up from Moghi's to see the show and drink and lay bets whether the boat would make it.

The blackleg didn't investigate. There were a lot of people up and down the walk. He was paying all his attention to the Grand, because if he turned around he had to see a lot of drunk and disorderlies and a lot of them were carrying hooks and knives and chains and bottles.

"Oh, Lord!" Min's voice shrilled from waterside, all bubbly with alcohol, "Altair! I'm sorry, I'm sorry—"

Min boohooing because she'd forgot the chips and drunk up the money.

And it was getting toward dark.

"It's all *right*, Min!" Jones yelled. "Just go on back to Moghi's, tell him send 'em, put 'er on my tab!"

Whole damn walkway was full of people. People were on Pardee's bridges and balconies. "How you doin'?" Jones asked, sweating, while Mondragon and the help were working away with the wrenches.

"Close," Mondragon said.

There was a *hoooo-ooo!* from the crowd. Something was happening. Jones bet on the blackleg before she ever looked over the rail, and it wasn't just one, it was four of 'em coming through.

"Your permit's expired," their original blackleg

yelled up at them, waving his stick, and the crowd booed and hooted. "Move this hulk now!"

Mondragon stood up again. Applause from the bridges and the boats round about. He said, "Tanks're empty. Got to send after fuel!"

"Move this thing!" the blackleg shouted. "Or you're under arrest!"

"Hey" Tommy shouted high and clear, "I'll lend ye, Tom!"

"I got 'er!" Jones said, and yelled down at Lewises' boat, that was near her skip: "Hey, Lewis, gimme up that spare tank from the hidey!"

"That's not enough to *start* this thing!" Mondragon yelled. "I can't get to the harbor on that! Can anybody sell?"

"Yo!" somebody yelled, "I got 'er!"

"Your time is running!" the blackleg yelled.

"Hurry it!" Jones yelled. "Anybody what's got fuel to spare, just pass 'er up an' ye gimme the tally later! We got ter move this thing!"

Cans appeared from boats round about, the crowd cheered the cans, booed the blacklegs, and Jones and Rahman and Tommy and Moghi's lads made a chain so they passed cans and dumped chugger down the tank fast as it would pour, long as there were cans.

"You're overtime!" the blackleg yelled. "Move it!"

"All right!" Mondragon yelled. "All right! Cast us off! Everybody clear in front!"

Lines thumped inboard, one after the other. The boat began to drift. Mondragon primed the motor. He spun the crank. It died.

A moan from the crowd.

He primed and cranked again.

It took. It roared. Water flew up like a fountain astern and people screamed and the 'runner jumped so they all went sliding—

"*Look out!*" Mondragon yelled as they shot right under Pardee Low Bridge with all the people screaming and cheering—

Jones scrambled for the rail, yelled, "Jump!" and planted her bare foot on the rail and dived as far from those screws as she could send herself—

Hit the water like it was pavement and went down in the Det, fighting the wake that tossed her—

Kicked and fought to the surface and saw other heads bobbing in the trail the boat left on its track diagonal across the Grand—saw that boat still going, and didn't see the man she was looking for—

"*Mondragon!*"

God, it was going to hit—

He hit the rail and dived out clear and clean as the 'runner plowed right into Foundry's canalside, right up the boatskid of that new mek shop—

Just carried the whole front in with it before all that fuel went boom! and lit up the Grand like a second sunset.

All them records, Jones thought cheerfully. All them debts.

Canalers cheered and nobody was running real fast to ring a fire-bell yet. They would. Nobody else on Foundry deserved to burn.

But Sword did. And the word was out what that bunch was.

She took a lift from Lewises' boat. They got Mondragon picked up, too, and Mary Gentry got her man Rahman and Tommy onto her deck, along with Moghi's boys.

Wasn't any need for them to hang around. Accidents happened. People scattered. People were real alert for that fire, them that were in on it, and Moghi was real quick.

Blacklegs came to Mondragon's apartment that night. They asked polite, respectful questions. They filled out their official forms. They said it was regret-table, but there was a fine and damages.

Mondragon said he'd certainly stand responsible for that: it was just the pushing to get through, of course. He had been terribly worried about the crowd and the drinking, and he had been trying to comply with the law.

The officer on the scene would be reprimanded, the sergeant said. Shook hands, wished Mondragon good night and hoped he didn't take the fever from his swim.

Jones held her heart when the door shut. She felt like she was going to faint right there.

Mondragon walked over to the counter and poured them each a whiskey.

Lifted his, chink! against the rim of hers. "Anas-tasi's men," he said, meaning the ones that had just gone. "Report's official now. Just jammed on us. Working too fast—"

"Damn ye f'r stayin' aboard—"

"Hey, I wasn't going to miss, was I?" A sip of whiskey, a whiskey-flavored kiss.

After which, no need of good sense.

# RUN SILENT, RUN CHEAP (REPRISED)

## *Leslie Fish*

Beyond sight of land the high sun flickered on the low waves of the Sundance Sea, throwing reflected fragments of light along the hulls and underside of the *I'm Alone Two*. She had no nets down, and was not really out fishing for deathangel.

Showered with light, rocked on the mild waves, Rif and Black Cal made love on the arrowhead-shaped deck. Much skill and patience that required, and they made the most of it, timing every stroke with the swell and slide of the waves. The sun hung still at midheaven, as if to give them all the time in the world.

A good hour and more slipped past before Rif raised her head, noticing the prickle of warning heat on her bare belly, drowsily worrying about sunburn in embarrassing places. She turned to look at Black Cal stretched out beside her, sunlight reflecting silver off his long back and thighs, and worried that his pale hide might take damage, too.

"Where'sa suntan oil?" she mumbled in his ear, sliding a lazy hand down his washboard ribs.

"Mm, basket," he murmured, not turning his head.

Rif rolled over, stretched, climbed to her hands and knees and went hunting in the picnic basket. The oil flask was hiding in the bottom, under the empty containers and last half-bottle of wine. She hauled it out, rolled back to Black Cal's side, unstoppered the flask and poured out a handful of it between her breasts. Black Cal, watching with one eye open, offered a hand to help spread the oil. Rif purred, and let him.

It took a good quarter-hour to slick down all of her skin, after which Rif sat up to return the favor, worried that she might have taken too long already; Black Cal's skin was pale as steel, too easy to burn. She started at his heels, worked the oil up his long legs and buttocks, finally sat on his back to spread the rest on his shoulders and arms.

It was from that vantage point that she saw something odd along the horizon.

Some hundred meters ahead and a few degrees to port the flat line of the water was humped by something stationary—but not quite still. Rif studied the oddity while her hands worked, remembering that the Sundance was shallow here and sandbars were common. Some fisherman might be out there, crab-trapping or possibly beached. The current was bearing the *I'm Alone Two* steadily closer; she'd have a better view soon enough. Rif watched, hands still, task forgotten.

Black Cal lifted his head. "What's happening?" he asked.

Rif pointed. "Someone out there."

He frowned, annoyed at the loss of privacy, wriggled out from under Rif's thighs and reached for the tackle box tied to the mast. Inside lay a collapsible telescope. He pawed it out, extended it and put it to his eye.

"What ye see?" Rif asked, noting his sudden tension.

"Lord," Black Cal whispered, frozen.

"What *is* she? Cal?"

He shoved the telescope into her hands, got up and scrambled toward the rigging. The mainsail snapped and rattled as he pulled it up from the boom. "Cat-whale," he panted. "Beached. And something . . something else . . ."

Rif, staring through the telescope, didn't hear him.

Yes, it was a sandbar. A cat-whale lay across it, long mottled-gray body struggling to roll free. The huge, catlike face bore an almost-human look of distress, and the long-toed flippers dug futilely into the wet sand. Another desperate rolling revealed the broad, pale underbelly lined with a double row of gray-furred breasts, some of them plainly abraded and sore from pressing on the sand.

Around the beached cat-whale, trying to help her roll off the sandbar, were . . . figures.

Clearly not human: short-legged, long-tailed, cat-faced, covered in mottled gray-black fur like their much larger . . . companion?

Mother?

But they had arms—and hands—almost like a human's. They pulled and pushed like a human work gang, and some of them held curved white sticks—no, bones from some big sea-creature—which they used like levers, trying to push and pry, trying to help the cat-whale back into the sea.

"Sweet Mother Jane," Rif gasped. "I think . . . Cal, I think those're her young! Nobody knows much about cat-whales. Maybe they go through stages, start with arms an' legs like that, then turn 'em ter flippers as they grow older . . ."

"They're using *tools*," Cal said, steering the tri-maran toward the sandbar. "They're intelligent, and the . . . young can use tools. Lord, what if the young ones can walk around on land, live on beaches or tide-marshes? What if . . .''

''We've got t'help 'er.'' Rif sat up, closed the telescope and put it away. ''They've seen us comin'. Look, some o' the young ones're shakin' those bones at us, must be scared. Got ter show 'em we're here ter help . . .''

''Careful!'' Black Cal warned, wondering if the cat-whale young could throw those . . . tools very far, or if they'd swim out to attack the boat.

Rif climbed to her feet and stood at the bow, arms held wide, hands wide open and empty in the ancient sign of harmlessness. Surely any tool-using creature could understand that, and humans had never hurt nor hunted cat-whales during all their centuries on Merovin.

The cat-whale cubs saw her, made no move to dive into the water, but darted up and down the sandbar squeaking among themselves. Their voices were high, catlike, oddly sweet and chirping, but didn't sound reassured.

*Puzzled,* Rif guessed. *Don't know what to make of us. But they sing . . .*

Inspired, Rif sang at them: a long, high, steady note that suggested greeting, calm, respect. Then another note that ended in falling trills, suggesting friendliness, sympathy.

Black Cal paused at the sail, watching the gap of water close, watching the cat-whale cubs, praying that their ears worked somewhat like a human's, that they'd understand the wordless meaning of the notes.

The cubs stood still, eyes and ears turned toward Rif, hands motionless. Their silvery whiskers quivered, and they chirped softly among themselves. If they didn't understand, at least they made no move to attack.

Sand gritted under the leading hull. Black Cal lowered the sail, grabbed an anchor and dropped it. So close now, less than ten meters from the mother cat-whale's broad spade-shaped tail—but even she was still now, head raised, watching.

Again Rif sang, another sympathetic trill. This time some of the cubs trilled back, imitating the sound.

*First line of communication,* Rif grinned. Very quietly she said: "Cal, gimme a long line, and anchor t'other end ter the stern."

Black Cal chewed his lip, but went to open the near hatch and pulled out a coil of rope. He could guess what she meant to do, but would the cubs understand? Had they ever seen something as simple as rope? He tied one end to a stay-bolt at the stern, and tossed the rest of the coil to Rif.

On the sandbar, the gray cubs flinched and muttered. Did they recognize the rope for a tool? Did they think it was a sea-snake, or a weapon?

Rif held up the coil, showing it to them, showing that it was inanimate, only a tool—and sang again: a lighter note, urging hope.

The cubs licked their chops with nervous pink tongues, watching.

Holding the free end of the rope, Rif stepped off the bow. She splashed lightly in the shallow water and waded toward the cat-whale's tail, trailing the line, singing steady soothing notes.

The cubs flattened their ears and crouched lower, ready to attack or run, as Rif strode calmly up to the cat-whale's side.

Black Cal quietly went to the pile of his clothes near the mast and pulled out his long-barreled revolver. If the cubs misunderstood, if they attacked Rif, he'd commit the first interspecies murder on the planet. Whatever that led to, whatever history would say of him, he'd not regret it.

Rif stopped, leaned forward, and gingerly patted the cat-whale's side. The wet fur was surprisingly soft under her hand. She sang quietly, soothing wordless notes, in time with the stroke of her hand.

The cat-whale raised her head further and watched, didn't move, didn't so much as twitch her three-meter-wide tail.

The cubs slowly raised their ears and stood up to watch.

Singing, patting, very slowly and carefully, Rif eased the end of the rope across the cat-whale's tail, just above the broad paddle. She paid out enough to drop in a coil on the other side, then stopped to sing and pet for a long moment.

*Now comes the hard part,* Black Cal thought, watching her.

Rif bent down and burrowed her hand under the thick column of the cat-whale's tail, trying to reach the rope on the other side.

*She won't make it,* Black Cal considered, measuring the distance with his eyes. The cat-whale's tail, at its narrowest point above the paddle, was thicker than Rif's body.

Still Rif dug, burrowed, reaching for the rope.

The cat-whale blinked her enormous dark eyes, mewed softly, and raised her tail off the sand.

Rif sang a note of joy, success, ducked under the lifted tail and reached for the rope. For a moment the tree-thick tail arched above her like a boulder about to fall, and Black Cal bit hard on his tongue to keep from moving or crying warning.

Rif rolled back with the other end of the rope in her hand, back to safety, still singing. She pulled in the slack and tied a sturdy double-shanked knot, tight enough to hold securely, easy to untie with the right pull.

The cat-whale slowly lowered her tail back to the ground.

Rif patted the smooth gray fur once more, then

backed away. "Cal," she called, softly enough not to worry the cubs, "Turn 'round and start pullin' 'er out."

Black Cal put the gun away, pulled in the anchor and backed the trimaran's bow off the sand. "Come back aboard," he said.

"In a minute," she promised, wading out along the rope's tightening length. "I might have ter show 'em how ter help."

Black Cal gnawed his lip, but turned the boat and reset the sail. The *I'm Alone Two* tacked into deeper water, and the rope pulled tight.

"C'mon, ye boys; pull!" Rif called to the cubs, showing her intention by tugging on the rope.

The mother cat-whale lurched onto her belly and began shoving at the sand with her forepaws, pushing herself backward, toward the rope's pull, toward the sea. She trilled peremptorily at the gang of cubs.

The cubs, understanding at last, scrambled toward their mother and pushed, levered, heaved toward the sea, squeaking and mewing wildly among themselves.

"Not enough!" Cal shouted back at Rif. "I'll have to use the engines." He quick-tied the rudder, pulled open the hatch and scrambled below.

"That'll take time," Rif muttered, pulling futilely at the rope. The bottom had grown too deep for her feet to find purchase. "I hope the kids don't lose heart too soon."

A quiet rumbling echoed through the water as the engine on the main hull turned over and began to spin. Black Cal popped out of the hatch and ran to the closed hatch on starboard hull.

"Aye, give 'er all three engines," Rif called, feeling the renewed tension in the rope.

On the sandbar, the mother cat-whale flailed harder with her paws.

Black Cal came up from below and ran to the last hatchway and engine.

The cat-whale heaved mightily, gaining a meter's distance toward the water. The sand boomed under her weight.

"That's it! She's comin'!" Rif whooped.

Groaning and mewing at the abrasion of sand on her belly, the cat-whale inched slowly backward into the water. The cubs' squeaking grew higher and fiercer as they levered and pushed. The cat-whale's tail and hind flippers sank into the welcome waves, and she heaved again, trilling in triumph.

On the boat, Black Cal listened to the engines' laboring, chewed his lip, let out more sail.

The cubs' squeaking took on rhythm as they pushed in chorus: heave, heave. The cat-whale gave another mighty shove with her forepaw-flippers, and splashed shoulder-deep into the sea.

"Again! Again!" Rif cheered to the cat-whale.

Again the cat-whale pushed, her back bowing with the effort. Water splashed up to her chin, and her forepaws went under the surface.

The rope suddenly fell slack.

The *I'm Alone Two* jerked forward, then came up sharply at the end of the rope. Black Cal ran to cut the engines.

"She's free!" Rif howled, and pulled herself hand over hand down the rope toward the cat-whale.

"Get away from them!" Cal bellowed, scrambling for the last engine.

"Gotta cut 'er loose," Rif called back, swimming well within range of the huge tail.

The cubs splashed into the water, surrounding her.

Black Cal retained enough presence of mind to cut the engine and toss out the anchor before he dived into the water and swam after Rif.

Big as a small gray island, the mother cat-whale

curled around in the waves and studied the woman approaching her. There was no readable expression on the huge furred face.

Swimming along the direction of the slack line, Black Cal felt a hand stroke his side. Thinking it was Rif, he surfaced—and found himself staring into a furry black catlike face, less than an arm's length away. The big dark eyes blinked, ears twitched, and a pink tongue absently licked a black button-nose.

It looked so much like a kitten that Black Cal automatically reached out to pet it.

The cub backed away, flicking its whiskers, and batted a paw at his hand.

For an instant, hand and forepaw met—and stopped in surprise.

*I'm shaking hands with an alien*, Black Cal marveled, feeling the leathery toe-pads, fuzzy skin, articulate muscle and intricate bone under the soft webbing.

Then the paw withdrew, the cub blinked at him, and ducked away in the water. Black Cal shook his head and went back to looking for Rif.

But where was the rope?

Black Cal dived, surfaced, searched while furred heads surfaced near him to watch, finally found the rope trailing loose in the water. It was dead slack. He swam along it, letting it play through his fingers, until abruptly he found the end. It wasn't cut; it had been untied.

"Rif!" he shouted, making several cubs dive away from the noise. "Where are you?"

"Here!" echoed across the water.

Black Cal turned toward the sound, and saw Rif bobbing in the water close to the cat-whale's enormous upturned belly. Her hands brushed over the abraded skin, wiping sand out of the wounds. "Come and help, Cal," she called brightly. "I think we've made some friends."

Almost dreamily, Black Cal swam toward her. Curious cubs darted through the water around him, poking their paws curiously at his bare skin. The mother cat-whale's gray body rose up before him like the side of a ship, and he caught up to Rif at last. "You all right?' he asked, though he could see that she was.

"Fine," she grinned. "Excep' one o' the cubs damn-near goosed me, lookin' ter see why I didn' have a tail. Ain't they cute, though?"

"Cute?" Black Cal mumbled, looking around him. Yes, come to think of it, those fuzzy kitten-faces *were* sort of cute. Under his hands he could feel the mother cat-whale purring like an enormous engine. "Nice kitties. Some damn kitties. What in the Lord and Ancestors' names have we stumbled on?"

"Friendly, intelligent aliens," said Rif, patting the last wound clean. "We should try ter keep 'em fer friends, Cal."

"Damn right," he started to say—then yelped in surprise as the cat-whale curled her bulk around him and ran her huge rough tongue across his leg.

"There, there . . ." Rif stroked the long furry jaw. "We're all bein' friendly. And they like my singin'." To prove it, she sounded a long rippling arpeggio— once above the water, and once ducking her head below the surface.

The mother cat-whale mewed and rumbled back. The cubs chirped and meowed in chorus.

Black Cal gave himself up to marvels. He stretched out on his back and floated on the low waves, listening to Rif sing with the cat-whale and her young while the deepening sunlight sparkled off the Sundance Sea. He considered that he might be dreaming, until curious cubs swam closer, batted at his feet, nuzzled his hair, licked his outstretched arm and mewed in his ear. He stretched out his hands to pet them, and a few of the bolder cubs let him. Their fur was wondrously silky and soft, their whiskers wiry and long.

Eventually the singing stopped. The cat-whale gave a deep, commanding *churrr,* and sank under the surface. The cubs trilled briefly and dived after her, surfacing once or twice, farther out on the water, to look back and mew again.

"They're leavin'," Rif sighed. "Guess they've got ter go fetch dinner." She raised a hand to wave toward the departing troop.

"We should do the same," Black Cal reminded her, reluctant to part with the day's wonder. The *I'm Alone Two* rocked at anchor not far off, and he turned to stroke toward it.

Back on board they hauled in the trailing line, pulled up the anchor and set the sails to head them back toward land, saying nothing until the sun had dried them thoroughly. Almost reluctantly, they pulled their clothes on and poked about in the larder for any leftover food, finding only the half-bottle of wine. Rif solemnly poured it out into glasses.

"Ter the cat-whales," she toasted.

"And to many more days like this," Black Cal added, clinking the glasses. "Another intelligent species, and all this time we've never known it."

"So much we don't know 'bout our own world . . ." Rif set the glass down, a wild glow coming into her eyes. "D'ye think the sharrh themselves knew 'bout the cat-whales?"

"Maybe . . ." Black Cal looked up, startled. "Do you think that could be the reason they wanted our ancestors to leave here? Because they didn't want us to hunt or harm the cat-whales? Could that be it?"

"Maybe, maybe . . ." Rif stared out over the empty sea. "But if this was s'posed ter be a—a game preserve fer the cat-whales, why didn' the sharrh ever come back ter see how their pets was gettin' along?

It's been six hundred years, Cal. Surely they would've come ter check up in all that time.''

"Maybe not. Who can guess how they think?'' Black Cal frowned. That didn't make sense to him, either.

"All the sharrh did was chase our ancestors off, then leave again. Never came back. Old story has it, nothin' but signs o' space-goin' tech drew their attention, and they don't care 'bout anythin' less. But why should that be?''

"They didn't want space-travel to or from Merovin.'' Black Cal shrugged. "They seemed to want this world isolated—maybe to keep the cat-whales stuck on it, too. Who knows?''

"What if . . .'' Rif sat up, a wide reckless smile showing her teeth. "What if this was a kind o' sharrh prison-planet? Maybe an exile-place fer . . . fer the cat-whales. What if the sharrh don't care 'bout humans; they just don't want the *cat-whales* gettin' technology, goin' inter space?!''

"Why the hell. . . ?'' Black Cal pondered. "What grudge could the sharrh possibly have against the cat-whales? And . . .'' A sudden thought struck. "The cubs! The adults have to live in water, but the cubs could live on land—use tools, build civilization, even get technology for themselves . . .''

"—Unless there's somethin' they lack,'' Rif took up, "Somethin' they'd need ter build their own tech, but can't get here, had to have imported . . .''

"But why—''

"Oh, think!'' Rif stared out to sea, speculations darting behind her eyes. "What if the cat-whales ain't native ter Merovin? What if their ancestors were colonists, too—colonists what did somethin' ter stir up the sharrh, so the sharrh didn't want 'em gettin' back inter space again? What if the cat-whales *are* the descendants o' the sharrh?!''

Black Cal thought that over for long moments. "Wild, crazy guess," he finally said. "We've nothing to go on. Hell, there could be a million other reasons that have nothing to do with the cat-whales."

"Sure there could," Rif grinned. "But think o' the possibilities, Cal. Think what the Janes could make o' this."

Black Cal shaped a soundless whistle. "I think . . . your friends just might have an antidote for Crazy Cassie and the deathangel fad."

"Damn right." Rif narrowed her eyes in calculation. "What if the Janes can claim communication with the sharrh?"

# APPENDIX

## From the files of Anastasi Kalugin, Advocate Militiar

### I

From Skit:

. . . Certainly Fon's Revolution has not moved as it held forth to do, to make Old Tech generally accessible to Nev Hettek. To a certain extent such attempts have been hampered by powerful interests and monopolies which fear the loss of their exclusivity: list A attached.

In part also the orthodox Adventist clergy have supported these objections, maintaining in closely held memos (document B) that to deregulate tech too rapidly would open the door to uncontrolled experimentation of a sort that might indeed attract sharrh notice.

### II

From Diver:

Organized opposition to Fon is basically centered in the Adventist Orthodoxy, who have thus far remained untouchable, and who have taken extraordinary precautions against covert action and assassination: Fon's

331

agents in the Sword and possibly in other clandestine groups have certainly attempted to gain control of the clergy and the brutal murder of Ellenby this summer is generally believed to be Sword action, but thus far the Moderates have maintained their influence in the Council.

Fon has asked for a two year extension of his extraordinary powers—see attached: the Emergency Powers Bill.

### III

From Redfin:
The official line since Mondragon's escape is that Mondragon was guilty so far as his involvement with the Sword and did participate in assassinations until the Sword included his own family on its list of targets: that he then sent word to Fon, and attempted to warn his relatives, but that he was apprehended on the grounds.

Mondragon therefore is recently given to be innocent of his own family's murder, but guilty of numerous others, including the assassination of Fon's father. The reason for this shift in the official line is not clear, but the same highly reliable source believes Fon has ordered the one set of charges dropped to keep the official inquiry into the escape from pursuing certain lines of investigation.

### IV

From Skit:
Most significantly, certain of the Moderates among the Families of Nev Hettek have shifted assets and personnel to their widely scattered estates, which has, in our opinion, been an effective tactic in maintaining their political effectiveness in the face of Fon's attempt to gain control.

The Sword has made some strikes in remote estates,

and in fact there are rumors of "bandit action" and "outlaws" attacking trucks and upper Det shipments, and there have been rumors of attacks on certain estates or villages belonging to certain key Adventist Moderates, which we believe is Sword action. However, though the Nev Hettek Families traditionally keep secret the extent of their holdings, we believe that this network of remote plantations and stations is actually growing at present. All such attacks and reports of numbers of casualties and losses are rumor put forward most likely by the Sword and exaggerated: the Families deny all such reports, denying the existence of outside holdings, as they have done throughout the past.

This scattering of assets and personnel, accelerating a trend actually beginning before the Revolution, has compelled Fon to moderate his tactics and his program in the Council.

Fon clearly sees his dilemma: he cannot strike simultaneously at such a diffuse and in many cases effectively concealed number of outlying holdings; neither can he strike at the Nev Hettek residences of such families: to do so would remove the center that ties the remote estates together, thus decentralizing the Nev Hettek economy and government, which is not at all to his advantage.

Instead he is attempting to seize control of and manipulate the moderate organizations, even to the extent of setting up opposition to himself—building the reputation of certain individuals, notably Ian Metcaff, who has been safe to speak vehemently against Fon and to stir up a popular following.

Metcaff is not a Sword member, or at least has no provable ties to Fon or to the Sword. Tracing this matter has been very difficult, but Metcaff's miraculous survival of two assassination attempts may not be luck: in the second, Simmons may have been the real target, and I do not put it beyond likelihood that Metcaff himself was working with the assassins.

This tactic, if it is a tactic, has advanced Metcaff among the Moderate leadership; and provided a focus and an apparent success that may influence certain votes; that may incline certain Families about to bolt Nev Hettek for the outback to maintain a strongly centralized power in Nev Hettek—in short, Fon has provided leadership to his enemies and so far while we can penetrate that cover we cannot discredit it.

## V

From Redfin:

Regarding your inquiries: the Mondragon family is extinct with the sole exception of Thomas Mondragon. The estates were confiscated by the government and by creditors. The possibility of outlying holdings exists, but if so, they were completely decentralized by the removal of the Nev Hettek branch and the confiscation of outlying estates and properties. Supply and trade would have betrayed their existence to other interests, and, if such ever existed unfound by Fon's agents, such outlying properties were probably secretly annexed by neighboring estates.

Regarding the trial records: we are still trying. On his escape: the most reliable source maintains it was from Karl Fon's residency: that Fon on numerous occasions over the five year term of his confinement had him transferred from prison to his residency under guard, for periods as short as a few hours and as long as three days, notably preceding his arraignment on various charges, and several times close to set trial dates. Trial was set six separate times and each time canceled for reasons ranging from illness of witnesses to national security and Fon's personal intervention. Regarding the nature of those interviews, our source indicates that Fon wanted names and details of Mondragon family business; and possibly locations of property. Fon's behavior at such times ranged from fits of anger, striking out at bystanders, to threats of bodily harm, to threats of his own suicide, with what provocation is uncertain, although our source believes Fon is caught between his necessary political action on the one hand in eliminating Mondragon from his Sword post and on the other, his long-standing attachment to Mondragon—which our source characterizes as emotional dependency. Regarding any possibility Mondragon is still working for Fon and that Fon himself engineered his escape: our most reliable source indicates this as unlikely, on personal judgment. A deep and elaborate cover is certainly within Fon's pattern, but Mondragon's disaffection from Fon seems solid.

Regarding public perceptions in the case: the initial charges, that Thomas Mondragon was prominent in a Sword plot to assassinate Hamad Fon and simultaneously eliminate and replace key councillors—is still believed in some quarters; but Karl Fon's quick midnight move to take control and attack alleged perpetrators, which of course eliminated others of his enemies—is regarded with less and less credulity—not that people in general believe that Mondragon was innocent, but that many believe that Fon, due to his close friendship with Mondragon and his family, may have had some advance knowledge of Mondragon's involvement with the Sword: the general knowledge of their personal relationship and Fon's currently growing reputation for clandestine maneuverings and sharp dealing has created suspicion centering on Fon's swift assumption of power—but Metcaff doesn't make that suggestion.

The general public attitude among Fon's supporters about Fon's involvement in his father's murder and his ties to the Sword of God, whether present or past, seems pragmatic: that regardless of how he came to office, Karl Fon is capable to govern and that he has brought a stability and prosperity to Nev Hettek which it would be foolish to disturb.

The Adventist clergy in opposition to him is shifting its line, abandoning the moral theme and emphasizing the dangers of Fon driving certain economic interests to decentralize from Nev Hettek.

Metcaff's general issue has always been that Fon is morally reprehensible, both politically and religiously: this is carefully constructed to draw the genuinely unbuyable opposition into one manageable camp; and also to set up the chief opposition to Fon on an issue designed to fail, i.e., one which seems sound but which ignores the political and economic realities of Nev Hettek politics. Fon is, we are certain, the real voice behind Metcaff: Metcaff's apparent freedom to speak is also Fon's proof that he tolerates dissent. We are seeking solid evidence, but so far nothing that will not compromise our sources. We are deep in Metcaff's operation. We have extreme options available.

## VI

Memo: A. Kalugin
Preserve all options with Metcaff. Pursue solid evidence.

## VII

From Skit:
Karl Fon has been in and out of the city for months, general rumor says, clandestinely moving about the region. It is further rumored that he is troubled by disaffections from his Revolution, and that he has been under pressure from orthodox Adventist clergy to dispel the persistent rumors that he has past links to Jens Chambers: Chambers' position as the figurehead director of the Sword of God remains unchanged, al-

though there is an indication of a shakeup in Sword ranks. Our Sources believe that Fon is still strongly in control of that organization and that this shakeup reflects Fon's determination to retain that hold against certain stresses within the Sword hierarchies.

## VIII

From Runner:

At station: 12 Septe; Meridien.

Plague this winter affects hundreds; however prevention and treatment have prevented disaster. Suggest extreme caution: spread into hinterlands and Det Valley likely by spring. Nev Hettek's advanced methods are better able to cope with this. . . .

## IX

Memo: A. Kalugin:

Joseph: see me.

## X

Memo: Pardee

I have secured a copy of an early writing of Exeter's: she was a junior aide to Bishop Lin Ramsey. The question involved the proposal for the establishment of general wire service in the city.

## XI

Memo: Exeter

On the proposed wire system:

As per your request for Impact Study:

I respectfully recommend rejection of the proposal on the following grounds:

1. The public presence of such wires would provoke curiosity leading to speculative experimentation with presently available technology in ways exceeding the application. The argument that the system uses only existing technology (generators, batteries, current-

carrying lines) fails: there is a non-existing compo-
nent, namely the use of power interruption as a
message-carrying signal and thereby the use of elec-
trics as voice-transmission and thereby speculative curiosity into wireless transmission, i.e., radio devices
which might easily be manufactured with commonly
available materials, once the College lifts the ban on
the general Type of such devices.

It is not the dissemination of banned knowledge that
is the hazard in this case, but the widely remembered
and very simple principles of radio communications.
The public justly fears that radio transmission might
bring sharrh attention: to lessen that degree of appre-
hension by granting College approval to a principle of
electrical message transmission might seriously un-
dermine that long-established abhorrence of electrical
communications in general which is our first-line protection against the random tinkerer in some outlying
village—or worse, some subversive—who might decide to experiment with wireless technology which
might be detected by orbiting monitors; and which
might represent a major threshold in the mentality of
the sharrh.

2. Historically, the advent of wireless technology on
ancient Earth produced profound societal changes, including a tremendous increase in the speed, spread,
and general accessibility of information; the availabil-
ity of minute unfiltered detail, hence the need for elec-
tronic storage; the proliferation of communications
devices in the hands of individuals and the proliferation of devices to monitor and detect such communication; increased efficiency of espionage; and
ultimately research into electromagnetic phenomena
of all sorts, which is a major step toward a potentially
space-faring technology.

This wireless system cannot be justified under Existing Technology. It contains a principle which does come under the Ban.

It must be rejected without comment, under College Privilege of Silence.

# INDEX TO CITY MAPS

## INDEX OF ISLES AND BUILDINGS BY REGIONS

**THE ROCK:**
**(ELITE RESIDENTIAL)**
**LAGOONSIDE**

**GOVERNMENT CENTER**
**THE TEN ISLES**
**(ELITE RESIDENCE)**

33. Elgin
34. Narain
35. Zorya
36. Eshkol

37. Romney
38. Rosenblum
39. Boregy
40. Dorjan

---

## THE SOUTH BANK

Second rank of elite
41. White
42. Eber
43. Chavez
44. Bucher
45. St. John
46. Malvino (Adventist)
47. Mendelev
48. Sofia
49. Kamat
50. Tyler

## THE RESIDENCIES

Mostly wealthy or government
51. North
52. Spellbridge
53. Kass
54. Borg
55. Bent
56. French
57. Cantry
58. Porfirio
59. Wex

---

## WEST END

Upper middle class
60. Novgorod
61. Ciro
62. Bolado
63. diNero
64. Mars
65. Ventura
66. Gallandry (Advent.)
67. Martel
68. Salazar
69. Williams

## PORTSIDE

Middle Class
74. Ventani
75. Turk
76. Princeton
77. Dunham
78. Golden
79. Pauley
80. Eick
81. Torrence
82. Yesudian
83. Capone

## TIDEWATER (SLUM)    FOUNDRY DISTRICT

## EASTSIDE (LOWER MID.)

## RIMMONISLE (ELITE/MERCANTILE)

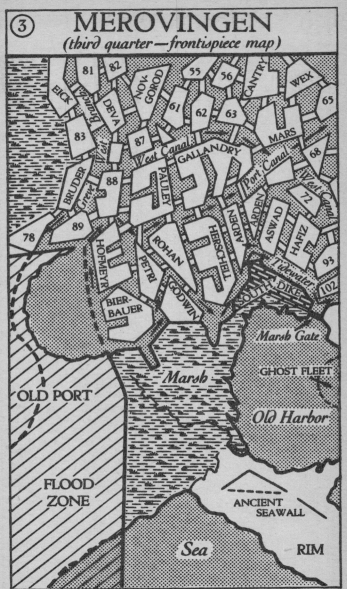

# ③ MEROVINGEN
## *(third quarter — frontispiece map)*

81 82

EICK

Vaspasi

DEVA

NOV-GOROD

55 56

CANTRY

WEX

Veit

Brauer

83

87

61 62 63

65

West Canal

GALLANDRY

MARS

68

BRUDER

88

PAULEY

Port Canal

West Canal

Grev

89

78

ARDEN

ARDEN

ASWAD

72

HOFMEYR

ROHAN

HERSCHELL

HAFIZ

93

PETRI

Tidewater

102

BIER-BAUER

GODWIN

SOUTH DIKE

*Marsh Gate*

GHOST FLEET

OLD PORT

*Marsh*

*Old Harbor*

FLOOD ZONE

ANCIENT SEAWALL

*Sea*

RIM

✳ NUMBERS INDICATE ISLES AND BUILDINGS LISTED IN INDEX

# ④ MEROVINGEN
## (fourth quarter—frontispiece map)

65

Grand Canal

Port

FOUN-DRY

NAYAB

MASUD

118

GOSSAN

PAR-DEE

CALLISTE

FISH MARKET

Snake

SALEM

WILLIAMS

VEN-TANI

Gut

TURK

YAN

75

DUN-HAM

MANTOVAN

DELARBE

EAST DIKE

RAVI

101

MEN-DEZ

SALVATORE

ULGER

FACTORY

107

CALDER

00 Grand

RAMSEYHEAD

New Harbor

102

Tidewater

SOUTH DIKE

BOGY GATE

RIMMON ISLE

105

DIKE

WHARF GATE

DEAD

WHARF

124

125

120

127

128

129

130

GHOST FLEET

Dead Harbor

RIM

Sea

# VENTANI ISLE
## (Canalside Level showing Moghi's Tavern)

LITTLE VENTANI BRIDGE

FISHMARKET BRIDGE

CALLISTE

Fisher Canal

BRIDGE PILINGS FOR UPPER LEVEL

1

MOGHI'S

VENTANI PIER

VENTANI WAREHOUSE

Grand Canal

2

STAIRS AND STORAGE (Ventani Family)

15

14

16

HANGING BRIDGE

PRINCETON LOW BRIDGE

3

RESIDENCES

13

RESIDENCES

12

4

MERRITT WAREHOUSE (cordage)

8

10

11

5

6

7

9

COFFIN BRIDGE

MAG'S LANE

Margrave

Ventani Gut

LOW VENTANI LANE

DUNHAM ISLE

| | |
|---|---|
| 1 LEWYT SECOND HAND | 9 TINKER |
| 2 WEAVER | 10 JUNK SHOP |
| 3 DRUG | 11 SECOND HAND |
| 4 DOCTOR | 12 SPICERY |
| 5 CHANDLER | 13 LIBERTY PAWN |
| 6 FURNITURE MAKER | 14 TACKLE |
| 7 KILIM'S USED CLOTHES | 15 MAG'S DRUG |
| 8 JONES | 16 ASSAN BAKERY |

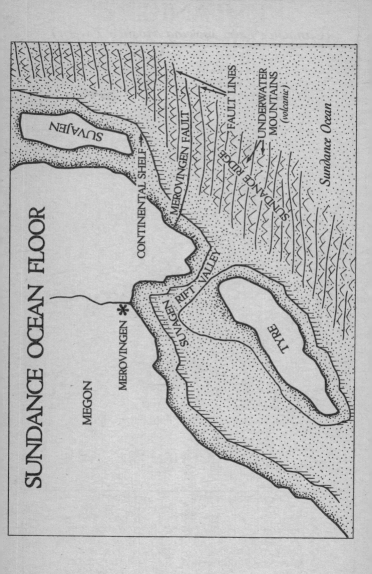

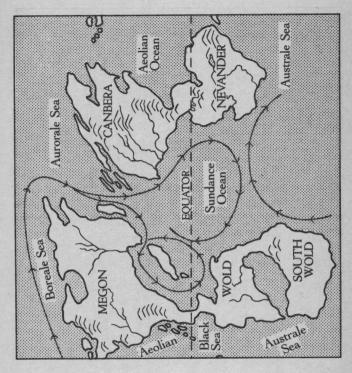

## MAJOR EASTERN OCEANIC CURRENTS
*(affecting climate)*

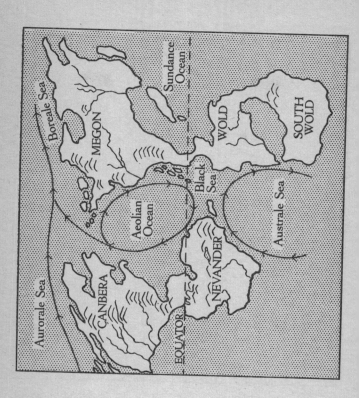

WESTERN

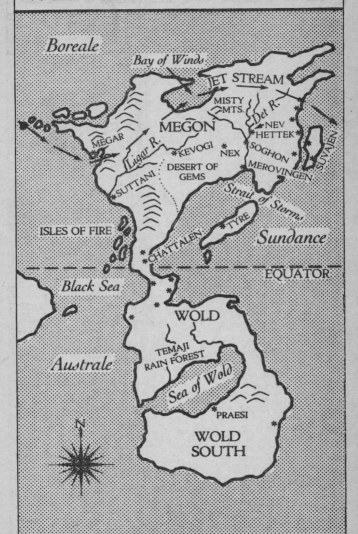

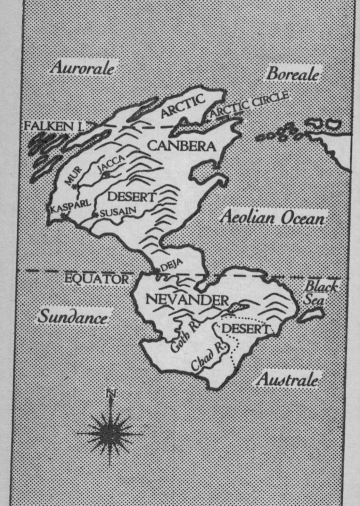

EASTERN HEMISPHERE

Aurorale

Boreale

FALKEN I.

ARCTIC

ARCTIC CIRCLE

CANBERA

Aeolian Ocean

MUR

JACCA

DESERT

KASPARL

SUSAIN

DEJA

EQUATOR

NEVANDER

Black Sea

Sundance

Goth R.

DESERT

Chad R.

Australe

N

DAW

# C.J. CHERRYH
## THE ALLIANCE-UNION UNIVERSE

**The Company Wars**
- ☐ DOWNBELOW STATION       (UE2227—$3.95)

**The Era of Rapprochement**
- ☐ SERPENT'S REACH       (UE2088—$3.50)
- ☐ FORTY THOUSAND IN GEHENNA       (UE1952—$3.50)
- ☐ MERCHANTER'S LUCK       (UE2139—$3.50)

**The Chanur Novels**
- ☐ THE PRIDE OF CHANUR       (UE2292—$3.95)
- ☐ CHANUR'S VENTURE       (UE2293—$3.95)
- ☐ THE KIF STRIKE BACK       (UE2184—$3.50)
- ☐ CHANUR'S HOMECOMING       (UE2177—$3.95)

**The Mri Wars**
- ☐ THE FADED SUN: KESRITH       (UE1960—$3.50)
- ☐ THE FADED SUN: SHON'JIR       (UE1889—$2.95)
- ☐ THE FADED SUN: KUTATH       (UE2133—$2.95)

**Merovingen Nights (Mri Wars Period)**
- ☐ ANGEL WITH THE SWORD       (UE2143—$3.50)

**Merovingen Nights—Anthologies**
- ☐ FESTIVAL MOON (#1)       (UE2192—$3.50)
- ☐ FEVER SEASON (#2)       (UE2224—$3.50)
- ☐ TROUBLED WATERS (#3)       (UE2271—$3.50)
- ☐ SMUGGLER'S GOLD (#4)       (UE2299—$3.50)

**The Age of Exploration**
- ☐ CUCKOO'S EGG       (UE2371—$4.50)
- ☐ VOYAGER IN NIGHT       (UE2107—$2.95)
- ☐ PORT ETERNITY       (UE2206—$2.95)

**The Hanan Rebellion**
- ☐ BROTHERS OF EARTH       (UE2209—$3.95)
- ☐ HUNTER OF WORLDS       (UE2217—$2.95)